Fire Born

Prince of the Netherworld

L.C. SON

Contents

About Fire Born: Prince of the Netherworld   ix

Prologue   1
Prologue   7
Chapter 1   13
Chapter 2   19
Chapter 3   23
Chapter 4   30
Chapter 5   35
Chapter 6   40
Chapter 7   45
Chapter 8   50
Chapter 9   55
Chapter 10   59
Chapter 11   64
Chapter 12   69
Chapter 13   75
Chapter 14   82
Chapter 15   87
Chapter 16   92
Chapter 17   97
Chapter 18   101
Chapter 19   109
Chapter 20   114
Chapter 21   120
Chapter 22   125
Chapter 23   132
Chapter 24   138
Chapter 25   143
Chapter 26   147
Chapter 27   151
Chapter 28   156

Chapter 29   160

Chapter 30   165

Chapter 31   171

Chapter 32   176

Chapter 33   180

Chapter 34   185

Chapter 35   191

Chapter 36   196

Chapter 37   201

Chapter 38   207

Chapter 39   213

Chapter 40   219

Chapter 41   225

Chapter 42   229

Chapter 43   234

Chapter 44   239

Chapter 45   243

Chapter 46   248

Chapter 47   253

Chapter 48   257

Chapter 49   262

Chapter 50   272

Chapter 51   280

Chapter 52   285

Chapter 53   290

Chapter 54   295

Chapter 55   300

Chapter 56   305

Chapter 57   310

Chapter 58   314

Chapter 59   319

Chapter 60   324

Chapter 61   332

Chapter 62   337

Changeling Epilogue   340

Stay Tuned! 341

More from L.C. Son 345

About L.C. Son 347

Copyright

Dedication

To my perfectly imperfect family.
Extended or near.
I love you.

About Fire Born: Prince of the Netherworld

Love. It's not something a Ferryman, a Prince of the Netherworld, ever hoped to attain. Yet, for Kharon Nyx, it's the one thing he is sure of. Rae Vereen loves him.

Despite his villainous past, her love kindled a fire deep in his soul.

But can she love him despite his present darkness?
As time is winding down to save his sister from the Netherworld, Kharon and Rae's love will be put to the test in ways neither of them thought imaginable.

With dark secrets revealed, the fragility of their world will expose whether their love can truly endure.
Will the darkness of his world douse their kindling flame? Or will their love burn brighter than before?

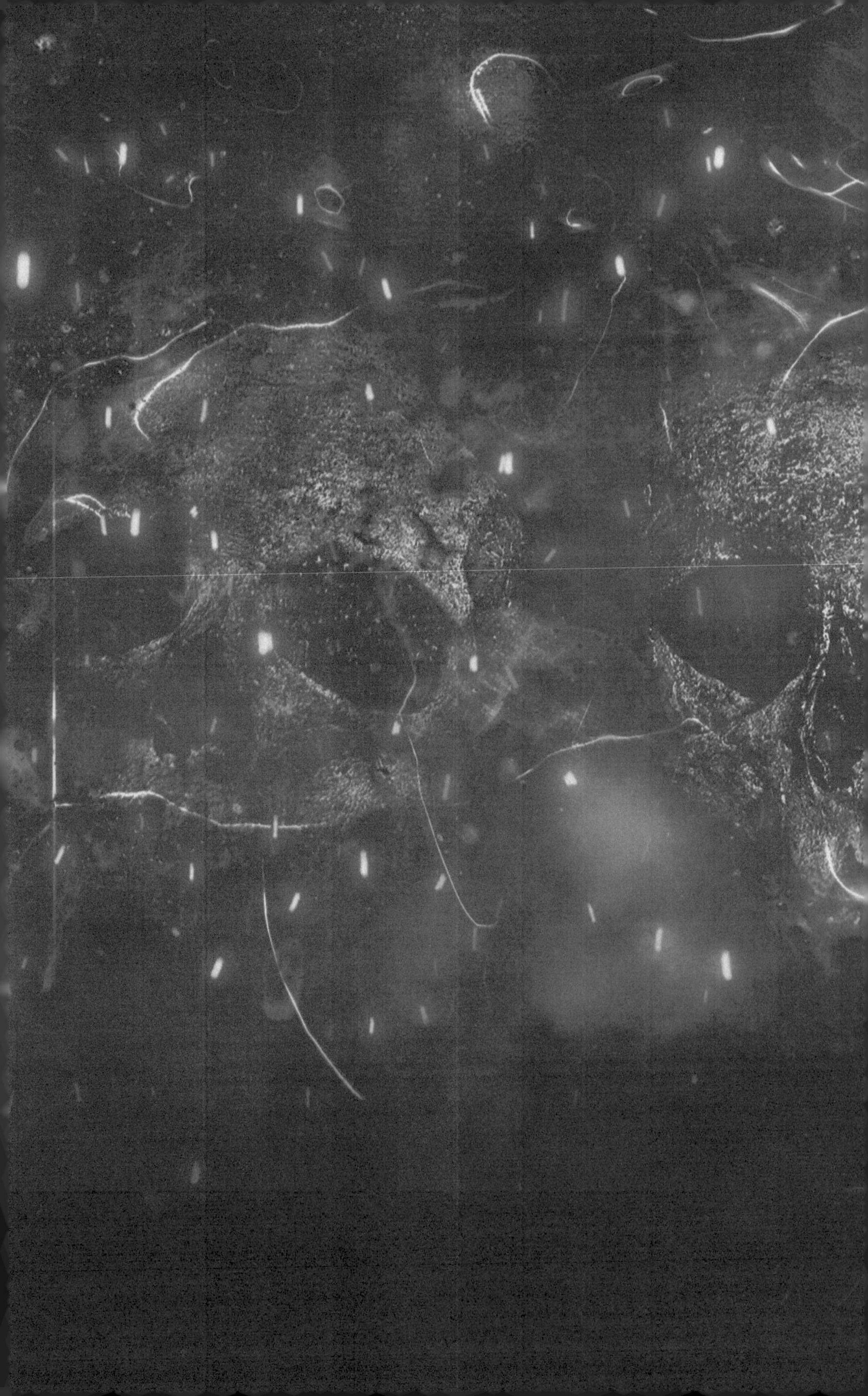

Prologue

KHARON

Before the First Bloom

"Woman, if I let you have your way, you'll make me the laughingstock of the Netherworld," I chuckle, shaking my head as I kick aside the mess of fabrics and flowers Rae managed to adorn the deck floor of my ship with. When I suggested she find a way to make my ferry less creepy, I had no idea she'd make it more in line with a parade float than one that shuttles the damned and the dead.

Laughing, Rae smiles, kicking her leg in the air as she tosses her lace panties at me with her foot. "Well, you weren't laughing an hour ago when you disintegrated my garments. I'm just surprised you didn't damage these."

Grabbing the small scrap of fabric, I hold it to my nose, inhaling the sweet scent of her nectar before stuffing them into my pocket. "That's because I plan on keeping these as a memento of our time together."

Scrunching her nose, Rae pushes herself to her knees, draping a rose-colored satin around her shoulders. "Am I missing something?"

Kneeling to her side, I brush her hair from her face, lightly kissing her forehead. Taking her face in my palm, I lift her chin until her eyes meet mine. I need to erase the worry I see there. "There's nothing to worry about, beautiful," I begin, stroking my thumb along her bottom lip. "Remember Cedric said he was bringing a friend who could help before we leave to rescue my sister? Well, his friend, Sincade DeLuca, is coming tomorrow. Until know what and who I'm dealing with, you need to stay away from the cavern. That is, until I'm sure he can be trusted."

"Oh," Rae mutters as her eyes flutter over her shoulder. "It's just, I thought—ugh, never mind." Pushing away from me, she leans back against one of the boney walls. I wish I could tell her how adorable she looks nestled between the bones of my ship, something I never envisioned she'd ever be comfortable doing, but noticing her unhappiness, I itch to know what's wrong instead.

"Hey, what's that face?" I ask, turning her face back to mine. "Come on, you know you can tell me."

"It's just...sometimes you talk like you're going to disappear. I mean, keeping things as a memento sounds like you're preparing to never see me again."

Taking her shoulders in my hands, I give her a squeeze, firm enough to get her attention, but gentle enough to reassure. "Rae, if I had ten thousand tongues, I'd say it all the same. I am yours, and you are undoubtedly mine. Do you understand? I don't know what more I can do to prove that to you, but please trust me when I say you are my life. My whole life. Do you understand?"

Thin, crescent droplets form at the corners of Rae's bright hazel eyes, and I want to wipe away every stain of doubt I see there. She nods, allowing a small, bashful smile before raking her fingers through my stubble and pulling my mouth to hers.

Her tongue collides with mine sweetly, and I can taste the remnants of myself hidden in the inner courts of her mouth. The thought goes straight to my manhood, reigniting the passion we shared only minutes ago. Lifting Rae into my arms, making her straddle my waist. She fists my hair as she twists our tongues together. Salty tears mesh between our mouths as she cries into our kiss.

My hold on her strengthens as I feel her quake in my grip. Although we've been together for months now, moments like these persist. Moments when Rae needs reassurance from me. Reassurance that we're together, that I'm not going anywhere. While everything in me wishes she knew my heart without a shadow of doubt, the shadows of our sordid past still linger.

For years, she watched me show feigned interest in her cousin while she felt like a hidden figure, lost in the background. Now that we're finally together, our love is still hidden. We're not at a point where we can make our affection public, and she has to hide her true feelings from the people she loves most, only so they may be protected from the dark plans of the Changelings.

In all of this, though, one thing is constant.

Rae's love for me.

She has given her all to me without regret. She loves me more than I've ever been loved. It almost feels unfair to have someone love me like she does. Withholding nothing, Rae gives me all I could ever need or ask for. Unselfish. Unrelenting. Wholly unapologetic.

All I want is to be a man worthy of the treasure trove of love she's bestowed upon me.

Tightening my embrace, I need her to know I've got her. I need her to know there's nothing that will separate me from her love, not now or ever.

Swiping my hands against my trousers, they crumble to my sides along with her pretty lace panties I had in my pocket. Masterfully as ever, Rae wastes no time sliding down my shaft, strumming up and down until she finds her sweet spot. Tossing her petite arms around my neck, she moans as she bounces, entrancing me with the bobbing motion of her breasts.

Warmth and flaming embers of fire shimmer beneath my skin, and I do what I can to hold back the flames. It takes more restraint than I could ever explain to Rae, but I fear what releasing my fire upon her would do. She's still mortal, without a trace of supernaturality. If I hurt her in any way, I'd never forgive myself, but it hurts, more than she'll ever know, that I can't give her myself in every way imaginable.

Still, I take pleasure in exploring her depths and sinking into her center, again and again. Rae's head falls onto my shoulder as her cries of ecstasy are only eclipsed by the sound of my own and that of the rushing waterfall serving as a backdrop to our lovemaking.

Resting my mouth against her earlobe, I whisper, "I'll never let you go." With one final thrust, Rae quakes in my arms as her pulsing core grips my girth like she feared I'd break away. A whimpering moan is all she manages in response as I feel her sweet nectar drip between our thighs, drenching the fabrics beneath us.

"I love you, Khar," Rae adds, running her fingers along my jaw.

"I know, baby, and I love you. Never forget that. If you do, I'll do all I can to remind you."

Lifting her head slightly, she offers a bashful smile. "Well, what if I like the reminders anyway?"

Rearing my head back, I look at her and smile. "My naughty little princess."

She taps the tip of my nose, a mischievous grin covering her face. "Only for you, my prince."

"Damn right." Narrowing my eyes, I give her a stare. Then, it hits me. Every time Rae needs reassurance, we end up like this. Perhaps I'm being played. Hell, if I am, if this is the game between us, there can't be any losers. "Well, I could start becoming more creative with *those reminders*, if you'd like."

Raising a brow, Rae sits up straighter, intrigued. Grunting slightly as she feels the strength of me still forged deep, her sexy lips part as her sweetness throbs at my base. "What kind of reminders, I wonder?" She stifles another moan, but her eyes betray her. I've got her right where I want her.

Rae's head sways back as I grip her ass, keeping our connection locked, ramming myself deeper into her. "If you thought you could simply goad me into another quickie, perhaps I should teach you a lesson in manners."

"A lesson?" Her eyes widen as I thrust upward, holding her tight, ensuring she feels every inch. Crying out, she shakes as I rock my hips, rotating and hitting her walls. In and out. Side to side. Up and down. "Khar!" she screams, clawing at my back and grinding in rhythm with my hips.

"One in which you learn to be careful what you ask for. You'll have to beg me to pull out of your sweet little hole. That way, you'll always be reminded that I'm always with you. When you walk, you'll still feel me inside you. Is that what you want, sweetness? You want assurances? I'll give them to you. I'll give them to you until you beg me to stop."

Rae's eyes brighten then narrow, and once more, a calculating grin covers her face.

"Well then... make me beg."

Game on, sweetheart.

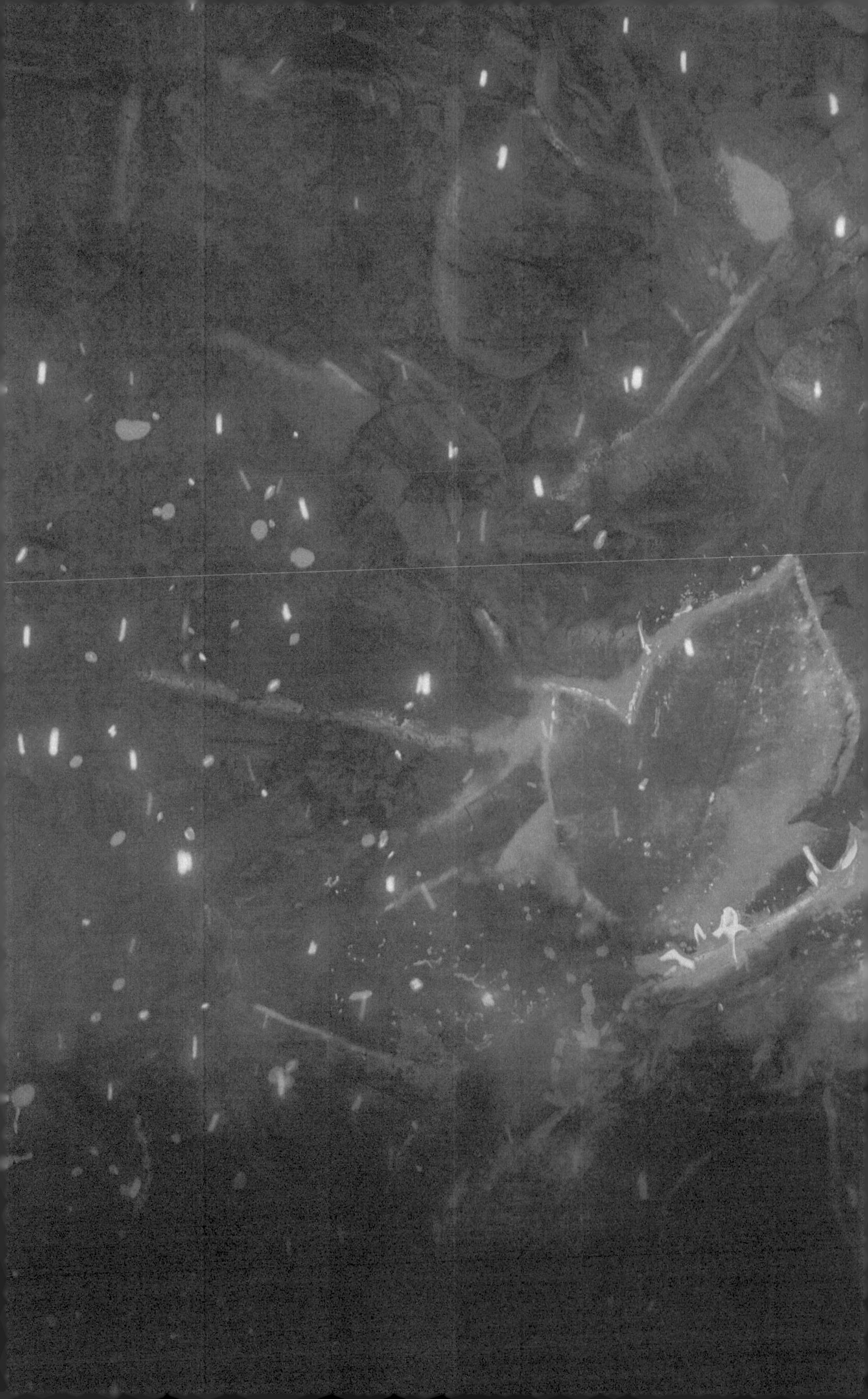

Before the First Bloom

KISSING the top of my head, Kharon nestles me into my pillowy soft bed and pulls my duvet to my chin. "Rest well, my princess," he whispers against my ear. "You got more than you bargained for today." Adding one more kiss, he runs his hands through my hair, smiling down at me with such a doting gaze, I can't help wondering how he would look putting our kids to bed.

Don't go there, Rae, I inwardly scold myself. That's a topic we've yet to discuss.

"At least I'll feel you with me always—every time I move," I say, wiggling beneath his grip.

Smirking, Kharon's dark brow raises, disappearing behind the wavy blonde hair covering his forehead. "That's what you get."

"I hope I get more." I smile and turn to my side. I may be teasing him now, but I'm truly tired. He wore my little ass out. Literally. While I wasn't truly challenging him just to get a rise out of him, I surely didn't mind the challenge.

Kharon made love to me like he owned me. His fervor was unrelenting, his need unquenchable. He's told me before that he's been holding back. If that's holding back, I can't imagine what else he has in store for me.

Unlike mortal men, Kharon's manhood doesn't diminish after a release. In fact, it appears to make him more ravenous. He says it takes all his willpower to stop. Tonight, however, it took my will. He had no intention of stopping until I begged him to do so, and make me beg he did.

On all fours.

On my side.

In my rear.

In my mouth.

Everywhere.

Eventually, Kharon finally took pity on me. Since I pleased him with more climaxes than I've ever had in a single bout, he said he knew I had, in fact, learned my lesson.

Learned my lesson I have, but it's an education I hope to experience again. *And again.* Perhaps not too far in the future.

Strumming his fingers softly against my cheek, he keeps his hand on my chin. "Who knew my little honeycomb could be such a vixen?"

I smile. "You bring it out of me, I suppose."

"Happy to bring out the best in you. For now, sweetness, you need to rest."

Reaching out from under the cover, I squeeze his fingers still resting at my chin. "But I don't want you to go. Please," I mutter.

Kharon's eyes soften as he stares down at me, still doting, as if I were his most prized possession. "What about your cousin? I think I heard her voice down the hall. We can't risk her seeing me with you."

My heart sinks. I've grown tired of this charade. While I understand why we must keep our love a secret, it still hurts. In fact, it sickens me to my core to act as if Kharon isn't a part of not only my world, but my heart. Over the years, Winter and I have shared everything. Not sharing this part of myself with her hurts me more than anyone could imagine. Even more, as happy as Kharon makes me, I should be shouting from the rooftops, not hiding in the shadows.

This isn't the first time I've begged Kharon to stay over. Each time, he's denied me. He's been right: Winter or my aunt inevitably make an appearance, making me happy they didn't catch him with me. Still, for one night, all I want is to lay in the arms of the man I love as I drift to sleep. I deserve that much.

"Please," I repeat as tearful pools cloud my view of Kharon's stately form. I really don't want him to leave.

Sounds from outside my window draw Kharon's attention, and he peeks between the blinds. Turning to me, he smiles again while reaching down to wipe my tears. "Well, it looks like you're in luck. I just saw Lux, Win, Abigail, and Cedric all get in the car."

"At this hour?" I frown, looking around Kharon's arm to check my clock on the nightstand. "It's almost midnight. I wonder where they could be going."

Sitting next to me, Kharon unwraps his ascot and his shoulders relax. "Well, you could continue to wonder, or you could slide over so I could hold you until you fell asleep."

A wide, Cheshire grin covers my face at the thought that I might finally get what I want. "Without the onyx sand?" I ask, sitting up on my elbows. In the few times Kharon has stayed in my room, he normally makes himself invisible. As sexy as that may be sometimes, I don't want him to be invisible. I want—no, I *need* to see him with me.

"Yes, without it. Just this once." Kissing the crown of my head, he gently scoots beside me, wrapping his arm around me. "Now lay down and try to get some rest."

Excited, I turn on my side, thankful to feel his strong arms holding me now. Tilting my head over my shoulder, I lean in for a quick peck, and Kharon seems almost too happy to comply as he lands a soft kiss on my lips.

"You seem too anxious to sleep," he laughs. "The agreement was for me to hold you until you do."

"Well, tell me a story. Anything," I add, wiggling my butt against him, happy to feel his rigid steel ready and waiting. I'm not tempting fate. I'm too sore to play that game.

"Okay, as long as you promise to stop seducing me. I don't think you need any more *lessons* tonight."

Throwing up three fingers beneath his hold, I laugh. "Scouts honor."

"Alright then. I'll tell you the story my aunt Clotho used to whisper to me along the Acheron River."

Softly, Kharon strums his hands through my hair as I nestle into the cradle of his arms. The cadence of his heartbeat is soothing, like a sweet melody lulling me to slumber. My eyes grow heavy as I inhale copious amounts of his sweet, smoky scent, relishing the feel of his arms draped around me.

With a dark, rich tone, Kharon's voice deepens as the melodic tenor of his voice sweeps over me like music, entreating me to my dreamscape.

In the beginning, there was nothing. A vast void of coldness and darkness covered the Earth until the first spark. Her name was Fotia. She was a kindling flame, sprung up from the center of the world, bringing life and light to all in her reach. Fotia's flame grew, covering the Earth until molten shores nestled against fiery seas. Everything in its path was scorched, turning it to ash. Then, out of nowhere, came Kapnos. He was smoke, but the smoke was not born of fire. It was sufficient within itself, hovering about like a gale, shifting the world on its axis.

Fotia's fire fought back, wishing for nothing but to continue its volcanic reign. What Fotia didn't understand, though, was that the smoke of Kapnos did not arise out of conflict but of love. For Kapnos knew that in Fotia's desire to burn, she would consume not only the world, but herself, and this was something Kapnos could not fathom. So, day after day, Kapnos remained unrelenting, so much so that when chance came, his smoke charmed Fotia's fire, teaching it to blaze without burning, to use its light to warm without scorching. Fotia soon came to understand her purpose. Even more, she learned her fire needed smoke, for the smoke would guide the fire's compass, serving as a warning before the fire held its sway. Finally combining as one, the fire and smoke lived in harmony, no longer consuming and suffocating, but warming and warning. It is said that until this day, Kapnos and Fotia lie in wait at the center of the earth, hopeful to one day conceive a child from their union.

*A child destined to be **Fire Born**.*

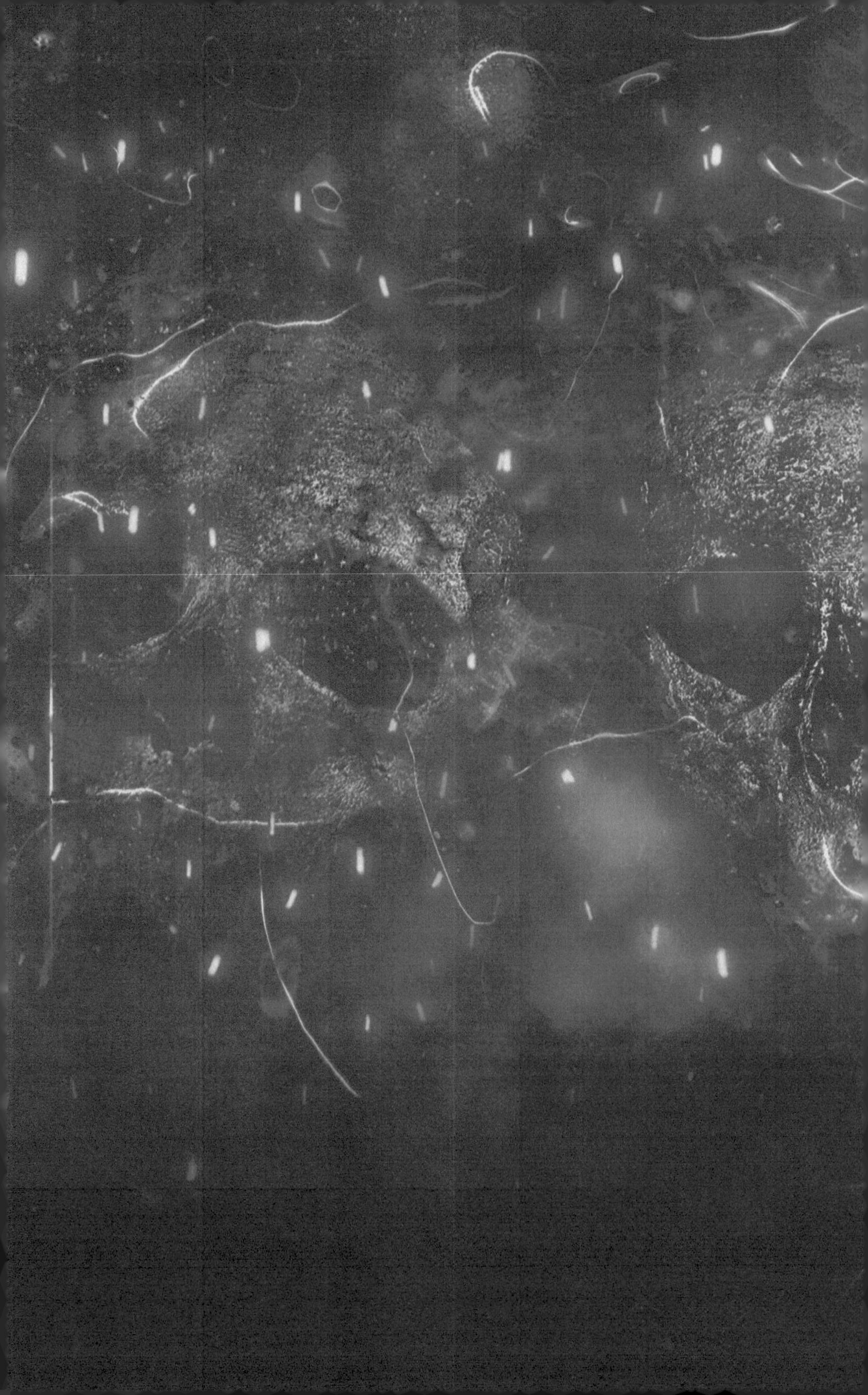

One

KHARON

THE AIR SMELLS different this morning. There's a harsh roughness knocking off the crisp winter chill I felt just last night. The wind was cool as we took flight over the pine-laden forest, making our way to Elysian Manor. It was so cool, in fact, that despite being wrapped in my coat, Rae's cheeks pinked as the chilly air hit her face. I recall noticing how adorable she looked nestled in my arms but also wanting to get her out of the cold.

The season is officially changing.

Spring is here.

Looking over the tree line, I notice small buds sprouting from the branches. Only another day or two before the heat of the sun awakens the sprouts into full bloom.

As much as I want nothing but to rescue Moirai from the hold of the Changelings, there's one lingering thought making me question my decision.

Rae.

I have no desire to take her anywhere near the Changelings or the Netherworld. While I admit a part of me is eager to show her my world, there's an equally more protective part of me fearful for how she'll react. Will it be too much for her? Will she think she's in over her head? What, I wonder, will she think of my home?

A chorus of questions swirls in my mind, tormenting my soul in an endless chord of despair. Yet, despite how ominous the chord might be, I know too well that as the Fates have decreed, so this tune must play out.

It was hard as hell to pull myself from her side. Rae fell asleep no sooner than I had concluded my bedtime story. I couldn't help admiring how beautiful she looked while she rested. Even her sleeping sounds, some combination of snoring and snorting, were the most adorable noises I'd ever heard.

Still, I left early because I couldn't risk her family catching me in her suite, not even Ross. While he's one of the few aware of our relationship, we're still doing what we can to keep a low profile. I hate that we must continue to endure this façade, but hopefully, once Moirai is free and our concern for the Changelings is put to an end, we can finally share our love with the world.

I don't have long to think about what it will be like to finally make our affection public – I detect the blood-curdling smell of a vampire as I land near the edge of my cavern.

This scent is different.

It's reminiscent of the stench I've grown accustomed to with both Cedric and Dalcour, although being pureblooded, their smell isn't as repugnant as Cedric's mate, Abigail. Mortal-made vampires like her, or Scourge as they are called, reek like spoiled, raw chicken.

What I detect now seems to be riddled with blood and ash. How, I am not sure, but with each step closer to my dwelling, I grow curious.

Small beams of light from the early morning sun illuminate my pathway as I take careful steps inside. Yet, when I see the form of a man dressed in a long, black leather trench, dark hair, wearing shades, I move from curious to angry.

"Who the hell are you?" I snap, watching the man lift a cautionary hand against a ray of sun . I watch in awe as his hand doesn't scorch or boil like most vampires. My hand, on the contrary, blazes with fire in my fists, preparing to strike this intruder down should he make even the slightest move. "What are you?" I grit out the words, still marveling at the stranger's ability to withstand a sliver of sunlight.

He lets out a sniveling cackle, revealing his fangs before plunging his hand into his coat pocket. "Well, I suppose that's one way to greet someone sent to be of assistance."

Stepping forward, I take him in. He's small, not even six feet. His features are youthful enough, although something tells me he's been around for longer than his boyish features would have me believe. Thick, wavy black hair frames his round, olive-toned face, and his skin shimmers with the usual Altrinion dew-kissed luminescence most mortals pay handsomely to obtain. Yet it's the faint black veins coursing beneath his otherwise-perfected appearance telling me there's more to this stranger than meets the eye.

"The name is Cade, Sincade DeLuca. I believe we have a mutual acquaintance." As I move into the direct sunlight, Cade removes his sunglasses, revealing wide eyes the color of a blood orange moon. Allowing another smile, still baring his fangs, he offers me his hand. "Cedric Decanter sent me. If now isn't a good time—"

Taking his hand in mine, the warmth of his palm surprises me. He's certainly not cold like a vampire. "No, now is as good a time as any," I say, offering a small smile to match the genuine one I see on his face. "I'm sorry. I just hadn't expected to see you in the daylight."

"Well Mr. Nyx—it is Nyx, correct?" He pauses, still gripping my hand firmly until I nod.

"Just Kharon," I answer, pulling from his hold.

Affixing his sunglasses to the collar of his dark blue shirt, his face relaxes into a more serious stare. "Ah, well, Kharon, since I don't have long on the island and I'd rather catch the next ferry, lest I run into any familiar faces, I figured daylight was best."

"Not interested in catching up with the domestics, eh?" I laugh.

Cade raises a thick brow, drawing his already-small lips into a thin line. "Precisely."

Taking off my coat, I wave my hand forward, leading us deeper into my dwelling. Touching the candles along the way, I light the flames with a flick of my finger.

"Interesting," Cade whispers, obviously shocked, or perhaps impressed by my fire.

Offering him a seat at my stone table, I look over my shoulder to ensure my sister's stone is still hidden within the wall. I used an enchantment to keep her safe, but I like to be sure. Her light flickers dimly behind the cavern walls, and I can only hope this stranger cannot see her. After she was taken by Dalcour's Guard, I fear someone else could do the same. Besides, since I spent the night with Rae, I have no idea how long Cade has been sniffing around.

"So, Cade, Cedric tells me you may have some useful information to help me in rescuing my sister from the Changelings."

He folds his leg over his opposite knee and leans back, his eyes flashing bright as the light of the flames intersects with the glow from his eyes. "Ah, but that isn't the question you really want to know, is it?"

I lean forward, my hands clasped together on the marble slab of my makeshift desk. "What are you?"

"There it is!" Cade throws up a hand, smiling broadly, apparently happy to get to the elephant in the room. "The million-dollar question—what you truly want to know. Well, kind sir, I'd be happy to oblige." Straightening his posture, he lowers his leg back to the floor and pushes himself to the edge of his seat so he's pressed against the desk, meeting my gaze. A few seconds of silence sit between us, and I watch the calculating dance of his eyes. He's obviously pleased to make me wait a moment longer until he notices a dark glower on my face. "You've undoubtedly guessed I am part vampire—my father was part mortal, part Altrinion. My mother, however, was a Changeling."

Gasping, I lean back in shock.

"Impossible! I've never heard of such a thing," I groan, wondering why I've never heard of a coupling across the species. Pushing myself back against the table, I study his face. "How is this possible?"

A small, dark laugh rolls through his chest as he looks at me. Sitting back, he once more folds his leg over the other, seemingly pleased by my response. "Well, I would think someone from the Netherworld would know nearly anything is possible."

"Yes, in the Netherworld, I would agree. Here on the earthbound plane, however, things always seemed rather black and white. Glad to see this side of the veil is just as unpredictable as my homeland." I let out a hefty sigh, still thinking about his reveal. Shaking my head, I force aside my desire to know more. Frankly, I could care less about his lineage. Spring is budding as we speak, and I need to know how he can help me. "I suppose that explains how you're able to withstand sunlight. I'm more interested in what Cedric thought you could provide to help me."

Cade's face darkens and his gaze narrows, but not enough to be threatening. "Ah, well, I suppose we have two very different interpretations of my reasons for being here."

I frown, annoyed my time may have been wasted. "Then pray tell, what are your reasons?"

"Whatever help I can provide is not for you, I'm afraid."

"Not for me? Then for who?"

He smiles, and I'm frankly frightened by what may spill from his mouth. "Why, your mate, of course. I'm here for Ms. Rae Vereen. She is my only reason."

A deep groan rumbles through my chest, and all I want to do is see just how much sunlight this hybrid can withstand. He's coming dangerously close to charting my ferry to the destination I alone can provide. *Hell.*

Two

RAE

"Mmm... Khar—" I whine beneath my sheets, reaching out to touch Kharon's beard.

The sound of laughter rolls around me, and I detect two voices chattering about. Although I can't make out their words, I jump up, realizing I'm not alone, and more importantly, Kharon is gone.

"Well, top of the morning to you too, sunshine," Ross chuckles, leaning against my headboard with one arm propped on a stack of pillows, staring at me. The incredulous smirk at the corner of my brother's face tells me he heard me call out Kharon's name.

Another burst of laughter blares from the corner of my room, near the bathroom. Through a sleepy haze, I wipe at my eyes, looking up to see Win peek her head out of our shared bathroom. Her shoulders bounce as she laughs while brushing her teeth. She tries speaking through her toothpaste, but she shakes her head, wagging her finger before returning to the bathroom.

"No worries, Pip. I don't think she heard your kinky cries for Kharon. She's been brushing her teeth for eons," he whispers, still wearing a mischievous grin.

"What are you doing here? In my bed? And where's—"

Covering his mouth and nose with one hand, he lifts his other, stopping me from continuing. "First things first, handle that morning breath. Your nether-honeybun may be accustomed to the smell of death, but I have no intention of enduring it so early in the morning," Ross quips, leaning away from me.

We both burst into laughter, and I cover my mouth, slightly embarrassed. Ross makes a good point. Kharon never seems to be bothered by morning breath, or at least he's never said anything to me. To be honest, he's never smelled bad to me. Either we're both totally whipped and oblivious, or we don't give a damn. I'm sure it's a mixture of the two.

"Now that's better!" Winter announces, adding a delicate dab to the corners of her mouth with a small white hand towel. "Glad to see you up and about, Rae. You seemed to be having a fit of sorts in your sleep. Is everything okay?"

Biting my lip, I share a bashful look with Ross, but he only hunches his shoulders and looks away.

"Yeah, I'm fine. Just a dream, I guess," I say, pushing my hair to one side.

"That's good," Win continues, walking toward us. She sits on the corner of my bed and reaches to grab my foot. Adding a little squeeze, her smile broadens as she stares at me. "I mean, you kept saying things like fire and smoke. It didn't make any sense—but I suppose dreams never do."

"Well, that's not entirely true." Ross pushes up from the bed, waving a hand in the air. "The other night, I had a super hot dream about my favorite lumberjack, only to wake up and be doing everything I saw in my dream. Now *that* made complete sense to me." Fanning himself, Ross falls back against the headboard, laughing.

Both Winter and I laugh, shaking our heads.

"All right then. Aside from lover boy over here, the rest of us know how erratic dreams can be," Win continues, shooting me a quick wink.

"Erotic, not erratic. There, I fixed it for you," Ross quips, reaching across me to playfully shove our cousin's shoulder.

"Okay, you two," I belt through their laughter. "Dream or no dream. Erotic. Erratic. None of that explains why either of you are in my room right now."

Ross grumbles something toward Win but folds his arms across his chest and sits back.

"Actually," Win begins sweetly, squeezing my foot once more. "We were thinking we could spend the day together. You know, go to Capers for breakfast and perhaps ferry off the island for a little shopping before—"

"Before what?" I quickly interject. Months ago, it'd be me, not my cousin, doing my best to pull her from work and off the island. Now that Kharon and I are together, though, I have little desire to leave the island.

"Before I leave for spring break with Lux. Since I've been knee deep in my studies, you in yours, and Ross finishing his hospitality management courses, we've spent very little time together. Besides, as much as I love spending my every waking moment with Lux, I miss our time together. With me traveling with Lux over the break, I thought now was as good a time as any. That is, if you're not busy. I certainly don't want to impose."

"Yeah, that's why we came over so early, Pip. We didn't know if you would be *busy* today." Ross gives me a look, and with the way he emphasized busy, I know exactly what he means. He wants to know if I'll be too busy loving on Kharon.

Shifting my gaze between my brother and cousin, I feel their pull on my heartstrings more than I have in a while. Truthfully, it feels good. *I've missed them.* A lot. Although I've purposely kept my distance so we don't alert the Changelings to my presence, it couldn't hurt to spend at least a day together.

"Let's do it!" I merrily announce, popping up to my knees.

Ross and Win's faces brighten, seemingly surprised by my response. Ross sits up, smiling wide as he leans onto my shoulder, nuzzling his nose against my arm.

"Perfect!" Win exclaims, rising from my bedside. "I'll get everything arranged and we'll meet you downstairs in a few."

"Yes, just a few minutes, Pip," Ross begins as he hops off my bed. "I've grown quite accustomed to Stephen's lumberjack breakfasts. I get hungry rather early these days. So unless you want me to get hangry, put a pep in your step."

Shaking my head, I give my brother a good eye roll. Jumping off my bed, I shoo both he and Winter to my doorway. "Okay, okay, just let me freshen up. You know, since my breath reeks of death and everything," I say, shooting a playful wink to Ross as I close the door.

Grabbing my phone from my nightstand, I shoot Kharon a text, hopeful he understands.

Three

KHARON

"What do you mean, *Rae is your reason for being here*?" I snap, quickly rising from my seat. Heat rises in my palms, and I know I could end Cade with the balls of fire in my fists.

Cade's thick brow raises, and he leans back into his seat, seeming unfazed at my fury. "Well, let me first say—"

"Wait!" I lift my palm when I see Rae's name dash across the screen of my phone.

> Rae: Morning babe! You left without saying goodbye. But that's a good thing.

I woke up to Win and Ross hovering over me.

Just Rae's sweet tone emanating through the text douses the raging fire within me. Little do either Cade or Rae know, she's the only balm capable of soothing my wretchedness.

> Me: Sorry I had to leave so quickly. You looked too peaceful to bother, and now I have a visitor.

> Rae: You have permission to bother me anytime. Who's there?

> Me: The friend of Cedric's. We just started talking, so I need to get back to him.

> Rae: Do you need me to come now?

> Me: No, stay put. Actually, it's a good idea to keep your distance, at least until I figure him out.

> Rae: You sure?

> Me: Yes, please. Nothing's wrong, I just need to feel him out first. Like I mentioned yesterday.

> Rae: Okay that's fine. Besides, Win & Ross want me to go off island for some shopping & eats.

I can't help staring at the phone. The annoying three dots pop up, and I know it's Rae worrying what's taking me so long to reply. While I'm happy for her to get time with her brother and cousin, I still don't trust what the Changelings could do if they discovered her—especially with Winter. However, I also know how much her family means to her. Soon, I'll take her memory of them from her mind while she escorts me to the Netherworld. I'm sure it won't hurt to let her have this moment. Honestly, I don't want Cade anywhere near Rae, either. Jury is still out on whether he can be trusted.

Crap! I took too long, and I see Rae's name flash once more on my screen.

> Rae: It's okay, Khar. I understand if you don't think it's safe for me to leave the island. I'll just tell them we should stay here instead.

Me: Absolutely not! Please, go with your family. Have fun! Feel free to use the card I gave you and spend to your lovely heart's content.

> Rae: Are you sure?

Me: Of course, baby.

> Rae: I suppose I could stretch my legs and get some good retail walking in.

Me: I thought I stretched your legs quite a bit last night, but retail therapy is good too.

Me: Okay, have fun. Keep a lookout for any broken twigs or rustling leaves. Never know when I might show up.

> Rae: Love you.

Me: Always, baby.

"Ah-hem," Cade belts a faux cough, breaking me from ogling Rae's name on my phone any further. "Apparently, we have varied interpretations. Perhaps we should wait until—"

Raising my hand in protest, I offer a small smile. A slight chuckle escapes me as I think how just a brief chat with Rae has eased my angst. Despite wanting to tear Cade limb from limb only moments ago, she has such a calming effect on me that I'm sure I'm grinning like a lovesick teen. "I know you're only here to help me. Forgive me if I jumped to conclusions, but you have to understand—"

"Oh, I quite understand. Ms. Vereen is your mate, and you'd do anything in your power to protect her. That I do understand." Cade pauses, clasping his hands together, offering another genuine smile. His eyes alone tell me he's no stranger to the power a mate can wield over even the most wretched of hearts. "All I meant was there is little I can offer you, since you are already from the Netherworld. Your mate, Ms. Vereen, on the other hand, is another matter entirely."

Scratching the stubble on my jaw, I grunt; he makes a good point. "Continue," I add, offering my hand, hopeful he'll explain how he can assist Rae.

"Well, as I mentioned before, I am part Changeling. However, I am also an orphan. I never knew my parents. I was raised by others —some who were also Changeling hybrids like me. They were itinerants, or, as mortals called them, gypsies." Pausing, Cade stares at me, likely to ensure I'm following. I am, although I don't yet understand how any of this helps Rae. Since he seems happy to share, and even more amenable to assist us, I force a slight smile, hopeful to show some measure of interest. Huffing a bit, he rises from his seat. Forcing a hand in his pocket, he saunters around the cavern, gliding his hand through the candle flames along the wall. Lingering on a candle closest to Moirai's stone, he stops his pacing and turns back to me. As he clears his throat, I notice his eyes are slightly glassy. I can only imagine what he's not telling me.

"As I was saying, I am an orphan. The gypsies taught me as much as they could, but being hybrids themselves, they didn't have much to offer. That is, except for this."

Pulling his hand from his pocket, Cade dangles a silver necklace with a purplish-blue stone at its center. Armored in a thick casing, the stone flashes as candlelight shines through it, revealing a bright light illuminating the dark halls of my cave.

"Derclanite!" I exclaim, surprised to see a rare stone, normally only found in the Netherworld.

"Ah, I see you know it," he smirks, dangling the necklace.

"How did you obtain such a find?" I marvel, taking a few steps forward for a closer look.

Pulling it back so I don't touch it, Cade lifts a hand in caution. Clasping the jewel in his fist, he removes it from my view faster than I can blink. "I'm sorry, Kharon, but I fear such a treasure cannot be touched by the likes of you."

A deep rumbling fills the hollow walls of my chest, and my nose flares as heat rises beneath my skin, wary of the darkened glare now forming along Cade's otherwise gentle features. My brows furrow, but I work hard to stifle the anger brewing within me. "The likes of me?" I grit through my teeth, digging my feet deep in the earth. It's all I can do not to throw a hard blow against his chin.

With his palm still lifted, a cagey grin smears the corner of his face. "Now, now, I meant no offense, Mr. Nyx. As I said, what I have to offer is for your mate, Ms. Vereen."

Cade keeps a watchful gaze as he regards me. Slowly, I work to pace my breathing that I hardly noticed was labored as I resisted striking him down. Obviously, however, Cade noticed. Looking at him, I'm surprised to see a thin sheen of sweat resting above both his brow and mustache. Sweating isn't a normal occurrence for vampires, but Mr. Sincade DeLuca is proving to be a rare creature all his own.

I watch as the softened features of Cade's face return as I relax my posture. While it's clear he's noticeably fearful, or at least wary of me, I know better than to take Cade for granted. I've never met anyone like him, and I have no idea what talents his breeding offers. Especially being part Changeling and Altrinion-Vampire, I can hardly lower my guard or assume I have the advantage. Although I am certain, bruised or not, I'd be the one walking out of this cavern intact.

"How so?" I grunt.

A broad smile stretches across his face, as though he were happy I finally asked. "Well, you see, Kharon, this Derclanite stone was one of the few things left for me when I was orphaned. I was told my mother provided it, should I ever wish to visit your realm."

"Yes, Derclanite has commonly been used by mortals over the centuries as a medium of transport. It's such a rare find that mortals scour the Netherworld for it to ensure they can stay, for without it–" My eyes grow wide as the truth becomes plain.

Cade's eyes darken, and his thin lips seem to vanish behind his mustache. "Now you see."

"I've always known taking Rae to the Netherworld was dangerous. My ferry only serves one purpose: death. I wasn't sure how I could take her. Doing so could prove deadly."

"Yes, I'm afraid so. Beyond the purpose of your vessel, there's the issue of the differences of the two realms. Time on the earthbound plane moves at a faster pace, so it's quite possible her mortal heart could give out under the duress of your homeland. While I am certain you have no need to keep her there longer than necessary, only this Derclanite stone can assure her safety. That is, as long as she wears it for the duration."

"While I appreciate your gesture, I can't ask you to part with such a heirloom."

A small smile curves at the corner of his mouth as he leans back on the cavern wall. "In all truth, I've never seen this stone as such. It's more of a constant reminder of what I lost. Seeing as I have no desire to seek out my kin in the Netherworld, or elsewhere for that matter, it serves far better use for Ms. Vereen than it ever could for me."

"Are you sure?"

Pressing his eyes shut, he offers a brief nod before reopening them. "Absolutely."

"What shall I repay you in exchange?" I ask, knowing that where I come from, no one ever does anything out of the kindness of their heart.

Stuffing the jewel back in his pocket, Cade's thick brow rises once more, and he smirks, now holding his chin between his fingers. "Well, I'm glad you asked."

I blow out a hard sigh, wondering just how heavy a price I'll have to pay.

For the safety of Rae and the rescue of Moirai, there's no cost too high.

Four

RAE

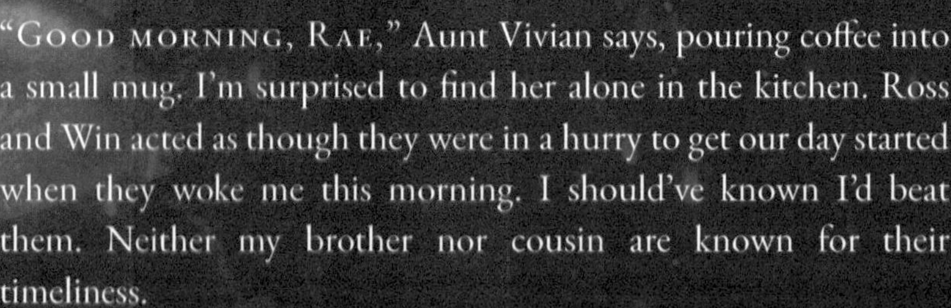

"Good morning, Rae," Aunt Vivian says, pouring coffee into a small mug. I'm surprised to find her alone in the kitchen. Ross and Win acted as though they were in a hurry to get our day started when they woke me this morning. I should've known I'd beat them. Neither my brother nor cousin are known for their timeliness.

"Morning, auntie," I reply, giving her shoulders a slight squeeze. "Where is everyone?" I ask, noticing how quiet the house seems this morning.

"Well, let's see," she begins, turning over a book on its face. My aunt never misses a quiet opportunity to read a good book, so I almost hate to interrupt her. "Your uncle left too early to tell, likely examining the pine fields for next season with Mel. Winter and Ross are outside with Stephen, warming the truck. I think Stephen is giving you all a ride to the port."

"Oh," I say, peering through the window to where I can see smoke from the exhaust blowing through the trees. The sight of it makes me think of Kharon. Often, when he goes invisible, only a whiff of smoke remains. Whether it be a cloud of smoke from a cigarette or a chimney, the mere sight of it is now synonymous with the captor of my heart. I smile at the thought.

"Rae?" Aunt Vivian questions. "Are you okay?"

Forcing myself upright, I realize I've clutched the back of her chair as I gazed through the window, my breathing a tad racy. "Oh, I'm sorry, Aunt Vivian. I'm just hungry is all. Leaning over isn't a good idea on an empty stomach, I suppose," I lie. That's all I can think to say.

My aunt's nose crinkles as she gives me her all-knowing stare. "Mmm-hmm," she huffs and takes a sip of her coffee. "Well, be sure to grab your coat, dear," she continues, allowing her forefinger to stretch away from the sides of her cup toward the coat rack. "Spring may be teasing us today, but the first flower has yet to bloom. It's still chilly out."

Nodding in reply, I pull my coat from the wall hook. Looping my arms inside, it hits me: spring is here. The thought wrangles my gut into knots. For the last few months, thoughts of going to the Netherworld have been nothing more than a nagging notion. Now, it is so much more. Now, it is a piercing reality.

The Netherworld. I'm going to the frigging Netherworld.

What in the entire hell was I thinking?

Talking tall with an iron-clad pair of lady balls I must've

borrowed from the shelf, apparently, because right now, there's nothing iron or clad about any part of me. No. Not at all.

Right now, I feel like a mouse who's found her cheese and is ready to retreat into her little hole in the wall.

But no, that's not my lot. I opened my big mouth and agreed to this, to go to the Netherworld to help Kharon rescue his sister, Moirai. I agreed to be by his side. I agreed to it all.

I cannot go back on my word. I must stay the course.

Either I grow a pair or borrow another set from the shelf, but whatever I do, I can't back down now. *Kharon depends on me.* Just knowing that Kharon needs me gives me more confidence than I've ever had in my life.

Now, *how* I can be of any help is beside me. All I know is that Kharon needs me. Even more, somehow, the Fates have decreed it. Perhaps I have a purpose beyond baked goods after all.

"Rae, darling?" my aunt calls me once more. Her tone tells me she's questioning why I'm standing here like a statue.

"Yes," I say, shaking my head, breaking myself from my musing. "Well, look at me acting like a gufflebup. I should get going. Ross and Win will come looking for me if I don't make my way out soon." Adding a quick peck to my aunt's forehead, I prepare to leave.

My aunt won't let me leave just yet. "Not so fast, my dear," she begins. Her eyes search mine, and I know she's trying to figure out what's gotten into me. I wish I could tell her it's all Kharon Nyx, but I'm pretty sure that's a tad inappropriate, more than she wants to know, and more importantly, not information I can share just yet. "Look, I know it's been a while since we've talked. I know you've been busy with school. Frankly, everyone has been too busy around here lately." Pausing, her eyes stare off distantly, and my heart sinks.

Thinking about it, every time I see her these days, she's alone. Normally, she is glued to Uncle El's hip or Winter's. Lately,

Uncle El has spent almost every waking minute with Melchior, likely trying to rebuild what they lost. With Win in school and enjoying her time with Lux, the two have had very little time together. Even Ross and I have been busier and away from the mansion more than usual. These days, my aunt has remained alone in the manor with her books. The thought pierces my heart. I hadn't thought about how she must feel. I, more than anyone, know how it feels to fade into the background. Despite our differences over the years, the thought of her alone sinks my heart.

Shaking her head, she forces her throat to clear, bringing herself back to the moment. "As I was saying, I know we haven't talked much, but I can tell you've been...distracted as of late. I just want you to know you can always talk to me. About anything." Taking my hand in hers, she gives it a squeeze. "I mean it, Rae. Besides, I know it must be difficult to see your brother and cousin all engrossed in their love lives. I told Winter they needed to find a way to be more inclusive of you. We are family first."

What? She told Win to take me out? What am I? A charity case?

I thought they wanted to spend time with me. This changes things.

Stifling an eye roll, I dig my nail into the side of my hip instead and bite my bottom lip. I can't believe I fell for Win's sudden interest in me. And Ross? I can't believe my twin brother went along with it.

Then, inspiration hits.

"You should come with us!" I exclaim, forcing my voice higher than the groan thickening in my throat. "It's a lovely day. There's no reason you should be held up in here all alone."

My aunt's brows lift and her eyes brighten, revealing the more youthful features hiding behind her otherwise no-nonsense expression. "Really? Oh–oh no, I couldn't. Today is for you young folk.

I'd just be in the way." Shaking her head, she turns away and reaches for her coffee. "You should get going."

Placing my hand over hers, I gently push her cup down before she has a chance to bring it to her mouth, offering the biggest smile when she looks up at me. With the way the sun shines through the window, my aunt's cocoa skin glistens, highlighting her youthful features as her smile reaches her now-dancing eyes.

"No, I insist, Aunt Vivian. It'll be fun. If I recall, you took me to Capers—just me and you—when you and Uncle El first took me and Ross in."

Her eyes widen in surprise as her berry lips part slightly. "You remember that?"

Nodding and taking her hand in mine, I smile. "How could I ever forget? That was the day I knew everything would be okay." Tears crest in the corners of my eyes, but I resist the urge to cry. That's not what this moment is about. But when I see glassy pools form in the eyes of my usually staunch and stoic aunt, I can no longer hold back.

Sharing a brief laugh as we both turn away from one another to wipe our tears, I pull my aunt up from her seat with my free hand.

"Well, I guess when you put it that way, how could I resist?" Aunt Vivian says, pulling me in for a hug.

"That's the point, Aunt Vivian. You can't." Squeezing her equally petite frame, another loose tear falls to my chin. Although my initial inclination was to stick it to Win, this just feels... *right*.

Five

KHARON

STILL RUBBING his chin with an incredulous grin, Cade's eyes bounce around the cavern before turning his attention back to me. "Let me first say that I won't ask you to go out of your way to repay me—if that's even what we want to call it."

My brow lifts, and I force my hands in my pockets. It's all I can do to keep my fire at bay. While he's shown me little cause to worry, I don't readily trust people, especially ones I've just met. "I'm listening," I mumble, too low for human ears, but enough so his Changeling-vampiric ears hear every word.

"When you reach the holding chamber, the place you'll undoubtedly find your sister, I need you to do something for me."

Groaning, I sigh. Although Cade is part Changeling, he's never been to the Netherworld, nor does he know how things work there. Just entering that chamber is dangerous enough–and with Rae with me, I'll barely have the time and strength to rescue Moirai. I certainly won't have a chance to free anyone else.

Before I have an opportunity to protest, Cade raises his palm. "No worries, good sir, I'll not ask you to rescue anyone. I just need you to call out a name."

My heart sinks as I witness the glassy pools in his eyes. I jumped the gun. Here I am, worried about protecting those I love, and this man stands before me, likely worried about the woman who gave him life.

"I'm sorry," I replied softly reply. "Please tell me your mother isn't a prisoner."

Scrunching his face, confused, he quickly belts a hearty chuckle. Shrugging his shoulders almost dismissively, he waves his hand again. "Oh, her?" he laughs again. "I haven't a clue. She could still be in this realm, for all I know."

"I don't understand. Your tone earlier–you seemed to care for this person." This acquaintance of Cedric's is quite a puzzle. It's been a long time since someone in this realm has confounded me. Then again, he *is* part Changeling. His speech is just as furtive as his kin.

"No, I'm sorry if I led you astray. I'll say it's not for lack of care, but probably not the level of care you have for your sister or Ms. Vereen."

"Ah, I see." Stepping away, I walk back to my desk and sit. I really don't have time for this man and his riddles, but I'll endure what I must, for no other reason than my sister and Rae's safety.

Slowly, he paces toward me as he fidgets his hand in the inside pocket of his coat. Pulling out a small intricately folded note card, he hands it to me.

"Origami?" I question. I can almost feel my brow brushing

against the hair hanging on my forehead. Cade's bright smile fades some as my annoyance becomes harder to ignore.

"No, sir," he answers, his tone a tad flat. Perhaps he's equally annoyed with me. I should care, but I don't. "Just a note, I'm afraid."

Looking at the paper shaped like a flower, I pull at one of the petal edges.

Reaching across my desk, his hand hovers over mine. "Please, my lord…" he says, staring around the cavern nervously. "Do not open it. *Not here.* Not yet." Cade remains with his hands shaking over mine, watching me carefully until I offer a small nod.

"You seem fearful, young one," I add, watchful of the sweat now glazing his mustache. It is an odd sight. Especially since vampires aren't known to sweat.

"And rightfully so, I'm afraid," he says, standing upright. Wiping the back of his hand against his forehead, he rounds my desk until he once more finds his seat.

"Look," I begin, trying hard to rein in my growing frustration. "While I appreciate you wanting to offer your heirloom, I'm beginning to think it may not be a good idea. Firstly, I don't know you. I hardly know Cedric enough to trust any acquaintance he offers. Seeing as I had limited options, I thought, what the hell. Now, however, I think–"

"Please, Kharon," Cade says, both his hands raised in caution. "I know I seem a bit off kilter, but I assure you, it's for good reason."

"How so?"

"Well, for starters, coming here is just as dangerous for me. I haven't a clue about my origins more than I've already shared. What I do know is that the Wretched Ones have not ceased their pursuit of Elysian blood. While it may appear they have vacated their hold on you, we both know better."

"Tell me what you know!" I say, pounding my fist against the desk with a sudden burst of energy.

"I know you've hidden an oracle stone behind you." Pointing over my shoulder, Cade pauses as my eyes glance at his finger. Withdrawing his hand, he clasps his hands together, resting them on his lap. "I also know the name in the paper will make no sense to you, but it will mean something to the Wretched Ones. In fact, it means more than you know."

"So why can't I open it?"

"I'd rather you didn't. That is, until you're in proximity where saying the name will mean anything. You'll also find a message only for the name you now hold in your hand. I assure you, it's no more danger than you'll already be in when you arrive at the Changeling hall. I promise. When you return, I simply ask you let me know if you were able to share the message."

"That's all?"

Cade presses his thin lips together tightly, before looking back up at me. "Yes, that's all."

Groaning, I fold my arms over my chest. "Why do I feel there's something you're not telling me?"

"Because *there is something* I'm not telling you." Pausing, he looks up at me a bit, likely trying to discern my mood. I keep a pointed stare, with just enough of a softened expression to make it safe for him to continue. Blowing out a sigh, he clasps his hands together before taking a deep breath. "Suffice it to say, whatever I am withholding would seem more like a side plot to your already enthralling story, as it were. More importantly, just as the Changelings used you to exact their measure of ill will toward mankind, I too know of their dark witchery. You and the Elysians may be one medium they used to break into this realm, but there are others. Some are even dearest to me. That is why I am offering my assistance to you now. Because one day, my lord, I fear we'll need to stand together, contending against the very darkness you now seek to face."

Looking at him now, only silence drifts through me. It's clear he trusts me just about as much as I trust him, so I don't fault him for not being direct with me. Still, it's also evident that we have the same enemy.

The Changelings.

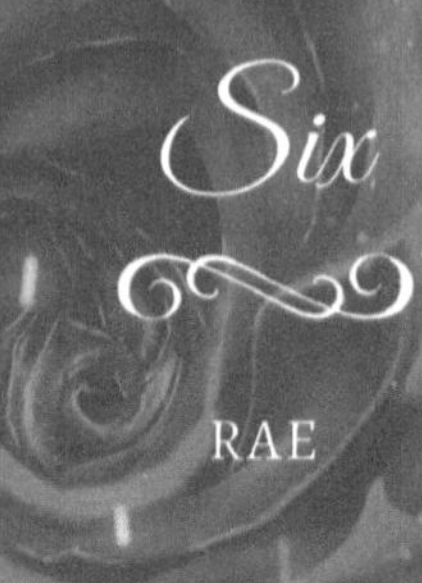

Six

RAE

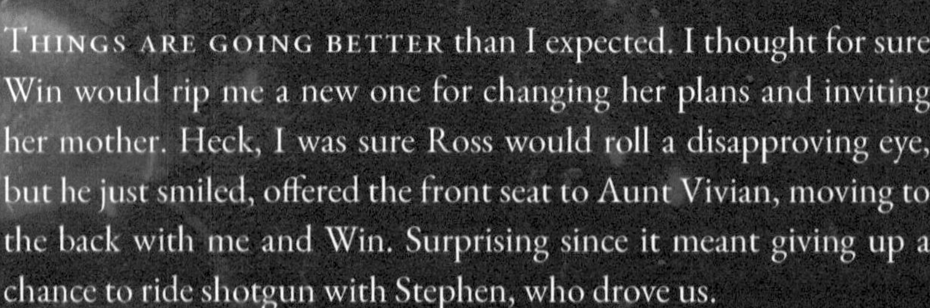

Things are going better than I expected. I thought for sure Win would rip me a new one for changing her plans and inviting her mother. Heck, I was sure Ross would roll a disapproving eye, but he just smiled, offered the front seat to Aunt Vivian, moving to the back with me and Win. Surprising since it meant giving up a chance to ride shotgun with Stephen, who drove us.

Then again, I don't know why I expected to get under their skin. Our family is used to doing things together, so I'm sure this wasn't the disappointing surprise I'd hoped to ruffle their feathers. Besides, I suppose the way my aunt encouraged them to take me out is no different than me bringing her along.

Breakfast at Capers is wonderful. If you ever wanted to experience bagels on steroids, you're sure to find it here. I always opt for the three-cheese omelet bagel. Sure, I can only imagine the thousands of calories I'm inhaling, but I hardly give it a second thought.

For Ross and me, this is certainly a treat. We're normally the ones who make breakfast for the family, so having someone cook for us is quite welcoming. Even more, it's our favorite meal of the day. This, of course, and *second breakfast.* You know, true to our Merry and Pippin roles.

"I am stuffed!" Win sighs, pushing away from the table and leaning back in her seat.

"Me too!" Ross adds while swirling his last piece of bacon in what remains of his egg. "I could eat this everyday," he croons, quickly forking a leftover crumble of avocado into his mouth.

Shaking her head, Aunt Vivian chuckles. "I really don't know how you eat those runny eggs, Ross. They're so slimy." She scrunches her face, her shoulders quivering with disgust.

We all share a laugh, and Win reaches over to squeeze my knee. *Thank you,* she mouths quietly, shifting a gaze over to her mom and back at me. Covering her hand with mine, I offer a small nod. I can't help inwardly scolding myself for wanting to somehow hurt my cousin. Not only was that a crummy thing to do, but I should've known someone as sweet as Winter wouldn't see this as an imposition.

"Well, auntie, we should hang out for dinner, too. I plan on devouring a cow mid-moo. Nothing but medium rare for me. I just love when the blood runs all over the plate onto my pomme frites," he jeers, making a mooing sound while nuzzling Aunt Vivian's shoulder.

She laughs aloud, and her face brightens. It's good to see her happy, and even better to see her smile.

"Aww, leave my mom alone!" Winter quips, playfully shoving Ross' shoulder.

"That's right, dear, you tell 'em," Aunt Vivian says, offering an approving nod.

"I mean, if my mom wants to eat tires and call it steak, that's her right!" she laughs.

"Hey!" Wagging a reprimanding finger, my aunt huffs playfully before laughing once more.

Just as our chorus of laughter rounds the table, the sound of the ferry horn blowing outside calls our attention.

"All right, party people," Ross begins, standing up from the table. "That's our cue. I'll settle up front and you darlings make your way to the ferry."

"Are you sure, Ross, dear?" Aunt Vivian questions, surprised by the gesture.

"While I might be the prettiest thing at this roundtable, my father would roll over in his grave if he thought his son anything less than a gentleman. Not to mention, Uncle El would have my hide, especially since he gave me the duckets for this little endeavor," Ross laughs, pulling out a wad of cash and zipping toward the cashier.

The news of my uncle having anything to do with our outing puzzles me. My uncle doesn't do kind gestures without a purpose. While everyone continues laughing, my mind wanders.

What, I wonder, is my uncle up to?

Maybe leaving the island wasn't a good idea.

Despite saying he'd accept my relationship with Kharon, I can tell he's still not sold on the idea. The few times he's seen Kharon over the last few months, he's kept the conversation short. Mainly, he only accompanies Melchior when he comes by to chat with Moirai's stone. Uncle El never comes into the cavern, but instead keeps himself perched outside, carefully watching his son and Kharon's every move. It's obvious he still doesn't trust Melchior alone with Kharon.

Although I'm sure he fears losing his son again, from the way he watches Kharon like a hawk, it's clear he still holds Kharon responsible for Melchior's disappearance.

Kharon has said Uncle El chooses to lay all the blame on him because it's easier than taking responsibility for the part he played in his own son's demise.

Still, I can tell Uncle El does what he can to make up with Melchior. He nearly bends over backwards to meet my cousin's every whim. While my uncle has appointed Winter to catch her brother up on the family business, Uncle El has used every moment in between to indulge in leisure activities with his son. From ice-river fishing to regular weekends at wine tastings and cigar houses, my uncle is making up for lost time as best as he can.

All of it makes it that much harder to be mad at him for his obstinance toward Kharon. *He'll come around*. At least that's what I keep telling myself.

"Rae?" I hear Win say my name while tapping my side.

"Huh?" I answer, shaking myself from my musing. Looking over my shoulder, I'm surprised to now find only Winter and I left at the table. "Where's your mom?"

A baffled stare is all Win offers before breaking into a sweet chuckle. "She went to the restroom, Rae. Didn't you hear her grumble before she left?"

"Oh, I must've missed that," I reply, quickly wiping my mouth and grabbing my purse from the back of my chair. "What was she grumbling about?"

Winter stands and slips on her coat, and I do the same. "You know, the usual. Something about her old lady bones and her bladder not being what it used to be."

Laughing, I smile. More so, I'm thankful I didn't miss anything major. "Ah, I see."

"Oh, I almost forgot. She also complained about the ferry restrooms being subpar. I guess she thinks Don Addy's boats aren't as nice as the ones that wretched Kharon had."

There it is. I was truly hoping the topic of Kharon wouldn't come up today. I should've known better.

Shrugging my shoulders, I look away, hopeful Winter doesn't catch my eyeroll. "Well, she's not wrong, Win. Kharon had the best fleet on the island."

Twisting her mouth into a frown, Win stares at me like she wants to say more, but chokes back her words. Swiping her curly tendrils from her forehead, she quickly zips up her coat, sighing hard as she does. She takes a step forward but turns back on her heel, stopping me short of running into her. "Okay, fine, that monster had a nice ferry. But I'd rather ride on a cardboard float across the sea before taking one step onto anything belonging to Kharon Nyx."

I want to say something. *I should say something*, but I can't. For her safety. For my family's safety. For the safety of everyone in this room.

She has no idea how much *saying nothing* is protecting her right now. She has no idea the same wicked creatures who captured her brother likely want to do the same to her or worse.

It's my job to keep that from happening. Mine and the *monster* she holds in contempt. To protect her, I'll stay quiet, like always. One day soon, I won't be so quiet.

Seven

KHARON

"You're the first vampire I've met with those," I say, changing the subject to point at the black veins beneath the skin on Cade's hand.

"Ah, so you *have* noticed," Cade answers, trailing his finger almost proudly along his black veins that seem to move beneath his translucent skin. "Yes, I suppose I am special that way."

"Courtesy of your Changeling origins, I presume?" This time, I'm not feigning interest.

He smiles. "That is correct."

"So, besides abiding a sliver of the sun and your veins, care to share any other differences?"

Tapping his fingers along my desk, he looks over his shoulder momentarily, then back at me. "Frankly, it's mostly aesthetic. The look of my skin and not scorching in the sun seem to be the major variances from my blood thirsty kin. That, and my heart still beats, albeit slower than a human heart, but it beats nonetheless. Other than that, I subsist on a normal blood diet and abide by all the other rules."

"That's interesting. I haven't ventured far from Nova Scotia since my arrival, so I've only been privy to the supernaturals on the island. Cedric and Lux are the first hybrids I've met on the earthbound plane. There are tons in the Netherworld, but you, I must say, are quite a find."

Darting an appreciative smile, his eyes dance slightly. He doesn't appear like someone accustomed to compliments. Interesting.

"Well, I appreciate that, Kharon. I suppose I can say the same of you. I've never met a *ferryman* before. Truly, I've only met a few stragglers from your homeland."

"Really? Who?" Now I'm really interested. I only know of a few who fled centuries ago.

Pushing up in his seat, his posture stiffens some. "Ah, I prefer not to say. Most are refugees. I'm sure they'd rather remain anonymous."

"Fair." I can appreciate his sense of propriety. "Is it safe to presume beyond Cedric, our meeting today will be kept confidential?"

Offering a quaint nod, Cade purses his lips tight. "No one beyond the mates of you and Cedric will hear anything from me."

"Thank you."

"Of course." Jumping up from his seat, he brushes his hands on his sides. "Well, if there's nothing more, I should get going. I'd still like to catch the next ferry."

"Right, avoiding the domestics," I say, standing up to walk him to the entrance. "Oh, but before you go–"

Turning quickly on my heel, I'm surprised to find Cade dangling the necklace. Once more, his eyes dance as the flickers of light illuminate the blood orange glow of his irises.

"Do you have something I can put this in? It's best if you don't touch it."

Huffing, I frown but make my way back to my desk. I grab the blue velvet fabric I've kept Rae's hair in and offer it to Cade. "Will this work?"

"Perfect!" he exclaims, carefully lowering it inside. "I'm sorry, good sir, but this gem is strictly for someone from the earthbound plane. When it was given to me, I was instructed not to let any other supernaturals touch it. Derclanite tends to be precious that way, I'm afraid."

"I see," I reply, gently folding the velvet over the jewel, careful not to touch it. "It is a rather precious stone. This is my first time seeing it up close. It's very rare."

"Yes, and from what I understand, the Changelings were responsible for hiding all manner of rare and precious stones across the two realms."

"Ah, you know your history," I answer, surprised.

"Some," he groans, stepping back. His brows turn inward a bit as he looks back at me.

"What is it?" His pensive gaze is giving him away.

"Well–it's just...I don't know you, and I'm sure you know what you're doing, but—"

"Spit it out." I work hard to keep my tone low. He's a grown man. By his speech and manner alone, I know he's older than his youthful face suggests. Still, I close the space between us. I need him to speak his mind.

"How do you plan to thwart the Wretched Ones? From what I understand, they ensnared you and held your sister captive. While I certainly can't pretend to understand the strength you may possess as a ferryman, I know better than to underestimate their power." A sheepish stare is all Cade offers in return for my pointed gaze, but he continues. "Please know, I mean no offense."

My posture softens. I won't say I'm wholly trusting of him, but he seems genuinely concerned. Taking a few steps back, I create a bit of distance as I pull my hand from my pocket. Opening my palm, a flaming ball of fire forms, growing into a shining orb. I'm careful to turn slightly, ensuring none of my fiery essence reaches Cade. He may be different, but he's still a vampire. I don't want to hurt him.

Stepping back, he puts on his sunglasses and rests his forearm against his mouth. Nothing but shock etches every corner of his face as he stares at me.

"How can you?" Cade gasps, now pressed against the cave wall. "Impossible!"

"Very possible," I say.

Relaxing his posture some, he steps away from the wall but maintains his distance. "Fire? Are you saying they can be killed by fire?"

Blowing a cloud of dark smoke against my hand, the fire douses as I slowly close my fist. "Let's just say this is only a fraction of my capabilities. Once I free my sister—well, Moirai is capable of more than you can imagine."

"Magnificent!" Cade exclaims, and I see what looks to be the makings of hope dancing in his eyes. "So you can destroy them? Once and for all?"

Grunting, I shove my hand back in my pocket. "I'm afraid, *destroy* is too broad a word. What I can do is free my sister and keep Rae safe; of course, with your aid. Unfortunately, the power of the Changeling witches is still a stronghold in my realm. It'll take more than the power I alone possess to end them entirely."

Cade's eyes fall, and I almost hate to douse the kindling hope I just saw only moments ago, but I rather not give him false hope.

My goals are simple: free my sister and keep Rae safe in the process. Everything else is secondary.

"I see," he mutters, fumbling with his collar. "Well, have you fought their kind before? Or at least know their weaknesses?"

"Do you?" It's not a retort. In fact, it's just the opposite. "What do you know of their weakness?" The gleam in his eye tells me he knows more than he's letting on. "Please, tell me."

Lifting a cautionary hand, his gaze bounces around, as though he were sifting through his mind for the right words. Pushing away from the wall, his face brightens. "Cedric mentioned you have encountered a Jinn jar. Do you have it?"

I nod. "I can get it.

"Good. You'll need it. As you know, the Changelings are bound in kind, marked by two."

Circling the area, I nod again in agreement. "Yes, we call them the Traveling Sisters."

"Interesting—the pair cannot be broken. If you were to open a Jinn, release it in their presence. It could disorient them enough for you to strike a mighty blow."

"Well, my new friend, I'll say this. You lied when we first met." Pausing, I watch as his brows tighten, but when he spies my forming smile, his expression softens. "You said you only had help for my mate. As fate would have it, you indeed offered the help I didn't know I needed."

Eight

RAE

Nothing like a little shopping to put us in a good mood.

The ferry ride was quiet, far quieter than I thought it'd be after such a nice breakfast. With my aunt's uneasiness on Don Addy's less-than-pristine ferry, Ross fawning over his call with Stephen, and the silent stand-off Winter and I shared, you could hear a pin drop.

What difference a little retail therapy makes!

Within fifteen minutes of strolling the promenade, we found ourselves laughing, shopping, and frolicking as though we never missed a beat. In fact, this is how I remember it always being: my aunt taking us out on the weekend to shop, have lunch, and catch up. Aunt Vivian never shied away from keeping us up on the latest fashions. She ensured we were dressed in nothing but the best. Although me and Winter do our best to stay trendy, my brother picked up our aunt's panache for finer things more than either of us.

That's why watching Ross and Aunt Vivian work their way through the stores is such a spectacle. Both Win and I normally stay entertained for a while before skulking off into our own corners of the shopping district. Win typically veers off toward home goods while I make my way to the jewelry.

I needed this.

I've been so absorbed in all things Kharon, pastry arts classes, and keeping my family from finding out about us that I've taken too little *me time* as of late.

This feels good.

While we'll inevitably find our way back to one another, I'm sure Win needed a little distance from Lux, just as much as my twin could use a breather from Stephen. My aunt, well, she most of all needed a reminder to do something she enjoys while my uncle reconnects with Melchior.

Taking a deep breath, I exhale, enjoying the cool breeze as I make my way along the gravel shopping court. There are a few table vendors in the center, so I leisurely stroll by, seeing if anything strikes my fancy. I'm not looking for anything in particular, but I'll know when it catches my eye.

Silk scarves! Buy one, get one half off! one kiosk seller calls in my direction.

Hand-painted pottery, perfect for your indoor garden, another shouts.

End of season sale on all mittens and toques! the first yells louder, vying for my attention.

She won't get it.

Aunt Vivian taught me well. I'm not an easy sell, and I'm

shrewder than my mild disposition suggests. I can haggle with the best of them and, much like my uncle, I can be stubborn as a mule. I continue my pace past the tables, making as little eye contact as possible.

A small, elderly woman is putting away bracelets in a basket. Odd. The shops haven't been open long enough to close for the day. Perhaps she's not interested in competing with her table neighbors today, or maybe the cool breeze blowing through the courtyard is disrupting her business. Either way, I pick up my pace, hurrying to her table, a few shiny trinkets catching my eye.

"Miss!" I lift my voice just enough to be heard, but not quite a shout.

She definitely heard me. Her face lifts just above a few decorative crates sitting on her table. A kind smile with eyes shoot to me, ones that seem too young to match the folded skin freckled with liver spots. I offer a wave to let her know I'm on my way.

From the corner of my eye, I catch a few scowls from the other vendors, but I pay them no attention; nothing they have interests me.

These sparkly things... *Yes*, they interest me greatly.

"Yes, dear," the woman, with a name tag that reads *Sophe*, begins. "Do you see something you like?" Her smile remains steady, but the lilt in her tone tells me she's happy to assist me.

My eyes scan her table quickly, looking at all the pretty things on display. "Oh, there's so many things. Do you have any specials? I don't see any prices," I say, flipping over a bracelet and pair of earrings, looking for sale stickers.

"Well, my dear, everything you see here is handmade. I'd hate for the tape to mess with these little lovelies, so here's a price list," she adds, pulling out a small easel from her storage trunk. I scan the sign and smile, noting how everything is reasonably priced.

Admiring the full display, my hands trail the edge of the table. "Everything's so nice."

"I think this one matches the lovely color of your eyes," she says, holding up a lovely banded jewel of silver with a pinkish hue.

"What is this curious color? It's like tie-dye with silver." My eyes scan the pretty stone in the center as the woman lifts her palm for me to get a closer look.

"This one is dipped in pomegranate oil while the silver is still warm." Turning her palm a bit, she shifts it side to side. I watch as the pinkish color seems to move like waves. "An illusion, of course," she says, answering the question she knows will likely come next.

"Is this a ruby?" I ask, pointing to the stone. "It's my birthstone."

"No, I'm afraid not, my dear," she replies, her face falling. Moving her hand to return it to the table, I can see she is sad to miss a sale.

Lightly taking her wrist in my hand, I smile. "Oh, that's okay. I still want it." Her smile broadens, and I watch her eyes dance in response. She grabs some tissue paper and puts it inside. "It's such a pretty bracelet. I may just need an extra clamp to fit it on my wrist."

Her shoulders shake as she laughs, lifting the bracelet out of the tissue paper. "It's an ankle bracelet." Peering over the table, she looks down at my feet. Her gaze flits past my canvas shoes where she can get a decent view of my ankles just below my denim cuffs. "It looks like it'll be a perfect fit!" she exclaims.

Pointing to a small folding chair at the side of her table, she gestures for me to put my leg up. I watch her petite frame saunter closer to me. She's small, even shorter than me. Her black hair is pulled into a low bun in the back as thick silver graces the crown of her head. Draped in a thick black afghan, I can barely make out the rest of her outfit as she shuffles faster than I thought possible behind the seat.

I place my foot in the center of the chair, and she seamlessly affixes the jewel to my ankle. Reaching down to touch it, I marvel at how warm the metal feels against my skin. I expected it to be cold, but its temperature is a pleasant surprise. I notice the pinkish hue still seems to swirl some, and I glide my forefinger along the edge, hopeful I can break the illusion. I notice a tinge of pink on my finger, and I wonder if it will stain my clothes. Good thing my pants sit just above my ankles.

"Don't worry about that, dear," the woman says softly. "I just made this one yesterday, so it still needs to set. Oh, and I forgot to add that the stone is actually a pomegranate seed glazed in crushed zirconia. Gives it that ruby-like glow." She rushes her words as she holds my hand steady while I lower my foot.

"It's so pretty," I add as I pull out the credit card Kharon gave me. I chuckle at the thought of the Ferryman of the Netherworld using such things, but I brush the thought away. He's been here for a decade; I'm sure he's had to use things like this to assimilate. "How much again?" I ask, looking for the price easel, but I no longer see it. When did she move it?

"My treat," she answers, clasping her hands together at her waist.

"Ma'am, please, I couldn't," I counter, reaching down to pull off the bracelet.

"I insist," she says, tugging firmly on my shoulder. "Besides, it's my fault. I forgot to bring my card reader. That's why I was packing up earlier. With the way it looks on you, it's obvious it was made for you. Think of it as an early birthday present."

If I had cash, I could protest, but she's right. It does feel like it was made *just for me*.

Nine

KHARON

"So, sister, what do you think?" Moirai's stone brightens at the sound of my voice. Offering my palm with the Derclanite necklace laying atop the velvet fabric, my heart quickens, hopeful my sister will give me good news.

Cade wasted little time leaving after discussing ways to best the Changelings. I got the eerie feeling he feared he'd bring too much attention to himself while at my cavern. It's obvious he has no desire to meet any of his dark kin, so I suppose lingering in my domicile was out of the question.

Once more, I call to Moirai, but her light only flashes in

"I–I'm sorry brother," her voice cracks, as though she merely had bad phone reception.

"Moirai, what's wrong?" I ask, worried. "Moirai!" I shout, banging my hand on the wall next to her stone.

"I–I'm sorry, Kharon. I'm not sure how much longer I can manage this duality. The power of the stone and that taken by my captors lessens my strength daily. I thought I could hold on until spring, but I fear I cannot."

The crackling sound of my sister's voice hurts me. I've never heard her sound like this before. Tired. Broken.

A loud roar erupts from me, and I shove my fist through the wall. Grinding my teeth, I work hard to stifle my ire. "What have they done to you?"

"Please, brother, do not trouble yourself. I will be fine. I only need some time for my strength to restore." Moirai's tone is calmer than before, but she still sounds winded.

"Do not worry, Moirai. Spring is here. You will see my face again. *Soon.* I will finally rid us of the curse our wretched father wrought upon us."

"It does me good to know this, Kharon. The dark ones have pulled from me more than usual as of late. The Great Eye seems almost veiled from me. I fear if they take any more, the power of the Great Eye will be lost."

Clenching my jaw, the thought paralyzes me with fear. Fates like my sister need the power of the Great Eye to see into the future. The power lives within each Fate to proclaim what shall become. If such power fell wholly into the hands of the Changelings, there would be no stopping them.

I suppose that's why the Fates were separated long ago to the four corners of the Netherworld. Many feared that should the Changelings capture all of them they would have access to unlimited power. Moirai is a Supreme Fate, which means she leads their order. Ever since our father, Erebus, sold us to the Changelings, the order has been scattered, leaderless.

This is why I must save my sister. She must be restored to her rightful place as a leader of her order. Doing so will ensure the power of the Great Eye remains, balance maintained in both this realm and the Netherworld combined.

I'd risk all that I am to save her, simply because she is my sister. I'll do that and more for the good of all. My soul may be dark and villainous, but it is not without honor.

"All will not be lost, dear sister. I will save you." Trailing my hand along the coolness of the stone, I work hard to see her face through the thick hazy chasm. I can only make out her silhouette, but I see her hand reach toward mine.

Our fingers press together along the stone, and the warmth I feel warms my heart.

"Soon, brother. Soon," Moirai whispers.

"Soon," I repeat.

"But yes, Kharon, the Derclanite stone is precisely what you'll need to ensure Rae can safely enter our realm."

"Enter and depart, you mean." My tone is gruff. Fates do not mince words. She said exactly what she meant.

Moirai's light brightens but she backs away from the stone and I can no longer see her frame. "Brother, just as I told you months ago, Rae will be safe."

"But will she–"

"Kharon, that is all I can say for now. Soon, you will see my face, and we'll leave this wickedness once and for all. Until that time, perfect your magic. I know it's been a while since you've had to use your skill. We will need it all–that and the power of Jinn. Until then, goodbye, brother."

Just like that, Moirai's stone darkens.

I'll never understand how Fates know what they do, but

hearing Moirai confirm Cade's idea of using the power of a Jinn to disorient the Changelings tells me I must be on the right track.

Unfortunately, I don't feel entirely good about the track I'm on.

From the beginning, I've known this would be a risk for Rae, and my time with Moirai didn't help matters. I know there's something she's not telling me, but I also trust my sister wouldn't willingly put the woman I love in harm's way. She, more than anyone, knows how much Rae means to me.

For now, I'll have to trust what the Fates have decreed for my life, even if it means trusting them with the only woman who's set my heart ablaze.

Ten

RAE

"RAE!" Winter shouts to me from behind. Turning around, I find her with Ross. Waving at me with multiple bags dangling from her wrist and clutched beneath her arms, I chuckle, knowing she's definitely made the most of our shopping trip.

Ross smiles, leaning against a brick wall wearing a new salmon-colored jacket he wasn't wearing this morning. With only one large bag at his side, which I make out to be shoes, I'm certain my twin has spent a small fortune on whatever is in that bag and on his back.

Looking around, I'm surprised I don't see Aunt Vivian. A large clock in the promenade says it's almost noon, and I wonder where the time has gone. It doesn't seem like we've been gone that long, but now it's almost lunchtime. My stomach grumbles just as I make my way toward my cousin and brother, and everyone laughs as I hold myself at my waist.

"Same here," Ross grumbles, rubbing his abdomen. "I've walked off everything I ate at Capers."

I nod in agreement. "Me too."

"Already?" Win smiles, looking between me and Ross. "You two are always hungry!"

"If we don't eat soon it'll turn into *hangry*," Ross whines, using his foot to push himself from the wall.

"Now see, Ross, that's because you're on a lumberjack's diet. All that time you're spending with Stephen has you eating just like him," I tease, bumping my hip into him. He offers a weak laugh in return, but his eyes tell me he's probably thinking of Stephen right now. The two have been inseparable. This is probably the longest they've been apart in the last few months.

"Yeah, I mean, you've even bulked up a little," Winter says, squeezing his bicep.

Laughing a little more, Ross raises a brow, offering his best *The Rock* impersonation. "Please, you know I've always had these guns." Flexing his arm, he shifts side to side, rolling his shoulders back, allowing his new jacket to fall to the middle of his back.

"Win, darling!" I hear my aunt call nearby, but I don't see her.

"There she is!" Winter says, pointing behind me.

"Who is she with?" Ross asks, picking up his bag from the ground.

Hunching her shoulders, Winter gives me and Ross a confused look. "I don't know."

With curious glances, we make our way across the courtyard of the shopping center toward Aunt Vivian. Her smile is wide as she watches us, but the woman at her side remains hidden behind a large fountain. It's not uncommon for my aunt to find someone she knows everywhere we go. She and Uncle El are well known on our island and many of the neighboring provinces.

"Whoever it is, they better have snacks," Ross gripes, leaning into my ear.

"Agreed," I whisper back.

Winter strides a distance in front of us. Aunt Vivian has raised her daughter to be at the heel of her every word, so it's no wonder my cousin's pace picks up. It's a strange dance between my aunt and cousin. Despite how jovial she's been today, Aunt Vivian is rather direct and cool with Winter. While my cousin works hard to appease both her parents, even well into her mid-twenties, it remains obvious that Winter holds her parents in high regard.

Being orphans, Ross and I do our best not to get caught up in the tango between Winter and our aunt and uncle. So, as is typical for us, we hang back a bit, for no other reason than to discern if we're walking into the hornet's nest or the honey pot.

For now, it seems it's the honey pot.

Aunt Vivian is all smiles as we make our way closer, waving us forward. I still can't make out the woman at her side, her face blurry from a distance. Odd. I don't need glasses, but I find myself squinting trying to see her.

Winter crosses the threshold to a group of small tables outside a row of fast-food shops. Ross and I try to make our way through, but there are lines forming and the area is tight.

"Ouch!" Ross groans next to me as he runs into a small woman with a cart.

"Oh, my goodness, I'm sorry dearest," a familiar voice chimes from behind the large cart. A few boxes lay scattered on the ground where a few pieces of jewelry now adorn the gravel pathway.

Stooping down to help the woman, I'm surprised to find Sophe, the woman who sold me my ankle bracelet.

"Ms. Sophe!" I exclaim, taking her hand to help her from the ground. I'm surprised by how smooth her hand feels in mine.

Despite the liver spots and chill in the air, her skin feels silky and warm. "Let us help you," I continue, gesturing for Ross. He tries to peer over the cart to get Winter's attention, but with the crowds, she can't see him.

"I'm so sorry. I couldn't see around this big rig. I don't know why they gave this to an old lady like me." She laughs, squeezing my hand firmly as she regains her footing.

"Mmm... pretty," Ross coos, holding a shiny silver necklace with a blue stone in the center. Handing it back to Sophe after he manages to put everything back in her boxes, his eyes dance as the lovely jewel shimmers in his palm.

Taking his hand in hers, she cups the necklace in his hand and offers a warm smile. "You keep it, dear," she whispers.

"I couldn't," Ross gasps, looking over his shoulder at me, then back at Sophe.

"I insist," she counters, squeezing his hand. "Besides, it's good fortune to give to twins."

Ross and I share a look and laugh. "How'd you know?" I ask, adding another box to her cart.

"It's not hard to guess. You have the same beautiful eyes," Sophe replies, taking my chin in her small fingers. "Like ambers of light dancing behind a forest of pine." Sophe's gaze deepens into mine, and for a moment, it's like we're the only two in the promenade.

A fluttering feeling flows through me, and I feel dizzy.

"Pip," Ross shakes me, and I lean into him. I feel faint. "Come on, sis, hang in there," Ross says, fanning me with his hand. "What's wrong?"

My stomach rumbles once more, and Ross chuckles, the worry I just saw in his eyes fading.

"Dearest, you should eat," Sophe adds, taking my hand in hers.

"Yes, we were just making our way to grab some lunch. Thank you, Miss–"

"Ms. Sophe," I groan, pulling myself together.

"How do you two know each other?" Ross questions, taking the bags from my hand. With a raised brow, he gives me a stern finger wagging when I try to take them back.

The clock strikes noon, and a loud chime blares through the courtyard.

"I must be going, I'm afraid," Sophe answers, pushing her cart away. Looking over her shoulder, she offers me a wink. "I'm sure we'll see each other again. Now, you two get something to eat."

Stepping in front of me, Ross looks me over, his brow still raised. "Yes, I can't have you fainting on me again. I don't need your ferryman breathing down my neck if he finds out. I'd hate to have Stephen whack him with his ax if he got all huffy with me."

Grunting, I twist my mouth to the side, shaking my head at my brother's insinuation. He's only half joking.

"Hey you two!" Winter's bright voice rings through the air as she approaches us. Peering around my brother's brooding posture, I look for Ms. Sophe, but I'm surprised to see her farther than I thought she'd be. "We have a table just over there," Winter says, smiling brightly.

"Good, because we're starving!" Ross blurts, looping our arms together and leading us away.

For some reason, I feel strange. For a reason I can't explain, I don't think it's my hunger.

Eleven

KHARON

I SPENT the remainder of the morning training.

It's been years since I've used any of my real power. I'm sure my sister suspects I've grown rusty in my time away. She wasn't wrong, but it doesn't take me long to work up my skill.

Harnessing my power is much like going to the gym. After a few repetitions, I grow stronger, building the muscle of my magic. If muscle memory exists in supernaturals, it is clear my muscles remember how to lift powerful spells strong enough to exact considerable damage. So much so, I nearly brought down the entirety of my cavern. Yet, just as sure as I almost brought it down

I used the magic flowing through me to rebuild it entirely. Stick by stick. Stone by stone.

One thing is certain: I'm much stronger than I remember.

Still, I don't waste time marveling at my skill. While I revisited my abilities, Melchior contacted me to let me know he's acquired the last of my obols. Melchior has used his treasure-seeking prowess to help me find a great deal of the obols hidden here on Earth. This time, we've contracted fellow adventurers to gather them. Elysian insisted on doing so, fearing losing his son to another expedition.

To my surprise, Dalcour Marchand offered considerable assistance procuring obols found in some of the most remote locations. While I can't say we're now friends, I do consider him an ally. Anyone who stands against the witchery of the Changelings is an ally to me.

Long ago, the Changelings hid the obols in this realm. Hopeful of keeping the ferrymen in their dark servitude, they scattered the obols so we would remain indebted. Much like the Great Eye gives power to Fates like my sister, the golden obols grant strength to the Sons of Erebus. Although each ferryman is granted their own signature stone, such as the one I wear, the smaller ones can still strengthen me.

Eighty-eight. That's how many I'll have once I collect the five Melchior has for me. No single ferryman has ever had so many in his possession. It is a hell of a lot of power for just one person, but since it is to hell I must go, I think it is appropriate.

"Damn it!" Elysian barks as I appear at his side. Even after more than three months, my old friend still gets shocked by my sudden appearances. "Must you do that?" Cringing, Elysian curls his lip as he brushes his shoulder and takes a few steps away from me.

"Never mind my father," Melchior greets me, seated in the

corner near his father's whiskey bar. "He still gets jumpy." Shaking his head, it's obvious Melchior takes a modicum of pleasure at seeing his father squirm.

Elysian has worked hard over the last few months to regain his son's trust, but despite his overtures, it is clear Melchior maintains his grievances.

Knocking his cane hard into the floor, Elysian paces toward his desk. There's a new vitality in his stride that I haven't seen for a long time. I notice that his knee seems to bend more than it has in almost five years. Interesting.

"My apologies, Lord Elysian. I didn't mean to startle you. I presumed you left the door open so I could make my way inside without too much attention."

Elysian grumbles as he saunters to his chair and plops down.

"Thank you for coming, Kharon." Melchior lifts his voice above his father's mumbling.

Closing the door behind me, I smile. "No, thank you. Both of you." I offer a reserved smile, but Elysian makes a point not to look in my direction. I do my best to shake off my irritation. Dealing with my old friend is like suffering through a bout of whiplash. Some days, he seems amenable, while other days, just the look of me seems to sour his mood.

Frankly, I could care less what he thinks about me. As long as his feelings for me don't transfer to how he treats Rae, I'll be fine. He could hate me until he took his last breath and I wouldn't bat an eye, but if Rae were shown an ounce of discourtesy, I'd ferry his soul to places that would make him wish for hell.

"We didn't do anything really," Melchior continues, now folding one leg over the other, reaching to grab his glass. Day drinking has become a regular habit for Melchior since his return. Although I know little about the man he was before, it's clear alcohol has become a coping mechanism. Tossing back the remnants of his drink, Melchior purses his lips, grunting a little as he leans back into the brown leather sofa. "The stones are in that case." he says, pointing to a small satchel on the side table.

As I open the case, the five obols glow brightly, larger than the last batch. Looking at them, I can tell they were found in a dry area. Those found near water tend to be smaller and not as bright as these. Although there's no difference in effectiveness, it's similar to the cut and clarity of a diamond. Some are rarer a find than others.

"Thank you," I say, closing the case.

"Aren't you going to affix them to your master obol?" Melchior asks, lowering his foot to the ground, moving to the edge of his seat. His eyes beam, as though he really wanted to see the power of the obol roll through me.

"It's a private pleasure, I'm afraid," I reply, winking my eye. "But thanks again."

Disappointed, Melchior shifts back in his seat. Shrugging his shoulder, he reaches for a bottle of Evans and Williams and pours some into his glass. "Then I suppose you have all you need to free your sister." He takes another sip, but his gaze stays locked on me.

Looking over my shoulder, I now see Elysian watching me intently. Something is wrong. I'm not sure what it is, but it's something.

"Well, not entirely," I begin, inwardly pondering the best way to ask for the Jinn jar.

"And there it is!" Elysian exclaims, throws up a hand and rocking back and forth in his seat.

Lifting a cautionary palm, Melchior's eyes roll as he glances over his shoulder at his father. "Please, Kharon, sit." Melchior gestures to the wingback chair adjacent to the window.

I'd rather stand, but I do as he asks for no other reason than knowing Moirai fancies him and Rae loves him. There's something going on with him today, and I really don't like it.

"So, what more do you need? I mean, you're already taking my little cousin with you to hell."

Ah, now I understand. I can't say I'm wholly offended. He's not wrong. Taking Rae to my realm is dangerous, *very* dangerous. Still, I work to rein in my frustration. I don't appreciate his tone.

Clasping my hands tight, I lean forward, shifting a gaze between Melchior and Elysian. "While I understand your hesitancy, please know I would never do anything to put Rae in danger. You, Melchior, of all people should know Moirai would never offer the notion if she thought doing so would put Rae in harm's way. *You know this.*" My last words are more of a whispering plea, but I know he heard me.

At my words, Melchior's stiff posture loosens. The tight scowl etched on his face relaxes, and he gently places his glass on the coffee table. "Kharon, I know you mean well, as does Moirai, but neither of you can assure Rae's safety. I've witnessed the horrors of your realm firsthand, and I don't want my cousin to endure an ounce of the cruelty that place can inflict."

My heart falls to the pit of my gut. He's right. It's not safe. There are untold dangers that not even Melchior, in all his years of captivity, could fathom.

Sighing hard, I sit up but keep my gaze fixed on Melchior. "Yes, the Netherworld is dangerous, but it is also beautiful, hauntingly so. In fact, I am certain my sister shared some of the beauty of our world with you. Did she not?" I pause, watchful as he concedes with a small nod. "Then believe me when I say, Rae will not be privy to only the darkness of my world, but its loveliness too, despite how dark it may seem. Just know, I will protect her with my very life."

Lifting his glass to me, Melchior takes another sip. "Well then, Ferryman, I should hope so. Despite my feelings for your sister, if you can't return Rae safely, don't return at all."

If he were anyone other than Rae's family, I'd strike him where he sits, but oddly enough, I agree.

Twelve

RAE

"Oh, what a pity," Aunt Vivian groans, peering over Ross' shoulder as we make our way to the table.

I'm surprised Winter has led us to such a large table. It's big enough for eight, and there are only four of us. Then again, we do have a lot of bags, so the extra room might be necessary.

"What's wrong, auntie?" Ross asks, looking behind himself and back again at my aunt. "What did we miss?"

"Leila Green," Aunt Vivian says with a bright smile.

"Leila Green?" Ross and I chime in unison, trading confused gazes.

Winter nods. "Yes, she is an old friend of my parents. To be honest, Mother, I don't quite remember her either."

My aunt grimaces. "Really?"

Winter shakes her head, chuckling as she looks between Ross and I. "No, mother, I don't."

"That is odd indeed. You weren't that young when Lila lived on the island. One day, without a word, she vanished. We were good friends. In fact, before Ms. Carrington became your father's assistant, Lila helped him organize his books and set up his contracts. We were all so close, thick as thieves. That is, until Kharon Nyx came around. After he affixed himself to your father, everything changed."

Aunt Vivian's eyes go distant, and Winter's brew like the eye of a storm. Ross bounces a glance between us as he squeezes my hand, keeping me calm. Every time I think I can relax, there's some negative mention of Kharon. Quite frankly, I'm sick of it. Everything in me wishes to blurt it out here and now. I'm tired of pretending Kharon doesn't matter to me.

"Well, that's all behind us now," Ross blurts out, tightening his hold on my hand. "I smell food."

"Yes, Ross is right," Winter adds as her face brightens. "Besides, I've planned a little surprise."

"A surprise?" Ross turns to me, shrugging his shoulders.

"Glad to know I can still surprise you, handsome," a heavy voice bellows from behind Ross. Turning away from me, Ross glares over his opposite shoulder, blurting an expletive as he does.

Dropping his bags to the ground, Ross throws his arms around Stephen as if he hadn't just seen him this morning.

"Now this *is* a pleasant surprise!" Ross coos, tugging Stephen's beard while leaning into his embrace.

"Well, not everyone is a surprise," Lux says, walking to Winter's side. He plants a doting kiss on her cheek as she loops their arms together.

Now more than ever, I'm glad I dragged my aunt along. Not that I'm upset Winter brought dates to a day I thought would just be for us, but at least I'll have my aunt to keep me company.

"And one more surprise," Win squeals with the widest grin stretched across her face.

My heart thumps. Could it be? Has Ross told Winter about my relationship with Kharon? Perhaps her little jab about Kharon earlier was all a ruse? Maybe my aunt is in on it as well. Is that why she brought Kharon up just a moment ago?

I know my cheeks are burning red, because I feel like I'm on fire inside. When I turn around, though, it's like someone dumped two gallons of ice on my head.

Seeing Don Addy's son Kevin is not who I wanted to see. Not at all. What the hell is he doing here?

Smiling, albeit awkwardly, with a handful of pink carnations, Kevin's eyes beam with hopefulness. "These are for you," he offers as his wavy brunette hair hangs at his dented jaw.

I don't take them. I just stand here brooding. Thinking. I hate pink.

"I'll take them." Ross reaches across me, taking the flowers. "She's actually allergic to carnations." It's a lie, but it will do.

"Well, why don't we all sit down," Aunt Vivian suggests, casting an awkward smile.

"Yes, let's." Ross leans into me, trying to catch my gaze, but my sights are set on Kevin.

Unfortunately for him, he's catching the full weight of my ire. It's meant for Winter, but I fear if I turn around to face her now, it will all come out. My true feelings. Everything. This isn't the time nor the place.

"Come on, Pip, you're making a scene," Ross whispers in my ear. I don't care. I'm tired of this charade.

Kevin brushes his hands through his hair nervously, and I can see how uncomfortable I'm making him. It's not his fault. He has no idea my heart belongs to another. I mean, sure, we danced at the summer solstice, but it was just a dance. A dance we barely started before Kharon snatched me away, for no reason than to ensure no one else could have me. I didn't understand it then, but I understand it now.

Even more, I know if Kharon was willing to do that when we weren't a couple, I can only imagine what he'd do if he saw Kevin with me now.

"I–I know–" Kevin begins, but I can't stand it any longer.

"I'm sorry, Kevin, but I need to go!" I snap, brushing past him and back toward the courtyard.

"Rae!" I hear my name shouted from behind me, and I can barely make out which one of my family members it is.

My eyes are a glassy puddle, and I can hardly see where I'm going. I just know I have to get out of here. Oh, what I wouldn't give to be able to fly, or just a few grains of onyx sand. Invisibility would be a perfect skill right now.

Turning side to side, I look for the least crowded exit, but my tears block my view. Thankfully, the loud sound of a ferry from afar pulls me in the right direction. I need to get back to my side of the island. Today was a mistake. I should have never come here!

In no time, I find my way back to the ferry. Although it's the Addy Ferry, at least I know Kevin is still with my family. I won't have to deal with him right now.

"Rae!" I hear Winter's voice as she tugs my arm, pulling me out of line. "I'm sorry, Rae," she cries.

"Are you?" I bite back, and I can tell my tone startles her as her eyes widen. "How could you?"

"It's just I thought you liked him. Remember the dance?"

"Oh, for goodness sake, Win! You danced with Herbert Frost at the same dance. You don't see me dragging him to lunch, do you? Do I look that desperate to you?"

"Of course not, Rae. After what you told me the night of the cotillion, I just wanted you to be happy. I know you had your heart set on Nyx, but that monster–"

"Okay, that's enough, Win! Look, I know you say you're looking out for me, but this is not what I need. I thought today was about us–you know, reconnecting. But you just couldn't help yourself, could you? All I wanted was time with my family. *With you*. With Ross. What was I thinking? I know the only reason you did this was because Aunt Vivian told you to."

"No, Rae, that's not true. Sure, she suggested it, but–"

"But nothing, Win. Look, you got your happily ever after and I'm happy for you, and I'm happy for my brother. Believe it or not, I'm happy for me–but you wouldn't understand that."

"I'm sorry, Rae," Winter protests as tears pour down her cocoa cheeks.

It pains me more than she knows to see the tears in her eyes, but for once, I need to steward my own tears. She has the strong arms of Lux waiting to comfort her, and if not him, I'm certain my aunt will be a welcome shoulder to cry on. Meanwhile, I'll have to wait for the cover of night to finally rest in the arms of the man I love, and I'll have to do so with the ones I love not knowing who truly holds my heart.

"I know you are, Win. I'm sorry too, but I can't do this. I won't. I love you, and I know you love me, but I need everyone to respect me enough to understand I know what's best for me. If I wanted a companion for lunch, I'd have one." I want to say more, but I restrain myself.

"Please, Rae, I'll send everyone away. It can just be us. We can grab a bite somewhere else. I'm sure Lux and Stephen won't mind. And Kevin, he—"

"Win, this isn't even about–" I sigh, stopping myself before I say too much. The ferry horn blows once more, and I see the line moving up the ramp. Pulling my ticket out of my back pocket, I turn back to my cousin. "It's okay, Win. I think I've lost my appetite."

"Ah-hem," Elysian bellows a faux throat clearing across the room.

Silence continues to sit between me and Melchior. While it bothers me to see us at odds, at least I know it's only concern for Rae leading his contempt. Elysian, on the other hand, is only concerned for himself. Whatever animosity he has for me has nothing to do with his niece.

"Yes, Father?" Melchior whips his head over his shoulder, his tone slightly exasperated, as if he's grown tired of his father's weak attempt of breaking up our forming stand-off. "What is it?"

"Well, wouldn't you like to know what else Mr. Nyx wants? It's not enough that he wants to traipse my niece through the underworld, or that we've nearly exhausted our resources to help him procure his precious obols–now, he wants more!"

"Lord Elysian, I've offered you more than what's reasonable for your aid. You've refused me!"

Jumping up from his seat, Elysian shoves his cane into the ground as he makes his way to the middle of the room. "That's because I have no desire to be indebted to the likes of you. In fact, I'd offer half of everything I own just to see you gone!"

A knot wells in the center of my throat. If I didn't know it before, I know it now. Kingsley Elysian hates me. The menacing glare he's giving me right now tells me that if he had even a fraction of my power, he'd strike me dead. Thankfully for him, the feeling isn't mutual.

Swallowing the hard air in my throat, I slowly lift from my seat. "Listen, old friend, I know you hate me, and I understand. I'm not a father, but if I had a son, I'd be just as furious. You lost time with your son, and that is a debt I can never repay."

"Yes, but that is not all," he grits through his teeth, twisting his cane further into the ground.

My chin lifts, and I work hard to restrain my frustration. I'll not apologize to anyone for my relationship with Rae.

"Rae and I love each other. We–"

Swiping his hand hard against the air, he turns to Melchior and then back to me. "Oh please, Nyx! Do not hide behind whatever depraved desires you have for my naive niece. You know what you've done. How could you?"

Elysian's words lash like a whip. If his eyes were daggers, I'd be a dead man.

"What are you talking about?" I grumble, doing my damndest to keep my cool.

"Come on, Kharon," Melchior says, rising from his seat. "You had to know we'd figure it out."

For the life of me I haven't a clue what they are referring to. Yet, before I have a chance to inquire further, Elysian's office door slams shut.

Both Melchior and Elysian's mouths hang open in shock, but I don't need to turn around to know who it is. I can smell her fragrance, taste her scent as her aroma explodes across my skin.

It's Rae. *The love of my life.*

What is she doing here? I thought for sure she'd still be out with her family.

Turning on my heel, my heart warms just seeing her face. It doesn't matter how torn I may feel right now; having Rae here seems to calm the raging storm brewing within me. While everything in me wants to pull her in my embrace, something tells me she's not happy.

I suppose walking in on us like this is not what she expected.

"Figure out what?" Rae's tone is flat as she steps to my side, instantly looping her arm with mine and threading our hands together. Just having her hand in mine feels good, but her posture feels stiff. Something is wrong.

"Baby, are you okay?" I whisper into her ear.

Looking up at me, the glassy pools in her eyes give her away. Still, it's the flush of red beneath her cheeks that tells me the truth. She's upset. No, she's angry. All I know is that for now, her ire is not set on me. I need to know what's wrong, and I need to know now.

'Rae?' I repeat, hoping to pull her attention from the torpedoes she's sending her uncle.

What did he do?

"I'm sorry, my dear niece, but we're trying to get to the bottom of yet another deception by your beloved ferryman!" Elysian barks, slamming his cane into the ground. That was meant for me.

Now I'm pissed. I don't give a rat's ass about whatever new blame Elysian chooses to lay at my feet. All I care about is Rae. I need to know what upset her.

"What are you talking about now, Uncle El?" Rae groans, leaning her head back.

Stepping in front of his father, Melchior turns to Rae. "Look cousin, we need to address this. I mean, I've been in your corner this whole time, but this–this is too much to turn a blind eye."

"*Forgive me, baby*," I whisper to Rae, and turn back to her uncle and cousin. "What the fuck are you talking about? I've stood here, taking your shit for the last few minutes, and frankly, I'm sick of it. Whatever the hell you're talking about, just fucking spit it out!"

"This!" Elysian shouts, dropping his cane to the floor. Slowly, he saunters around his office with his hands outstretched. Taking long strides, he does a heel spin, and his blazer flares as he turns about.

"Uncle El!" Rae gasps, covering her mouth. Her eyes widen, and she looks up at me and back at her uncle in shock. "Oh, my goodness! How is this possible?"

His knee buckles, and Melchior rushes to his side to offer his father his cane.

"Well, my dear, that's a good question. Possibly one that your beloved ferryman can answer." Elysian's eyes stay glued to mine as he leans into his cane.

"We know what you did, Kharon," Melchior mumbles with his arms folded across his chest. "But why?" Melchior purses his lips, shaking his head.

Squeezing my bicep, the feel of Rae's petite fingers trailing my arm is the only thing keeping my wits in check.

"Khar? Is this true? Did you do something to Uncle El?" Rae's words are soft, like a feather sweeping across my face as she turns to me with confusion in her eyes. Her hands fall slowly from my arm as the look I give her says all she needs to know.

Shit. This isn't how this was supposed to go.

"It's a withering spell," Melchior chimes in, closing the

distance between us. "The Changelings put the same spell on me. That's why, when I first arrived, my legs were wobbly. Over time, however, the spell wore off."

"That's precisely what the man you claim to love did to me." Elysian says. "But it's why you did it that's the most disturbing part."

Looking between me and her family, Rae locks her gaze with mine. "Please tell me this isn't true, Kharon. Don't tell me that you–"

"Yes, Kharon, tell her! Tell my niece how you withered my bones for the sick purpose of bringing Winter closer to you and your duplicitous schemes!"

Throwing her face into her palms, Rae mutes her screams. "Damn it, Khar! Is this true? You did all this for Winter?" She pulls her face from her hands, and the disappointment in her eyes hurts more than she'll ever know.

I want to tell her the truth, but I can't. Not here. Not like this.

"Yes," I lie. What other option do I have? Telling her why I did it won't change anything. I did it, that much is true. Just not for the reasons they think.

"You know this is fucked up, right?" Melchior exclaims, circling the space where he stands.

Elysian frowns, shaking his head. "Son." It's an admonishment. He's no fan of swearing.

Melchior hunches his shoulders, gesturing his hand toward me, making me the reason for his expletives.

"So, let me get this straight," Rae starts, resting her hand at her chin.

She paces back and forth, and I take a moment to admire how adorable she looks in the denim pants and leather bomber I made her. Everything hugs her in all the right places. When she cuts her eyes up to me, I rein in my thoughts. She's mad at me. Still, I take a moment to study how she looks when I'm not her favorite person.

I want to know how to discern her every mood. I'm sure it'll come in handy in the future.

That is, if we have a future after this.

"You injured my uncle so my cousin could return from school all in the hopes that you two could get closer?" Rae frowns, but if I had to guess, I can tell she's not buying it.

I won't give up my pretense, at least not yet. "Yes. It was the only way to rescue both Melchior and Moirai." Not so much a lie, but it is definitely a half-truth.

Rae halts her pacing, but keeps her gaze locked with mine, studying my face. Twisting her mouth to one side, she lifts a brow, sucking her teeth. "That was the *only* reason? To save Melchior and Moirai?"

"Oh, for mercy, Rae!" Elysian cries out. "Don't tell me you're buying this?"

"My dad's right, cousin. I mean, he hurt my father just to get closer to my sister. That's twisted!"

Whipping her head toward Melchior, Rae frowns. "To save your ass! Did you forget that? Everything Kharon did was for his sister and for you, Mel! Besides, even after Win came home from college, Kharon barely made a move. It wasn't like he was trying to get that close."

"Then why do it, Rae?" Melchior whispers, dipping his head low as if it pains him to say it. Gripping her shoulder, he uses his free hand to lift her chin to meet his eyes. "I mean, I get you wanting to see the best in the guy, but he went through an awful lot of trouble to bring Win closer. I just don't want to see you get hurt."

Everything in me wants to pull Rae into my arms and tell her the truth, but I'm frozen. Fearful my dark deeds have caught up to me, I don't flinch. I refuse to do anything more to set her off.

Rae tugs herself from Melchior's hold. Her eyes bounce around before landing back on her cousin. "Well, lucky for you,

Mel, no one is forcing you to watch. Besides, I've grown a little tired of you and your sister thinking you know what's best for me." Rae sidesteps next to me, once more tethering our hands together. "Khar, get me out of here."

Grabbing the briefcase, I tuck it under my arm. Pulling Rae into my chest, I twist my foot into the floor, where I sprinkle a dusting of onyx sand. Kissing her forehead, I mutter, "As you wish."

Fourteen

RAE

M y mind is a muddled mess, and Kharon's chest is wetter than a waterfall. Pools of tears flow like a river from my eyes as he carries us back to his cavern.

When I woke this morning, I never imagined today turning out as it did. A part of me wishes this was nothing more than a bad dream, but I know the truth. This is my life. *My hell.*

Kharon holds me tight as we stand at the entrance of his cave. Despite me wiping copious amounts of snot on his silk shirt, he does nothing to dissuade me. Instead, he holds me like he never wants to let me go.

I'm sure he's reeling about what I just learned, but really, I could care less. Right now, I'm just pissed at how screwed up everything is. I can count on one hand how many times I've been mad with Winter, but this hurts more than I care to say. Even more, I'm afraid to tell Kharon what happened, for fear of what he'd do to Kevin if he found out. I may not like Kevin in that way, but I'd hate for him to take a boat ride to hell on my account.

If I didn't know better, I'd think I felt a tear fall from Kharon's eye when I feel water hit my cheek. No, I know better. There's no reason for Kharon to cry. I'm sure it's just condensation from the cave walls. I've grown used to it over the last few months.

Though the thought of pulling out of Kharon's embrace pains me, I need to. I need something more. Looking up at Kharon, I can barely see him through my tears. I've bawled my eyes out so much today, I'm sure they're puffy and hideous, but I don't care. I need what only Kharon can give.

Kharon rests his palm on my face and I rest there, enjoying his warmth. His thumb swipes across my bottom lip, and I part my mouth just enough to suck on the tip. He grunts at the feel of my tongue grazing his nail, and I moan, knowing this isn't the only part of him I want on my tongue.

"Baby," he grunts, using his free hand to pull me close. Instantly, I feel him harden, and I know he wants what I am all too eager to give. "We should talk, Rae," he groans, as his hand curves around my butt.

"Later," I coo, planting kisses along his hand and wrist. My phone buzzes in my back pocket and Kharon pulls it out.

Waving the phone at me, Kharon, pulls away. "It's Ross."

Unzipping my jacket, I yank it off and throw it to the ground. My shirt is next, followed by my bra. Kharon's eyes darken, and all his attention locks at my waist. Biting his lip, he drags his gaze along the length of me as I lower my pants to the floor and kick off my shoes.

"Later, I said." Wiping my face, I release my hair from my messy bun.

Lifting his hand toward the cavern entrance, Kharon utters *Prīvātus*, and an iridescent curtain, reminiscent of a waterfall, covers the rounded entryway, giving us the privacy we need.

Kharon clothes are off no sooner than my eyes look at our barrier and back at him. Now, he's standing there just how I love to see him. Tall and proud, with glistening skin, golden tresses that only highlight the perfection of his stately form, and his iron-hard member aimed straight at me.

Before I can ogle him further, Kharon lifts me in his arms and carries me to the large poster bed I pestered him for weeks to get. As rough as we go at it, I was tired of my knees scuffing along the stony ground. Although Kharon saw no reason for a bed since he needs little sleep, he finally obliged when I showed him the scrape on my leg. Knowing it infuriates him to see me hurt, I knew it was the only thing that would coax him along.

Laying me down, he scoots me to the edge of the bed while he kneels in front of me. Parting my legs, he locks his eyes on the core of my femininity. Half crazed. Half hungry. All mine.

Smirking, he glances at me before licking his lips. "I'm famished," he growls as he thrusts his tongue deep inside me. Kissing. *Sucking.* Biting. Shifting his finger against my sensitive spot, he continues feasting on me as if he wanted to swallow me whole, and it's everything I need.

I need Kharon to make me forget all my pain, my fear, doubts... everything. I just want him.

Lifting his face, his fingers continue their assault. "Come for me, baby. I need it." He goes back in for a lick, swirling and twisting his tongue inside me, and I come undone. "Rain for me, Rae."

"Khar!" I scream, tugging at his hair.

"That's it, baby," he moans against my lower lips. "You look so beautiful when you come, sweetness. I wish you could see what I see. So beautiful." Kharon keeps his fingers lodged tight until my final spasm is complete. Pulling away from me, he brings his fingers to his mouth and sucks them clean. "You taste so good."

I need more. So much more.

I push myself back until I'm in the center of the bed. Rising to my knees, I turn on all fours, until nothing but my ass is in his view.

"Ahh, so that's what my baby needs?" I can almost picture the gleam of his perfectly white teeth as he dashes his cocky grin. He's fully aware of the sexbot I've become in his presence. These days, I'm always on, and he doesn't even have to flip a switch. He *is* the switch.

His hands are on my hips in a heartbeat, thrusting his rock-hard length into me without regret. Mercilessly, Kharon thrashes against me, until I can do nothing but claw at the satiny fabric beneath me. It's the only way to keep myself from slipping. I muster all my strength, digging my nails into the sheets, doing all I can to take everything Kharon is giving me.

"Damn, baby!" Kharon growls, rotating his hips, ensuring he hits every spot. "You know you own me, right? You fucking own me!"

"I do?" I whimper beneath the strength of him as my knees falter. Then it hits me. *It all hits me.*

I feel Kharon pull himself from me, and he flips me over. "Baby, what's wrong?"

Crap! My eyes are leaking again, betraying me in what should be an intimate moment. I can no longer hold it back. As much as I wish I could, I need more than getting my back broke.

Hovering over me, Kharon leans on his arm and strums the side of my face with his hand. "Please tell me. I can't fix it if you don't let me know what's wrong."

Palming my face, I mute my cries. "I'm trying to be strong, Khar, I am."

Kissing the top of my head, Kharon gently moves my hands from my face. "You *are* strong, Rae, stronger than you give yourself credit for. Right now, it's okay to let me be strong for you. Tell me what's wrong, please."

I sniffle. "It's what Melchior said. Really, it's what everyone says."

"About what?"

"I mean you hurt my uncle to bring Winter close to you. Am I really your second choice?" There go my tears again.

For the first time, I witness something I never thought I'd see: tears in Kharon's eyes. One drips down his cheekbone, and it's unlike anything I've ever seen. Like a shimmering diamond, it hangs there until it slowly soaks into his warm flesh. His eyes remain glassy pools, and everything in me wants to dive into those depths and lap up everything that is Kharon Nyx.

"I am sorry, Rae. I know I keep saying that, and as sure as I sit before you now, I know I'll probably say it over a thousand times in our lifetime. I am sorry. I did what I did because it is what I thought I had to do, not because it is what I wanted to do. I hate that the shadows of my past hang over us, but if you let me love you, I promise the light of our love will one day outshine all the shadows. Please don't you ever say you're second. You are first in my heart and soul. I meant what I said, Rae Vereen. *You own me.* If you told me to go to hell right now, I'd do it. If you told me to fly to the moon and back, I'd do it. Do you understand me?"

Thick droplets rush from my eyes, and I swipe them away as a small smile wanders from behind my frown. "Pluto's moon," I mutter, pulling Kharon's hand to my mouth as I kiss his knuckles. "Only Pluto's moon."

Brushing one last tear from my face, Kharon smiles. "So let me take you to the moon, baby."

Fifteen

KHARON

WE MADE LOVE FOR HOURS.

It feels so good holding Rae like this, like nothing else matters but our love, like the stars could collide and the Earth stand still, and nothing would matter but loving her as I do now.

As much as I want to keep her in my arms, though, I cannot. We have responsibilities. To each other, to our family, and more importantly, to the life we want to build. We'll never be able to truly build that life if we don't do what needs to be done.

Strumming my thumb across her face, I kiss the top of Rae's head as she lays on my chest. I'll never love anything more than the sight of her wavy tendrils spread across my chest while her legs lock with mine as her soft, naked body nestles against me. This is probably the closest to heaven I'll ever get.

"Rae," I whisper into her hair, inhaling her scent.

"Yes," she says, delicately tiptoeing her petite fingers up my chest until she finds my beard.

"You should go make up with your cousin."

Instantly, I feel her body tense, and she begins to pull away from me. I maintain a firm hold around her back, keeping her as close to me as I can.

"Khar, I–"

Tapping my forefinger on her pouty lips, I stifle her protest. "Just hear me out."

Looking up at me, Rae's eyes widen and even water a little. I know she wants to say more, but she bites her lip and nods for me to continue. "I'm listening," she grits out, narrowing her eyes at me.

"While I'm obviously not a fan of anyone trying to set my woman up with another man–if you can even call that boy a man–her motives were pure. She just wants to see you happy."

"I am happy, Kharon. *With you*."

I smile. She has no idea how happy she makes me. "Yes, baby, and I am happy to be with you, but your cousin is not privy to our happiness. I'm sure if she knew the truth–if she truly understood what we meant to each other—things would be different."

"She won't understand, Kharon. As long as she thinks you're the villain who stole her brother, she'll never understand." A few drops fall from Rae's eyes, and I quickly brush them away, planting a soft kiss on her forehead.

"I know, baby. That's why you have to go to her and make things right. Tomorrow, we leave for my realm. The two of you need to be on good terms in case–"

"Something goes wrong." Rae's words sting. The thought of anything happening to her because of me shakes me to my core.

"It's okay, Kharon, I heard you talking with Mel and Uncle El. Once I got off the ferry, I took a long walk back. I thought I heard your voice, so I kinda–"

"Eavesdropped?" I smirk, raising my brow, although I'm not surprised. Rae has always been inquisitive. Over the years, she's used her ability to blend into the background. It's no wonder she'd do so if the opportunity presented itself.

"I'm sorry, Khar. I heard how Mel was talking to you and I didn't like it."

"Neither did I, but he wasn't wrong, Rae. Taking you to the Netherworld isn't safe. Don't get me wrong, I trust Moirai. If she said you'll be okay, I believe her, but I also know the dangers that exist in my world. If anything happened to you, I'd never forgive myself. That's why I want you to be on good terms with not only Winter, but your whole family."

Rae rolls her eyes, huffing and pouting like she's about to throw a tantrum. She's quite sexy when her inner brat comes out.

"What difference will it make? You're only going to erase my memory when we leave."

Taking her chin, I lift her head until her eyes lock with mine. "It matters. To your family, it matters. Gods forbid anything should happen, you'll want their last memory of you to be those of happy times. It would hurt them more than you can understand if they were left with regrets or what they could've done. I've ferried countless souls in my lifetime. Every time, their lasting thought, whether monster or man, is that they wish they'd left the ones they love in right standing. Trust me, beloved, you want to make things right."

Rae's cheeks redden and her eyes well with tears. I know how much she loves her family. Being at odds with them hurts her more than she even wants to admit to herself. Despite how much her family may despise me, nothing matters more to me than seeing their reconciliation. Besides, it'll only make things that much easier if or when they ever accept me into their family.

Taking in a deep breath, Rae exhales hard, blowing her hair from her face. "When you're right, you're right." Pushing herself up against the mountain of pillows she begged me to purchase, she pulls the satin cover across her chest. I know it's a tad chilly in the cave when I see the indent of her perky nipples. It's sexy as hell, but I try to force my longing thoughts aside, or she'll never leave this place. "It's cold in here," she says, clutching her arms.

I scoot closer to her, pulling her to my side. Being a fire born soul of the Netherworld, I'm naturally warm. As much as I'd like to think she just likes cozying up next to me, I'm sure that's the main reason. She wants my heat.

"You know, Kharon, when everything is all out in the open, we're going to have to consider a real place to make our own."

That was unexpected.

I frown. "A *real* place?"

Her eyes flit over my shoulder and her mouth twists to one side. "I'm sorry, baby, I'm not trying to be rude, but I mean, I'm human. I have human needs. There's no television, no living room, and most of all, no kitchen. Where am I gonna cook?"

I nod a little. "Valid point. You should have your own kitchen."

She gives my hand a little squeeze before pulling her hair up into a bun. "What about when we have kids? I'm not sure I want our little tikes running around a cave. I mean, the river is right there. It's not safe."

For the first time, I feel cold inside. All the warmth I've ever known seems to evaporate, and I'm left in a bone chilling repose.

"Kids?" My mouth remains parted, shocked. I don't know why I wasn't prepared for this conversation. But what man truly is?

"Yes, Kharon, kids. Look, I know we never discussed having kids before, and I'm not watching the hand of my biological clock or anything, but I assumed one day we'd want to start a family of our own."

Rae searches my face, likely looking for any indication of agreement. I'm sad to say, she won't find it, not now, not ever.

Jumping up from the bed, I quickly wrap the duvet around my waist. Normally, I wouldn't care that I'm naked, but I'm actually freezing.

"Kharon?"

"Look Rae, you know I love you. You know I want to spend my life with you."

A nervous frown covers Rae's face as she stares up at me. "Yes, I know. I want the same thing."

"No, you don't. I don't know why it never crossed my mind before, but what you want and what I can give are two very different things." I pause, fearful of what I have to say. Swallowing my angst, I continue. "I can't give you children, Rae. I can't give you a family."

Sixteen

RAE

Today has officially gone from bad to worse. Being with Kharon was supposed to make me feel better. Right now, it's doing anything but.

"Kharon, what are you trying to tell me?"

Grunting, Kharon runs his hands through his hair, pacing back and forth. Stopping when he makes his way to my side of the bed, he exhales hard. "I'm not *trying* to tell you anything, Rae. I'm telling you I can't give you what you want. I can't give you a family."

My heart sinks below my gut and drops to the floor. How is

this possible? At every turn, just when I think I've found happiness, I'm sucker punched in the gut.

"What do you mean, you can't give me a family? Are you saying you don't want kids?"

"I'm saying it isn't possible for me to get you pregnant."

I smirk, twirling my fingers through the curls in my hair. I reach for the duvet at Kharon's waist, yanking him close. "I'm sure with all the practice we've been having, you're sure to get me knocked up sooner or later. I'm surprised it hasn't happened already."

Gently batting my hand away, he steps back. "That's because it's not possible, baby."

Frowning, I work hard not to shoot daggers at him. "Not possible? How so?"

Gulping hard, Kharon purses his lips, clenching his jaws tight. "Simple physics, I'm afraid."

"Kharon, you're not making any sense."

He stares at me for a few seconds until it becomes clear I truly don't understand. "I'm from the Netherworld. You are earthbound. Our makeup is different. Being earthbound, your biology is made to produce life. Mine is the opposite. Everything about me—everything that makes me who I am—is nothing more than the personification of death. No matter how great our love is, Rae, there is one thing I can never give you. *Life*."

My eyes thicken with so much water, I can barely see Kharon's face. I want to say something, anything, but I can't find the words. Even more, I can hardly breathe.

"Rae, baby, please say something," Kharon pleads, reaching out for my hand.

For the first time, I withdraw my hand from him. I don't even know why, but I do.

Side-stepping him so I can climb out of the bed, I keep the

sheets wrapped around me until I find my clothes where I left them at the entrance of the cave.

"Rae, don't go, please. We need to talk about this."

"I–I don't have anything to say. I need to go." My words are garbled, but I know he understood me.

"Look, I know I should've said something before now. It's just, I've waited so long to have you in my life, I didn't think everything through."

"Yeah, well, I can see that. I just need to go. You know, so I can think. I need to think!" I shout, looking around for my shoes. Kharon steps closer, holding my canvas shoes in his hands. He offers them to me, and I reluctantly take them. "Thanks," I grumble.

Grabbing my wrist, Kharon holds me until I look at him. "I'm sorry I didn't say something sooner. Look, I know my timing is horrible, but I'll understand if this changes things between us. I'll even understand if that means you don't want to come with me tomorrow. I won't ask you to risk your life for someone you're no longer sure about."

Once more, I find glassy pools in Kharon's eyes, and it rips me in two. I want to comfort him and tell him I'm not going anywhere, but I can't. Not now. Not yet.

Still, he holds his emotions in check, refusing to let his tears escape. Slowly, he releases his grip, and the loss of his touch stings me in ways I've never imagined.

Dropping my shoes to the floor, I work hard to slide my feet inside, but I'm such a mess that my coordination is all over the place.

"Let me," he says, dropping to one knee.

Watching him now, thoughts of him proposing race through me, and a flood of tears stream down my face. With as messed up as things are now, I have serious doubts *that day* will ever come. Besides, it's Winter who always dreamed of a Cinderella moment. I said I wanted a monster. Sure, it sounded bold and sexy in my mind, but here, with the weight of it all, I may have bitten off more than I can chew.

Gently taking my foot in his hand, he glides it inside my shoe. Just the motion sends goosebumps up my spine, and I inwardly berate myself for even being upset. Still, as much as I want to say it's okay and crawl back into his arms, I can't. Not yet. All I ever wanted was to share a life with Kharon Nyx, and for me, that life included having a family with the man I love.

"What's this?" he says, taking my other foot in his hand, examining my new ankle bracelet. "I've never seen this before."

The way his eyes scan my ankle annoys me, and the thought of being annoyed by Kharon makes me sick inside. What the hell is wrong with me?

Frustrated, I yank my foot from his hold and shove it into my shoe. I can barely push my heel inside, but I let it stay out of my shoe, flopping as I walk away.

"I got it at the market today." I want to tell him about the kind woman who gave it to me. I even want to tell him how she was nice enough to give Ross something after he almost knocked her down, but I don't. I won't. He doesn't deserve a feel-good story from me right now. Right now, he deserves my silence.

Standing up, he gives me a look. I don't know what to make of it, so I roll my eyes and turn away. Then, my brat comes out to play. "Well, Kevin Addy didn't give it to me, if that's what you're worried about."

His face darkens, and a flicker of flame twinkles in his eye.

Ah... the desired effect.

Kharon parts his lips to say something, but he presses them shut, narrowing his gaze. He takes a small step forward, lifting his hand in caution. "Rae, I know I've given you a lot to think about, and I know the timing couldn't be any worse, but I'll say this, and you can be on your way. At dawn, I'll be at the riverbank. If you still want to come with me to save Moirai, I'll meet you there. If not, I understand. Your choice."

A few seconds of silence sit between us, and I wait, wondering if he's going to say that he wants me to go with him. He doesn't. He says nothing. If I didn't know better, I'd think he was cool if I didn't go.

Maybe he is.

I suppose it's the same way he's cool with not giving me children – he's cool leaving me behind. My eyes sting with the threat of tears wishing to erupt once more, but I choke them back. I've done enough crying for today.

Seventeen

KHARON

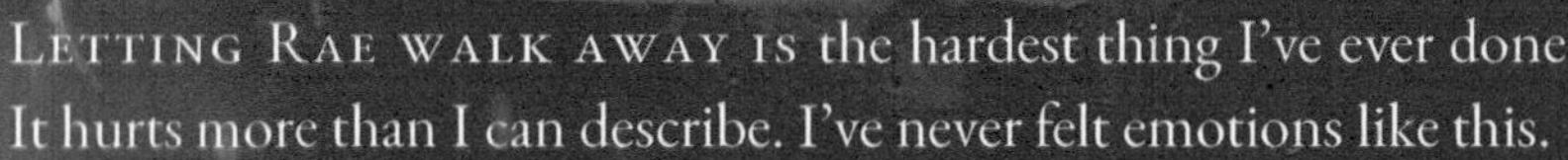

LETTING RAE WALK AWAY IS the hardest thing I've ever done. It hurts more than I can describe. I've never felt emotions like this.

Conflicted. Confused.

Is this normal for human relationships?

Sure, I dated women in the Netherworld, but not like this. Outside of fulfilling my carnal needs, I never thought much of finding a mate, much less love. Yet here I am, wholly in love with a human who has my heart in knots.

A loud roar blares through me, and I shoot a few flames across the room. I race to the opposite side just in time to allow the brunt of the fire to hit my chest. Grimacing at the pain of the flames searing my flesh, I cry out, knowing this is likely how I made Rae feel.

Why I never thought to discuss the matter of children before now is beyond me, but it may very well be my undoing.

Times like this make me long to speak with Moirai, but in her current state, she's probably not in the best shape to give advice. Outside of Rae, my sister is one of the only women I'd even consider asking for advice.

I can only hope Rae and I find a way to work things out.

"Knock, knock!"

Turning quickly, I'm surprised to find Melchior now standing at the entrance to my cave.

"Well, I suppose if you had a door, I would knock. I just never know what to do in these situations," Melchior laughs, digging his hands into his pockets. Rocking back and forth, he scrunches his face some, waiting for an invitation to enter.

I grumble a bit then walk to the side where Rae added a dressing curtain. I told her we didn't need one, since I like seeing her naked, but moments like this make me glad she didn't listen.

"Come in!" I shout over the curtain.

"Thank you," he says, splashing the heel of his boot against the puddles of water as he enters. He's the only person who does that. Rae always steps over them. I suppose he gets some kind of child-like amusement every time he does it.

It doesn't take me long to get dressed. I'm surprised to find Melchior seated at the marble bench adjacent to my desk. Normally, he goes straight for Moirai's stone, but not today. Interesting. Maybe his earlier irritation with me has spilled over to include his affection for my sister. Either way, after our run-in today, I hope his visit is brief.

"Why are you here?" My tone is brusque, but I don't care.

"Ah, so right to the point, huh?" Melchior casts a nervous grin my way, and I wonder what's really going on. Then again, I don't care. I'm not in the mood.

"I think you said everything you wanted to say to me earlier."

I can tell he wants me to sit, but I keep myself planted against the wall, arms folded and fully annoyed.

"About that," he pauses, rubbing his five o'clock shadow. "I came to apologize. The way we came at you earlier–that wasn't cool, especially not from me. Man to man, I came to offer an apology."

Fuck. He threw me a curveball. I had every intention of being pissed off for the rest of the day.

My posture betrays me as my arms drop to my sides, and the tense pressure in my shoulders relaxes. "Come again?" I whisper.

"Oh please, Nyx," Melchior offers a restrained smile. "You're certainly not going to ask me to say it twice, are you?"

Laughing, I push away from the wall. "It's just that the acoustics in here are horrible!" I laugh, twirling my hand around.

"Acoustics my ass," he laughs, popping up from his seat, pacing to the center of the floor before giving me a firm handshake.

"Thank you," I say. "I appreciate it more than you know."

Patting my shoulder, Melchior smiles. "We're all good. Besides, I know we can come across a little gruff. I shouldn't have let my father get in my head. I know you better than that."

My brow lifts. "Oh really?" I muster an appreciative smile.

"Come on now, I spent the last decade watching you agonize over the whole thing. I know you never wanted to hurt my family. I get it, you know, the whole Winter thing with the withering spell. I mean, don't get me wrong, that's my sister and I don't want anyone taking advantage of her, but I get it." Melchior rocks back and forth on his heels, twisting his mouth slightly. I can read between the lines. He trusts me, but he's setting a boundary. That's fair.

For the life of me, I wish I could tell him the truth, tell him how little it had to do with Winter, but it's a truth I'll have to bear alone, at least for a little while longer.

"Whatever your reasons, I'm just happy we're on good terms. You have no idea how much I need that right now."

He smirks. "Oh, I can only imagine. I caught a glimpse of my cousin walking up the road. She looked pretty pissed , and to be honest, pretty scary. I've never seen Rae angry, so I just kept my distance. I'm not even sure she saw me, that's how mad she was. I don't know what happened, but I'm guessing you're not in her good graces."

My head dips, and I bite my lip before nodding my head in agreement. "Oh, I am certainly the furthest from her grace right now."

"Well, I'm sure whatever it is, you'll work it out. She loves you."

"You think? I don't know. I think I messed up royally."

Melchior shakes his head, chuckling. "If she didn't love you, she wouldn't be bothered enough to be upset. Just give her some time to cool down. My grandmother always said when she and my granddad got into it, she'd wait until he was asleep and then she'd talk to him. Something about good people don't dream angry or something. At any rate, just trust in what you two have built these last few months. You have to believe that at some point, you'll finally reap a harvest from all the love you've sown."

I watch as Melchior's eyes grow distant. Something tells me that the last part was more about him and Moirai than me and Rae. Either way, I appreciate his sentiment.

Just when I thought I had no one in my life I could trust for advice, I find I was wrong.

Eighteen

RAE

Wow. Our first fight, if that's even what you can call it.

I'm mad. Steaming, actually.

I can't believe he just let me walk away. *Rae, I'll never let you go.* My ass. He just let me walk away like it was nothing. Ross always said men will make promises in a moment of passion that they never intend to fulfill. I guess he was right.

He didn't even offer to lift me back to the manor. Rude ass. I can count on one hand how many times Kharon has let me walk back. Even most of those times, he at least escorted me halfway, albeit invisible with onyx sand.

Not this time. Nope, he just let me leave like I was a visitor, after telling me we couldn't have kids like it was no big deal, like I am supposed to accept it and move on.

Then again... maybe I *am* overreacting a bit. Maybe he was waiting for me to talk it out?

Well, then he should've said so.

Perhaps he tried. Crap! Did I just mess this up?

"Pip?" Ross' tone is anything but *merry* when I hear him call my name. Standing with Stephen at the side entrance to the kitchen, he looks at me like I tied a kitten to a tree. "Well, come on, missy. You can add a little more pep to that walk of shame."

Grunting, I clench my jaw, giving my brother a hard eye roll. "I'm not in the mood, Ross."

"Why don't I give you two some privacy?" Stephen says, offering me a stifled smile as he nods at Ross and walks toward his truck.

Before I have a chance to say anything, Ross raises his hand. "Nope. Not a word," he says, holding the door open and gesturing for me to come inside.

I do as he says, but mostly because I'm chilly. I'm not in the mood for one of his lectures right now.

"Want some tea?" he begins, holding up my favorite teacup.

Surprised at the gesture, I feel a smile trying to make its way out, but I hold it in. "Yes, please."

Staring at me for a moment, Ross offers a quick wink while rummaging through my tea bin. "I think we'll bypass the Earl Grey. A little honey chamomile seems more appropriate."

He read my mind. The last thing I need right now is something bitter. I need something calm and sweet.

Ross remains quiet as he makes my tea. Although he knows I normally prefer the whistle of the kettle over the Keurig, he wastes little time preparing everything. He's seated across from me, gently pushing the cup forward as he rests his chin on his hands, biding his time. My eyes scan the table, looking for the honey, but also trying to avoid direct eye contact with my twin.

"Here you go," he says, his voice softer than usual as he pushes a jar of honey next to my cup.

"Thanks." My voice is hardly above a whisper, but I know my brother heard me. I quickly drop a dollop of honey into my tea, still keeping my eyes off Ross. Only acknowledging me with a slight head tilt, he keeps his hands nestled under his chin, biting his lip. I know he wants to say something, but right now, I'm happy for the quiet.

The warmth of the tea covers the coldness creeping over me, and it reminds me of Kharon. Kharon always makes me feel warm and cozy. Every time I'm with him, it's like sitting next to a fireplace, like you never want to leave.

That is, until today. My eyes go glassy at the thought.

"Sweetheart," Ross begins, just as a lone tear rolls to my chin. My hand shakes, but Ross gently places his hand over mine, slowly lowering my teacup onto the saucer. "Do you want to tell me how you're feeling? What's going on in that pretty little head of yours?"

Taking a deep breath, I sigh. I barely know where to begin. Nervously, I look around. I wonder if we should go to my room. I don't need anyone knowing about me and Kharon or our problems.

Ross squeezes my wrist, regaining my attention. "Don't worry, it's just us. Melchior is off committing to his day drinking I'm sure, and our aunt and uncle left to go to dinner."

"A date?" I chuckle, wiping my face.

"I know, can you believe it? It was actually his idea."

"Wow!" That deserves another sip of tea. My uncle never takes my aunt anywhere. I wonder what got into him. Whatever the cause, I'm sure my aunt is grinning from ear to ear. "Good for them."

"And the lovebirds, Win and Lux, they're out doing whatever it is they do." Pausing, Ross narrows his gaze. I can tell he wants to say something more, but he's trying to be sensitive to my feelings. "Look, Pip, you don't have to tell me everything going on with you. I know you have to keep so much under wraps these days, but let me just say, I totally understand if you felt blindsided today. I had no idea Win was going to pull that little stunt. I mean, I get it, she really just wanted all of us to spend a little time getting to know Lux, since he's not coming back with her when she returns from Spring break. Good intentions, bad methods. It would've been fine if she hadn't brought that snot nose Kevin Addy. I mean, of all people—an Addy?"

We both laugh. Ross and I have enjoyed a decade-long inside joke about the Addy family. I've never met another group of people who always seem to be sniffling.

"Anyone but an Addy," I laugh, taking another sip of tea.

"Please, honey," Ross groans, pushing my hand. "Who do you think you're fooling? You aren't thinking of anyone other than your nether-honeybun."

Twirling my hair between my fingers, I can't help blushing at the thought of Kharon. Then, I remember I'm mad at him.

"Whoa—wait a minute! What's that face?" Ross takes my chin in his hand, lifting it until our eyes meet. He searches my face hard as if he were trying to count my freckles. "Spit it out, missy."

Pulling from his grip, I throw my face into my hands. "Ugh! This is all so frustrating!"

"What happened?"

Taking another glance around the kitchen, I stand and walk to the door. Looking out the window and peering down the hall, I make sure I don't hear or see anyone. Ross is nearly jumping out of his skin, waiting for me to spill.

"It's everything, Ross! I mean, you saw what happened with Win. Then, when I got back on this side of the island, I overheard

Uncle El and Mel lashing out at Kharon–so I had to get us out of that–"

"Why? What? Hold on, I thought Mel was on your side?"

"Yeah, me too."

"Well, what changed?" Ross asks, now standing with his arms folded.

Throwing my head back, I swallow hard. I don't know where to begin or if I should say anything at all about the withering spell. "To be honest, Ross, I couldn't tell you what changed with Mel. Our uncle, well, he's just looking for any excuse to get Khar out of my life." It's an omission, not a total lie.

Ross doesn't seem to mind as he rolls his hands a few times, insisting I continue. "And?"

"Okay, so I was casually mentioning we consider finding a real place to call home because as romantic as his place is, it's not really compatible with human needs."

Nodding in agreement, Ross twists his mouth to one side. "You're not wrong. I mean, it's a cute little love nest and all, but where do you even go to the bathroom?"

I dart him a look. "Don't even get me started on the particulars."

"Got it. TMI. Alright, continue."

"So out of nowhere Khar says, *'oh yeah we can't have kids, I can't give you a family.'*" I'm air quoting and doing my best grungy Kharon voice, but Ross is just staring at me. "Did you hear me, Ross? He just blurts it out like I'm supposed to be cool with the fact that he's telling me we can't have kids."

Dropping his hands to his sides, Ross leans against the pub chair. He stares at me for what feels like a full minute, biting his cheek. "Well, Pip, did he say why you can't have kids?"

"I don't know. Something about being from the Netherworld, him being death and me life. Gave me some line about our biology and whatever–"

"And whatever?"

"I mean, the balls, right?" I groan, offering a hand to Ross, looking for a sign of agreement.

"Yeah, I'd say so." His voice is quiet, almost too quiet for my liking.

"So, I just had to get out of there."

"Wait a minute! You mean to tell me this man told you he can't give you kids because of something he can't control–his biology–and you walk out on him? Damn, Pip, you've got a steel pair of lady balls indeed!"

My heart sinks. If there was ever anyone to see my side of things, it's Ross. The way he's looking at me now makes me feel like I'm skating on an ice cube.

"Damn it, Rae! Come on, sis, I know you're better than that. I mean, I get breaking loose at lunch today and maybe with whatever our uncle had up his butt, but walking out on a man who just told you something I'm sure was hard to say–that's just cruel. It's not like you to be cruel."

"Ross, but I–I–"

"Not buts, sis, not this time. I can't believe you don't see anything wrong with what you did!"

Now he's ticking me off. "With what I did? What about what *he* did? We've been together for over three months, Ross. Three months! Not one time has he thought to tell me."

"Oh yeah, because you're totally handling it like a mature adult right now." Ross glares at me, bores his eyes into me the way he does when he's dug his heels in. We're both stubborn, but Ross even more so. Sighing like he's just about through with me, he throws up a hand, waving it around a few times before dropping it to his hip.

"Wow, Ross, of all people, I thought I could come to you with this, but I guess I was wrong." I get up to leave, but he jumps in front of me, blocking my path.

"Yep, you were wrong, Pip. I'm just surprised you of all people can't see *why* you're so wrong. I mean, it's exhaustingly amazing how my own sister can't see the error of her ways, which is surprising because you don't screw up often. Ever really, if I'm being honest. I guess you held out for a big one, huh?"

A knot wells in my throat. Words fail to form a witty comeback, the kind I'm used to when Ross and I go back and forth. This time is different. The look in my twin's eyes is as though I walked out on him, not Kharon, and it feels like my soul got yanked from my body. I feel void and empty inside.

Ross' eyes glass over, but he holds his tears back. "Of all people, I thought you understood."

"Understood what?" My words are wispy, cracking through the knot welling up inside me, almost too afraid to say more.

His eyes tenderly search my face, looking for any trace of comprehension. "Family isn't only biology, Rae. That's what I thought you understood. I thought you understood that one day, your brother, *your twin brother,* would be faced with the same dilemma. Stephen and I both understand we'll have to do so without the comforts of biology. I mean sure, I wish I could ask my very female, painfully hetero sister to help us in that endeavor, but I'd hate for you to pass on any of this nonsense to my child."

The weight of my brother's words smack me in the face. Hard. I cup my hands over my mouth, astonished at just how foolish I've been. How did I not see this?

"Did you ever stop to think how hard it must've been for him to keep that secret? To hold on to something so painfully personal? To look in the eyes of the woman he loves and tell her he can't give her what he not only knows she desires, but likely does himself, only to have her walk out like he's the problem? I can't imagine how he feels. Alone in this realm, no friends, no confidant, *no siblings,* just alone with his insufficiencies. He may be a strong, warrior prince of the Netherworld, but today, dear sister, you made your handsome prince feel like a frog."

Nineteen

RAE

"THAT'S ALL RIGHT, baby girl. Cry it out, it's okay." Ross' arms are almost everything I need right now. *Almost.* Kharon's arms would be better, but these are the arms I've leaned on since I learned my own name.

Planting my face deeper into my brother's hold, I let out all my frustration and fears. I can't believe how foolish I've been. How could I be so cruel, so insensitive? This isn't like me. Anyone can have a bad day, but this takes the cake.

Laying on Ross' chest, I'm surprised at how solid my usually lanky brother feels as I nestle into his embrace. Winter was right:

Ross is bulking up a bit. I suppose spending his days chopping wood with Stephen is adding more muscle to his usually svelte frame.

Reaching behind me, Ross grabs a linen cloth from the table. "Here you go. This will be far better to use than my shirt," he grumbles, kissing my forehead. I take the napkin from him and wipe my face and nose. "Much better, Pip," he coos, moving my hair from my face.

"He probably hates me right now," I groan.

Ross smacks his lips, raising a brow. "Yep, probably."

"Ross!" I shove his shoulder.

Scrunching his face, my brother maintains his pretense for a few seconds before bursting into laughter. "Fine, he probably doesn't hate you, but he doesn't particularly like you right now, I'm sure."

"How do I fix this?"

"Um, people usually lead with I'm sorry, or I'm sorry for being an ass. You know, something like that," Ross chuckles as he makes his way to the fridge. He pulls out an IPA, pops the top off, and chugs it down. "Now see, fooling around with you has driven me to drink. I'm sure your honeybun is popping off a few bottles right now."

"You think?"

"I know I would." Ross takes another swig and smiles. "Just apologize, Pip. He'll understand. He loves you, and he knows you love him. Besides, you two can talk about the creative possibilities of having a family once you reconcile. As a matter of fact, Lux told me he has friends in Louisiana who foster supernatural children. There must be a kid or two who could use a loving home. You know, just like we did when we were orphaned."

"How did I not think of that?"

"Because you were being an ass." I throw a punch toward my

brother's arm, but he pulls me in for another hug. "It's okay, sis. Plenty of kids have asses for parents, I'm sure of it."

We both laugh, and for the first time since I was in Kharon's arms, I feel the weight of today slowly slip from its tight hold on my soul.

"Thank you, Ross," I say, tapping his chin. "I couldn't do this life without you, you know."

He shoots me a wink and leans his head on mine. "Oh, I know. Neither could I."

I sigh. "Before I can deal with Kharon, I should at least make up with Win. Even my *honeybun* said I need to make things right with her."

"Agreed," Ross says. "We always said we'd never let anything come in between us. Nothing. Making up is definitely the priority. There's no way you can leave things the way they are and then head off to the Nether—"

"The Netherlands?" Winter's small voice whispers from behind us. Ross and I share worried glances, wondering just how much Winter overheard. "You're going to the Netherlands?"

The Netherlands? Then it hit me – she didn't hear Netherworld. Thank goodness!

"Um, yes. Rae has been selected for an apprenticeship at a confectioner's program in Amsterdam. She leaves tomorrow!" Ross has always been a good liar. How he just ripped that one out of thin air is beyond me.

"Tomorrow?" Winter gasps. "I didn't know you were even considering leaving."

"Well, I didn't want to talk about it too much. You know, in case I wasn't selected." Maybe I'm not such a bad liar after all.

Winter's eyes are still glassy and wary as she regards me, but her bright smile gleams from ear to ear. "That's wonderful news, Rae!" she exclaims, taking a few small steps toward me.

Breaking away from Ross, I inch my way toward her, my tearful eyes clouding my view, but I press my feet into the kitchen floor.

"I'm sorry!" both Winter and I blurt in unison. Throwing our arms around the other, we alternate between tears and laughter.

Win pulls back first, keeping her hands fixed to my shoulders. "Rae, I am so sorry. I know I've been totally dismissive of your feelings and dreadfully inconsiderate."

"Please, Win, I've been quite a monster myself today. I know you love me."

Winter's eyes are a pool of tears, but it's her infamous loving smile currently tugging on my heartstrings. "Yes, I love you, but bringing Kevin Addy was totally inappropriate. I'm so sorry. I just couldn't bear having you feel like a third wheel. I don't want you to feel like you're shuffled to the background. You belong front and center."

"I just belong with my family, because with you, I'm never in the background. I know that now," I cry, extending my arms for both my cousin and brother.

"Aw, now that's how we're supposed to do things," Ross adds, wrapping his arms around both of us.

Quickly wiping her tear-stained face, Win sighs hard, forcing her tears aside. "Look, Rae, I want a do over. Whatever you want to do tonight, I'm in."

I give Ross a look and we both share a laugh. "Movie night!" Ross and I holler.

"Perfect," Win agrees, grinning hard. "I can hang out until 11 or so, but we leave at midnight. Taking the redeye to Louisiana. Cedric and Abigail can only leave in the cover of night."

"Oh, they don't do the whole coffin thing, huh?" Ross asks, trading glances with me.

Winter laughs. "Only in the movies, I'm told. Lux said some of the old ones have crates that slightly resemble coffins. He thinks that's where the legends come from. Anyway–are you sure we're good, Rae?"

Adding a kiss to her cheek, I look up at Win and smile. "Positive. We are more than good. We're family."

Twenty

KHARON

It was nice talking with Melchior. While we've always been cordial, today was the first time we just talked. From everything about the wickedness of the Changelings, to his strained relationship with Elysian, it was nice connecting with him on a deeper level. Surprisingly, the topic of Moirai never came up. There were a few times I wanted to mention her, but my instincts told me otherwise. Still, it was good catching up.

Not only did I learn he was still experiencing night terrors from his time in captivity, but I understand why he's taken to drinking. He confessed he knows it's not the best way to manage things, but he really feels like there's no one he can talk to about it. I told him

I'll always lend an ear and work to get him support before things get too far gone.

Oddly, Melchior still feels like an outsider. I understand. He's lost more than a decade. His family has changed in his absence. With him and his father's relationship vacillating by the day, it's not quite the reunion he hoped for. Although he puts up a rather believable front, it's evident he doesn't feel like he fits.

I suppose that's why when Ross texted Melchior to join them for a movie and snack night, he politely declined. He said he had to work, but something tells me he doesn't feel like one of the gang.

For me, however, it was good hearing Rae was with her family. Knowing she's at least reconciling with her cousin makes me happy. I do wish I knew if she decided whether she was coming with me. My gut says she will but I'm not a man who likes leaving things up to chance.

That's why when Melchior called to tell me I could retrieve the Jinn jar once he made sure the coast was clear, I took flight to Elysian's chamber. Melchior had it ready for me as soon as I arrived, and I thought of heading back to my cavern and preparing for tomorrow's journey, but I just couldn't pass up an opportunity to see her.

I needed to see her. Be where she is.

So, after cloaking myself in invisibility, I made my way to the manor. I stood outside, gazing into the family room as she and her family watched The Holiday. This isn't the first time I've seen the three of them watching it together. It warmed my heart watching her laughing, singing along with Jack Black, even tearing up when Jude Law's character cried. She's told me on more than one occasion that this was one of her favorite films, but we've never had the pleasure of watching it together. As much as it pains me to watch as a spectator, I'll take what I can get.

Watching as Lux and Stephen joined them made me jealous I'm not afforded the same opportunity. I studied Rae's face as she forced an awkward smile at the loving couples. I can only imagine how much she wished I was there.

When I saw her head upstairs alone as Winter left for her flight with Lux and Ross pulled Stephen up to his quarters, my heart ached for her. Why should the woman I love be alone? Why should we be denied the love we've longed for?

Following her every move, I smile, watching her text me. She whispers my name as she types into her phone, and I wish I knew what her message was. I didn't bring my phone. I only hope she doesn't need an immediate response. Even more, I hope she's not writing to me to say it's over. Little does she know, I'm never letting her go.

"You're mine," I whisper, my cold breath blowing out like smoke.

For a minute, she looks around the room, as if she heard me, but she shrugs her shoulders and continues going through her drawers, as though she's looking for something.

She pulls out a few garments I made her. Hanging them on her wall hooks, she judges between two, likely trying to decide which to wear. I want to tell her it doesn't matter because she's lovely in everything, but when she starts undressing, my attention shifts from the clothes to the beautiful naked creature standing before me.

She hums as she collects items for her shower, and the alluring bounce of her bottom and breasts nearly hypnotizes me. It's been a while since I've been invisible in her room, but at least in those moments, she knew I was there. Even in the instances of my hauntings, I remained outside her room, peering in from the window, only entering her dreamscape.

This time, however, she doesn't know I'm here.

This should feel wrong – stalking her, watching her nakedly stride through her bedroom while I envision all of the things I could do to her. Just my thoughts alone as I gawk at Rae now should avail me a place in the uttermost parts of hell. But . I don't care. For her, I would devour hell. I'd consume it whole if it meant I could be a part of her life.

Besides, if she doesn't come with me tomorrow, who knows if I'll live to behold her beauty another day.

So, I greedily watch as she soaps up her body, carefully moving the sponge along every delicate curve and crevice, singing a melody like she's a siren to my soul, entreating me to surrender.

My manhood responds, nearly bucking out of my pants. The strength of me juts against my inseam, and I fear I'll reveal my presence with just the crown of my member, peeking out past my cloaking spell. The thought chokes me up and I grab my steel shaft, eagerly stroking as I watch the woman I love. It's a wonder I haven't exploded just watching her. I can't. There's only one place I can even imagine powering through my own eruption: inside my beloved.

Rae is out of the shower within minutes, but just when I think she will grab her robe, she doesn't. Instead, she rubs oils into her body, and the scent is heavenly, like vanilla and jasmine, sweet and comforting, just like Rae. Patting dry, she's quickly out of the bathroom.

She goes to pick up her phone, likely checking for a return text. Her mouth crumples some at my lack of response, and it pains me to disappoint her. As she shakes her hair from her messy bun and sits on her bed, I consider leaving. I should text her back. I don't want her to worry.

But when she pushes herself to the middle of her bed, showing me everything I've already claimed as my own, I can no longer move. I'm frozen.

She owns me.

"Khar," she moans, motioning her fingers over her nipples, her eyes closed tight. She bites her bottom lip as she gyrates on her bed.

Slowly, her fingers make their way down her body until she finds her sweet spot.

I groan as I watch her rub along her sensitive skin, calling my name between incoherent mewling sounds. It's taking every bit of my willpower not to make myself known to her.

Rae grabs her knees, parting her legs, revealing the pretty pearl that has both my heart and my rock-hard member leaping for joy.

"Baby, please," Rae moans, swerving her perfect body around.

I take a step forward, my need for her growing with each stroke of my erection. I want her. I need her.

"Please, Khar," she whines, circling her finger inside her glistening hole. "Are you going to make me beg?"

My pacing halts, and I look around the room and back at Rae. As I do, her gaze locks on me. I look over my shoulder into her floor length mirror, ensuring I'm still cloaked. I am. This must be her private pleasure, her way of letting her imagination run wild. I'm just thankful to know I remain at the forefront.

I take a few steps closer. Desperate to see her reach her climax, I wait like a kid in a candy store, thankful for a front row seat.

"Ahh," Rae whines, flicking her finger harder against her sensitive spot.

You're almost there, baby. Keep going, I inwardly groan.

Her build-up is beautiful to behold. Normally, I'm in her, so I don't get to see it like I am now. I might make this a regular part of intimacy.

"Kharon, please, I need you baby. I need you!" she screams, now tugging at her nipple. Her eyes pop open and lock right in my direction. "I know you're here. Please finish this like only you can."

I won't make her ask twice. Just as I begin to take my trench off, revealing myself, Rae sits up.

"Wait!" she says, lifting her hand.

Staring, her hooded eyes glaze over me, and I wonder if she really can see me. Rae bites her bottom lip, parting her legs wider.

This time, I can see everything. Rae knows exactly what she's doing. If she didn't know it before, she knows it now. She fucking owns me.

Her smoldering gaze stays locked on me as her lips part slowly. "I want you to stay invisible."

As you wish.

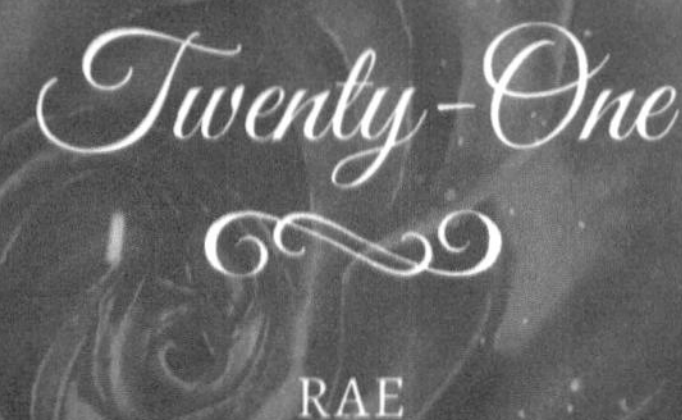

Twenty-One

RAE

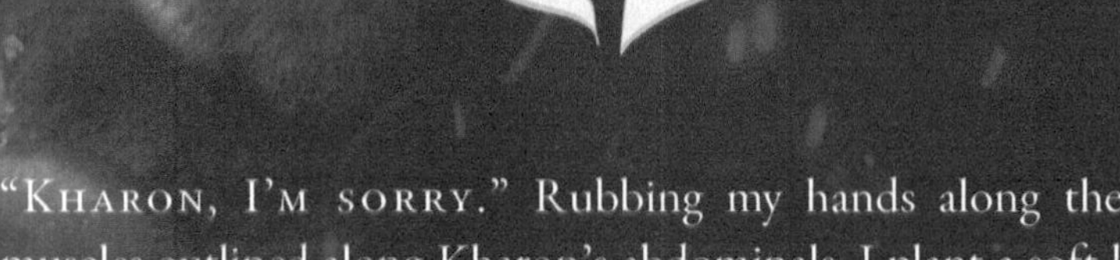

"Kharon, I'm sorry." Rubbing my hands along the eight muscles outlined along Kharon's abdominals, I plant a soft kiss on his chest.

Moving my hair from my face, Kharon casts his typical doting gaze as he looks down at me. A small smile curves at the corner of his mouth before he kisses my forehead and tightens his arms around me.

"There's nothing to forgive," he says, squeezing me tight.

I love us.

I want to stay like this forever.

Unfortunately, I need to own my faults. I can't very well be in a mature relationship with someone like Kharon Nyx and still act like a petulant child when things don't go my way.

"But there is," I continue, pushing up and out of his hold. Frowning some, Kharon's dark brows crowd the center of his forehead. I know he wants to protest, but he tightens his lips, nodding for me to continue. "It was wrong of me to storm off after you shared something so personal. I know it wasn't what I wanted, or even what I expected to hear, but I know that's not how I would want to be treated. For that, I'm sorry."

Taking my chin between his fingers, Kharon lifts my face and kisses me softly, but the strength of his tongue swirling over every inch of my mouth feels like he's taming me into submission. It's as if he's bending my tongue to his will, ferrying me to places only he can take me.

"Thank you, baby," Kharon whispers into our kiss. Holding my face between his large palms, he kisses me once more, then holds us so the crown of our heads are pressed together. "I appreciate that more than you know." Releasing me a little, he pushes himself so his back is against my headboard. "I also owe you an apology. I should have told you sooner. Besides, I think with the day you've had, your response was appropriate."

"Yeah, but I'd sure hate for you to break up with me because I act childish."

Kharon's eyes flicker, and he groans hard. Taking my shoulders in his hands, he grips me harder than usual, and the heat I feel coming from him would burn if I didn't know he was restraining himself.

"Do you not understand what this is, Rae?"

"Wh–What?" I stutter, slightly fearful of the darkened glare now marring Kharon's face.

His grip loosens some, but his eyes flash once more, and I see the same all-consuming flames I've seen since our first night together.

"We are forever, Rae. Forever. There is no breakup or any of that meddlesome human shit. If we don't like something, we say something. There's no leaving, no breaking up, no divorce. Nothing. You've given yourself to me, so there's no going back. All that I am is now yours. Do you understand? I meant what I said before; you own me, Rae Vereen."

Holding me until my eyes spark with understanding, Kharon's eyes slowly flicker once more before returning to their normal, storm-cast hue.

"And you own me," I whisper, strumming my hands through his beautiful blonde tendrils, hoping to calm the tempest I still see brewing in his eyes. "Besides, who knows—maybe down the line we could consider adopting?" My words come out more like a nervous whisper.

Leaning back some, his brow raises as he searches my face. "Adoption, huh?"

I don't really know what to make of the look he's giving me now, but I forge onward. "Well, you know the same way my aunt and uncle adopted Ross and me when our parents died. Ross said there are plenty of supernatural kids out there who need loving homes."

Taking my chin between his fingers he lifts my face to meet his eyes. "My aunt raised me too, you know. I think adoption is a great idea. Any child fortunate enough to have you as a mother would be the happiest child in the two realms." Kharon smiles, wrapping his arm around me, pulling me back into his hold. "Still, I guess that means we really should start looking for somewhere else to live. I can't have our family swashbuckling it with me forever," he laughs.

"There's no one else I'd rather swashbuckle through life with," I tease, nudging his jaw. "But it will have to wait, at least until we rescue Moirai."

Kharon leans away from me. His face is a mix of confusion and admiration. "You still want to go with me? Are you sure?"

"Swashbuckle, remember?"

Shaking his head, Kharon laughs again. "You are one amazing woman, Rae Vereen. To risk your life for someone you've never met—that you don't know—"

"I know you. That's all that matters. Besides, she's your sister. It's like I told you on our first night together: I'd do anything for my brother. I will do anything for you."

"And I, you—" Groaning, Kharon utters something in a language too haunting to understand. Resting his mouth on the top of my head once more, he kisses me again before pulling away. Stepping out of the bed, Kharon finds his clothes on the floor and dresses quickly. "I need to take care of a few loose ends before we leave. It'll be dawn soon. We'll need to travel before sunrise. Do you think you can be ready in time? Say your farewells?"

"Yes, I can. I'll just see Ross. He'll give the news to my uncle."

Kharon's brow raises. "Really? Where do Winter and your aunt think you're going?"

"Well, Win will be traveling to Louisiana with Lux, and Ross will tell Aunt Vivian I'm off to an apprenticeship in the Netherlands. At least, that's what we told Win earlier."

"Think she'll buy it?"

"I'm sure she'll be suspicious, but everyone knows Ross wouldn't let me out of his sight unless it was important. I think we'll be okay."

Kharon stares at me for a moment, but I can see something else spinning behind his eyes. "As long as you're sure."

Making my way to the side of my bed, I wrap the sheet around myself and sit on the edge. Kharon comes to my side, his eyes full of worry.

"I'm sure, Khar. Please don't worry. Everything will work out just as it should, and when we get back, our first order of business will be getting the naked truth out in the open."

Kharon stalks toward me, his eyes flashing once more. This

time, it's not his grumpy fire. If I didn't know better, I'd think he was enroute to devour me whole. *Oh, how I wish he would.* No, we've got Moirai to think about. I can't let him get me all spun up in his sexy stallion ways.

Taking my sheet in his hands, he opens it, baring me to him. Dragging his eyes over the entirety of me, I hear a low rumble move through his chest. "Well, my sweet, this naked truth is for my eyes only. Is that clear?" Licking his lips, Kharon's eyes greedily take in every part of me, from the top of my head to the tips of my toes. Kneeling in front of me, he looks up, giving me a doting gaze that has my lady parts buzzing. "One day soon, I'll drop to my knees and offer you the world."

Threading my hands through his hair, I rest my palm on the back of his neck. "I don't want the world, Mr. Nyx. I just want you."

"Already done." He smiles, taking my hand in his and kissing my wrist. "But I need you to do me a favor."

"Anything."

Rising to his feet, he gives my hand a squeeze. "Once you've decided which one of these to wear, remove anything from the earthen realm. Your earrings, bracelets–ah, yes, and your newest bracelet," he says, pointing to my anklet. "It's important that nothing from this realm enters the Netherworld. When you board the Erebus, I'll give you the derclanite stone Cedric's companion provided for your protection, but most importantly, wear nothing from this realm."

"I heard you clearly. Wear nothing. Sounds easy enough."

Shaking his head, Kharon gives me a stare as he pours the sand into his palm. "Too tempting, Ms. Vereen. Too tempting, indeed." With a wink, Kharon spins on his heel, sprinkling his onyx sand and disappearing.

Twenty-Two

KHARON

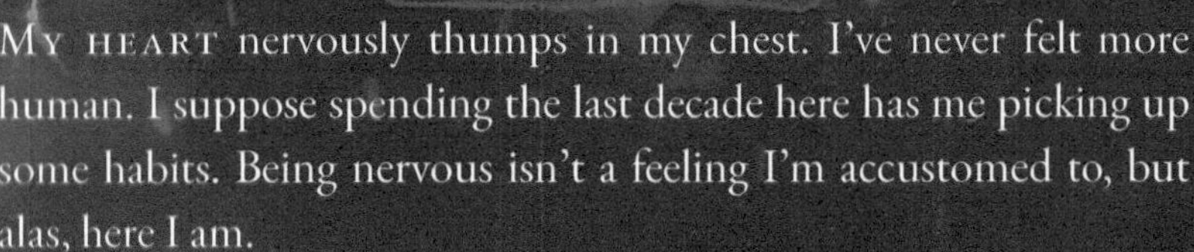

MY HEART nervously thumps in my chest. I've never felt more human. I suppose spending the last decade here has me picking up some habits. Being nervous isn't a feeling I'm accustomed to, but alas, here I am.

Pacing back and forth along the ship deck, I worry whether I've covered all my bases.

I've closed off the cave, ensuring no one can enter. I even reached out to Melchior, letting him know of my pending departure. He wished me Godspeed, and for me to take good care of his cousin. Although I was surprised he made no mention of Moirai, I let it go. Whatever is going on between them isn't my business. I even scoured my contacts to find Ross' beau, Stephen. I sent him a message intended for Ross, but not one I wanted him to see until after Rae and I departed. Since the twins can barely keep secrets from one another, I hope Stephen can get him the message without Rae knowing.

Burying all my Earth-bound belongings within my cave, with the hopes of retrieving them upon my eventual return, I locked away all that remains of my time in this realm. As much as I've relished the last decade here, the time has come for me to return to a life I've long since lived.

I can only hope doing so won't sully the life I hope to build with the woman I love.

A brisk breeze blows through my ship, and it carries her scent in the air. Turning to see her as she makes her way along the bank of the river, my heart races with both excitement and dread, knowing I'm taking her to the Netherworld.

My home.

How will she respond? What will she think?

A fluster of thoughts race through me, but I do what I can to set them aside. I need to be strong for her, and I refuse for my worry to become hers. In fact, I never want her to worry when I'm near. I only want her to feel safe, loved, and protected at all times.

Ross and Stephen are at her side as she nears the ferry. Her eyes glance up at the cavern, likely surprised to see everything closed off. Rae's brow raises as she looks at me, hunching her shoulders in the most adorable way, smiling as she mouths something I can't quite make out.

I'm too distracted.

She's adorned in a teal georgette gown that hugs every perfected inch of her, and my eyes scan her in pure awe. I wondered whether she'd pass as a creature of the Netherworld, but looking at her now, I am sure she is too beautiful for either my home or this Earth.

The gown is long, sweeping the ground so gracefully as she walks, I can barely see her feet. When I do see her toes peeking out from under the lengthy fabric, I'm happy to see she's wearing the sandals I made for her some time ago. Although she admitted they weren't quite her style when I first gave them to her, I'm glad she's wearing them just the same.

She looks beautiful!

I do what I can not to let my thoughts drift too far as she takes careful steps toward me, but all I can think about is how lovely she'll look on the day we join together in covenant. Groaning a bit, I rein in my inhibitions, tucking my zealous thoughts for her aside until our task is complete.

"Alright, Mr. Ferryman, do well to ensure my sister is returned to me in one piece," Ross chides as they reach my ship. "And alive! I know you're used to only ferrying the dead, but this one here needs to be an exception to the rule. Do you understand?"

"Ross!" Rae grumbles, shoving her brother's shoulder. He ignores her, mumbling something under his breath before he pulls her in for a hug. "It's okay, Merry, I'll be fine. I promise," she says, rising to the balls of her feet to kiss his cheek.

"You had better be, Pip. I'm serious," Ross whispers, hugging her tighter.

"Come on you two, Rae needs to get going," Stephen adds, nodding at me with a wink I can only hope means he received my message.

"Okay, okay, lumberjack!" Ross whines. "Let's see how you do sending your only sibling off to some godforsaken land–"

"Ross," Stephen grumbles, raising a brow. I can barely see the twist of his mouth under his mountainous beard, but his jaw shifts enough to know he's giving Ross a gentle warning.

"I'm sorry," Ross snips, rolling his eyes and poking Stephen's shoulder. Stephen pulls him into his hold and kisses his forehead.

"Well, I guess that's my cue," Rae says, looking up at me. "At least I know Ross will be in your very capable hands, Stephen. I know you won't let him get into any trouble."

Stephen smiles down at Ross and back at Rae. "Not on my watch, Rae."

"Shall we?" I offer my hand to Rae, lifting her up inside the ship. She latches a strong grip to my forearm, and I pull her up in one quick stride. "No worries, Ross. I will keep your sister safe. I will bring her back very much alive and in one piece. I swear it to you."

"Okay, big guy, I believe you," Ross begins, leaning on Stephen. "Rae, I love you, sis. You are literally the half that makes me whole. Be sure to come back to me. Promise?"

Rae leans over the boney railing of the ship, waving at her brother as I loosen the sails. "I promise, Ross. I love you, Merry!"

"I love you, Pip!" Ross waves wildly in the air.

Stepping behind Rae, I wrap my arms around her small waist, nestling her into my embrace. "And I love you, Rae Vereen."

Looking over her shoulder, she tilts her head up and plants a soft kiss on my lips. "I can't believe we're doing this," she chuckles. Goosebumps erupt over her arms, and I tighten my hold on her, hopeful to keep her warm.

"Yes, we are, beautiful. I couldn't imagine doing this with anyone else."

Turning to me, Rae rests her head on my chest. "I have to admit I'm a little nervous, Kharon."

"Perfectly normal. Besides, I must admit, I'm slightly nervous as well."

Rae rears her head back in surprise. "You? I've never known you to be nervous about anything."

"Well, I suppose the need doesn't arise often, but having you venture to my homeland is quite unnerving. Not only am I bringing you somewhere not entirely safe, I wonder what you'll think of it all."

"If it has to do with you, I'm sure I'll love it."

I hope so. I only smile in return, bringing her back to my chest. "You look lovely, by the way. The gown I made for you fits perfectly."

Stepping away from me, Rae does a little twirl. "You make such beautiful garments, Khar. You should really consider starting your own clothing line."

I can't help laughing. "I'm not sure that's in the cards for me, but I'm glad you like it. Truthfully, I only like dressing you."

Wrapping her curly tendrils around her finger, Rae smiles. "Well, I like when you dress and undress me, so there's that."

"Tempting, Ms. Vereen. Too tempting," I smile, stuffing my hands in my pockets before I act on my impulse to claim her right here and now.

"I only aim to please, Mr. Nyx."

"That you do, beautiful." I pause and take her in. She is such a beautiful sight to behold, but I have to get a few things out in the open. "Before I let you tempt me, we need to discuss some things."

Scrunching her face a little, Rae plops down on the bench near the side rail. "Aye-aye, Captain. Ready for instruction," she says, adding a faux salute.

Her breasts bobble a bit and my cock instantly twitches in response. I want to tell her we can include this in our role play once this is all over, but I know mentioning it will lead us off topic.

"At ease, princess," I start, taking my seat next to her. "I just wanted to go over a few things. First let me say, thanks for leaving your earthbound things at home. It'll be enough for me to cloak you and bring you into my realm. If you had anything still bound to the Earth, it might not take. The results could be dire. It's a good thing we don't have that to worry about."

Rae fidgets a bit at my side, tugging on her gown at her feet. Her face crumples a bit, too. She must be cold. I pull a thick fabric we keep onboard from the chest next to us and wrap her in it.

"Is that better?"

Her eyes bounce around a bit, but she forces a smile. I think her nervousness is starting to set in. "I'm fine, Khar. Thank you," she says, pulling the fabric to her chin as she smiles at me.

"Good, because the next part is a bit different." The ship begins to sway as we move over the rocks. Once we pass the waterfall, we'll be near the cliffs, where we'll make our descent into the Netherworld. "The Netherworld operates differently than the earth realm. Without the sun's influence, time creeps along much slower. I've been here for ten years, but where I'm from, I've barely been gone a month. That's why we must be expedient. That's where this comes into play." Pulling out Cade's derclanite necklace, I offer it, still in the velvet casing, to Rae. Her eyes pop up to mine and back to the stone. "I'm afraid I cannot touch it. You'll have to clip it on yourself."

Taking it from the velvet case, Rae brings the necklace to her neck. "What does it do?"

"Primarily, it adjusts your heart rate to that of my realm. More importantly, it keeps your heart beating."

Rae casts me an awkward glance as she affixes the jewel around her neck. "You did promise to bring me back alive, so that's a good thing, I suppose."

"Indeed. However, I am going to make a few adjustments. I'll mark the stone using a chronos incantation. That way, as the color of the stone fades, we know when we need to get you back to your realm, no matter where we are in terms of rescuing my sister. I will not risk your safety."

"How long will the stone be good for?"

"I'm marking it for no longer than three months. It'll feel like a day or two for us, but back here..."

"It will seem longer. I understand." Rae's eyes fall a bit, glassing with tears.

Taking her chin in my hand, I lift her face to mine. "Rae, is this too much? Just say the word and I will take you back to Ross."

"No, it's not that—well yes—but..."

I furrow my brows in concern. "But what? Please, you can tell me anything."

"Well, it's just–*ugh just spit it out Rae*–is this when you take my memories from me?"

Ah, now it all makes sense. She doesn't want to lose her memories.

Wiping a fallen tear from her cheeks, I let my thumb slide smoothly against her soft jawline. "Yes, we'll be getting to that part in a moment, but don't worry. I'm tying the magic to this realm. The minute we return, all your memories, plus those you gain while you're with me, will return to you. This is only to protect you and your family from the Wretched Ones."

"Yes, I understand, Khar. Okay, so let's get it over with–"

I shake my head. "Not yet. There's one more thing. Afterward, I'll set the incantation and cloak your mind; that is, if you choose to stay after what I need to say next."

"Oh, so you saved the worst part for the end. Great. Can't wait to hear it." Folding her arms and leaning back, Rae pins her eyes to me, waiting for me to continue.

"I wouldn't say it's the *worst thing*, just something harder to describe."

"Come out with it already, Khar," Rae sneers with a quick wave of her wrist. There's a cute smile laced under her pouty expression that lets me know she's teasing, but it does little to ease my angst.

Here goes nothing.

Twenty-Three

RAE

I'M DOING my best to play it cool. I can only hope I'm convincing Kharon.

All I want him to know is that I'm here, along for the ride, ready for whatever we have to do to save his sister. What I don't want him to know is that I was unable to take off that blasted ankle bracelet.

I tried everything. Wire cutters. A hunting knife. Scissors. Nothing worked.

I even considered reaching out to Stephen to see if some of his lumberjack tools could help, but I didn't. If somehow it didn't work, that would've been all it took for Ross to lock me up. With how things have been with Uncle El, I have no doubt he would have assisted in keeping me from Kharon. He would have said it was because of the bracelet, but I know better.

Truly, I'm just thankful the gown I'm wearing covers my feet. With the way it pools around my feet, there's no way he should be able to see it. Sitting just above the sandals he made me, I'm happy how much the anklet seems to blend in.

Although I'm inwardly freaking out that I might burn, melt, or combust upon entering Kharon's realm while wearing something earthbound, I have to keep up the pretense. I promised Kharon I'd go with him, and I'm not letting anything stand in my way. After acting so foolishly yesterday, it's time I stick by his side no matter what. Even if that means my own life.

So, while he's obviously wrestling with whatever it is he has to say to me, I'm sure it pales in comparison to my own internal struggle.

Taking my hand in his, Kharon gives it a squeeze, regaining my full attention.

"When we cross into the Netherworld, you're going to see things. Creatures. Monsters. You'll see beings you've never seen before. I know you're accustomed to vampires and wolves, but being earthbound, even they retain shadows of humanity. Not so in my world. There are winged creatures and some with two heads or four arms. There are gorgons and hydras, too."

My curiosity piques. This is better than what I thought he'd say. "What about dragons?"

Kharon's face falls some. "I wish. I had a few good friends who were dragons, but the Changelings hunted them to extinction. There remains a few of their kind–griffins and scions."

"Griffins? Scions? I have no idea what those are."

"You may or may not see them on this trip, but that isn't my main point. What I really wanted to say is that you'll also see a monster when you look at me, but only when we chart the ferry."

Releasing his hold, Kharon searches my face. I know he sees the worry there.

"What do you mean, Kharon? I thought Moirai said I can see you for who you really are because of the love we share."

Cupping my face in his hand, Kharon smiles. "Yes, Rae, but my employ, my vocation in life, as it were, even our love isn't capable of keeping that at bay."

"How is that possible?"

"My vocation as the Ferryman is just that–my job. I am a prince to many, but to others, I am the thing they fear, the one slated to carry souls to the bowels of Hades in the underworld."

Wait a minute, Hades is real? The fact Kharon says it with a straight face is even more unsettling.

"Okay, I get you're the Ferryman, Kharon, but I'm really not following."

"What I am trying to say is that once we cross onto the rivers of my realm, I'll look different."

"How so?" My voice is small, but I know he heard me.

Rising from his seat, Kharon waves an arm around the ship. "Do you see these bones? These are the remnants of the ferrymen who came before me. When we ferry the shores of the Acheron and Styx, we become bone. No flesh. No face. A skeleton hidden in a cloak."

"But–but what about our love? Won't I still be able to see the real you?" I ask, fearful.

"It doesn't work that way, I'm afraid. The ferrymen have always charted the rivers as such to protect our identities. Others in my employ, like Reaper and Grim, whom we call Roark and Thelios, shield themselves as well."

"Why?"

Kharon lets out a small laugh. "In our profession, it's better if we're not directly associated with the death dealing we alone provide. It's better for us to remain an ominous presence even though we are also princes and lords of our own lands. Does that make sense?"

"I suppose so. What does that mean for us? I mean, you'll look like a skeleton the whole time? Will I be able to touch you? Talk to you? Anything?"

A sweet smile crosses Kharon's face as he paces back toward me. He extends his arm, gesturing for me to take his hand in mine so he can bring me to his chest.

"Firstly, you'll always be able to touch me, beautiful. Second, it only lasts while we're on the ship. Once we step onto dry land, you'll have your Khar back. I promise."

Nuzzling deeper into his embrace, I inhale his smokey scent. "That's good to know."

"I don't talk much when I'm in my ferry form, but that's not to say I can't. I've just never had a need. Ah, I almost forgot–" Kharon leans away from me, still holding me at my waist. "Once we reach my shores, I may appear a tad larger than you're accustomed."

My eyes widen. "You're way past six feet as it is."

The wind blusters, and he runs his hands through my hair. "Let's not worry about that. Whatever size I become, I'll always be able to hold you in my arms."

I can't help smiling at the thought. "I guess there's a bright side after all. Is there anything else?"

"I'm sure I'm forgetting something, but we'll deal with it as it comes."

I shake my head and laugh. It really doesn't matter if he's forgetting something. I'm in the thick of it now. There's no turning back.

"You are one amazing woman, Rae Vereen. Are you certain you're okay with this?"

Fisting the collar of his trench, I tug him close. "Will you stop asking me that? I'm not going anywhere, I promise."

"Ah, that's a promise from me and now from you. I think we're now matched, promise for promise."

"So, are you going to take my memories now?" I hate to ask, but I want to get it over with.

Kharon's eyes narrow and his lips tighten. "Are you ready?"

A small nod is all I have to give.

At my insistence, he steps away from me. He whispers something almost lyrical, and a group of cream and gold fabrics emerge from the chest near the bench. "Why don't you lie down? I'll need you to be comfortable for this to work."

Gently, Kharon lays me down as he kneels near my head. Placing his hands at the crown of my head, he continues his enchantment. "Try to remain still, Rae. I'm linking the stone between realms."

The necklace warms a bit before turning icy cold. Kharon motions his hands over me, and two intersecting lights shine around the stone, reminding me of the northern lights. It's that beautiful.

"Rae, it's time to cloak your mind. Do you feel relaxed? That's the only way this will work."

My eyes flit up to his, and a small smile curves at the corner of my mouth. Fluttering my lashes, I twirl my hair between my fingers. "I only know of one way to truly relax me."

"Rae," Kharon gasps, sitting back on his knees. "Come on, we have to do this right."

"I'm counting on it," I say with a sly smile.

Kharon's eyes darken, kindling with the same flame that gets me there every time. "You are incorrigible, you know that, right?"

"Well, let's see. You're planning to take my memories of the only people beside you I hold dear. We're going to a place that's akin to hell to wrangle your sister from some sinister sadistic creatures. I think I need all the relaxation I can get. Besides, once you've turned into either a skeleton man or some giant primordial prince, who knows when I'll be able to feel your hands on me again."

Straddling my waist, Kharon runs his hands through his hair, pushing it away from his face. "Fair point, Ms. Vereen."

"Fair point indeed," I grunt as I feel the strength of him jutting against my abdomen.

"Well then, I suppose I should, um, relax you now. Clear your mind a bit, at least enough the only thought running through your mind is how it feels to have me inside you. Do I have your permission?"

"Permission for what?"

He pushes my dress up some and I feel his iron-clad member nudging at my sweet spot. "Permission to make love to the most beautiful woman I've ever known."

I whine, grinding against him. "Yes, Kharon! Permission granted!"

Twenty-Four

KHARON

DRIVING MYSELF INSIDE MY BELOVED, my heart races as I pound into her until her eyes roll into the back of her head.

It's not often we make love with our clothes on, but I suppose there's an exception to every rule. The last time we made love fully dressed, I hadn't seen her in almost two days because she'd been so busy with school. The minute she wandered into my cavern, I bent her over my desk, lifted her dress, and filled her sweet little hole.

I was unrelenting, and so was she, but this is different.

She needs something different from me. This isn't one of those "I can't wait any longer" fucks. This is a mix of "take all my pain away" and "protect me forever."

I need her to know I'll give her all of that and more.

Rae's legs are wrapped around my waist like she thinks I'm going to disappear if she lets go. Her sex has a death grip on my manhood, and if I didn't know better, I'd think she had no intention of me ever moving out of her again.

"Khar!" she screams as I hold her wrists above her head. I still need to keep her from moving too much so I can cloak her mind.

This is indeed a first. Never have I been intimate while issuing an incantation, but I suppose there's a first time for everything. I intend to spend a lifetime of firsts with the woman I love.

"*Quiescis animo*," I begin. I feel Rae's movements settle beneath me as I continue rotating my hips in rhythm with the sway of my ship. Slowly, she gyrates against me as I feel her pulsing core grip my length.

Shit! *She's milking me.* She's never done that before.

It feels so damn good. She'll end up stepping onto the shores of the Netherworld dripping with my cum. What a beautiful sight she'll be! Perfectly marked as mine.

Now it's me who needs to quiet their mind.

"Damn, Rae. Baby, you feel so good. *Too good.* You're so wet, so sweet."

My grip loosens on her wrists, and she glides her hands through my hair. "I love you, Khar," she whispers, still working her body against mine.

"I love you, Rae," I say into her mouth, pulling her in for a kiss. Thrusting in and out of her, I feel her lock onto my girth, crying out my name. "That's it, baby. Let it go. I've got you."

Looking over my shoulder, I notice we're at the end of the rock formation, nearing the cliffs into my realm. The ship will descend, but I need her to feel protected and safe.

"Hold onto me, baby," I groan into another kiss. She does as I ask, and I press our heads together. Finally, I feel her relax in my arms, but I don't withdraw. I'm far from done.

Whispering the ancient word of forgetting, *Dedisco*, I glimpse memories of her family flick through her mind. Capturing each thought, I pull the faces of each from her mind. I've done this for countless others over the centuries, but never for someone I've loved.

I start with her uncle, then her aunt, then Melchior. I even sift away thoughts of random relatives who live on the island. When I get to Winter and Ross, though, it gets harder, like pulling a grain of rice from a baby's hand. Rae holds on for dear life.

I know what I need to do.

Picking up my pace, I thrust harder, rocking her side to side until she's making those mewling sounds that always turn me into a firehose.

Fucking my beloved hard and steady seems to do the trick, and she writhes beneath me, coming again until I feel her sweet honey drench the fabrics on the deck. As she does, I'm able to pull the thoughts of Winter and even her parents from her mind.

I leave Ross in place. I could never take him from her. I just hope it doesn't backfire on me.

I hold her tight as the ferry dips over the cliff and we descend into my realm. She's still coming as we do, and the feel of her tight around the strength of me feels better than anything I've ever felt, even more so as we struggle against gravity. I use the sacred words of my ship to hold us steady.

"Ah... right there!" Rae cries out, scoring her nails at my back as she convulses under me.

Splash!

The ship hits the water hard, but I don't know if the splashing I heard was the water or Rae. She's that wet. The thought makes me ravenous, and I slam into her sweet center once more, this time filling her with everything I have.

This time feels different.

Rae's eyes pop open and she presses back some. Her eyes widen and her death grip on my manhood relaxes.

"Khar?" Rae's voice is small, almost inaudible. Slowly, she reaches to touch my face, but she's hesitant, as if awaiting permission.

I move to take her hand in mine, but now I know the reason for her caution. Seeing my large, boney fingers gripping her tiny hand, I know she finally sees me.

The Ferryman.

I pull my hand back and try to push up, but Rae locks her legs around my waist, holding me still.

"Oh no you don't, Mr. Boatman," she coos, biting her bottom lip. "I'm not letting you get off that easy."

Shaking my head, I try to work a smile, but the tremor in her body tells me I probably look more frightening than the man she fell in love with.

Still, she keeps her hold around my waist firm. Although I know I could easily get out of her grip, I stay still. If nothing else, I need to let her get used to this side of me.

Wrapping her arms around my back, she pulls me close, planting a kiss on my jaw. Running her tongue along my jawline, she firms her hand along the back of my neck as she sucks and gnaws along my boney face. *Ugh.* I've never felt anything like this. What is she doing to me?

"I want more," she whispers at my side, where my ears would be.

Rae reaches between us and takes my length in her hand. She doesn't seem to mind the large bone now void of flesh. Instead, her eyes are dancing. Lining me up at her entrance, Rae lifts her hips, grinding against me, pulling me back inside her soft center. Rolling her hips a few times, she motions for me to let her on top, so I do.

Now, here I am, in the darkness of my realm, still beholding the closest vision I'll get of paradise as Rae Vereen straddles me. Taking me deep, she looks like an angel as her hair blows in the wind as she rides me.

Hard.

Surprise and awe overtake me, but I don't want this to stop. I've never been intimate like this before. Honestly, I never even considered whether this was ever an option.

All this time, I feared how she would react when she saw the monster I am. Here with her now, she's awakening a new monster in me that I don't think she'll be able to contain.

Twenty-Five

RAE

I JUST FUCKED THE FERRYMAN. Like, for real this time.

Not the cute and sweet roll in the hay on a ship at the dock of the river. Not even in the quietness of Kharon's cave.

I found pleasure in allowing his *bone* to explore my depths in ways I never thought possible.

I don't know what kind of kinky monster that makes me, but I know one thing: I want it to happen again.

And again.

Although I could tell Kharon was hesitant, he made no move to stop me. In fact, he seemed to rather enjoy himself. I know I can't say for sure, but if I didn't know better, I am sure there was an apt skeleton grin stretched across his face.

The feel of his fleshless palms massaging my breasts, every stroke of him inside me, sent me into back-to-back orgasms, orgasms so strong, Kharon had to cover my mouth as we made our way into the Netherworld.

Who would've thought this normally quiet and shy girl would enter this dark realm of the Ferryman getting rocked to near heaven? But here I am.

Yet, for as pleasurable and surprising an experience as it is, it's not the only thing that has my mouth dropping open.

We're here. In the Netherworld.

Just as I reach my climax, we reach the shores of a realm I never thought I'd live to see. I'm still straddled across Kharon's waist when we arrive. Sitting up, Kharon caresses my face, holding me against his skeleton chest. I admit I was surprised with just how comforting it still felt to be in his arms. Different, but comforting just the same.

Even more, I'm thankful I didn't combust despite wearing this anklet.

Gently lifting us up from the deck floor, Kharon motions his hand for me to look around. Before I do, I notice how much taller he is now, almost nine feet if I had to guess. He doesn't talk, but I can tell it's still him beneath it all. A part of it feels spooky, but after the love we just made, there's no room for fear.

Walking to the bough of the ship, I take in the grandeur of it all. A violet sky, reminiscent of a summer sunset, shimmers against the waterfall veil, separating us from my realm. I've never seen anything so beautiful before.

This world is bigger than the one I belong to. I've never felt so small. The golden, sandy shores seem to rise as water the color of silver splashes against its edge, leaving behind a glittery diamond-like dust. Out beyond the shores are mountains, large, all-consuming mountains, ones I'm sure rival Mt. Olympus itself. It feels like I sailed into a fairytale world.

Opening a small door on the side of the ship, Kharon gestures as if it was time for us to leave.

"Not without you," I nervously say, looking back at him.

He only nods, motioning his hands around a few times as I watch the sails retract and the skeleton crew recede back into the ship walls. Lifting me in his arms, he carries me down the narrow staircase until we reach the glittery, sandy shore.

Carrying me until we are no longer near the water, I feel his hands tighten around me as they return to flesh.

Lowering me to the ground, he smiles wide. "Welcome to the Netherworld, Rae Vereen," Kharon announces, having returned to his stately, handsome self. "So, what do you think?" His voice seems more melodic now as his smile stretches from ear to ear.

"Kharon!" I exclaim, like I haven't seen him in weeks. Wrapping my arm around his waist, I notice I can no longer rest my head at his chest. He's taller now. My lady parts tingle when I realize the only place my head can rest is his literal nether region.

Good to know.

Laughing, Kharon rubs my shoulders. "You seem much smaller than I remember, Rae."

Stepping back, I smile. "Yep, I'm still an even five feet. I believe it's you who's grown. Every part of you, I'm sure." Dragging my eyes over the entirety of Kharon Nyx, I'm pretty sure my thoughts are obvious.

"About that," he starts, leaning down until he reaches my ear. "Are you too sore?"

A sly smile covers my face, but I sway a little, trying to seem bashful. "Whatever do you mean, sir? Because I had your entire bone in me?" I laugh, and his eyes flicker with the fiery hue I've grown to love. "Well, it was a new experience, that's for sure."

"For me, too," he whispers. Kharon's confession surprises me, but it makes me happy to know we experienced it together.

"Good to know you've saved some firsts for me, my prince. Seriously, I'm okay. I mean, it felt different. It hurt a little, but in a good way."

"As long as you're okay," he says, searching my face. He's more worried than me.

"Yes, I am. I promise. Now, show me around," I laugh, shoving his shoulder.

Smiling, Kharon rips off his trench coat and guides it to the ferry with a wave of his hand while recalling a satchel he had on the side of the bench to himself. Speaking sacred words of privacy, he waves his hand along the outline of his ship, and it disappears. As he does, I'm surprised to find him dressed in more regal attire.

My eyes betray me as I take him in.

Kharon shrugs his shoulders while adjusting the satchel around him like it's no big deal. "Ah, yes. My clothes. Just formalities, I'm afraid."

Looking him over, I almost feel underdressed. He's adorned in gold pants and a shimmering white shirt that looks like it was made with dragon scales, and I stand in awe of the man I've come to love like no other.

Seeing him now, I know he isn't just the man I love.

He's a Prince of the Netherworld.

Twenty-Six

KHARON

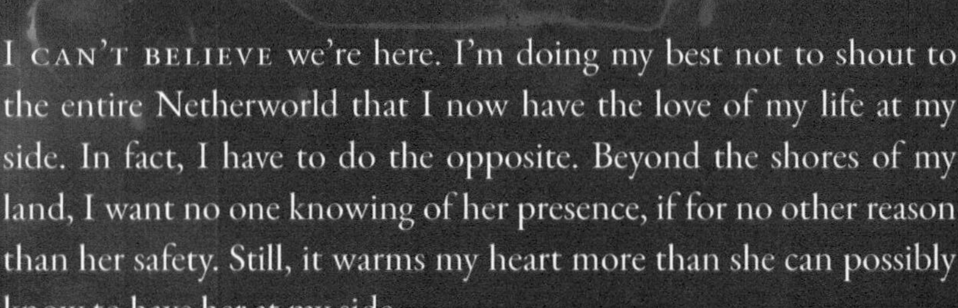

I CAN'T BELIEVE we're here. I'm doing my best not to shout to the entire Netherworld that I now have the love of my life at my side. In fact, I have to do the opposite. Beyond the shores of my land, I want no one knowing of her presence, if for no other reason than her safety. Still, it warms my heart more than she can possibly know to have her at my side.

"Do I look okay?" Rae says, now fidgeting with her dress.

Rae has no idea how adorable she is. "You look beautiful," I reply, stilling her motion.

Giving me a stare, she twists her mouth to the side. "You're not just saying that, are you?"

I gently take her face in my palm. "Of course not. It's the truth, Rae. You are stunning. You'll fit right in."

"Doubtful. I'll be the shortest thing here," she chuckles.

"How is that any different from any other day?" I tease.

Rae pokes my shoulder before looping her arm in mine. "Very funny, Khar–or should I say, Prince Nyx?" Looking up at me, the child-like innocence in her gaze freezes me.

"Beautiful, you can call me whatever you wish. You own me, remember?"

"Oh, okay. I'll call you Mr. Boat Cakes."

Maybe I spoke too soon. I truly hope she's joking. "Boat cakes? Um–I'm not sure about that one."

She laughs, leaning her head on my forearm. "I thought I owned you?"

"Let's just stick with Khar. I like that one."

Winking up at me, she smiles again. "As you wish."

Damn. Now she's even using my colloquialisms. This woman can have anything she wants, except the boat cakes thing.

"There is one thing," I begin as Rae turns to look at me. "We need to adjust your dialect." Before she can respond, I take hold of her neck with one hand, caressing her face with the other. Her eyes bulge some, slightly fearful as she stares at me. "Trust me," I whisper, kissing her forehead and uttering an enchantment.

Rae struggles to breathe slightly, but just as she releases a wispy moan, I blow a gale of smoke toward her face. As I slowly release my hold around her neck, she works to catch her breath, clawing a bit at her neck.

A sharp curse in Nether-tongue rips from her mouth as she looks at me. "What in the entire hell, Khar, was that? Are you trying to kill me?"

"Well, only slightly, I'm afraid," I groan, patting her back as she works to control her breathing.

Shaking my hands from her, Rae backs away. "What the fu–"

Lifting my hands in surrender, I step closer. "It's as I told you before, to be 'Nether' is to be void of life. I had to pull you to the brink and breathe the shadow of my native language into you so you'll be able to understand us. No one speaks English here, Rae."

Blowing out a hard sigh, Rae brushes her hair away from her face. "You could've just warned me, Khar. I mean, I trust you, but damn it."

Coming to her side, I take her shoulders in my hand. "Only life announces itself, beautiful. Death, on the other hand, isn't as courteous. Still, I am sorry for scaring you."

Resting her hands on her hips, Rae throws an eye roll my way. "Be very glad I love you, Kharon Nyx. Don't you ever do that again!" she says, jamming her elbow into my side.

Holding up three fingers, I smile. "Scout's honor."

"Mm–hmph," she grumbles, offering me her hand. Taking it, we make our way past the shoreline. Reaching the cobblestone path to my city, Rae looks around and back at me with a concerned stare. "So, where is everyone? It's much quieter here than I thought it would be."

I take a deep breath. There's so much to explain; I barely know where to begin.

"This is Theogony Island. My home, Purgia, resides in this province. It is thought to be the birthplace of primordials like my parents, Erebus and Nyx. Many say the sands of these shores contain the genealogy of both our realms. I call this place home. Things may seem quiet now, but when we walk through the gates just up that road, it can get very loud."

"It's just so beautiful here. I'm surprised no one comes to this beach."

I chuckle a bit. Times like these remind me just how *very human* Rae is.

"Well, it's not quite a beach, Rae. It's a sacred place where few are permitted to travel–or even reach. The body of water here is made of pure ether. There are few who can enter it and live, which brings up a good point. Never touch or ingest the water here. It's deadly. Do you understand?" I pause until Rae nods with understanding. "Also, never accept or eat anything offered to you unless it comes from me."

She affirms with a quick nod. "Got it. Only eat from your hand. Can we go in there now?"

I give her wrist a squeeze. I need her to understand the seriousness of our situation. "Rae, I'm serious. Do you understand?"

"Yes, Kharon, I understand."

Exhaling, I had no idea I was holding my breath. Swarms of wretched possibilities fill my mind. If Rae even attempts to dip her toe into the dark waters, it could cost her her life.

"All right, then," I begin, leading us forward. "Let's show you around Theogony Island."

Rae tightens her small hands around my forearm as we make our way down the gravel path, and I hear her let out a small breath. I can tell she's just as nervous as I am, maybe even more.

As we reach the end of the pathway, we stop in front of the gate. Rae looks up at me, her eyes wide with curiosity as she leans into me, almost hanging from my arm.

"*Resero,*" I whisper against the iron railing covered in golden pothos and ivy leaves.

A thick, smoky cloud rises from the ground, pushing the doors open. This time is different. Although I've opened these gates a thousand times, this is the first time I'll enter with the woman I love on my arm.

Twenty-Seven

RAE

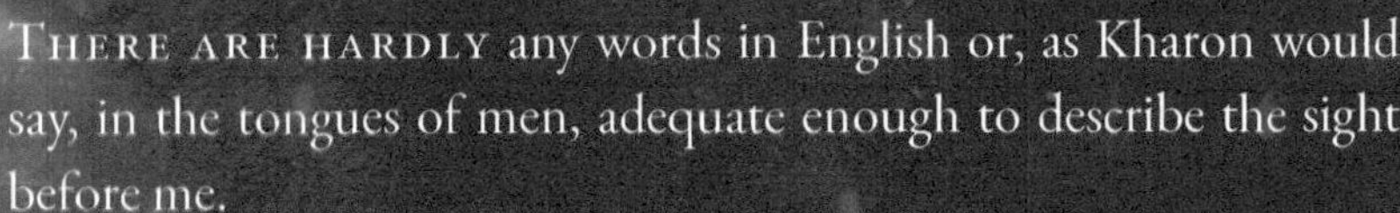

THERE ARE HARDLY any words in English or, as Kharon would say, in the tongues of men, adequate enough to describe the sight before me.

The moment I stepped foot on Theogony Island, on this Netherworld, I knew I was indeed in a different world. From the hazy, purplish-blue sky, to the poisonous ether, to the view of the most massive fortified city my eyes have ever seen, this is other-worldly.

This is more than I expected.

As soon as the gate opened, the sounds of what have to be a celebration ring loudly in the streets. Creatures I've never seen before wander about, singing, talking, and carrying on as you'd find in any earthbound city.

Still, this is different.

I know Kharon tried to prepare me for what I'd see, but nothing could prepare me for this.

Seeing what I presume is a man with four arms and six eyes should freak me out, but it's the falcon-headed merchant on the side of the road, enticing passersby with something that looks like a feather-covered soccer ball, that first catches my attention.

"It's called a Pluma Pila," Kharon whispers into my ear, pointing to two, troll-like children playing on the side of the street. "A feather ball of sorts. Typically, it's used during–shit! I can't believe I forgot what season this is." Tightening his hold on my wrist, Kharon takes runs his free hand through his hair. "Damn it! I really don't have time for this."

"Time for wh—"

Before I have a moment to say more, the sound of blaring trumpets roars through the city streets. A troop of six uni-horned women with peacock-like feathers coming from their backsides dance with tambourines and flags, making their way toward us. Cloaked drummers march behind them, faces like Ghostface from those slasher films. Still, it's the sight of circles of fire hurling toward us that have me retreating behind Kharon's massive frame.

Shielding me with an arm behind his back, Kharon utters something I can't make out, as the fire flares along the city streets. If we weren't in the Netherworld, I'd fear for everyone's safety, especially the cute little troll children. They all clap and cheer as the fire seems to merely shimmer against their skin like morning dew, though, so I know they're not the ones in danger.

I am.

The warmth of the fire washes over me, oddly cooling my angst as I hover behind Kharon.

"Our prince has returned!" a thunderous voice hails from afar, and the crowd cheers in response. I want to peer around Kharon's frame to see who's speaking, but I fear another round of fire will come rolling down the street.

Once more, the trumpets blow, and onlookers roar with enthusiasm. Streamers fizzle like firecrackers as they fall from the sky. I look up to see a group posted on a balcony above, tossing streamers onto the street, each one whistling as they pop and burst on the ground. I only hope Kharon can keep the fire at bay. Lifting his arm, he waves at the swarm gathered around us.

"Welcome home!" one woman screams from the balcony, releasing a wad of streamers from her basket. Lifting his arm, Kharon's forearm takes the brunt of the crackling, shaking his arm and blowing the smoke from his sleeve as if it was no big deal.

"My, have we missed you." I hear the thunderous voice once more, but I'm still too fearful to move from behind Kharon to see who it is.

"Thelios!" Kharon exclaims brightly. "It is mighty fine to see you, too." Kharon shifts a bit in front of me, seemingly trying to shield me. I still can't see anyone, but as Kharon moves, a dark, foreboding shadow hovers over us.

"Why, Kharon, who is it you have hidden back there?" the one called Thelios asks. Darkness creeps over us, and a painted skeleton face peers around Kharon's side. Luminous green eyes stare at me as black and red lips crest into the most haunting smile I have ever seen. "What a pretty little one you are!" Thelios breathes, circling where we stand.

Kharon moves me to his side, draping his arm around me, holding me tight, my head locked at his waist. "This is Rae Vereen," he says, looking at me with a proud stare.

"Ah, so you're adding to your collection, I see. Well, I already curated a nice grouping for you for the festivities, but we can certainly add this little morsel to the set," Thelios mumbles, almost annoyed. He snaps his fingers and two burly men, dressed in nothing but fig leaves covering their private areas, rush to his side. "Calis, Dane, take this one to the harem lair. Tell Pella to have her properly groomed and fitted for our prince."

A loud growl rumbles through Kharon's chest, and I feel his arms squeeze around me. As he does, another hand grabs my wrist, tugging me from Kharon's hold.

"Dane, take your hands off of her!" Kharon shouts, his eyes flaming bright like fire. Quickly yanking me back to his side, the warmth of his hands nearly sears my forearm as heat emanates from his palm. Without a word, Kharon pounds his fist into Dane's chest, sending him to the ground. His body goes limp and pale as he falls.

Crap! I think he killed him.

"Did–did you kill him?" I cry out, turning to Kharon.

Instead of finding the doting, kind gaze I usually see when I look at Kharon, I only find a menacing scowl etched on his face. I haven't seen that expression since the night it was revealed he held Melchior hostage. In fact, it's an expression I hoped never to see on his face again.

Rushing to kneel at Dane's side, Thelios holds his wrist to Dane's forehead. "Well, he'll certainly be of no help for the festivities. My prince, if you wanted to escort your damsel yourself, you only needed to say it. Now look at him!"

"Thelios, she is no damsel, nor will she set foot in any groupings you've prepared."

"But my prince!"

"That will be all, Thelios!" Kharon's growly tone leaves no room for protest.

Standing and offering a reverent bow, Thelios steps away from Kharon. "Calis, have Dane taken to a dead-and-wake cell. Should he not revive, have him tossed in with the others."

"Yes, my lord." Calis shuffles past me and Kharon, throwing Dane over his shoulder and carrying him away.

Turning quickly on his heel, Thelios turns back to us, offering Kharon a broad smile that stretches the painted lines of his skeleton grin from ear to ear. "Well, now that we've gotten that out of the way, shall we enjoy the festivities?" Kharon nods and Thelios spins, adding a flourish with his cloak as he marches forward.

Kharon's jaw tightens and his gaze narrows as he regards Thelios, but he gestures for us to follow. Looking between the two of them, I can't tell whether they're friends or foes, but I seem the only person even remotely unnerved by what just happened. Everyone else continues dancing, as if Kharon didn't just strike a man down for touching me.

While the irony of continuing down this shimmering golden road isn't lost on me, I do finally understand Dorothy Gale. I'm certainly not in Kansas anymore.

THIS IS NOT how I wanted this to go.

The plan was to bring Rae to the Netherworld safely, rescue Moirai, show her around my homeland a little, and return Rae just as safely as she came. Now, I can throw my entire plan into the Styx.

As we follow Thelios up the pathway to my castle, Rae's eyes are a mix of awe and fear as she takes in the grandeur of it all. From the stone relic in the courtyard to the triple-wide iron gatehouse and drawbridge with serpents swimming in its moat, I know it's a lot to take in.

Still, I'm impressed Rae hasn't begged me to take her back or run away from me altogether. I know she's frightened, but I'm thankful she's holding it together. Mostly, she's holding on to me, like she's afraid of letting go. Little does she know, it's her hold keeping me from losing it.

The wide doors of my palace open, and a large red carpet seamlessly rolls out for us as we walk, arm in arm. More fire ratan streamers are thrown our way, but I'm thankful they pop and burn without getting close to us. Some shiny confetti is heaved into the walkway, and Rae giggles as a few pieces land in her hair.

This part, I could get used to: walking through my castle with the woman I love on my arm. Yeah, that's not something I ever considered before, but with Rae at my side, I'm starting to consider things I never knew I wanted.

Thelios extends his hand to my throne room chair, but I give him a look, giving a quick nod towards Rae. He snaps his fingers and instantly, attendants bring out my sister's seat and places it next to mine.

Escorting Rae to her seat, she slowly sits but keeps her hand fisted in mine. I take my place next to her and extend my opposite hand to Thelios to proceed.

"Kharon, what is going on?" Rae whispers through her teeth.

Leaning over my shoulder, I kiss her wrist. "I'll explain in a moment. Hold steady."

"You didn't tell me you lived in a palace," she grits as her eyes wander about. Her gaze shifts from the seraphim creatures standing like living sconces along the walls to the life-like painted cherubim decorating the darkened ceiling. "Like, a whole frigging palace!"

I smile back, bringing her hand to my mouth once more. "What did you think I meant when I said I was prince?" I add a few small kisses, and she smiles.

"Well, I didn't think–"

"Ah-hem, Prince Kharon," Thelios says, issuing a faux throat clearing. I shoot Rae a quick wink before returning my attention to Thelios. "Shall we begin the opening ceremonies?"

"First, where is Pella?" I shout across the room. A small firefly, about the size of my thumb, hovers in front of my face. With bright, twinkling lights and a fiery tail, I am happy to see Pella, one of the last horned sprites, flickering in my view.

"Yes, my prince?" she answers, only loud enough for me to hear. "It's good to see you."

"It's good to see you too, Pella. Can you please set a place for Rae?" I say, waving a hand toward Rae. Pella smiles, and the soft outlines of her pale green face brighten with a child-like glow. Pella is one of the few to wish a mate for me. To her, Rae is an answered prayer of sorts.

"I'll see it done, Prince Kharon." Pella flutters to Rae, pausing briefly as she stares at her, chuckles, and then looks back at me. Rae's eyes widen as her gaze shifts between me and Pella. Pella nods, bowing at her waist before flying away.

"You may begin," I say to Thelios. He grins widly and turns, clapping his hands. As he does, the sound of a leer and trumpet blare through the room, getting closer each second.

Yanking my arm, Rae pulls me to her. "Okay, Kharon, you really need to tell me what's going on," she demands. Her eyes narrow as she regards me, but she gives a weak smile at Thelios and the few court attendants. "First, who is that man?"

I follow her pointed nod to Thelios. Smiling, I squeeze her hand. "Oh, that's Thelios Mirth, my Grim. Don't mind him. He's a far gentler creature than he seems."

Rae grunts, rolling her eyes. "I bet he's just a ball of sunshine. You mean to tell me he's the Grim Reaper?"

"Not quite. He is the Grim, the dark one. He can vacate a soul or send it to the great abyss. My Reaper is Roark. You haven't met him yet, but he's the one who executes death orders and serves as General of my dark guard."

The sounds of merriment grow louder, and Rae's eyes scan around the hall. "Sounds like a fun bunch." Her face crumples into a smile. "I take it there's a celebration today?"

Taking her hand in mine, I force aside my instinct to give full attention to what will soon burst through the double doors of my court. "It's Festivus."

"Festivus? What's that?"

"I can explain it all once we're alone, but for now, think of it like the Dia De Los Muertos but with a twist. Instead of a day to honor the dead, here in the Netherworld, it's a day for the dead to present tributes with the hope of being pardoned from the Underworld."

The music and revelries grow closer. As much as I want to explain it all to Rae, I know I need to stay focused on what or who will come through that door. This is all happening too fast, but I have no way of slowing it down.

"Why would they need to be pardoned from the Underworld? Isn't Purgia their home?"

Damn it. I should have done a better job preparing Rae for what she would encounter when we arrived. Instead, I drowned myself so deep in her love, I barely came up for air.

"Not quite," I begin. "Purgia is more like—"

The court doors swing open and the look on Rae's face tells me one thing: I've fucked up.

Twenty-Nine

RAE

Wʜᴀᴛ ɪɴ ᴛʜᴇ whole hell is this mess?

The sight of about fifteen naked women strolling through the large double-wide golden doors, wearing nothing but a few feathers covering their nipples and genitals while dancing seductively, is not something I expected to see.

Kharon palms his face, his elbow resting on his armrest. He's embarrassed, as he should be.

Why in the world would he bring me here? I thought he was a cursed ferryman. Instead, it seems instead like he's some hedonistic pig.

Four of the women are dancing on poles carried by a few

others, while the remaining women perform moves meant to arouse every carnal desire imaginable.

My skin warms, and I know my face is blushing red. I'm pissed. "Kharon, what is this?" I bite through my teeth. I'm trying to stay cool, but I don't know how much longer I can sit through this. Despite some women having three eyes or four breasts, it's clear they're doing everything possible to gain the attention of the prince.

My prince.

"Please, Rae, I'm sorry." Kharon's clenched jaw and glassy eyes alone tell me of his remorse. He's likely more embarrassed than sorry for parading these women in front of me. Still, he doesn't take his eyes off the women. "Just let me–"

Once more, the loud sound of clapping from Thelios reverberates through the room. "Now our Great Prince can make his grand selection!" Thelios starts, turning back to Kharon with a wide skeletal grin. "As is his custom, Prince Kharon will now choose his first Tribute to be added to His Highness' royal harem." A series of claps and shouts from the court attendants echo through the hall, and my stomach sickens at the thought of it all. "Prince Kharon, I hope you are pleased with the grouping I've assembled for you on this great day. Knowing your predilections and your particular tastes, I've curated quite an eclectic mix, if I don't say so myself. From Mara, the Sea Siren, to Krill, the Huntress of Cayman, and of course, Lyra, the last daughter of the Leviathan order. I'm told Lyra here is quite prolific with her fourth tongue," Thelios whispers over his shoulder to Kharon.

Looking around the courtroom with the throngs of onlookers and women clamoring for Kharon's attention, the large hall grows small. Suffocating. I feel like I can't breathe. Gazing around, I look for an exit. I have no idea where to go, much less where it's safe to go, but I know I can't stay here.

Slowly pulling my hand from Kharon's grasp, my eyes search

for a way out. I hear Kharon whisper my name through the roaring sounds around us, but I'm too fearful to look him in the eye. I need to get out of here.

A green and orange light flickers to my left like a beacon, and I take its cue. Jumping up from my seat, I run toward the light. My eyes are glassy with tears, and I can barely see anything in front of me. Still, I keep my gaze locked on the guiding light hovering in the darkness, hopeful for relief.

For the first time since I've been here, I feel small. Insignificant.

Boisterous laughter rings aloud as I make my way down the side aisle, and I swear they're all laughing at me. Pointing. Ridiculing. Mocking me as if I were nothing more than a worthless plaything on the arm of the prince.

Maybe they're right.

Not once did Kharon tell them who I am to him. Then again, *who am I?* His girlfriend? I don't know; we've never used such terms. I'm certainly not his wife.

In fact, I can't say what I am to him. We've never given what we are a name.

I thought it would be different here. I thought this would be the one place I wasn't relegated to the shadows, hidden in the background like always. Instead, here I am. Unlike those girls who met the love of their life and got engaged all in the matter of twenty-four hours, the man I've pined after for years, given myself to entirely, has yet to declare who I am to those who matter most to him.

For months, I've told myself this was the route we must take, but now, I'm not so sure. In fact, I'm not sure about anything anymore.

The fiery light flashes bright as I get closer, and I realize it's the small creature Kharon called Pella. Following Pella's light, two narrow doors open, leading me into a large room. Flustered, I turn about, still bawling my eyes out and trying to take in my surroundings.

There's a large poster bed with sheer drapes in front of a large balcony overlooking a lovely fountain. Instead of water, the fountain empties a black substance reminiscent of oil, but with a shimmery haze that's almost mirror-like. It's beautiful but haunting.

Still, I don't take much time to ponder the grandeur of it all or this stately room. I want to throw myself on the bed and cry, but the bed seems like it's ten-feet tall and I'd need a ladder to climb onto it. Surely, it's not made for humans.

For as wide as it is, larger than at least four California King mattresses combined, it's probably meant to entertain the horde of heifers who were just showing their all for Kharon.

Leaning against the legs of the bed, I ball into a knot on the floor, doing my best to console the stabbing ache in my heart.

Pella's light continues to hover about, flickering and flashing, trying to get my attention. Through tearful eyes, I peer up to see the face of a small feminine being. I think she's trying to say something, but as small as she is, I can't understand her. Instead, her words are nothing more than a buzzing sound ,like a bee.

"I can't understand you," I tearfully confess, cupping my face in my hands.

Once more, Pella's light brightens, but this time, it's almost blinding. Sharp flashes of gold and green beam through the room, and I cover my eyes. The flashing comes to a halt, and I feel a small pat on my shoulder. Slowly peering through the gaps between my fingers, I see an angelic, moss-hued face smiling back at me.

Startled, I press myself against the large wooden pole at my back. "What–who?"

Her smile widens as she raises her palm that seems to leak with some kind of pixie dust. "Please, don't be frightened. I'm Pella, last of the Horned Sprites of Viridian. I'm also High Aide to his Highness Prince Kharon, which means I am at your service, my lady."

She bows at her waist, and her small, iridescent wings flutter at her against her back. Even with the singular gray horn surrounded by long purple hair in the center of her head, her smile is the most pleasant thing I've seen since we've arrived.

"It's nice to meet you, Pella," I force a smile toward the only courteous creature I've met so far. Using the hem of my gown, I wipe my face. "I'm sorry you're not meeting me at my best." I try to force a laugh while Pella offers her hand to help me from the floor.

Straightening my dress, I'm happy to find Pella is about my height. Perhaps an inch or two taller, but just enough so I no longer feel like the only ant in the Netherworld.

"Are you okay, Rae?" she asks, still rubbing my shoulder.

"I'll be okay, I guess," I say, but my smile isn't as forced as before. I part my mouth to say more, but when the door swings open and I see Kharon's flaming eyes glaring at me from the threshold, I know whatever niceties I had for Pella will have to wait.

Thirty

KHARON

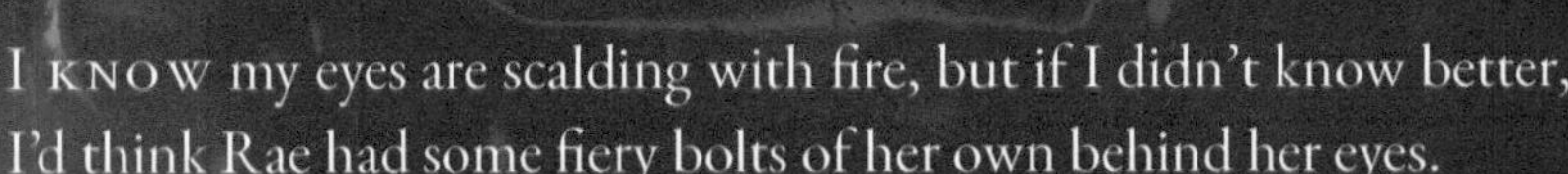

I know my eyes are scalding with fire, but if I didn't know better, I'd think Rae had some fiery bolts of her own behind her eyes.

Damn. I know I've screwed things up royally, but her behavior is totally unacceptable.

"Rae Vereen!" I shout from the threshold, too fearful of what I'll do next to take another step.

She doesn't answer. Instead, she just stands there, all folded arms and condemning eyes, looking at me as if I owe her an explanation. I do, but I still don't appreciate the stare, especially in front of Pella.

"What the hell, Pella?" I bark, coming into the room and slamming the door behind me. "You know better than to reveal your true form! What if someone saw you?"

Pella takes cautious steps past Rae, fidgeting with her fingers. "I'm sorry, Prince Kharon. I–I just thought since she's *your mate*— I mean, she *is* the one, is she not? The one your heart has always sought to find? I assumed since you've never sat anyone next to you except Moirai–and with the way your eyes danced–I–I..."

Rae's eyes widen before returning to a full scowl as she steps forward, placing herself in front of Pella. "So, great prince, you heard her. What am I?" Folding her arms, she leans her head to one side, twisting her mouth as she drags her gaze through the entirety of me.

"Pella, out!" I demand.

A bright flash of light blares through the chamber, and Pella returns to her normal sprite form before flying out of the balcony.

"Why did you yell at her? She was just trying to console me. Something you were too distracted to do, might I add," Rae bites back.

I'm doing all I can to keep my composure. The last thing I need to do is heap the full weight of my fury upon Rae. She deserves better, much better than I can give.

"What in the hell do you think I'm doing here right now? You think I left my courtroom on a whim? I came to check on you."

Rae's stiff posture softens a little, but she keeps her daggered stare marked on me. She's not letting me off that easily.

"You never answered my question, Kharon–or should I say, Great Prince. What am I to you?"

Huffing hard, I circle around the chevron pattern of black and gray on the marble floor. *Stay cool, Kharon.*

"What the hell kind of question is that, Rae? You are my everything. My fucking everything. You already know this. How many times must I say it? Damn it!"

"Damn it, is right, Kharon! Sure, you've told me plenty of times, most notably when you're screwing my brains out," she shouts back. Her cheeks blush, and I can tell even saying the words awakened her sensuality in ways only I can. Still, she digs her heels in, biting her lip, forcing her thoughts aside. "What about everyone else, Khar? Do you not care to tell the world who I am?" Rae's tone may be quiet, but her words snake around my heart like a cobra, fisting it tight.

I take a small step forward. I need to close the distance between us in more ways than one. "You are my world, beautiful. I love you."

Rae's eyes swim in a pool of tears as she regards me, but she looks away, swiping her chin against her shoulder, wiping her face. "But not enough to tell anyone," she groans, now nibbling at her knuckles resting at her chin.

This time, I nearly leap to her side. Small steps be damned. "I'll tell the whole fucking world if you want me to." Taking her shoulders in my hands, I turn her so she's facing me. Her eyes slowly trail up to mine, and the pain I see in them crushes parts of me I didn't know existed. "I'll write our love like fire in the sky. I need you to know this, baby."

Rae shakes her head, pulling herself from my grip. It hurts to let her go, but I'll give her a little space, at least for now. "So then why haven't you said anything? I mean, do I have to hide what we have everywhere we go? I thought at least it would be different here, but it's more of the same. And on top of everything–everything, Kharon–we're greeted by a dancing orgy. What is that about? Did you expect me to just sit by and be cool with that? What kind of fool do you take me for?"

She's right, on all sides, but she doesn't understand everything.

Reaching out, I take her chin between my fingers. "You're far from a fool," I whisper, holding her face firm in my grip until her eyes meet mine. "If there's a fool here, it's me. Please don't take my lack of declaring my love for you to the whole of the Netherworld as some measure of my love. Quite frankly, I'm just as disillusioned as you are."

Rae's mouth twists some as she twirls her curls between her fingers. "How so?"

"For starters, I forgot about Festivus altogether. It's been ten years since I left the Netherworld. Sure, it's been only a little over a month for everyone here, but as I'm sure you can understand, a lot has happened. Although my goal was to rescue Moirai, I'm not surprised my sister ensured I was back in time for Festivus. She knows how important this time is for my city."

Pacing the floor, Rae stares up at me as she continues to tussle with her hair. I can see a thousand questions racing through her mind.

"Okay, I'll bite. What is Festivus?"

I smile, thankful that maybe she hasn't given up on me completely. "Well, as I was beginning to tell you earlier, Festivus is very similar to Dia De Los Muertos, the difference being the dead beg to remain in Purgia instead of being ferried to the Underworld."

"I don't understand. Why can't they just stay in Purgia? Why would they need to plea? To who?"

I can't help laughing. "To me, baby. I am the Prince of Purgia." I smile wide, offering a bow, and she stifles a laugh. I know I'm getting to her, but she's still mad at me. Straightening my posture, I pace with her at her side. "It may help if you think of Purgia for what it is—purgatory."

Gasping, Rae stops in her tracks. "Purgatory! This place is limbo? I thought it was the Underworld."

"No, I'm afraid the two are quite different. The Underworld is a place of final judgment. For some in the Netherworld, that outcome can be perilous."

"So, you ferry them to the Underworld? To Hades?"

Moving a little closer, I stop and meet her eyes. "Yes, unless I find them worthy of pardon and they remain as full citizens of Purgia."

"How do you choose who gets to stay?"

I sigh. "These days, I only choose those who will be given court access. Some of my lower guards and adjutants, like Thelios, Pella, and Roark, they select a few, too. It's kind of like a talent show of sorts. Those seeking a pardon must offer distinct talents that would lend themselves to Purgia."

"Like naked, dancing heifers." Rae's tone is sharp, but it's the cut of her eyes that slices me in two.

Gulping hard, I force down the froggish knot growing in my throat. "Well, you may have heard Thelios earlier say he curated a grouping on my behalf. He normally does so to add to my harem."

She steps back from me, creating more distance. "You have a harem?" Her brow raises and her nose twitches. *Shit.* She's pissed. I've really messed this up.

"Had. Past tense." I will fix this.

Rae's eyes travel the length of my body. She's not buying it. "What do you mean past tense?"

"Had you not run out of the courtroom, you would have heard my decree to disband the harem. I don't need it."

Rae's wide eyes fill with tears as her thick lashes flutter, trying to hold them back. "You don't?"

"No, Rae, I don't. Truthfully, I've never needed it. Now that I have you, I'll never need it again. Besides, I'm sure Thelios and Roark have far better use for his *curation* than me."

Shaking her head, Rae sways side to side. I know she's trying to make sense of all this.

"I just don't understand you, Kharon. Your whole life in the Netherworld is one big mystery to me. First, I learned we can't have kids because you're death and I'm life or whatever. Next, you turn into a skeleton and nearly choke the life out of me. Now it's

Festivus and orgies and purgatory. Kharon, you know everything about me. Everything. My life has been an open book, and you've been there for the better part of it. Yet, in all this time, I know so little about you. I don't even know you–"

Rae's voice trails off as she muffles her cries, palming her face.

She's right about everything and wrong at the same time, but none of that matters now. Watching her cry into her hands is painful to witness. After doing everything I could to protect her, it's clear I've broken her heart.

Now I have to figure out how to put it back together.

Thirty-One

RAE

"Rae, please. Let me try to explain," Kharon begins, tugging my hands from my face. I almost hate to let him see me like this. I'm sure I am beginning to look like a crybaby, but truly, what is the appropriate response to everything I've endured?

"Kharon, I love you, and I know you love me, but there's a world between us. I can't remain a hidden figure forever. Not here. Not in your life."

"I understand, but I need you to trust me when I say it was never my intention to keep you hidden. Things just happened so quickly once we arrived. More importantly, for your safety, I can't just go shouting your name through the streets of Purgia. While this may be my city, the Changelings have spies everywhere. If they discovered your existence–"

"Then they discover it! I'm tired of living in the shadows, Kharon! I've done it long enough in my realm. I'll not be the pathetic girl in the background of the man I love."

Kharon winces at that, his lips curling as he runs his hands through his hair. "Pathetic? Never! Can't you understand I just want to keep you safe?"

"Listen, the Fates decreed I come to the Netherworld. Why would they decree such a thing if they didn't think I could handle it? I know it may seem like I run off crying at a whim, but perhaps the Fates see some strength in me even you don't see."

Kharon's face nearly pales at my words, but he sucks in a breath and stays calm. "I don't need anyone to see what I already know about you, Rae Vereen, what I've always known about you. Yes, the Fates may have decreed for you to come here, but it is my decree to keep you safe." Once more, Kharon's eyes grow dark, and it's the same menacing glare from earlier.

"Oh, and does keeping me safe include knocking men out for merely touching me?"

Kharon's gaze darkens and he draws his mouth into a thin line. "That's exactly what that means."

Throwing my hands in the air, I pace again. "I can't believe you're cool with hurting someone so easily."

"No, Rae, not hurting. Killing. I killed him."

Gasping, I grab myself at the waist. "Please tell me you're kidding."

"I wouldn't joke about killing someone."

"But why? Because he touched me? I've been touched by other men before."

Folding his arms, Kharon nudges his chin, donning the arrogant smirk that normally has my head spinning. Right now, it's doing anything but.

"The only men in your life other than me are all related to you. This man, however, was trying to take you from me. I won't allow that."

"Only because Thelios told him to. Why didn't you strike him down?"

Kharon hunches his shoulders almost dismissively. "Because Thelios didn't touch you. Don't worry–it was only a dead-and-wake. He'll be fine in time."

"A *dead and* what? Okay, now I'm confused. Didn't you just say you killed him?"

"Yes, but technically, everyone here is already dead. The term kill is relative. Here, we call it a dead-and-wake. He's dead now. He should wake soon. If he touches you again, it'll be the true death."

Running my hands through my hair, I lean back. I can hardly believe my ears. "See, Kharon, this is what I'm talking about! I've never heard of a dead-and-wake before. There's so much I don't know about you!"

"Look, you're right. I haven't done a good job explaining everything to you or even preparing you for what we could encounter. I take responsibility for that, but you have to understand that I spent years, *long* years, desiring you, wanting you, *needing you*. When our time finally came, the last thing I wanted to do was take the focus off us. I wanted to bask in your love and bathe in the entirety of you. When I said you owned me, I meant it. I nearly forgot I was a prince. The only thing, the only one I thought of these last few months was you, Rae Vereen. Only you."

I want to believe Kharon. *I do believe Kharon.* Still, there is so much left unsaid.

"Kharon, believe me when I say the time we've spent together has meant everything to me. I spent those same long years desiring and wanting you, but that doesn't change the fact that you've told me so little about who you are."

Growling hard, Kharon marches toward me, his heavy feet

hitting the marble floor hard. Lifting me in his arms, Kharon cradles me in his embrace. He utters something in some unknown tongue and walks us across the room.

Turning my head, I notice he's heading toward the bed. Banging on his chest, I shout and protest. "Kharon, no! We're not going to fix this with sex. I'm not going to let you fuck your way out of this one."

He stops at the side of the bed. A smug look forms on his face while his dark brow raises behind the golden blonde tresses hanging against his forehead. "Is that what you think I've been doing? Fucking my way out of it?" A sly grin slides to the side of his mouth, and I feel my lady parts dancing.

"Kharon, please, we need to talk." I can only hope my deadpan tone hits the mark.

He resumes walking, his steps heavy as we near the center of the bed. "What if I don't want to talk?"

"Is this how it's going to be? Every time we find ourselves at odds, we fuck it out?"

Licking his lips, he looks down at me and kisses my forehead. "I really don't see the problem. I rather like the idea. Think how much better our worlds would be if we all just fucked it out. There'd be much happier folks walking around, I bet."

"Kharon!" I shove his shoulder, trying my best to retain a shred of self-control.

"Well, if you're done tempting me to *fuck it out*, as you say, maybe you'll be up for a tour," he says, passing the bed and leading us to the open balcony.

"A tour?" I rasp, slightly relieved and disappointed, looking up into his steely stare. It's taking every bit of my restraint not to ask him to throw me on the bed.

He offers a little nod. "Yes, baby, a tour. You said you don't know much about me. Maybe we'll start with a tour of my home-land. You're right: there's much I've left unsaid. I need you to understand I've been alive more than six-hundred earthbound years. There's a lot of ground to cover, and I've got centuries worth of information to share. I can only hope you know I've told you the most important thing: I love you."

A river of tears race to my chin, and I bury my face in Kharon's chest. "I love you too, Khar."

Kissing the crown of my head, Kharon smiles. "Don't worry, beautiful; I'll make it just like one of your favorite cartoons and show you a whole new world."

Brushing a loose tear from my face, I smile, taking hold of his chin. "What? No carpet?"

"Not necessary," he smiles back.

I feel Kharon's grip tighten around me, just as I hear Thelios shout his name. "Your Highness, there's still a litany of tributes left to see!" Thelios yells, running into the center of the room.

Kharon only looks down at me, smiling again. Tilting his head just over his shoulder, he whispers, "You can see to it. I'm giving the love of my life a tour."

With that, he lifts us from the balcony floor up into the indigo, star-covered sky.

Thirty-Two

KHARON

FINALLY, this feels right.

Rae is nestled in my arms where she belongs as we soar, rising to the tip of my castle. The air is mercifully comfortable, void of its usual humidity, a brisk breeze carrying us to the gable dome.

Landing on the roof, I lean against the black crystal owl overlooking the city. Rae is still in my arms, holding tight around my neck. Although it's not her first time flying with me, she's still not a fan of heights.

"Please don't drop me, Khar," Rae squeals, looking away from the ground and pressing her face into the nape of my neck.

Kissing her forehead, I lift her face so her eyes meet mine.

"Never, baby. I've got you."

She squirms, as if there was a deeper cave for her to crawl into inside my arms. "You promise?"

"Of course, beautiful. Now come on, you said you wanted to know more about me. Well, now is your chance. Come on, take a look."

Slowly, Rae stares out into the dark abyss I call home. "I know there's no sun here. It's always night and it–"

"It's beautiful!" Rae breathes, now pressing her face against my jaw. I wish she could see how lovely she looks as the wind whips through her hair, and I capture it all for my memory.

"You like it?"

"Khar, I love it!" she coos, kissing my cheek.

I point out important spots from my life in the darkness. "To your right is the Eye of Night. It's the watchtower of our keep, named after my mother, Nyx. I can't tell you the number of days I spent as a rascal, running through the watchtower. My aunt Clotho could barely contain me."

I feel Rae's eyes dancing as she stares at me, but I keep her in my periphery. It's not often I recount the days of my youth.

"I bet you were a handful," she says, threading her hands through my hair.

Nodding in agreement, I smile. "Something like that." I throw her a quick wink.

"I still can't believe you're a prince." Rae whispers, looking around.

I shrug my shoulders. "That was never a secret."

Rae flits her wide eyes up to mine, a curious smile behind the escaped waves of her hair. "Yes, but a castle? All of this? It's just so much to take in."

"Take it all in, Rae. My world is now your world."

"Our world." She smiles, running her hand along my forearm. Just as she parts her mouth to speak, something catches her eye over my shoulder. "Oh! What's over there?" Rae asks, pointing to a large red tent. "Is that a circus?"

"Close, but not quite. It's a Soleil court, where all the fabrics of Purgia are produced."

"How is that like a circus?" she laughs with a quirked brow.

Now *this* is right up my alley. "I'm glad you asked. Let me show you. Hold on tight."

Burying her face once more into my neck, Rae screams as the wind carries us through the sky to land at the Soleil court. An echo of oohs and ahhs pour through the courtyard; most Purgians are likely surprised to see me. I've been gone for a while, but it's been even longer since I'd last visited the Soleil. Now, I'm here with a mortal in my arms.

"Prince Nyx!" Gao, my Chief Steward, gasps as Rae and I land in the middle of the court. "It's so good to see you, Your Highness," he adds, bowing at his waist. Those in his charge offer formalities as well, but I lift my hand, smiling to let them know it isn't necessary.

"Please, Gao, don't let us stop you," I say, watching as he and his wife, Oru, gather troughs of fabrics into a bin just outside the tent doors. "I see you are busy."

Oru steps forward, a wide smile gleaming as she looks at Rae in my arms. I put Rae down, bringing her to my side, our hands still clasped together. The golden leaves scattered across Oru's gown cascade from her shoulder to her toes. Even her sandals are embroidered with small golden leaves, and there's a matching one in her coal black hair, just above her ear. Gao only has one golden leaf clasped at the top of his tunic, but the diamond-like cresting of his clothing is just as radiant.

"We're never too busy for you, my prince," Gao answers with a broad smile. "And that goes for your–" He pauses, waiting for me to reply.

"This is Lady Rae Vereen. *My mate.*" There it is. The first time

I've said the words out loud. I want to call her my wife, but not yet, not until she says yes.

Their smiles grow wider, but that's because they know all too well what the word means here in the Netherworld. Our souls are tied. We are tethered together like woven threads of fabric, bound forever. No one understands such a notion more than the stewards of the Soleil.

Quickly taking Rae's hand in hers, Oru flashes her perfectly white smile. Her golden eyes dance as she brings Rae into her arms for an embrace. Rae's eyes bounce to mine, surprised by the gesture, but she lets out a cute little chuckle that always makes my heart leap.

"It's so very nice to meet you, Lady Vereen," Oru begins, looping Rae's arm in hers. "I am Oru. We are delighted to have you here. Please, won't you come join us in the Soleil?"

Rae looks over her shoulder at me, and I nod for Gao and Oru to lead us inside.

"Please pardon the mess, Prince Nyx. We've been busy getting everything ready for Festivus," Gao explains, pushing aside a few loose fabrics on the floor.

"There's nothing to forgive, Gao. I know this is the busiest season for you. I just wanted to show Rae around a bit."

"Well, then let us give Rae a fine showing. After all, it isn't every day we are fortunate enough to entertain such a beautiful guest," Oru sweetly adds, lightly strumming her hand against the side of Rae's face, leaving behind a trail of golden dust.

Slowly, Oru releases Rae from her hold and Rae steps back into my waiting arms. As she does, Gao raises his arms and fire shoots from the sides of the tent. Three sets of rings drop from the ceiling, revealing an array of fabrics hanging from each.

"Kharon, what's going on?" Rae murmurs, nudging my side with her elbow.

Firming my grip around her, I smile. "Just wait and see."

Thirty-Three

RAE

I'VE NEVER SEEN SUCH a spectacle in my entire life.

Three women in long flowing gowns, wrapped in gold, pulled fabric cords hanging from the rings, causing it to unravel into distinct threads. Each thread, carried by a gale of its own making, circled the tent until it enclosed us in silk.

Beams of light radiate through each thread, creating a cosmic glow in the center of the red tent of the Soleil. I've never seen such vibrant colors. Twirling where I stand, I try to take in the wonder before me, but I am awestruck as the magical threads fuse together like bolts of lightning.

"This is beautiful!" I gasp, still in awe.

"Go ahead, my dear," Oru says sweetly, now at my side. My eyes linger a bit on the golden dusty glow emanating through her skin. "Touch a thread."

I look to Kharon; I need to know this is safe. Smiling, he gives me a nod before sharing an appreciative smile with Gao, who is almost just as tall as Kharon. Oru isn't short, but I'm thankful she's not as tall as the men.

Carefully, I stretch my pointer finger toward a bright red thread. "This one?" I whisper to Oru. She smiles, blinking in affirmation. Touching the thread, a prickly, warm sensation rivets through me. Instinctively, I pull my finger back. "Oof!"

"It's okay, beautiful," Kharon says. "Let me help you." Winking down at me, Kharon folds his large palm over my wrist, guiding my hand back to the thread. "What you want to do is pull it toward you. Guide it where you want it to go." With his hand over mine, Kharon pulls my hand back after I connect with the red thread once more. Shifting his hand side to side, he yanks it until the thread is all that is left. "Now, envision what you want to see," he breathes just above my head.

Closing my eyes tight, I try to picture what I'd like to see. I don't have a clue what I'm doing, but the first thing that comes to mind is Kharon and how much I love the smart way he wears his ascots.

My eyes pop open, only to find the wide grins of Oru and Gao staring back at me. Kharon leans over my shoulder and turns my chin up to meet his storm-cast gaze. "Something strike your fancy?" My head bobbles, and I chuckle as he takes my free hand in his. "Stretch your fingers to the length and width you desire."

I do as he says, lengthening my arms as wide as I can while gaping my palms open for the width. Shimmering fibers mend together, cross stitching across the sky in one fluid motion.

Gently, Kharon moves my hand as we watch the fabric come

together. "Now, we let the magic take its course," Kharon whispers in my ear, wrapping his arms around me from behind.

"Beautiful," I sigh with my hands over my mouth, watching the fabric weave like magic in the sky.

Once more, Kharon lifts my hand back up, and the fabric slowly falls into my palm. It's as light as a feather, but softer than silk.

"It's lovely, my lady," Gao says as he and Oru walk toward us.

Oru hovers her finger over the red cloth, smiling sheepishly as she looks up at me. "What is it?"

I smile, looking over my shoulder at Kharon. "It's an ascot. For you," I reply, handing it to Kharon.

Kharon's cheeks blush beneath his dark stubble, and his bright smile beams from ear to ear. "Thank you, baby." Quickly, he wraps it around his neck. It doesn't match his clothes, but he seems happy to wear it.

"Just another one to add to your signature look." I shoot him a wink as I sigh dreamily. "This is all so beautiful."

Gao waves a hand, laughing as his shoulders shake. "You haven't seen the half of it," he adds, snapping his fingers.

As he does, the three women take hold of the fabric, climbing up to position themselves within the rings. With acrobatic precision, the women move around them using the fabric. I watch in awe as the threads still hovering around us bloom like flowers into thicker wads.

Taking my shoulders in his hands, Kharon leans over me and points to the woman in the center. "That is Korah. She is a base threader. She's responsible for holding the threads together. The other two are weavers. They use their weaving magic to thread the fabrics into fashions one could wear."

"Weavers?" I tug Kharon's wrist and look around the tent. "Does that also make you a weaver? I've seen you thread fabrics, too."

"Is he a weaver?" Gao snorts with a faux chuckle. "Prince Nyx is the best weaver this side of the Styx. That is, only second to you, my dear." He winks at Oru and gives a knowing smile to Kharon.

"Just a little Nether-magic, huh?" I shove his shoulder playfully. I can't believe Kharon played down his magical abilities. He's more than a mere carrier of souls!

"Only a little," Kharon smiles, holding his thumb and forefinger just above my face. "Keep looking," he continues, pointing to the rings.

The three women begin to sing, and more rings sprout from the ceiling. Now there are more weavers funneling fabrics around the Soleil. As their song nears its climax, a small man, shorter than me, pushes something into the center of the room. I watch as shirts, dresses, and trousers fall into a bin.

"Wow, Khar," I whisper, wrapping my arms around Kharon's waist. "This is all so beautiful. How is this possible?"

"It's like I told you before: Aunt Clotho taught the silkworm and the spider to spin silks and satins. She taught some of us the same. Gao was her apprentice and Oru , of the Midas clan, is a Siphoner of gold and jewels. Oru can fashion any rare finds onto our clothes."

"Even dragon scales?" I ask, running my hand across Kharon's chest.

He smirks, his chest swelling with pride. "Ah, so you noticed?"

"It's kind of hard to miss. Why didn't you ever wear that in my realm?"

"Our magic must align to the rules of the realm. Dragons aren't a part of your realm, so no dragon scales. Here, almost anything is possible."

My eyes drift back to where the finished fabrics fall into the bin. Gao steps in front of me, catching my attention. "This is how we collect the clothes. Later, they'll be prepared for distribution throughout Purgia."

"This is incredible. Thank you for showing me around." I offer a hand to Gao and a hug to Oru.

"Wait one minute!" Kharon says with a bright smile, flames dancing in his eyes. "I want to weave something special for the woman I love." Cracking his knuckles, he flashes a smile that meets his eyes, and I know I'm in for a treat.

Thirty-Four

KHARON

CRACKLING sounds like fireworks pop and fizzle as I guide my hands around Rae's torso. Her smile outshines every flash of light as I weave enhancements into her gown so that she's matching me. I want everyone in the Netherworld to know she is mine.

With Oru's help, diamond-encrusted dragon scales now adorn Rae's gown. Gao even provides a thin red sash to complement my ascot. Rae twirls about, amazed by the overwhelming display of Nether-magic in the Soleil.

"Kharon!" Rae rasps, still twirling, admiring her gown. "It's lovely!"

Taking Rae's hands in mine, I look her over. *Beautiful.* "I'm glad you like it."

"Thank you!" Blowing a kiss to Oru and waving at Gao, Rae's eyes dance as she glances at her dress once more. Staring at her, I notice Oru has managed to add a light dusting of gold to Rae's face and skin, highlighting every perfected inch of her.

"It was our pleasure," Oru blows a small kiss in return.

Nodding at Gao, I give Rae a look, signaling it's time for us to leave. "Shall we?" Looping her arm in mine, I lead us toward the exit. Rae turns and takes one last glance around the Soleil before offering me a reluctant smile and squeezing my forearm.

As we depart, the ring bearers and weavers continue singing, belting in harmony until each thread is knitted and woven as one. An almost overflowing trough of clothes sits in the center of the Soleil, and Gao's attendant moves the bin outside next to another. Stepping outside the tent into the courtyard, Rae takes in the sights and sounds of the Netherworld. Heaving a deep breath, she looks up at me and smiles.

"I think I'm ready for another adventure!" She grins.

"Another? Already, Bilbo?" I laugh. As I scoop her into my arms, she giggles, as if she were surprised by the gesture.

Taking my chin in her hand, she scratches at my stubble, pulling me in for a small kiss. "I'm Pippin, remember?"

Shrugging my shoulders, I laugh and push off the ground. "You're mine," I growl into her ear.

Rae locks her arms around my neck, once more digging a hole into the cavity of my arms. Her curls blow in the wind, cascading through the sky like an amber cloud, and it's the prettiest sight in the Netherworld.

I zip around to a few points of interest in Purgia. From the gold-capped Midas mountains to the shipyard and docks at the Styx, I do my best to show Rae places that matter most to me.

Her curiosity keeps her distracted enough not to be fearful of heights. She seems just as interested in learning how I navigate my fleet as she is to understand how we mine gold as a primary commodity in the Netherworld. Even more, Rae is markedly shocked Purgia doesn't seem as dark and cruel as she thought it would be. Although I assure her my realm is certainly no fairytale, it doesn't take a genius to know she's assessing whether she could make a home here with me.

Inevitably, I knew this topic would come up. For as much as I want to be wholly open with her–and tell her I have a duty to my people here–I fear what it will mean for us.

Still, I promised Rae the truth, so here goes nothing.

Gently landing back on the balcony, I keep Rae cradled in my arms. "I hope you enjoyed the tour."

"I loved it, Khar. Thank you for showing me your world."

Kissing her forehead, I lower her to the ground. "I'm glad you liked it. I hope perhaps you'd consider it becoming your world, too."

There it is. My fucking heart. Out in the open, like an exposed wound.

Rae looks up at me, her eyes bouncing around a bit as her fingers twist through her hair. *Please be gentle, Rae.* Don't rip the bandage off too quickly. I wonder if she knows she could literally crush me if she's not careful.

"How would that work? I'm human, and from the looks of it, this stone is already starting to show signs of waning," she says, rubbing her thumb over the derclanite.

Shit. I hadn't looked at that damn stone since I put it around her neck.

Bending over, I stare into the stone. She's right; it *has* dimmed a little, though thankfully not enough to worry. I'm sure we have more time.

"Look, if I have to command an army to look for more derclanite, I will. I'll dig up every ounce of it if it means having you here with me."

Rae's eyes go misty, but I can tell she's working hard not to cry. "What about my home? Ross? It's just the two of us. I can't leave him."

"I'd never ask you to abandon your brother, baby, but as you see, we could stay a decade in your realm and still come back here and barely miss a beat. It'll be up to us how often we come and go."

"Kharon, you're a prince. You have responsibilities to your people. I can't ask you to–"

"You don't have to ask me a damn thing. I want to spend my life with you."

Stepping away from me, Rae walks to the threshold. "It's just too much, Kharon."

"For who? Not for me. I've waited an eternity to find you, Rae Vereen. There's no way I'm letting what we share go because we can't decide between the winter and summer home."

Rolling her eyes, Rae laughs, although not as merrily as I'd like. "Oh, please! I think this is a bigger decision than a winter and summer home. Besides, what about the other obvious stuff–"

I raise my brow. "Like what?" I have no idea where this is going.

Pacing back and forth, Rae's hands settle on her hips. She's giving me a look like I'm in trouble. For the first time, I wonder if this rawhide stare is what she'd give our kids. *Damn it. Don't go there, idiot.*

She makes a hard stop when she nears the bed. Still, she doesn't turn to look at me. Instead, she whips her head over her shoulder. "You're a frigging primordial, damn near immortal. What happens when I get old and wrinkly, and you don't want an old lady on your arm? It's not like we can grow old together."

"I suppose I'll just wither my bones and age along with my wife."

Spinning on her heel, she turns to face me. "Your wife?" Her hands quickly cover her mouth when she finds me now down on one knee. Rae's eyes widen as she stares at me, her hands starting to shake.

"Khar? What are you doing?" Her voice is barely above a whisper, but she knows I can hear her.

"Rae Vereen, owner of my heart, lover of soul, dictator of my dreams, would you do me the honor of becoming my wife? I promise to faithfully walk this life with you, hand in hand, until the end of time. Please make me the happiest man in the two realms. Be my forever."

Extending my hand to her, I turn my wrist downward, a normal gesture of submission during a proposal. With my head also facing down, she can't see my face, and for that, I am happy. My eyes are puddles, and whatever she says next will either crush or create the man I hope to become.

I had planned to ask her back in her realm. I wanted her family there to witness it, but who knows when they'll be willing or ready to accept me. Something tells me that beyond Ross and perhaps Melchior, it will be an uphill battle for us when we return. Despite her fears, looking at her tonight, I know she considered what our life could be together.

"Khar, are you serious?"

"Very," I reply, slowly shifting my eyes up to her.

Her eyes are dancing. Hopeful. Happy. But there's still something else there: fear.

You have nothing to fear with me, I whisper in the ancient tongue. Rae's eyes shift a bit, but it's almost as if she understood me.

"I love you, Rae. I know there's so much to decide, but we'll work it out. I don't want you worried about living here or growing old. Hell, I don't even want you worried about death itself. I'd crawl in your coffin and stay until your eyes opened in the High Place, until I knew you were safe."

Her head tilts a little, and she takes a few steps closer. "The High Place?"

"The only place appropriate for your beautiful soul."

"And what about your soul? Will you be there with me?"

Turning my hand over, I offer her my palm. Closing the distance between us, she places her hand in mine. "I'll always be with you. Death can never separate true love. Not even Hades himself."

Loose tears fall to Rae's chin. "I want that, Khar. That's the kind of love I've always wanted." Her eyes run like a river, but she tightens her grip.

"That's the only kind of love I have to give."

Cracking a wispy smile, she covers her mouth once more with her free hand. "Then yes, Kharon. Yes! I will be your wife!"

Pulling her into my arms, I hold her face in my hands as I crush her mouth to mine. Devouring her kiss as if it were my last, I fist her hair tight, craning her so she has no way of escape.

Thirty-Five

RAE

I'VE NEVER FELT SO happy in my entire life.

All I ever wanted was to be in Kharon's life, to be his woman. *His wife.* To think only a little while ago, I wondered whether Kharon even wanted to tell anyone about me, and now he's asked me to be his wife. Sure, I have no idea how we'll sort out every-thing, but I know that together we can make this work.

Sweetly, Kharon's hands caress my body as he gently nips at my bottom lip. His eyes stare into mine, and there's a joyfulness emanating through him I've never seen before.

"You have no idea how happy you've made me." Lifting me from the ground, Kharon wraps my legs around his waist. He sits us on the edge of the bed, and I marvel at how easily he sat on the titan-sized mattress. "Woman, I love you so much," he growls into my ear, fisting my hair and pulling me in for another kiss.

"I love you too, husband," I breathe into our kiss. He gives me a half smirk, half lust-filled smile, like he wants to rip my clothes off. Running my hands along his stubble, I smile. "I just had to say it at least once."

"Taking it for a walk, huh? I get it," he groans, alternating kisses from my neck and face.

Once more, I feel my lady parts dancing, wetness gathering at my core. I'm all too familiar with what comes next, but this time, I'm a little worried.

"Baby, maybe we should wait," I say, as I feel his hands under my gown grazing my thigh.

He stops short of grabbing my butt, and I shake a bit. I know if he touches me there, there'll be no stopping us.

"I'm not waiting for a priest, if that's what you're thinking." He peppers kisses just above my cleavage. He shifts us around so I can feel him at my sweet spot, Kharon's chest rumbling as his hands make play across my body.

"But you're so big," I mumble, almost embarrassed.

Kharon lets out a hiss before pulling back some and looking me over. A sly smile rests at the corner of his face, but it's the calculating dance of his eyes that has me worried. "You're worried it won't fit?"

"I'm worried you'll rip me in half."

Licking his lips, he smiles. "I don't think you give yourself enough credit," he says, and I feel him opening the fasteners of his pants. "You did just tell me you'll be my wife. I feel like celebrating, and what better way to cap off the night than having you at least sit on my crown?"

I bite my nail, bashful eyes darting up to him. "You want me to sit on it?"

His eyes darken. "Yes. Then I want to feel your nectar run down my shaft until I'm completely covered in you." Kharon's hands glide to my breasts, and he works his thumbs against my nipples through the silky fabric. "I want to hear you call me your husband while you cum."

"Is that all?" I moan as I feel him align himself with my entrance.

"Why don't you slide that pretty little pearl on me and find out? I know you're not wearing panties."

I whimper, feeling his thick knot knock at my entrance.

Kharon firms his hands around my waist, forcing our connection. "Shit," he growls. "Now I know how fucking wet you are. Damn it, Rae! You'll make me the happiest man when you let me in."

"Khar!" I cry out, lowering myself on his tip. It's big, bigger than usual, and it hurts. But it also feels good. I roll my hips a bit until I feel his girth take up every inch of space inside me. I can barely move, he's so big, but I bounce around just enough for him to hit the right spot.

"That's it, baby! Grind that sweetness all over me." Pushing up, Kharon forces another inch of his thick, hard length inside me. My arms hang over his back and my head falls to his shoulder as I try to move. Reaching his hand under the top of my gown, he flicks his fingers against my breast as he pushes more of himself inside. "Come on, baby. You know I need to hear it. Give me that pretty little gift."

Rolling my hips hard, my thrusts become desperate as I feel my climax nearing. The feelings I have for Kharon and his continual confession of love for me swarm through my mind, and I grind harder, faster, until that knocking, exhilarating feeling overtakes me.

"Husband!" I cry out as I lock onto his girth, and I feel him releasing all that he has inside me like a firehose. Pressing me down some, his eyes spark like fire as he grits his teeth. "It hurts, baby! Oh!" I shout, scoring my nails across his back as he fills me up.

A blazing torch of fire burns in his eyes like I've never seen before, and the sight of him freezes me still. "Give it to me!" he shouts, pumping hard, hitting places I never knew existed inside me. It feels good. *Too good.* In all our love making, I've never felt anything like this. His hands are warm against my skin, almost burning. "Mine!" he growls, yanking my dress down in front, exposing my breasts, lapping at them like a thirsty man. I dangle in his arms like a ragdoll, my back arched over his forearms as he fucks relentlessly into me.

"Khar!" I scream as I feel another orgasm roll through me. He's filling me with at least half of his shaft, and I fear he'll rip me half. "Please," I mumble in between tremors.

Slowly, Kharon's eyes fade to his normal storm cast-hue, and his eyes grow wide with worry. "Rae?" he says, as if he's surprised to see me.

"Baby," I moan, limp like a noodle hanging over his arm.

"Damn it!" he begins, pulling me to his chest. He peckers kisses over me and shifts a little to slide out of me. The relief I feel when he pulls out causes me to sigh hard. I wince at the slight pain, but I also know I've never felt anything so good—ever. "I'm so sorry baby," he continues, placing me on the bed.

I'm spent. Falling onto the pillowy soft mattress, I rest on the bouquet of pillows Kharon brings to my head.

"I lost control. Shit. Fuck." Kharon paces the floor, alternating between looking at me and palming his forehead.

"It's okay, Khar."

"No, it isn't! I could have hurt you, really hurt you. I can't be that careless, reckless, or greedy with you."

"Greedy?" I breathe with a raised brow. I try to lift my head from the pillow, but I don't have the strength.

"Yes, greedy. I knew better, but I wanted it anyway. I can't treat my wife like that. You deserve better. For that, I am sorry."

I force myself to sit up. "Baby, please come here," I say, extending my hand to him. His thick brows cave together as he watches me. Reluctantly, he returns to the bedside and takes my hand. "I know you never meant to hurt me, and if I'm being honest, I liked it. Although I'm glad you let up, you're certainly not getting any complaints from me."

"I could have done worse."

"You love me too much to hurt me. I'm not a porcelain doll, Kharon. You can't break me. Even if you could, there's no one else I'd trust to put me back together."

Thirty-Six

KHARON

I HELD Rae in my arms until she fell asleep.

This feels good. Right. Just as it's supposed to be. I know she said I can't break her, but she has no idea how wrong she is. I *can* break her. Hell, I could do a whole lot worse, but I won't. I refuse to be that man. Instead, I'll be the man she deserves. A man who will put aside his dark desires and love this woman the way she should be loved. Tenderly. Compassionately. With everything I am.

The last thing I want to do is hurt her out of some ravenous desire to bend her body to my will. Sure, it's a tempting thought, but it could turn disastrous for my very mortal mate.

Correction: my soon-to-be wife.

While the word fiancée is not native to Nether tongue, I'll ensure everyone around me understands who and what Rae Vereen means to me.

She is my everything.

A buzzing sound from outside the door catches my attention, and I see Pella hovering about.

"Come in," I whisper, careful not to wake Rae.

"I'm sorry for the intrusion, Prince Kharon," Pella begins, fluttering just in front of my face. "But there seems to be some disturbances from–"

Rae wiggles against my chest, murmuring incoherently. She giggles a bit, murmuring her pet name for me before squeezing my waist and burying her head into my arm.

"Please, Pella, just ask Thelios to see to it." My tone is still quiet, but I cover Rae's ears just in case.

"But your Highness," Pella protests, her wings flapping rapidly as she hovers just beyond my nose.

Lifting my hand, I shake my head. "Whatever it is will have to wait," I counter.

"Even the High Serpent Queen?" I hear a familiar voice bark into the room from the threshold.

I am surprised to find Roark here. "Roark?" I groan as quietly as possible, pushing up some from the headboard. "What are you doing here?"

Pella buzzes around a bit, her pensive, sea-green eyes shifting between me and Roark.

"It's good to see you too, my prince." Roark throws a jaunty grin my way.

Moving inside, his hands fixed at his waist, holding tight to his scythe on his hip as he always does as if he were afraid it would disappear, the heel of his brown leather boots clank hard against the floor as he strides across the room. I'm surprised to find his long brown hair swept into a bun as well as a thick beard covering his face. Roark is normally as clean shaven as they come, with his hair hanging to the middle of his back. There's definitely something different about him. Whatever it is, it will have to wait.

"What do you mean Raja is here?" I bark. Her arrival is the last thing I need right now.

"Henches on the lookout spied her enroute only minutes ago, a few kilometers from the Soleil."

"Yes, your Highness," Pella interjects, her eyes still traveling nervously between me and Roark. Interesting. I ignore the thought and give her my attention. "Thelios has indulged in quite a bit of mead while commuting tributes since you left your courtroom. I doubt you'll want him to be the first face Queen Raja sees when she enters your court."

A low growl churns through me, and Rae pushes up from my chest. Her hazy eyes mull around the room for a few seconds before she looks up at me.

"Khar?" she rasps, rubbing her eyes. "What's wrong, baby?"

"Baby, is it?" Roark scoffs, covering his mouth as his shoulders shake in laughter.

Pella throws her finger to her mouth, trying to get him to settle down. Fluttering to his ear, she whispers something, but I don't bother trying to hear as I help Rae sit up.

"Oh my!" Rae gasps as her eyes pop open. "I didn't know we had company." Forcing herself upright, she combs her hands through her hair a few times. Cupping her hands around her mouth, she leans into my ear. "Do I have drool?" She points at her mouth as her eyes drift around to Pella and Roark, then back to me.

Smiling, I shake my head and run my hand over her cheeks. "You look perfect." Rae offers me a small smile while quickly crossing her legs, attempting not to look too relaxed.

"We can wait in the hall," Roark quips with a sly smile. I'm sure after my anti-love talks over the years, he's getting a kick out of seeing my head totally spun. He always called bull on my tirades against love in the past, so I know he's waiting for the right moment to wag a self-righteous finger in my face.

Standing up from the bed, I give a quick nod to Rae. She smiles, nodding in return. No words are spoken, but I'm glad she understands I must return to business. "That won't be necessary, Roark. I'm sorry I haven't had the opportunity to introduce you to Lady Rae Vereen. My mate."

Roark's eyes grow wide, and he gulps, shifting a look between me and back to Pella. "Your mate?" he hisses in surprise. He changes his posture some, motioning his hands to his holster, to the air, then back again. Swallowing whatever questions he has, he chucks his legs together and folds his arms. "It's very nice to meet you, Lady Vereen," he adds, bowing deep at his waist.

"Same to you, Roark," Rae says sweetly. Pella flutters toward her, and Rae waves, whispering a quiet hello.

"Your Highness," Roark continues, his voice now more restrained. "Queen Raja. How would you like me to procced?"

"We have to let her in, that's for sure. She's not one to visit during Festivus. I can't imagine what she's doing here."

"Do you think the Changelings are involved?" Pella asks, now flying to my side. "Perhaps they know you've returned, my lord."

"Doubtful," Roark quickly replies.

Stepping forward, I rest my chin against my fist. "Roark's right. The Changelings are wary of Raja. Her venom and Leviathan familiars are one of the few things the Wretched Ones fear."

"That much is true, my prince. Still, whatever she wants can't be good. Today most of all," Roark groans in agreement.

Offering Rae my hand, I help her off the bed and bring her to my side. "I know one thing: the High Serpent Queen better have a damn good reason for me to take my mate out of my arms. If not, she'll surely have hell to pay." With Rae's hand in mine, we head toward the door.

Roark races to my side, grabbing my free arm. "Are you sure you want to tempt the High Queen? Do you think it wise, my prince?"

I grunt. "The only unwise thing I've done so far is pull Rae from my chest, so the High Queen better make it worth my time."

Thirty-Seven

RAE

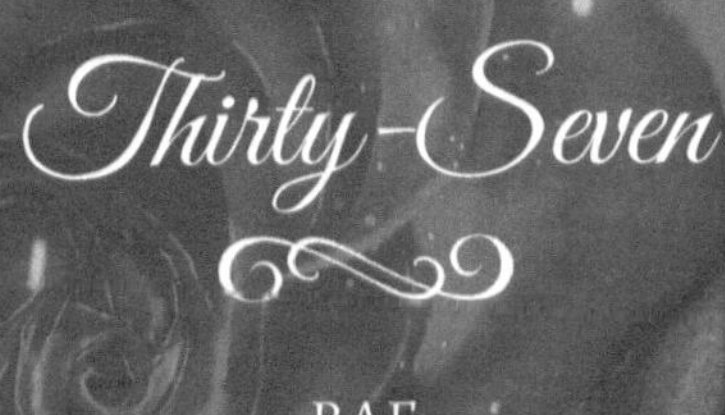

KHARON CURLS his large finger tight in my palm as we make our way down the long galley. It's brighter than I recall when I bolted from his courtroom earlier, adorned with flame-filled sconces and a stately gothic revival look. I feel like I'm seeing Kharon's castle with new eyes.

Not to mention, Pella intermittently blows something resembling pixie dust on my face as we walk. It smells like a mixture of spearmint and lavender, and the aromatic scent implodes my nostrils and tickles the back of my throat. I can barely make out her face; if I didn't know better, I'd think she winked at me after that last dusting. Perhaps, like Ross, she recognized I woke up with the breath of death. Who knows? Either way, I'm thankful.

"Would you like me to post a few patrols around the citadel?" Roark asks as he walks at Kharon's side. While he's not as tall as Kharon, he's not a small man. Burly and broad as a Netherworld door, there's not an ounce of fat on this Herculean wonder. Despite his musculature, I'm surprised how human he appears. He's the first person to have a distinct accent since I've been here. Scottish, perhaps? I'm not sure how that's possible here, but it's one of my favorite accents, so I don't bother asking.

"Not necessary," Kharon answers, keeping his face straight and his jaw strained. He's been quiet since we left the room, and I can tell there's tons running through his mind.

We're near the courtroom, and I can hear the same loud revelries from before. This time, though, is different. This time, those sounds don't bother me. While I hope the naked women are gone, or at least fully clothed, I'm not worried.

Kharon has done all he can to assure me of my place in not only his life, but his world. All I have to do is trust in that love. I need to trust in us.

Stopping just before we cross into a corridor separated by a sheer cream curtain leading to the courtroom, Kharon gestures for Pella and Roark to go ahead of us. They quickly exit, leaving just us two.

"Rae," Kharon says, taking both of my hands in his large palms. "I can't hardly prepare you for what you'll see when we enter the courtroom. I just ask that you trust me and know I love you." His eyes narrow as he stares at me, but it's the worry I see in his eyes that is more troubling.

"Of course, Kharon—I mean, *my prince*," I self-correct. I need to do a better job of addressing him properly, especially in front of his people. "I need you to tell me what's wrong. Is it the Queen?"

Kharon sighs, brushing his hair away from his face. "No. In all honesty, I'm not really worried about Raja. I *am* worried about my sister. We came here to rescue Moirai. Instead, I'm ransacked by Festivus and now the High Queen. Meanwhile, Moirai is still being held hostage. Every minute we spend here is another minute she remains in peril."

My heart sinks.

I can't even imagine how he feels. This has nothing, or at least very little, to do with the High Serpent Queen, whoever the hell she is.

Being a twin, I understand a sibling bond better than most. There's nothing I wouldn't do for my brother. It pains me to know I've put Kharon through my own trifles since we've arrived, taking him away from our true reason for being here.

"I'm sorry, Kharon. We'll get Moirai. Some way, somehow." I rise to the balls of my feet, stretching until I reach his chin. I pull on his beard just enough to draw his eyes down to me. He cracks a weak smile, nodding as he leans down to kiss my hand. "You just need a little faith."

Kharon's face crumples a bit. "This is the Netherworld, beautiful. There's not much faith down here, I'm afraid."

"I don't believe that, Khar. The whole point of those like your sister is to give you faith. You have to trust that when Moirai saw us coming, she knew everything we'd face. Even more, she knew that between Festivus and surprise visits–*and even proposals*–that somehow, some way, it would lead to her rescue. Now, my prince, it's up to you to believe that, too."

Kharon's jaw tightens, and a small smile pulls on the left side of his face. His stormy eyes search my mine for a few seconds as he firms his grip on my hands.

"Well, I know one thing. Moirai knew I needed you here with me. Nethers knows I needed to hear what you had to say. Thank you, baby."

Bowing my head, I smile. Although I still see the makings of concern drifting in his eyes, I'm thankful to provide even an ounce of consolation.

"Alright, it's time." His voice is more growly than it was just a moment ago. A loud horn blares through the courtroom, and he gives me a nod. "Just stay close. Queen Raja will be surprised to see a human in the Netherworld. She has a sordid past with humans, so I'm not sure how she'll respond. No matter what she says or does, don't offer any response. She's a wild card, and you never really know which hand you're dealt until it's too late. Do you understand?"

Biting my lower lip, I glance up at Kharon. "Do nothing. Stay quiet. Yep, I've got it."

I can tell he wants to say more, but he just smiles and squeezes my hand tight.

As he leads us through the curtain that seems to flourish without wind, we make our way onto the throne risers. The sound of horns grows louder, as do what I make to be harps. I gaze around the large hall, wondering where the music is coming from. Overhead, I see a balcony where I finally spy an ensemble gathered.

Gold confetti falls from the ceiling, but it disappears just as quickly as it comes. The courtroom is more crowded than it was earlier. My eyes roll a bit when I notice the naked women remain, albeit now slightly covered by an array of feathers. But there are also other creatures here I hadn't seen before. I barely have a chance to take in the sight of twin gorgons, a reptile woman, and a burning man holding a bow, when the horns lift an octave, and the double doors open wide.

Securing my hand in his, Kharon hurries me to my seat before taking his own. Roark takes his place at Kharon's side, while Pella remains buzzing just above my shoulder.

Thelios, wobbling a bit as he makes his way to Kharon, clangs his flaming rod into the floor, quieting the room. "What shall I say, Your Highness?"

Kharon shakes his head, his nose wrinkling as he takes a whiff of Thelios. "Take your place and leave it to me."

"You reek!" Roark gnashes through his teeth, waving his hand at his nose.

Kharon growls low, darting an eye to both men. Thelios ambles back to his place, and Kharon's mouth hovers to the side as he fixes his eyes on the double doors.

A loud hissing sound draws my attention to the entrance. My eyes nearly pop from my sockets when two large, black snakes slither inside. Their wide, venomous mouths hiss open while their forked tongues strike out toward the onlookers standing on either side of the courtroom. Unlike me, most don't seem surprised, but they do flinch at the sight of the serpents as they coil their bodies across the marble floor.

Yet, it's the sight of a large creature resembling something between a crocodile and a dragon making its way between the snakes that strikes fear in my heart. With glowing green eyes and a long, slimy, thick forked tongue, the creature glides through the entrance in an almost regal stride.

I see why.

Perched in a gold saddle, a woman with a large gold crown encrusted with rubies sits atop the creature. Her beautiful pecan skin shimmers with a gold dusting like Oru, but not so much that you can't see the perfect brown hue underneath. A mixture of snakes and thick black coils hang to her shoulders, outlining her black leather fitted gown capped with dragon scales.

She is beautiful.

Dangerous.

As she enters, Kharon stands, bowing at his waist. I quickly rise and do the same, as do Thelios and Roark. Pella flutters, but I swear she offers a curtsy as well, though it's hard to make out.

"High Queen," Kharon begins, the court bowing in reverence.

"What a pleasure!" he exclaims, forcing a bright smile that extends the width of his face.

More hissing echoes through the hall, and the Queen dismounts her scaly creature. Taking slow, sensual steps forward, she leans against the mouth of the beast, dragging her hand along its sharp fangs. She smiles wide, revealing pointy fangs of her own. Shaking her hair some, the rattling sound of snakes whisks through the air, and the crowd slowly rises with all eyes on the Queen.

"Prin-*sss*-e Kharon," she seethes, the *s* sounding like nails on a chalkboard. The Queen takes a few steps forward, her golden eyes scanning the throne, landing on me for a second longer than I'd like. A wicked smirk crowds her face as she regards me, but she drags her eyes back to Kharon when he clears his throat slightly. "The courte-*sss*-y of your hall has le-*sss*-end of late. I thought today was a day of jubilee!"

Looking to his left, Kharon claps a hand, and a man brings out a large chair. Queen Raja quickly takes a seat, making a show of her long, curvaceous legs as she crosses them slowly. Roark groans some and Pella quickly flies to his side, buzzing in his ear. Thelios surprisingly remains steady, and Kharon doesn't react at all.

Slowly, Kharon takes his seat. He motions for me to sit, and I do. Turning his attention back to the High Serpent Queen, he forces another smile. "Great Queen, please forgive me. We weren't expecting you, but we are glad to have you with us. How, praytell, may I be of service?"

Her eyes dance for a few minutes as she taps a pointy black nail against the arm of the chair. "It's Fe-*sss*-tivu-*sss*! I've come for Tribute!"

Thirty-Eight

KHARON

TRIBUTE?

What the hell kind of game is Raja playing? Whatever it is, I really don't have time for it.

I can't recall the last time she visited during Festivus, much less requested a tribute be made in her honor. Traditionally, tributes are only allowed by myself and those of my court. Every so often, however, I'll allow one to a neighboring royal, but that hasn't happened in quite a while.

"Is there something wrong, Great Prince?" Raja sneers, hissing through her forked tongue.

I force a smile, shifting slightly in my seat. "Of course not.

207

You've just caught me a bit off guard. Thelios was just presenting a tribute to me. If you would, allow us to continue. I'll be more than happy to hear your request."

Raja's lips curl as she shakes her long leg over her knee. Dragging her gaze over the length of me and along my charge, she casts another wicked smile. Her fangs lengthen, and her eyes glow brightly. I almost worry she'll try to induce us with her own brand of witchery, but when her sights rest on Rae, the glow in her eyes dims.

"This is a curious one, Prince Kharon," she continues, a long, pointed nail aimed at Rae. "Human?" She sniffs the air, her hair rattling as Rae's sweet scent arouses her curiosity.

Without looking over my shoulder, I stretch my arm over my chair. Rae keeps her eyes set on Queen Raja, but she instinctively guides her hand into my palm. The warmth of her hand calms the anger warring within me, and I take a deep breath.

Exhaling, I squeeze Rae's hand. "This is Lady Rae Vereen. My mate."

Gasps echo through the courtroom. A chorus of murmurs ring around us from the floor and above, all eyes on Rae. I feel her hand go cold in my grip, and she pales as everyone's gaze pins to her. Squeezing her hand once more, I bring it to my mouth, planting a small kiss on her wrist. Her eyes flit to mine, and I offer a smile. She cracks a faint one in reply.

A series of claps sound to the right of us. Rae's eyes brighten when she sees Oru and Gao clapping. They turn to those around them, remarking on how beautiful Rae looks, riling the room up so that everyone is cheering in kind.

Raja's eyes circle the room. I'm no idiot. She is not a fan of another woman getting more praise than her—especially in her presence. Still, she remains observant as she turns a calculating stare back at Rae.

"To Prince Kharon! To Lady Vereen!" Thelios jaunts, lifting his flaming rod high as the room bursts into a jovial uproar.

Queen Raja stands quickly, and the room goes silent. With her two serpent familiars as escorts, she slithers slowly to the steps of my throne. Her darkened gaze flits between me and Rae as she swirls her fingers at us.

Her long tongue juts from her mouth, licking the corner of her face before slowly grazing her fangs. I firm my grip on Rae's hand; Raja has been known to feast on human flesh in the past. If she makes a move against Rae, I'll release the full fury of my flames where she stands and take everyone down.

I have no desire to kill anyone, but for her, I'll kill them all.

"Well, well, Great Prince," Raja hisses. "If I had known you had taken a mate, I would have come bearing gifts. A wedding present, at least," she sneers, slithering in front of me. "And such a pretty, pretty mate she is. Quite a delectable little morsel, isn't she?" she snarls to the serpent hovering over her shoulder. "And a *sss-isss-ter*! Had I known you delighted in darker berries—oh, the fruit you could have had." She shoots Rae a look, daring her to react. "But I suppose the time for that is well past."

"Thelios!" I shout, needing a way to distract both Raja and Rae. I know Raja is trying to get under Rae's skin, and Rae is doing all she can to maintain her cool. "Bring the next grouping."

Banging his staff against the ground, he offers me a quick nod. I'm not even sure if he has another grouping prepared, but Thelios is the best bullshitter I know. Whether he has something planned or not, he'll make it happen.

Clapping his hands, a grouping appears, and a horde of other creatures enter the room. I nod for Roark to reposition the Queen's seat at my other side. He does as I ask, and Raja seems more than happy to take a front and center seat. For all I know, that was her plan all along.

A group of centaurs trot before us, as do two male gorgons.

Queen Raja is quickly distracted by the gorgons displaying their strange talents. Instead of merely shifting objects to stone, they can shift things into any other hard surface, like glass or marble. The Queen is impressed with their abilities, so much so that she pays little attention to the shapeshifting prowess of the centaurs.

The courtroom is once more alive with merriment and song as a few others come to offer their tributes. Everyone, including Rae, is so enthralled with the festivities that no one seems to notice when I ask Pella to investigate the Queen's arrival.

"Check the registries. There must be someone here of great interest to her. I need to know who it is before she asks," I whisper to Pella; she quickly affirms with a nod and takes off.

Roark casts me a curious gaze, but his eyes follow Pella as she buzzes by him. "Where is she going?" he mouths to me.

Although Pella can take care of herself, there's a familiar protectiveness in his eyes I know all too well. I have no idea what's going on between them, nor do I have the opportunity to dig further. Tilting my chin in Pella's direction, I signal for him to follow her, and he backs out of the room without much notice.

Thelios and I make needless chatter with the Queen, trading comments about who we believe offered tributes worthy to remain in Purgia. For a moment, it's almost reminiscent of times long past as Raja and I carry on as we did when we were young. She was a different woman back then, kinder. Alas, her father turned her into the ruthless queen she is today. His wickedness was known throughout the Netherworld, but I dare say, his daughter has surpassed him. So much so, she took his head to gain the throne. That's why I'm careful with my words. It's not that I fear for my safety, but I do fear for my very mortal mate.

Thankfully, Raja is too engrossed in our conversations to pay much attention to Rae.

Rae's eyes, however, are bright and full of wonder as the centaurs take turns shifting into various animals. They seem almost too eager to bear their brawny chests in front of Rae, flexing and brandishing smiles at my woman; I should have their heads on a platter, or at the very least a strong-fisted dead-and-wake. I'm almost proud of my restraint. It would appear so is Rae when one of the men flexes a little too close to her seat. She gives me a quick nod, and my jaw tightens, but I keep my cool.

However, when another shifts into the Queen's slithering adjutant, Raja hisses aloud. "Blasphemy!" She points a condemning finger, and the room once more falls silent.

The four stags falter backwards, fearful, but that proves to be a fatal mistake of one as it falls into the waiting mouth of her leviathan, Lucien. Shrieking in amusement as Lucien's sharp teeth ensnare the helpless soul, the snakes in Raja's hair rattle once more as she leans forward, savoring each bite Lucien takes.

Most in the courtroom look away in disgust, while others continue on as if nothing happened. The stags back away from the throne, fearful of what fate awaits them.

Rae's nails dig into my forearm as her eyes remain locked on Lucien. I know she's doing her best not to fret but I wouldn't blame her if she wanted to run out of the courtroom in tears again.

"Is this how your tributes dare treat a queen?" Raja jumps from her seat, her eyes glowing bright.

"It was a regrettable and foolish mistake. That will not happen again," I quickly say, rushing to her side.

Her eyes are still full of contempt as she stares at me, but her posture softens, and she settles back in her seat.

"Prince Kharon," Rae's voice surprises me from behind, and Raja whips her head over her shoulder. Clenching my jaw, I fear what Rae will say next. I thought we talked about her keeping a low profile in front of Raja. I nod for her to continue as I return to my seat. "Perhaps it would please Queen Raja to move forward with her tribute? Since these were presented in such bad–shall I say–taste." She cocks her head over to Lucien and offers a sly grin. "It may best not to waste the queen's time with any further unkempt displays. Wouldn't you agree, Great Prince?"

My heart nearly stops. How have I missed the cunning ways of Rae Vereen all these years?

Rae wants Raja gone. What better way to get rid of her than to oblige her request?

Queen Raja presses back into her seat, her hands fisting the arms of her chair. "The little human makes a fair point. I'm certainly not interested in sitting through another litany of these mediocre displays."

"Very well then," I say, motioning my hand to Thelios. "If that is what my queen wants," I say, dipping my head to Raja while darting a wink to Rae.

"Indeed," she adds, crossing her legs and folding her arms across her chest.

Rae tilts her head to the side, and I now notice Roark and Pella waiting at the back entrance. I'm not certain when Rae noticed their departure, but I'm thankful she alerted me to their return.

I wave them forward, and Pella buzzes the news in my ear. Roark's brow raises, giving me a knowing glance as I look up at him after Pella shares her intel. Now that I know why Raja is here, I have to wonder whether Moirai truly meant for us to return when we did.

This all feels wrong.

Still, I do my best to hold onto a shred of faith. Next to Rae, it's all I have left.

Thirty-Nine

RAE

"Thelios! Let's excuse these groupings for now. I'll select my tributes once we've met Queen Raja's request. I can wait." Kharon's fingers tap against his chin as he looks out into the room. "As for the rest of you, if your tributes are not accepted, you'll be deferred to the lottery, as is our custom. If it be your lot, you shall remain. If not, you shall meet your fate. So, go. Enjoy your last night in Purgia. After the Eve of Repose, Festivus begins, and your life shall be set." Kharon's tone is darker now as he speaks to the onlookers, but his posture has softened.

I can only imagine how difficult it must be. I'm sure if he could, he'd make a place for almost everyone in Purgia. The look in his eyes alone tells me how tough this is for him. On top of that, he's got to deal with the High Serpent Queen.

The hall grows quiet as the centaurs and gorgons are removed. A few other creatures who remained in the background, including the naked women, also vacate, leaving only a few in the throne room.

Queen Raja almost seems disappointed to see the room emptied. It's clear she prefers an audience. Still, I sense whatever news Kharon just received has him in protective mode. With Roark now standing between me and Kharon, Pella hovering just to my left, it's clear Kharon has enlisted them as my personal detail.

Thelios seems to command a dark brood of faceless sentinels now flanked at various points around the room. I'm not sure what's going on, but Kharon clearly isn't taking any risks.

Raja's eyes scan the hall, and a sly grin curves at the corner of her mouth. She's no idiot. She knows Kharon doesn't trust her. Strangely, however, she appears content to let it play out, which probably means whatever she wants is a big deal.

Looking around, I still see Gao and Oru in the hall. I presume most of those remaining are court royals. I'm starting to see a difference between those of Purgia, like Kharon and Roark, and those who offer tribute to gain permanent residency. Most are dressed in colors of gold, red, and silver, like Kharon, while those offering tribute seem a bit more plain clothed.

There's one person who catches my eye. A kind-faced elderly woman, cloaked in a creamy fleece wrap, stands near the thick Corinthian column, talking with a few others. It seems normal enough, but odd just the same. Everything about her feels familiar, yet unassuming. Her bright blue eyes look like a crystal sea, more youthful than her face suggests. Still, I shrug it off. I don't know anyone here.

Rising from his seat, Kharon saunters to Queen Raja's side "My queen, are you ready to request your tribute?"

Staring around the room, she clicks her thin, pointy heel against the base of her seat. "You've kicked everyone out. I thought the whole point of the tributes was crowd engagement. You know, so others could see who loses and who wins?"

Kharon's shoulders shake as he covers his laugh. "Not quite. It's meant to be celebratory, yes, but not humiliating. Besides, I figured you'd prefer privacy."

Standing from her seat, her two serpents hiss at her sides. "You figured wrong." Her eyes narrow as she stares at Kharon, but he doesn't flinch. He's done playing her games, and he's surely not going to bow to her in his own kingdom. "Fine! Let's get this over with!" she bites, marching down the steps to take her place next to Lucien.

"Very well then," Kharon says, remaining on the staircase. "Who shall we bring for tribute?" She parts her mouth to speak, but Kharon lifts his hand in caution. "But be advised, Great Queen, the finality of the tribute is left to my discretion. If your charge isn't deemed worthy, or has already been handpicked by Hades for judgment, they will meet their fate in the underworld."

Raja's eyes darken. "Surely there must be some leniency for a High Queen."

"Even my leniency has limits," Kharon answers. "Please, submit your request before my court."

Looking over her shoulder to Lucien, Queen Raja clasps her hands at her waist. "I request three tributes be charged to me, Prince Kharon, Son of Night."

"Three!" Thelios shrieks, whipping his head over his shoulder. Raja's snakes rattle loudly as she hisses in his direction.

Kharon motions for Thelios to settle down. "I'll hear it."

"Thank you, Great Prince," she offers a slight bow of her head. "For my first, I offer Bosam, the Iron-Toothed One."

As she says his name, Kharon looks to Thelios, and he waves his rod in a circular motion. The flame of his rod flickers, and a thick smokey haze opens something that resembles a portal. A wobbly, hairy creature, with beady red eyes and a singular, long, iron tooth ambles out of the murky chasm. It's the most hideous creature I've ever seen. For a moment, I feel pity for it, but then it catches a whiff of my scent. Its red eyes widen, and it makes an atrocious gurgled noise as it lunges toward me.

Before I have a chance to scream, bright flames hurl from Kharon's hand, burning a hollow hole through the torso of the creature. Bosam falls to the ground, withering into an ashen husk at Raja's feet. Her eyes quickly flit up to Kharon, and I wonder if she's angered by Bosam's death. When she steps into his ashen remains, closer to the thrones, I see she doesn't care.

"I'm afraid you'll have to offer another tribute," Kharon says, wiping the smoke from his hands. Smirking, he rolls his head over his shoulder and winks at me. Sexy and cocky. I like it.

Raja's brow raises, impressed. She drags her eyes through the entirety of him before curling her lips as she looks over Kharon's shoulder to me. "You behave more kingly than your predecessors," she says, her eyes glowing bright.

My hands tighten at my sides, wishing I had the same powers to burn a hole through her chest. She has a lot of gall, flirting with Kharon in front of me. It's obvious she's trying to get a rise out of me, but she'll have to get used to disappointment. I refuse to give her the show she so obviously desires.

"You have two more tributes, Great Queen. I do, however, hope it doesn't go as poorly as your last offering." Stepping back, Kharon eases himself into his seat. Reaching over the arm of his chair, he offers his hand to me once more, and he leans over, kissing my wrist.

A low hiss churns through her, but an appreciative smile spreads across her face, as though impressed. Clasping her hands together, she shoots a look to Lucien, and he snarls back.

"It's no matter. Bosam was a long stretch. Just practice. He spent many of his days feasting on the blood of younglings. I see you still have a soft spot for children."

Kharon groans, slowly pulling his hand from mine, but I firm my grip around his large pointer finger. I know this is just Raja's way of taunting me. She wants me to know she has some sort of a history with Kharon. Whatever their history, it doesn't matter. It's history. I'm the present.

My eyes bounce over to Kharon and I offer him a small smile. I need him to know he has nothing to worry about. Queen or not, I will not be moved by anything she has to say.

"Your tributes, Great Queen. The Eve of Repose will soon be upon us all," Kharon grumbles.

This is the second time he's mentioned the Eve of Repose. I have no idea what that is, but it must be serious enough to move her along.

"Indeed. I have no desire to be here for my annual repose," she grits through her fangs, rolling her eyes. "For my next offering, I propose a grouping. Hestas of Serpentine Falls and Krillen—Lucien's son," Queen Raja says with a brighter lilt in her tone than I've heard from her so far.

Once more, Thelios motions his hands, using the flaming rod until the smoky veil opens again. This time, a creature, smaller than Lucien but similar in appearance, slithers through the portal. Quickly making its way next to Lucien, the two lock their slimy tails in what I assume to be some sort of embrace.

A whistling sound calls our attention away from the endearing moment between the creatures, followed by the long, leathery stride of a tall yet brawny man wearing a black flowy cassock with red tubing along the sides. His hair is curly like Raja's but void of snakes. He's handsome, but he carries the same menacing glare in his eyes as the Queen.

"Prince Hestas," Roark rasps, looking over his shoulder at Kharon. "The Bastard Prince!"

"You will watch your tongue!" Queen Raja lashes as her tongue whips across her face.

"Roark!" Kharon growls.

"Yes, my prince," Roark groans, tightening his posture and lowering his head.

"Sister!" Hestas exclaims with open arms, but his tone is more cynical than his gesture suggests.

Rearing back, Queen Raja's hand strikes a hard blow across Hestas' face. "Bastard!" she seethes, pressing against his chest with now elongated claws.

Screeching in pain, he clenches his jaw tight. "Raja, please!"

"Yes, brother, beg for mercy! Because of your whims, here I am, nearly begging a prince—a fucking prince—for a tribute. For your life. For Krillen. He's only in this lot because of your foolishness. In fact, you should thank the darkness for Krillen. I'm here at his father's behest, not yours. Is that understood?"

Groaning, Hestas crumples to one knee. "Yes, sister. Mercy!"

Ripping her hand from his chest, black blood drips from her fingertips, and she holds them to Lucien as he licks them clean. "You should be so thankful!" she mocks him, laughing as she rubs her hands together. "I know he's not much, Prince Kharon, but if you would accept him, I offer my brother, Hestas and his familiar, Krillen, as tribute."

The room goes quiet, and Kharon shifts in his seat. Rubbing his jaw, a low growl rumbles through Kharon's chest. Rising from his seat, he takes one step down. "I'll think about it."

Forty

KHARON

Loud hissing and snarling rattles through the hall.

Queen Raja rushes to the edge of the staircase, but two faceless guards flank the sides of her serpents, using long poles with rounded ends that wrap around the mouths of the snakes to stop their lethal forked tongues.

Lucien snarls, slithering forward as low embers whirl within his mouth. Krillen maintains his place at his father's side. Hestas, however, remains kneeling before his sister, still gripping his chest in pain while a sinister grin frames his face.

Raja's fangs lengthen, and her eyes brighten as her claws extend at her sides. "How dare you!" She lunges forward, but her brother raises an arm at her waist. "Get off me, Hestas! I shall not cower before a lesser being!"

Moving away from Rae, my body flashes like fire, and my full form is revealed as I tower over everyone in the room. "Lesser being?" I roar back. "You may be a High Queen, but never forget who I am. I was made of night and born in darkness. Your mouth may be venomous, Great Queen, but death itself moves through my veins and boils in my blood. I am a Son of Erebus. We are not the same."

Gnashing her teeth, Raja doesn't wholly back down, but her posture softens, and she takes a small step back. Lucien snarls once more at her side, lashing his tongue at the faceless guard.

"You come here, on the guise of Festivus, but for all your subtleties, you'd seek to set Hades against me and the whole of Purgia!" I lash my words hard like a whip. Raja knows what she is asking of me. She knows the position she's putting me in, and she doesn't care. "I've stood by, looked the other way over the years while you've lived out your tyranny. I did so because there was a time, Raja, daughter of Mollusk, when your way was kinder. There was a time I called you my friend, but a friend would never ask what you are asking me to do."

"The bloody imbecile is my brother, Kharon," she whines, looking down at her brother in disgust and kicking him so hard, he flails backward into Krillen. "Would you rather I leave him to rot or worse at the hand of Hades?"

Blowing out the hard air in my throat, my stomach turns to knots when I see the pool of tears in her wide eyes. "Raja," I whisper so only those close to us can hear. "I understand the lengths of a sibling's love more than you know, but what you are asking me to do–to commute Hestas, found guilty of treason against Hades himself, and allow him residency in Purgia? It is known that anyone found in treason is marked–" I growl through my teeth.

Grabbing Hestas by his collar from the floor, I pull him close and turn his head to the side. There it is. The mark of Hades, just below his right ear.

Raja's eyes grow wide, and her tears threaten release, but she hisses at me instead, her long tongue lashing at my face. She misses me intentionally, but it's definitely a threat. Rae jumps up and paces to the landing, but Roark holds her back. I want to tell her everything will be okay, but I don't. Right now, I can't promise anything.

"You will save my brother!" she demands.

Thelios steps to my side. "Queen Raja, after you took your father's throne, *after killing him*, you had all of your brothers executed. Their heads sit on pikes at the Serpentine citadel. Why save this brother?"

Placing my arm across Thelios' chest so he doesn't get closer, I keep my attention on Raja. She may only threaten to hurt me. She won't hesitate to kill him.

"Why Hestas, Great Queen?" I ask, searching her eyes, hopeful to see a glint of the girl I used to run with along the Styx.

"The others were *his* sons, my mother's captor, the one whose vile contempt brought me into the world. Hestas however, has the eyes of the only person who loved me. My mother. I couldn't bear to never see those eyes again."

"Wait, are you saying–"

Finally shaking himself free of my hold, Hestas stands up. "What my sister is trying to say is Salem Serpentine was not my father. I was born of Mollusk and her true mate, Hildrach."

Heaving a hard sigh, I pace in a circle. I don't have time for this. My only focus should be saving Moirai. Instead, not only do I have to deal with Festivus, I'm lodged in the makings of a war between Raja and Hades. To make matters worse, I've brought Rae here. She deserves a better life than this dark world I've exposed to her.

"Still, Queen Raja, what you're asking of me..." Turning away from her, I'm surprised to find Rae now standing behind me. Raja hisses some as she looks down at Rae, but Rae keeps her eyes set on me. Her petite hand rubs the small of my back, while the other takes my forearm. Roark is right behind her, his eyes keeping a close watch on the serpents, Lucien, and the Queen.

"Prince Kharon," she says sweetly as my gaze locks with hers. I want to tell her she doesn't need to call me prince, but as sweet as it sounds coming from her lips, she can say it a thousand times over. "Perhaps there's a way we can help the Queen. For as many mishaps as Ross has pulled me into over the years, I know I'd do anything to help him."

"You have a brother?" Raja asks, her eyes roaming the entirety of Rae. Her expression sits somewhere between intrigue and annoyance.

"Yes, Great Queen. My twin," Rae answers with a bright smile. "His name is Ross."

The hall stirs, and Ross' name surfs through the air like echoes in a cave. The thought alone unnerves me, wondering who else may hear it. I know I should have taken Ross from Rae's memory, but I couldn't bear to do that to her.

Raja steps forward. "See, Prince Kharon? Even your human girl understands my peril." Casting another glance at Rae, she sucks her in a breath, her tongue glazing the corners of her fangs. I can't tell if she fancies Rae, wants to eat her, or both, but I'll shut that shit down before she even lets the idea crawl up her scaly back.

"Rae is my mate!" I shout, turning her attention.

"Give me what I want then, Great Prince, and I won't touch a hair atop her pretty, pretty head."

My eyes flame with fire. "Are you threatening me? My mate? In my court?"

"Yesss!" she sneers, the snakes in her head rattling.

"Prince Kharon!" a small, yet familiar voice calls out to me from the side column.

All eyes turn toward an elderly woman with bright blue eyes wearing a creamy, white fleece as she steps into the middle of the hall. Her eyes shine like crystals from afar, and everything about her seems familiar, but I can't place her. I've been away from the Netherworld for a while, but I hardly forget a face.

"Who dares speak to the Prince without permission?" Roark growls, stepping in front of me and Rae.

Tugging my arm, Rae looks up at me. "Kharon, I don't know how it's possible, but I think I know that woman."

My brows furrow, but I don't answer. Roark is right. All Purgians know it is death to address my court without permission. Whoever this woman is, she should know better.

"Tell us who you are!" Thelios demands, banging his rod hard against the floor. Thick gray smoke rises from around his feet, but the woman doesn't flinch. Interesting. Most Purgians are well aware of Thelios' ability to throw anyone into the abyss for a thousand years. Hell, he's done so just because someone bumped into him. Surely, someone demonstrating such insolence is fair game.

The woman steps forward, and her eyes drift to Rae, and a small smile reaches her eyes. I step in front of her; I don't know who this woman is, but whatever her intentions may be, I'll not allow any harm to come to Rae.

Looking over my shoulder, I stare at Raja. She steps back, lifting her hands in protest. "This old crone isn't with me," Raja sneers, hissing as she turns her attention back to the woman. Lucien snarls, Krillen matching his father's tongue lashing, but the woman remains unmoved.

"Who I am is the only one capable of giving you what you seek, Great Queen," the woman breathes in a tone barely above a whisper.

Stepping forward, a small growl rips through me. She may be elderly, but I'll still tear her apart if need be. "The only one capable of giving Queen Raja what she seeks is me, old woman!"

Murmurs echo through the courtroom. Everyone knows this woman has crossed the line. Thelios stirs a grim-chasm at his side, just waiting for me to give the word. The woman's eyes narrow some as she regards Thelios, but she snickers, smugly looking away.

"Perhaps," she answers quietly, hunching her shoulders. "But if Queen Raja wishes to commute Hestas from his inevitable lot in the Underworld, there's only one person here who can do so."

"Only Hades himself can pardon those who trespass him. Perhaps too many nights have befallen you to remember?" I say.

"Well then, Great Prince, who shall pardon your beloved? It would appear her fate is set," the woman says, pointing at Rae.

Rae gasps, and I wrap my arm around her. Roark growls, pulling his sword from his side, ready to lunge. Thelios wields a grim-chasm with his rod, ready to drown the woman in the murky flume. Even Raja hisses back at the woman, stepping in front of Rae almost protectively. I'm surprised by the gesture, but I keep my gaze on the woman.

Others in the courtroom back away. They know too well what will come next.

Someone is about to die.

Forty-One

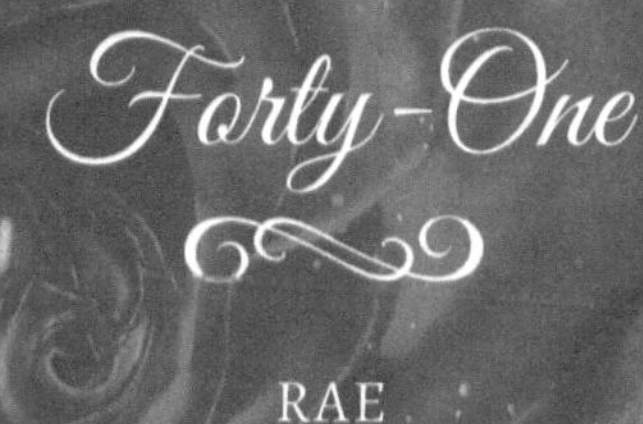

RAE

My heart pounds madly in my chest. I've felt threatened since I took my first step outside of his ferry.

Being nearly choked to death by the man I love, naked women, fearing his love for me, and even a serpent queen, I've gone from one threat to the next. This time, though, the threat feels real.

A warm feeling rides up my spine, like an inferno burning within me. My hands feel hot, tingly, like my blood is boiling within me.

"Khar," I stammer, almost breathless. Shaking, I nearly fall when Roark catches me from behind. Pella buzzes near my ear, but I can't make out what she's saying.

"Sire!" Roark shouts. "She's burning up!"

Kharon scoops me from Roark's arms, holding me close to his chest. "Hold on, Rae! I've got you," he says, whispering unknown words over me.

"Witch!" Thelios scornfully shrieks, and the faceless guards release their hold on Raja's snakes to turn to the woman.

"Release her from your witchery!" Kharon roars, cradling me, still whispering an unknown prayer.

Queen Raja joins Kharon, reciting the same words. Hestas comes to his sister's side and joins in. Looking to Kharon for permission, he removes his black leather gloves, hovering his hands over my head. Almost reluctantly, Kharon nods in approval, and a white light emanates through Hestas' hands as he places them on my forehead.

For a minute, I feel somewhat cooler, but it doesn't last. The boiling feeling grows stronger.

"Your light fire won't work, young one," the woman croons in a singsong voice, stepping closer. Raja's snakes hiss at the woman, and she lifts her hands at her side. "Sleep," she whispers, and they fall to the ground. Queen Raja's tongue lashes out at the woman, but she grabs it, holding it in place.

"Impossible!" Roark and Thelios cry in unison.

"Tell me your price!" Kharon mutters. "Whatever it is, plus the whole of my kingdom–I shall give it to you. Please, release Rae from your spell."

Bending down toward Kharon, the woman still holds Raja's tongue in her hands, dragging the queen with her. "Well, that's all you had to say, *Kharon*." The woman's face crumples into a sly smile. Not calling him prince was intentional, but Kharon lets it slide, looking to both Thelios and Roark so they stand down. Slowly, she releases Raja's tongue, allowing it to pop hard back into her mouth. Lucien quickly makes his way to his queen's side, allowing her to lean against him for comfort.

Waving her arms over me, the woman murmurs something I can't understand. As she does, my skin cools, dousing the burning feeling radiating through me only seconds ago.

"I–I'm okay, Khar," I say, pushing myself up. Still, Kharon keeps me firm in his grip, holding me on his lap.

"What. Do. You. Want?" Kharon's words are hard. The heat I feel coming from him tells me his ire is still kindled.

The woman paces the floor, looking at Hestas, then back at us. "It is as I said before, I alone can help you."

"You may have the witchery of the old ones, but against Hades, you will not prevail. For me to let this man reside in Purgia–against the will of Hades—it is folly."

"But what if I could remove that pesky mark?"

"Impossible!" Thelios exclaims.

Raja steps forward. "Can you?" Her voice is small. Quiet. I don't know if it's sincerity or whether her mouth still hurts from the pulling.

"Perhaps, with a little faith," the woman adds, darting a quick wink to me.

"Enough with the riddles!" Roark groans.

Kharon looks down at me in his arms, and I sit up. "Where have I seen you before?" I try to make out her face, but my mind is muddled.

Her smile fades as she looks over my shoulder to Kharon. "You cast a spell of forgetting?"

I look at Kharon, confused, but not worried. For some reason, I feel like I knew this already, but I truly have no idea what memories I may have lost.

"Even if he did, you are of the Netherworld. This is Lady Rae's first visit to our lands," Roark says, helping me and Kharon from the floor.

Wiping the dust off his leg, Kharon grumbles. "But you have been to the earthbound realm."

"Why yes, Great Prince. In fact, Lady Vereen and I met yesterday at the marketplace. That's when I gave her that lovely jewel at her ankle," the woman says, pointing down to the floor.

The gown I'm wearing shuffles against the floor; I've been tripping on it ever since I put it on. The only reprieve I get is that when I walk, it seems to move, flourishing outward just like the curtains did when we walked back into the courtroom.

Quickly, Kharon yanks my dress, revealing my ankle. The anklet sit tight against my leg. "Rae!" he growls. "I told you not to wear anything from your realm."

"But I–I–"

"She has not, Great Prince. This is a fire born trinket, made right here in the Netherworld," the woman says. "Made of the purest seedlings. Pomegranate."

Everyone shrieks in shock, rearing back, their eyes full of fear as they stare at me.

"No!" Kharon screams.

"Oh no, my prince," Thelios breathes. "I'm so sorry."

"Prince Kharon, I–I should have never brought my troubles to you–" Queen Raja says, backing away.

"Khar, what's wrong? Please, I'm sorry. I can barely remember anything. I think I just couldn't get the anklet off."

"Later," Kharon grits through his teeth, his eyes flashing with fire as he looks at me.

Turning to face the woman, Kharon huffs, and I swear I see steam leave his nostrils.

"Persephone," he growls. "I should have known it was you."

Forty-Two

KHARON

How the hell did this shit get so out of control?

I'm doing all I can to keep my cool. So many things have gone awry, and now I've learned Rae has kept something from me. While I know she didn't mean any harm, I will have to redden that sweet little ass of hers so she knows never to put herself in danger like this again.

That is, if we make it out of whatever game Persephone is playing.

She's been known to court others into the trifles between her and Hades over the years. I've done what I can to keep away from their foolery. *Not anymore.*

Slowly removing her creamy cloak, iridescent lights beam around Persephone, revealing her true form. Gone is the face of an elderly woman with wrinkled skin and liver spots. Instead, a beautiful woman with eyes like an ice blue sea and long dark raven hair stands before us now.

"What do you want, Persephone?" I grit out, throwing aside any formalities. Queen Raja stands behind me along with Roark and Thelios while Pella continues fluttering beside Rae.

"Firstly, let me say, you needn't fear any retribution from me for your beloved. I am not here to harm her," Persephone says in a soft tone.

"Do not take me for a fool. You've bound her with your seedlings. She is human, and now you've committed her to a life in the Netherworld!"

Rae cries out. "No!" Her voice is so loud, the crystal sconces around the hall shakes. Although this is not how I wanted us to share a life in my realm, hearing her disdain at the thought of it tells me she's not remotely interested in being here a second longer. I can't say I blame her.

"I assure you, Great Prince, that will only be her lot if you do not meet my wishes."

"And there it is!" Roark exclaims, waving a hand around.

Sucking in a breath, I try to hold my composure steady. "What are your wishes?"

Persephone chuckles, as if it's no big deal. "We'll get to that, but not in front of mixed company, I'm afraid." She bats an eye to Raja then back at me. "As I said, if it be your desire to see Hestas and his familiar released from the Underworld, I will release them from their obligation."

"I thought only Hades was able to cast a pardon?" Thelios leans into my ear.

Laughing once more, Persephone rolls her eyes. "Yes, I'm sure that is what my husband would have you believe. I assure you, young ones, I can do that and more. Besides, shapeshifting and parlor tricks are hardly the extent of my repertoire." Winking at Thelios, she gives him a smile that makes him blush beneath his painted skin.

"Are you saying you'll release my brother and Krillen from their fate?" Queen Raja asks.

Nodding in affirmation, Persephone keeps her eyes on me. "Only if Prince Kharon is amenable."

Whipping her head so the snakes shake almost violently, Raja hisses once more. "Will you?"

My gaze bores into the Queen of the Underworld. "What assurances do I have that Hades will not reign his terror upon me? In fact, I don't even know what they did to deserve such a fate. Perhaps their deeds warrant the hell of Hades."

"If my dire deed is that I did not kneel at the annual coronation, then I swear I'd do it again," Hestas protests.

"You fool! In his temple?" Raja scorns, swiping a hard blow against her brother's back. He shrugs, smiling carelessly. The young ones have little respect for the way of things in the Netherworld. Still, if that is Hades' grievance, perhaps it merits some grace. That is, depending on what the Queen of the Underworld wants from me.

"You have my word, Son of Erebus. Believe me when I say Hades has more pressing matters than to worry over one insignificant trite." Persephone's tone is convincing, but I still fear the trinket she's bound to Rae.

"And what of my beloved? How can she be freed from your entanglement?"

Persephone casts a look toward Raja and her brood. "As I've said before, not in front of mixed company."

Taking a deep breath, I war against my better judgment. I know better than to cross Hades, but I also know not accepting Persephone's help will inevitably mean invoking Raja's rage. I can't afford a war with Serpentine Falls or the Underworld.

Heaving a hard sigh, I step back so I am once more standing near my throne. "Fine. I'll accept Queen Raja's offering of both Hestas and Krillen."

Persephone waves her hand, and the mark of Hades fades from their flesh. Thelios bangs his rod against the floor, and a dewy mist envelops Hestas and Krillen.

Immediately, Hestas' dark clothes brighten, as do Krillen's dark eyes. Both look at one another in shock, and Queen Raja covers her mouth in awe.

Rae's eyes grow wide, and she looks at me and smiles. I can't smile yet. I still don't trust what Persephone has up her sleeves. What's worse is the saddened look on Rae's face when she doesn't receive a smile from me in return. I want to share in the merriment, but only when I'm certain she is safe. I don't give a damn about these two feigns who I'm sure did far worse than hurt Hades feelings. He marked them for a reason. I can only hope nothing comes of it. The only one I care about here is Rae, and I'll do whatever I must to see her safe.

"Thank you!" Queen Raja declares, throwing an arm around her brother. Although she's never been big on public displays of affection, it's clear Raja is indeed happy for her brother.

"You are now a resident of Purgia," Thelios announces. "As Prince Nyx has formally accepted you as tribute, you must uphold and endear the sacred ways of our land. On the morrow, at the dawn of Festivus, you will become official Purgians, bound to the Son of Night, the last Son of Erebus. Now, pledge your fealty to him, and him alone!" Thelios strikes his rod against Hestas' waist and he bows as Krillen dips his head.

"My Prince," Hestas declares, falling to his knees. "My fealty is yours and yours alone."

Queen Raja's eyes grow dim as reality sets in. Her brother is no longer in her charge. He is mine to do with as I please, but even she knows being in my hands is better than the alternative. Still, she wastes no time with tears or long farewells. Quickly mounting Lucien, she makes a hissing, whistling sound, and her serpent familiars are revived. Hitting Lucien on the side, he turns to leave, and she looks over her shoulder to grant me one final nod.

This is farewell for now, but I know it's not the last I'll see of the High Serpent Queen.

Right now, however, she's the least of my concerns.

Forty-Three

RAE

KHARON REMAINS QUIET. Brooding. If I know him like I do, I'd say he's pissed off.

At me. At Persephone. At Hestas. At Raja. The Changelings. Everyone.

As we wait for Queen Raja to leave, Thelios and Pella escort Hestas and Krillen out of the hall. Only Roark and the faceless guards remain in the courtroom with me and Kharon. I get the feeling you couldn't pay Roark to leave Kharon's side.

I'm glad Kharon has him, and Thelios for that matter, even though he comes across way more mysterious than Roark or Pella.

"Out with it, Persephone!" Kharon barks in the quietness of the hall.

"Mind your tone, Son of Erebus. I haven't released your beloved from my magic just yet," she warns, her eyes glowing. Kharon growls, smoke seeping out of his flared nostrils as she taps his shoulders, smiling wickedly as she does. "That's much better, young one. Now, just because I haven't released Rae from my hold does not mean I do not wish to do so. I only ask that you do something for me."

"What?" he seethes, still breathing hard.

Still smiling, she crosses her arms across her waist and paces around the empty courtroom. "Oh, it's quite simple. I'd like to chart two passengers on your ferry."

"There's only one way to chart my ferry and you know it, Persephone."

"Well, I'm sure you can make exceptions. How else do you explain bringing Rae from the earthbound realm?"

Kharon doesn't answer. Even Roark casts a speculative gaze, but he remains quiet.

"Prince Kharon, you and I both know you can do far more than you've led us to believe. Your power and magic are far reaching. You have the blood of the ancients in you."

"Dark fire, that's all I have. Rae is my mate. There are certain allowances that extend to her."

Persephone curls her mouth into a sly grin. "Of that, I have no doubt," she smiles.

Kharon sighs. "First, tell me why you bound Rae? Why? What were you doing there?"

"My business is my own, Son of Erebus. You'd do well to mind your place."

"Perhaps." Kharon is mocking her. I don't know why he's tempting fate, but I can only hope he knows what he's doing. "But until you tell me your reasons, I will not help you."

Persephone's eyes grow violent, like lightning bolts in the eye of a storm. "Then your mate will die!"

Kharon *is* the storm. "Yes, and I shall die beside her, along with your reasons for wanting to chart my ferry. Now out with it, Dark Queen." He's not backing down.

The fury in Persephone's eyes simmer, but tiny flashes of light remain. She almost looks like she's about to cry, but something tells me she'd never allow herself to do so in front of us.

"Persephone," Kharon begins in a softer tone. "You promised to tell me once we were out of prying ears. Rae is the love of my life. If you're going to threaten my very reason for living, then you better start talking."

"It's the Changelings. They've usurped Moirai and are now using her power against the Underworld. Ever since Hades broke allegiance from his brethren, his powers have been minimal at best. That's why he marks so many to the Underworld. He hopes to gain their powers for himself. For a while, it worked, but as of late, it does little to rekindle his strength."

"Are you saying–"

"Hades is dying." Persephone's words cut like a dagger. Now it makes sense why she pardoned Hestas. His arrival in the Underworld would mean very little.

Roark and I share a look. Even he is shocked.

"But that would mean–"

"Yes, Son of Erebus, the power of the Underworld would fall to the Changelings. They must be stopped!"

Gasping, Kharon, runs his hands through his hair. "This cannot be! But wait– you wanted to chart my ferry? Are you and Hades seeking to escape to the earthbound realm?"

"No, of course not! Hades and I have no use for such a mundane existence. But we do have someone we'd like to return to the Underworld. However, this passenger cannot stop in Purgia and wait for the next annual of Festivus. She must have a direct route to the Underworld to claim her rightful place, for only then can she rule in her father's place."

"What about your other children?"

"Desephone is our first born, the only one born of a time when we were in love." Persephone's voice is quiet as she holds herself at the waist. "She's the only one not corrupted by the darkness of our realm. Prince Kharon, please. I have no desire to harm Rae. If I had, I could have given her to the Changelings long before now."

Gnashing his teeth, Kharon heaves hard gulps of air. "What do you mean?"

"I met her at the marketplace. While there, I discovered she was being tracked by a Changeling incarnate."

"Impossible! There can't be an incarnate, not without a host. The way is too guarded by the vampires and wolves to allow it."

"Oh, but it is possible, Son of Erebus. I saw it myself. There was a woman, Leila Greene as she was called by Vivian Elysian."

Kharon's face pales, and he ambles backward. Something has him spooked. "Leila Greene? Are you sure, Persephone?"

"Positive. But you needn't worry. I kept Rae and her brother from harm."

"That's it!" I exclaim as fuzzy memories take shape in my mind. "I remember you. You bumped into Ross as we were walking. I–I just don't recall much after that." My head hurts trying to remember, as if I keep hitting a blank brick wall.

"Yes, my dear, that's when–"

Kharon grabs Persephone's wrist, stopping her short of telling me more. "Whatever it is can wait." Persephone nods with understanding, slowly retracting her arm. "All I know is that if Leila Greene was there, we need to expedite our plan and get Rae back to the earthbound realm."

"But, sire," Roark interjects, "it is the Eve of Repose. There'll be no movement until dawn breaks."

"Fuck!" Kharon roars, pounding a heavy fist into the chair Raja sat in. Splintering into a hundred pieces, it collapses to the ground.

"Your Highness, if I might add, this may be a blessing," Persephone says, her eyes full of hope.

"What do you mean?" I ask, my eyes steady on Kharon. He's reaching his limit.

"There's one thing I haven't told you, something I should have led with. I did not happen upon you, Lady Vereen, by happenstance. I was sent by Moirai."

Forty-Four

KHARON

This is a surprise. Why wouldn't Moirai tell me? She could have prepared me, saved me some grief. Then again, that's not how things work.. I know this. Still, it doesn't change how frustrated learning of this makes me.

Hope springs in Rae's eyes. "Khar, did you hear that? Moirai sent Persephone to help us." I don't want to dampen the spark I see in Rae, but I also don't want her to let this faith in our destiny cloud her judgment.

"Not quite, my dear," Persephone admits. There it is. The rug of hope is quickly pulled out from under Rae's feet. Looking at me, she continues. "What Moirai did say was that you could help me, Kharon, if I protected your beloved, that you were coming here to rescue her from the hold of the Wretched Ones."

"By what means did she appear to you?"

Persephone lets out a mild chuckle. "You didn't actually think you were the only one afforded a seeing stone, did you? Hades' health may be failing, but he has access to every seeing stone in the five kingdoms. In this instance, it was Moirai who called upon me. She knew we could help each other."

My arms remain folded across my chest as I pick at the hairs on my chin. "I see."

"Dark One," Roark begins, "you mentioned the Eve of Repose–"

"Ah yes," she exclaims, clapping her hands together. "At the eve, everything goes still in the Netherworld. All the land is quiet as we lay in our deathly, hollowed slumber, even the Changelings. It may be the opportune time–"

"To strike!" Roark and I bellow in unison.

"Or at the very least, rescue my sister," I say, as a tiny air of hope bubbles within me.

"There's more." Persephone grabs my hand. "You mentioned earlier that you have dark fire. There's only one thing that counters dark fire–"

I know where she is going. "Light fire," I answer, my eyes searching her face as we come to the same understanding.

"Khar, what does that mean?" Rae asks, now standing between me and Persephone.

"Yes, sire!" Roark exclaims, clapping his hand. "It so happens that you just spared the life of one born of light fire."

"Hestas!" Roark and I once again declare in unison.

"I'm not sure how keen he'd be going into the Changeling chambers after narrowly missing the Underworld, but it's worth a try," Persephone says.

Roark laughs haughtily. "It doesn't matter how *keen* he is on the matter. He's sworn fealty to his prince. He's obliged to go whether he wants to or not."

Rae steps in. "I don't understand what the Eve of Repose is, but it sounds like even you will be asleep, Kharon. How do you plan to rescue Moirai?"

"Well, by nature of my employ, it's the one night a year where I normally take souls to the Underworld. I don't typically rest as long as the others. I don't need it."

"Yes, Lady Vereen. On the Eve of Repose, only those who meet the true death are permitted to move. If say, a small band of us take a voyage with the Ferryman, we too will be seen as dead men, at least long enough to help him carry out his mission," Roark adds.

Rae's eyes glance over the three of us. I can tell she is worried, but this is the plan. "Okay, so when do we leave?"

"Absolutely not!" I snap. "You're not going anywhere near the Changelings' chambers."

Frowning, Rae's mouth twists to the side, like she always does when she gets mad. "Moirai's specific instructions were for me to join you."

"Actually, beautiful, her instructions were that you come with me to the Netherworld. She never specifically said you had to come to the Changelings' chambers. The last thing I'll do is deliver you on a silver platter."

"Khar, you're not making any sense. Why would they want me?"

"Because you're–" I stop myself. She doesn't even remember the Elysians. I took those memories from her. "It doesn't matter."

"But Kharon, you just can't–"

Grabbing her wrist, I lead her to the edge of the hall. "Listen, Rae, we still have the business of you coming here knowing you had something on from your realm."

"Kharon, I barely recall meeting Persephone or the anklet. You can hardly blame someone who's obviously shy a few memories. The forgetting spell, remember? Yes, I remember that part." Her eyes narrow, and the defiance I see there only serves to kindle a flame in my belly.

"I don't care what you remember. I'm locking you in your chambers until I return safely with Moirai. If I don't return, Thelios will have express instructions to send you back to your realm. Before I go, I need to teach your sweet little ass a lesson in manners." My eyes flash with fire, and Rae's cheeks blush.

"Khar," she rasps. "We're not entirely alone." Her eyes flit over to Roark and Persephone, who are feigning a conversation. I know they're listening.

"I don't care who's listening, beautiful. Besides, if you ever disobey me again, the whole of Purgia will be privy to your *education.*"

Rae gulps, her face still flushed and her fingers now digging into my palm. I can almost smell her arousal. Still, after what happened earlier, I won't push us too far. I also won't leave her, for what could be the last time, without having at least one stolen moment. If I die in the Changelings' chambers, I'll die a happy fucking man.

I turn back to Persephone. "Here's the deal. Once I rescue Moirai and return Rae safely, you'll see to releasing the anklet after I bring your daughter to the Underworld. Deal?"

Persephone takes a small step forward. "She will have a guest. The deal is to bring her and her mate safely."

"Consider it done!" I shout. "Roark, inform Thelios and Pella of my plans. Get the guard in formation. We will leave soon."

Roark nods as he and Persephone share a knowing glance. "Yes, my prince."

Turning back to Rae, I quickly lift her over my shoulder and give her ass a good swat. "I've got things to tend to."

Forty-Five

RAE

"Kharon!" I shout, banging my fist against his back. "Put me down!"

He swipes his heavy hand against my backside once more. "As you wish," he says, tossing me onto the bed. Raising his hand, he waves it in the air and the double doors of the bedroom close. Motioning toward the balcony, the terrace doors close, and two thick curtains cover the doors, giving us privacy.

I squirm on the bed, trying to get up, but Kharon holds me steady with his free hand. "Kharon, you're not locking me in here."

"Fight all you want, but I've told you the plan. You stay here." Pushing my legs open at my knees, Kharon's nostrils flare and he growls, looking at me like he wants to devour me whole. I try to kick and push my way up, but he holds me down. Lifting my leg in the air, he grabs my ankle. "You see this right here?" Kharon grits through his teeth, pointing at the anklet. "This is what got you in trouble."

I settle a bit as I look at the worry in his eyes. "Kharon, I said I was sorry. I don't even remember Persephone giving me this anklet. I only have a hazy memory of trying to get it off. Obviously, I couldn't."

"It's not that you couldn't get it off. It's that you didn't bother to tell me. Do you understand?" Kharon's tone is rough, but all I see is worry in his eyes.

I nod, my hands now lightly grazing his. "Yes, I understand."

He grunts and bites his bottom lip, restraining himself. "Good."

I flutter my lashes, hoping my charms are working on him. "So now you'll let me go?"

"No. Now, I eat." Kharon stills my hands and binds them above my head.

My breath hitches. "Eat what?"

Kharon throws my gown up to my waist. His dark brow raises, and he licks his lips. "Open wide for me."

"Kharon," I moan as my legs fall open. "Baby, we should talk."

His hands move up my thighs until the pad of his finger finds my entrance. He runs two fingers along the sides of my outer lips. "There's been enough talk for one day. Right now, these are the only lips I want to see move. Besides, I need to make up for how I hurt you earlier."

"I told you I'm okay," I croon, enjoying the feel of his thick finger working inside me.

"I'll be the judge of that. Now, I told you I needed to eat, and that's what I'm going to do. You're going to lay there and beg me to let you come."

"Khar–" I go to speak, but he reaches his hand up and covers my mouth.

Lifting my legs over his shoulder, he plants his face at my sex. Licking, twisting, sucking, Kharon feasts on me like a starved man. "Damn, you taste so sweet. Don't you dare fucking come."

As he flicks his tongue in and out of me, I writhe against his face, holding my hand in his hair. I'm dripping, and I feel so much wetness between us, but that only seems to turn him on more. He's kissing me like he's kissing my mouth, nipping and sucking the sensitive skin.

"Baby," I cry out, desperate for release.

"Don't. You. Dare," he growls against my entrance before thrusting his tongue back inside me. He's holding my hips down with his forearm, and I can barely move. My core tightens, and the feeling of a seismic tremor builds inside me. Pulling from me, he looks up from between my legs, his gaze hooded in passion. "Oh no you don't, beautiful."

Quickly, Kharon lifts me from the bed, wrapping me around his waist, suspended just above his erection. I take a moment to admire the love of my life. His stormy eyes. His dark and seductive smile. I reach to graze his jawline, but he shifts to the side and bends me over his knee.

"You're so beautiful, Rae," he whispers against my hair, as his hands rub my ass. "But I have to teach you a lesson."

"Khar, please," I say, hiking my ass higher. He knows how much I love the stinging pain of his hand.

I take a deep breath as his hand crashes to my ass. "You like this, don't you? Me giving your little ass a spanking."

"Yes, baby!" I cry out.

"I know, my little honeycomb." He plants another searing swipe on the opposite cheek. "You make me want to fuck the disobedience out of your sweet little hole."

I try to lift my hips higher, but he folds one arm under my

waist as his other grabs my sex. Plunging his finger inside, he growls. "*Mine.* All fucking mine." Swirling and pulling, he flicks the pad of his finger against my sensitive nub until my knees grow weak. "Look at that pretty little thing. You think I'm going to let you walk this pretty little pearl all over the Netherworld uncovered? The fuck I am!"

His fingers thrust in and out, side to side, exploring every sensitive wall until I feel the throbbing of my orgasm grow inside me.

"Kharon, please!" I cry out.

"Not yet," he breathes, removing his finger. Turning me over, he lays me back on the bed. "Not until I've finished my meal." Once more, Kharon Nyx is feasting on my sex, eating me out like a crazed man. My legs are limp, and my eyes roll to the back of my head. I go to scream, but he pushes a finger into my mouth. "Suck," he directs, ensuring I taste myself on his finger.

Relentless, his tongue glides masterfully, touching every sensitive spot. Just when I think he'll finally let me come, he sits up on his knees and licks his lips. "Now that was delicious. If this had to be my last meal, at least I can say I dined sufficiently."

I'm still writhing, desperate for my release. "But I haven't," I moan, reaching down between my legs.

He grabs my wrist. "Oh no you don't. No touching what's mine."

My eyes pop open. "But I–I"

Hovering over me, Kharon's eyes darken as he holds my hands over my head. "You disobeyed me. This is your punishment."

I feel his erection pressing through his pants against my sweet spot, and I start moving against him. Rocking and grinding, I try to find the path to my climax. His eyes grow heavy, and I know I'm getting to him.

"You keep moving like that, and I'm drenching you in my cum," he moans against my ear. "And I still won't let you come *or* leave."

Heat rises in my cheeks, and my movement comes to a screeching halt. "That's cruel, Kharon."

Hunching his shoulders as he sits up, he smirks, wiping my arousal from his mouth as he moves off the bed. "So is putting yourself in danger."

"Kharon!" I shout, sitting up on my knees.

He walks to the door, then turns to me and smiles. "There are some things and snacks on the table over there to keep you occupied. The door stays closed. Open it for no one. Pella is the only one allowed inside, and she can fit through the keyhole. When I get back, trusting I make it out alive, and depending on if you've learned your lesson, we can see about getting you that orgasm." Winking at me, he blows me a kiss and whispers something in an unknown tongue, before closing the door behind him.

Forty-Six

KHARON

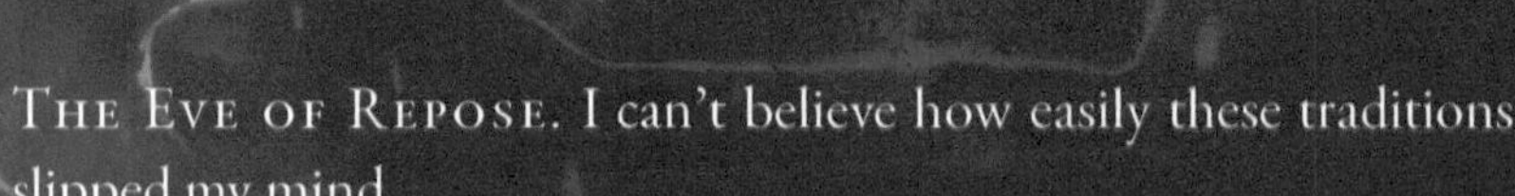

The Eve of Repose. I can't believe how easily these traditions slipped my mind.

Sitting in my chamber, the air feels cold as the shadow of death slowly creeps over the Netherworld. It's the one night where only the dead move, when those appointed for the Underworld board the fleets of their finality while those spared lie in wait.

Festivus is tomorrow, and those pardoned from the Underworld will rejoice, celebrating through the streets. While some will equally grieve their loved ones, the mourning doesn't last long.

However, this will be the first year I may not be able to share in their merriment. If I am unsuccessful in rescuing my sister from the Changelings or die trying, the Eve of Repose will be my last night in Purgia.

More importantly, tonight may be my last night with Rae. The thought is unsettling.

After I left her chambers, I closed out the tributes with Thelios while he officiated the lottery. Those who aren't pardoned by either tribute or lottery will begin boarding the ships to the Underworld.

Silence stirs around me as the possibility of never seeing Rae again sickens me to my core. Even more, knowing I left her unfulfilled makes me want to fulfill her in ways only I can.

Unfortunately, with the Repose setting in, everyone is dead to slumber, even Rae. I checked in on her some time ago and tucked her under the covers. I chuckled seeing her hands at her crotch. Knowing she fell asleep frustrated, trying to reach her climax, made me want to wake her and help her finish, but even her humanity can't keep her from the effects of the Repose. She drifted asleep just as anyone in Purgia.

Still, I wish I could hold her in my arms just one more time. Maybe...

A haunting. I haven't haunted her dreams since our first night together. I haven't needed to. Before, I haunted her dreams as the only way of sharing a modicum of intimacy with her, albeit in her dreamscape. I wanted her to know how I felt about her, but with me forced to pursue her cousin, it was the only inconspicuous way to do so.

Tonight, however, may be my only chance to show her one last time how I feel about her. Besides, I'd hate for her last memory of me to be denying her an orgasm.

With only a little time to spare before Roark comes for me, I close my eyes, musing for a moment until I capture her dreamscape.

There she is, resting in bed, holding the soft duvet to her chin. She stirs a bit, grumbling as she turns on her back, and her eyes pop open. "Khar?" she moans, surprised to see me.

"Hello, beautiful." I smile down at her, running my hands through her wavy tendrils.

Rae's eyes bounce around the room. There's a sliver of sunlight beaming in from the terrace, and she squints, shielding her eyes with her forearm. "I thought the sun wasn't a thing here."

I laugh. "It's not. You're dreaming."

She sits up. "Wait. What? But how–"

"I'm haunting you," I croon, nestling myself to her side. I take her face in my hands, pressing a soft kiss to her lips.

"But all the times before felt like—"

"I know they didn't feel real. That's because I didn't want you to know how much I wanted you. Needed you. Now, you know how much I love you."

Rae grabs my head, pulling me closer, sealing her mouth to mine. "I love you, Kharon Nyx."

Once more, Rae's kiss is strong yet sweet. Even in my dreams, she tastes like wild berries and honey. "I don't have much time, but I thought I could help you with something before I go."

"With what?" She smiles up at me, still running her hands through my hair.

"I'd like to make love to you now." My voice deepens, and my eyes lock with hers. There's a reflection of the flame of my irises resting in hers, and just the sight of it wrangles my heart.

Rae flips back the duvet, revealing her perfectly naked body. "I'd love nothing more."

"Already naked for me? I like that."

"Then you'll love this," she begins, guiding my hand to her entrance.

"Already wet, too? Damn, Rae. It's like you knew I was coming for you."

"Well what else do you think I dream about?"

Fuck. She knows she owns me.

Motioning my hand at my sides, my garments evaporate. Rae's eyes widen, hovering at my erection. "Don't worry, baby. It's your dreamworld. You make the rules."

Reaching toward me, she takes my hard length in her hands. With both hands, she strokes me up and down, writhing beneath me as she does.

"So, you're saying that even though I could barely fit this monster inside me before, I should be able to do so now because I make the rules?"

Using my knee to part her legs wide, I smile as her pretty petals open to me, revealing everything I've claimed as my own. I line myself at her entrance, and she grunts as I take a moment to just enjoy the lock and tether of us together.

Even in our dreams, Rae feels good.

I don't thrust hard into her as I usually do. No, I take my time, slowly sliding inside my beloved, enjoying the gentle caress of her tightened walls along my shaft. Our kiss deepens as I roll my hips, grinding into her until I feel her core lock onto my girth, milking me as she did on my ship.

Rae's hands drift along my back until she's gripping my ass, deepening my position as I shift side to side. I want to touch every wall, every nook and crevice. I need to feel all that she is—even if it's only a dream.

It feels so real and so damn good.

Raising her hips, Rae rocks beneath me, drawing me in until I'm buried to the hilt. Her eyes roll back as she cries out in both pleasure and pain. "Yes! Right there!" she shouts as I feel her throbbing center pulse along my girth.

She explodes with a seismic orgasm, rivaling anything I've felt before. Rae's hands grip my waist, her nails digging into my hips as she bucks against me, riding out another wave of pleasure.

I'm kissing her neck, working back and forth between her nipples when I thrust hard, unloading all I have to give, coating her with everything I've got. I know that even if she never saw me again, she'd remember tonight.

The night when I made sweet love to her in a place only I am permitted to go. Her heart.

Forty-Seven

KHARON

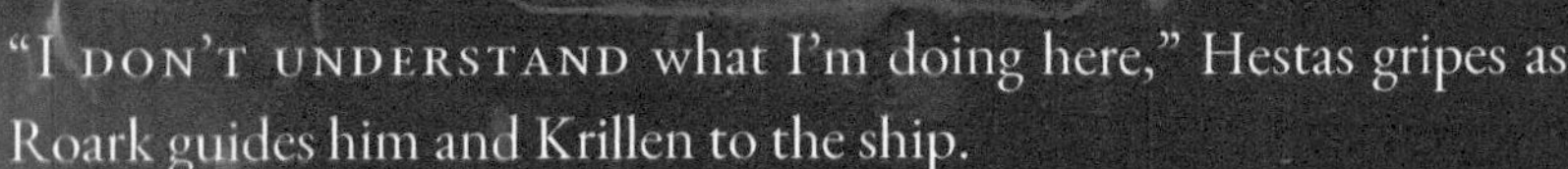

"I DON'T UNDERSTAND what I'm doing here," Hestas gripes as Roark guides him and Krillen to the ship.

"You swore fealty to Prince Kharon, Son of Erebus. You'll do what you're told!" Roark says, shoving Hestas forward while pointing his scythe at Krillen, directing him to follow.

"Now, now, Roark," I say, walking along the dock. Both men turn, surprised to see me. "Hestas has a right to know what's going on."

"If you've deceived my sister with every intention to take me to Hades, I promise, there'll be hell to pay," he bites back.

Roark lifts his scythe to Hestas' neck, growling, finally

revealing his long canines. "Just say the word, sire!" Stepping into the ship, Roark instantly shifts from his mortal-like state into his ghastly skeletal form with fragments of flesh hanging loosely from his bones.

Hestas grimaces some, curling his lip as his eyes glance from Roark to the now flaming scythe at neck.

Shrugging my shoulders, I laugh. Thanks to Rae, I'm in a damn fine mood. Placing my hand over Roark's blade, I nod for him to lower it. He does, but not before issuing a cautionary snarl. Hestas' eyes glow in return, but he shifts his focus back to me as he settles in his seat.

"Since I'm in a rather tolerant mood, I'll be brief. I'm not taking you to Hades, but I do require your assistance, and you're going to give it to me."

Hestas looks over his shoulder to Krillen then back up to me. "I'm listening."

"You have light fire, yes?"

Hestas nods, shrugging his shoulders as though it were no big deal. "Yes."

"Well, I need your light fire to rescue my sister from the Changeling keep."

His eyes grow wide and he shoots up from his seat. "Absolutely not!" Roark jabs his hand into his shoulder, pushing him back down. "Your Highness, please do not trade me from one dreadful demise to another. The Wretched Ones have been known to imprison those with light fire."

"I won't let that happen."

"Ah, yes because that worked out so well for your sister."

A low rumbling moves through my chest, and my jaws clench tight as I step into my ship, returning to my skeleton form. "The situation was different. I was not at my full strength." I take a moment to flex fire through my body, careful not to incinerate the ship. "Now that I have full power working through me, I am strong again. I also have this." I pull the jinn jar from my satchel.

Krillen's eyes glow, as do Hestas'. His familiar hisses at him, speaking in their shared tongue, and Hestas looks back at me and smiles. "I suppose this changes things."

"Good boy." Roark forces a smile, now running his finger along the blade of his scythe.

Hestas ignores Roark but gives me a cagey grin. "I guess it's the least I can do as repayment for my pardon."

"Oh, I'm pretty sure it's beyond the least you could do. Don't worry, I'll ensure we get you back to Purgia."

"Thank you, sire," he nervously bows his head.

"However, let me assure you that should you cross me, endanger my sister, or fail to provide aid, it will not be the Changelings nor Hades you need to fear. I'll have Thelios send you into the darkness of the abyss for a thousand years, and when you return, I'll have Roark split you in two. Then, I'll put you back together and we start all over again. Is that clear?"

Hestas' lips quiver, and he sheepishly lowers his head. "Yes, Great Prince."

Roark's smile widens from ear to ear. "That's more like it!" He shoves Hestas' shoulder, and the group of us walk to the helm of the ship.

"Prince Kharon!" I hear Thelios yell from afar.

Turning to see him, I'm surprised to find Pella fluttering at his side. Looking over my shoulder, I notice Roark's eyes dancing again. Sighing hard, I choose to ignore what my gut is telling me, at least for now. I'll deal with this later.

"I just wanted to let you know all the ships have departed for the Underworld. I've awakened the skeleton crew to man the fleet."

"Very well, Thelios. Please be sure to keep an eye on anything here. As I've already told you, if we don't make it back by the dawn of Festivus, send Rae back to her realm immediately. I don't care if she protests. Just do it."

Thelios nods in affirmation. "I swear it will be done."

"Pella," I say, turning my attention to her flickering light at Roark's side. "I'm surprised to see you here. Shouldn't you be in repose?"

"Ah yes, my prince. I–I just wanted to make sure you didn't need anything else from me." Pella's eyes brighten as she offers the same friendly smile I've always known. Yet, something tells me this smile isn't just for me.

I keep my thoughts to myself, crossing a look between Roark and Pella. "Thank you, Pella. Please, don't trouble yourself with anything further tonight. Do keep an eye on Rae for me. Don't leave her side. You're the only one I can trust."

Her wings flap hard, and she offers a small curtsy. "Yes, my prince. I will continue my repose at her door. I'll be there when she wakes. I promise to keep her safe."

Zipping past my nose, Pella loops quickly near Roark before flying back toward the castle.

"Good journey, Great Prince," Thelios says, bowing at his waist. "You too, Roark," he snips, laughing as he turns and walks away.

"Are you ready, sire? If we leave now, we'll make it there before dawn."

"Yes, I'm ready. It's time to free Moirai."

Roark sets sail, uttering the sacred words of the ferry as I stand at the bridge, my eyes fixed on the castle.

I love you, I whisper in the wind, hopeful the shadows of night carry my sentiment to Rae's ears. I only hope that I'll be able to say it to her myself.

Forty-Eight

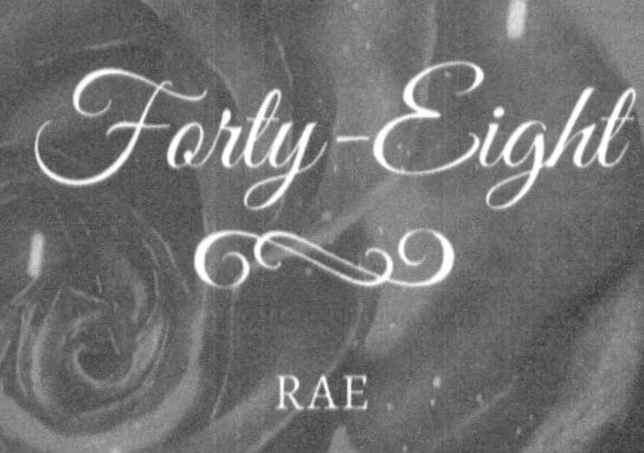

RAE

"Good morning!" Pella's voice startles me as I turn to find her sitting across the room. She jumps up, quickly bouncing to my side. "I thought you'd sleep the day away."

Rubbing my eyes, I look around the room, trying to get my bearings. Everything feels strange to me, like a dream. Although I know I spent the night in the Netherworld, I'm having a hard time wrapping my head around it all.

Especially after the *haunting* Kharon gave me last night. Biting my bottom lip, I wince, wondering how it's possible for me to still feel him, as if our lovemaking were more than a dream. At least, I thought it was a dream.

"Come on, sleeping beauty!" Pella's buzzing, singsong voice echoes through the room.

Groaning, I push myself up against the massive headboard. "Just give me a minute."

Pella's eyes fall. "Oh, I'm sorry. Am I troubling you? Do humans require more time to adjust from slumber? Seeing as we don't require as much sleep, it's not something I'm accustomed to. I understand if you need more time to adjust, Lady Vereen."

She moves to get up, but I lightly touch her hand. I'm surprised how soft her skin feels, like silk. "No apologies are needed, Pella. I'm just not a morning person–well, I suppose it's morning," I say, looking over my shoulder toward the terrace. "It still looks dark out. What time is it? How can you tell if it's day or night here?"

Pella laughs and bounces off the bed. Quickly flying to the terrace, she pulls the curtain back. "Do you see the skyline?" She points up toward the castle gable. "That pink hazy mist?" She stops to see if I'm following. I nod. "We only get that in the morning. Once that bluish-gray veil you see in the distance closes in, it's night."

"So, no sun? No moon?"

Tightening her lips, Pella folds her arms over her pewter chiffon leotard. Lifting from the ground, she hovers, looking out the window. "Ah yes, we do have a moon. I had to think about it for a minute. It only shows every so often. I think it's when the earth realm has an eclipse." Strange enough, that makes sense.

Before I can ask another question, the loud sound of horns and music from outside blare through my room. While it sounds lovely, it's loud, and I'm still trying to wake up. "What's going on out there?"

"It's Festivus!" Pella exclaims, clapping her hands, fluttering back and forth. "Come see!" She waves her hand, gesturing for me to join her on the terrace.

Sighing, I grab a robe I notice at the edge of the bed. Looking at it, I smile. I'm sure Kharon had something to do with it. My eyes quickly notice an array of gowns hanging on the side of a dressing screen, and I shake my head at the thought of Kharon preparing garments for me. I'm not sure when he had a chance to do this, but I'd know his style anywhere.

Tossing the robe on, I grab the bedpost, gracefully trying to make my way down. My foot slides on the robe, and I fall from the bed. Thankfully, Pella zips to my side before my head hits the floor.

"Oh, Nethers me!" Pella cries out, cradling me in her arms. For someone as petite as she is, her hold is firm. "Are you all right, Lady Vereen?"

She sits us up, helping me stand. "Thank you, Pella. I'm such a gufflebup sometimes."

Covering her laugh, her eyes search mine. "Excuse me, a what?"

I smile. "Oh, it's just something my brother and I say. You know, when we mess up."

"Ah, I see." Still looking me over, Pella circles where I stand. "Are you certain you're okay? Prince Kharon would have my head if anything happened to you."

Taking her silky hand in mine, I give it a squeeze. "I promise, I'm okay." I shoot her a wink. "Now, you wanted to show me something?"

Jumping up and down, she claps her hands. "Yes! Come see!" Looping our arms together, she escorts me to the terrace.

Pulling back the curtain, my mouth drops. It looks like a mixture of Carnival and Mardi Gras. From the loud music to the dancing in the street, the merriment of Festivus is in full swing.

"This is the perfect spot to see everything," Pella begins, her wings fluttering rapidly at her back. "Prince Kharon, Roark, and I normally watch everything from up here. The prince likes to wave at the people. Thelios, on the other hand, likes to be in the center of it all. He normally leads the caravan. Look! There he is!"

Pointing down, I see Thelios seated upon a large black cloud, lightning bolts swirling around him. We watch in awe as he takes small cords of lightning and tosses them into the streets. Children catch them, laughing as the tiny bolts fizzle in their hands.

Just behind Thelios, I see the same acrobatic women from the Soleil. They're carrying large rings they twist around their arms and down the back of their necks, flipping gracefully as they do. I notice a golden arm reaching through one of the rings, and see Oru and Gao stepping out of the largest one. Gasping, I turn to Pella, wholly in awe with how the couple came out of the ring.

"Nether-magic," I swoon, peering out the terrace door. Pella smiles wide, offering a nod.

The tiny man I saw with the trough of fabrics from the Soleil marches behind Gao and Oru. He and what looks to be six identical sets of himself pull clothes from the large bin and toss them to the crowd.

With outstretched arms, the onlookers readily grab the clothes, instantly changing from their plain, drab apparel into the glittery silk. Pella claps excitedly at my side, seemingly happy for them.

Stepping away from the door, I look at her smile. "This is all very exciting!"

"It's my favorite time of year," she says, squeezing my shoulder. Her eyes are still dancing, but something catches her attention below, and she shrieks. "Watch out, little one!" she yells. Pressing her face against the glass, her eyes grow wide with fear.

Looking out the terrace, I see one of the tiny men from Gao's caravan grab one of the troll children and return them to their guardian.

Turning her back to the door, Pella swipes her hand across her forehead. "That was close! If that youngling had fallen into the fountain..." Her words trail off as I stare down at the fountain I saw last night.

"Is it also made of ether like the river? Kharon told me it was lethal."

"Yes, it is lethal, just as the Great Prince has warned you, but it's so much more." Pella pauses and takes one more look at the fountain. Her eyes flit back to mine, and I nod for her to continue. "The term death is relative here in the Netherworld. So when our time comes to meet the true death, if we are not pardoned, we are ushered to the Underworld, where Hades takes the power of our souls, leaving us to wander in limbo. Yet, even in that there is mercy. Thelios can cast a grim-chasm, an abyss so dark, anyone caught in it goes mad. Roark is the master of the dead-and-wake, tearing souls apart from their bodies until they reemerge and awaken. The Fountain of Night, however, is from a time long before the primordials. Many believe it is the original source of Fotia and Kapnos, the original bringers of fire and death."

Gasping, my eyes grow wide, staring over Pella's shoulder at the fountain. "Then why is it not covered? I mean, that child almost fell into it."

Pella heaves a hard sigh. "It remains in Purgia as a warning, that life in Purgia is a privilege, *not a right*. Anyone caught in treachery or betrayal of any kind will be thrown in, where there is no limbo, no reawakening, no madness. It is a finality. A cessation of all things. A true death."

Forty-Nine

KHARON

"Is everyone good on the plan?" I bark, fastening my satchel over my shoulder.

Roark and Hestas nod in affirmation, as does Krillen. Three of my ghostface sentinels remain posted at the bow of the ship. They don't respond. They can't speak, but I know they heard me as they click their heels together, squaring their shoulders.

"Are we certain about this one, sire?" Roark says, shoving Hestas' shoulder. "I mean, aren't you curious as to why he didn't agree to lend his aid until after he learned about the Jinn jar?"

I take a step down onto the deck floor. "No, Roark, I'm not worried. I know he only did so because the Son of Mollusk understands that only two Wretched Ones can occupy the same space. Introducing a Changeling Jinn will disorient them long enough to give us a chance to escape. His light fire will be all we need to keep us safe. Isn't that right, young one?" I look down at Hestas, and he looks to me with understanding.

"Yes, Great Prince." Hestas dips his head gracefully

Concern fills the void between Roark's eyes as he stares at me. "My prince–"

I lift a palm in caution. "No worries, Roark. If Hestas tries anything untoward, I shall do far worse than return him to Hades. No, that'll be too good for him. There is always the Fountain."

Roark's eyes dance with fire as he rubs his hands together. "Indeed."

Hestas stands quickly, raising both hands in protest. "No, my prince. I am indebted to you. Believe me when I say there is no malintent brewing within me."

Leaning in to Hestas, I growl, and smoke flares from my nostrils. "I should hope so."

Nervously nodding, Hestas squeezes his eyes tight. Although I have no problem serving him up as bait if he risks the safety of my sister's rescue, I don't think I have anything to worry about from him. At least, not on this voyage.

My eyes scan the isle of *Men-an-Tol*, the southern keep of the Changelings, Siofra and Xana, the Wretched Ones. There are Changeling helms in all five provinces of the Netherworld, but the southern ones are known as the cruelest, the most vile and vicious. So vile, in fact, that every limerick or tale of Changeling cruelty can be traced to this pair.

Scattered in the darkness long ago for treachery against mankind, and all realm-kind, they were cursed by Apophis to wander formlessly, void of substance, made only stronger in mirrored form. From that moment, the Changelings lived only in pairs, seeking the power to once more unite themselves without fear of reaping the chaos they've inflicted for thousands of years.

I can only hope to trap the third changeling here, leaving them in chaos for all time, unable to cause any further harm to my province, Purgia, and those I hold dear.

Swallowing the tight air in my throat as my sails lower, I know this is the only chance I have to save my sister and keep us safe, once and for all.

As my ferry nears the docking post, I notice how eerily quiet it is. While Purgia is likely in full swing, it's still night here, so the Changelings should still be in repose. This is one of the rare times I'll have any leverage over them, while they lay in slumber.

Stepping off the ship, my guard goes first. Hollowed beings that they are, they have no flesh, no soul, and therefore, they feel no pain. They are lethal, and even harder to kill.

We let them pace a few leagues before we follow. As we disembark, both of us return to our mortal form while Roark leads us, keeping his scythe at his side. Hestas and Krillen follow, and I take the rear.

Roark turns, waving at me, pointing to the entrance of the dark cave of the Changeling chambers. I've only been here once before, when Moirai and I were first taken, but I'll never forget what it looks like, what it smells like. Dank. Cold. Empty.

Just as we enter, two harpy guards shriek, but my sentinels thrust their gloved fists, forged in ether, into their mouths, and they fall to ash. As we make our way further into the cave, more harpies hang upside down in repose. Hestas opens his palms, releasing his light fire, and the shimmering glow covers the gangly creatures, burning them instantly.

"Well, I guess that was the easy part," Roark scoffs, turning to me and Hestas. As he does, a large, black winged creature, an Aswang, soars down and lifts Roark from behind, clamping its fangs onto his padded shoulder.

"Roark!" I shout, shooting flaming embers from my hand. The Aswang dodges my fire, shifting side to side, working hard to tear Roark in two.

The sentinels circle, shielding me as they scan the area, looking for any other creatures.

"I can't get a shot, sire," Hestas says, looking for a clean hit without injuring Roark.

Krillen races up a small stump, roaring aloud and breathing fire at the Aswang's back. The winged creature makes a shrilling cry and loosens its grip on Roark just enough for him to turn and swipe his scythe. The scythe separates the soul of the Aswang from its body, while its wings flap chaotically. Hestas throws light fire into the soul of the creature, watching it combust while I shoot my flames directly into its body as it falls to the ground.

Landing on his feet, Roark whips his blade one last time over the Aswang, this time cutting off its wings as its hollow corpse lays ashen on the ground.

Breathing heavy, Roark rolls his shoulder, smirking as he does. "Like I said, easy." Laughing, he pats Hestas on the back. "Not bad, young one."

Hestas snorts, patting Krillen on the head. "Not bad yourself, old man," he says looking at Roark.

"Straight ahead," I order. The time for niceties will come after I've rescued my sister and ensured Rae's safety. "Roark was right. That was the easy part."

Leading the way with Roark at my side and Hestas and Krillen on our heels, I march through the narrow cave as my guard flanks our rear.

"Sire, I see a light," Roark whispers, pointing to our right. Quietly, we follow the lit pathway.

For the first time in what feels like a thousand years, I see my sister. I see Moirai.

Trapped in a golden cage, she lays on the floor, hugging her knees. She's scarcely clothed, but I give every man a look, ensuring their eyes don't betray them. As soon as I get her out, I'll cover her in my trench. For now, I just need to find a way to free her.

"I–I don't like this, sire. It feels too easy," Hestas says, his eyes scanning the area.

Looking around, I see a few more cages, but I turn my attention back to Moirai. She's all that matters to me.

"He's right, my prince. We need to get her out and be on our way," Roark groans with his blade lifted high.

Krillen growls at my side, licking his lips. His eyes flash to me, but then he turns to nip Hestas on his heel. Grimacing for only a moment, Hestas' eyes widen as he understands his familiar.

"Prince Kharon, Krillen's bite has light fire. Let him gnaw at the cage a bit, and then we can pull her out. I'll offer an enchantment."

"Stay your ground, sire. The sentinels and I will keep watch," Roark affirms, nodding at Hestas as the guard encircles Moirai's cage.

"Moirai," I whisper, hopeful I can wake her. "Sister, it's me."

Her small fingers move first, clawing at the dusty floor as she tries to sit up. Slowly, Moirai's head lifts, and her bright eyes pop open in surprise.

"Imposter!" she sneers, crab walking away from me.

I raise my palm, hopeful she'll lower her voice. "Moirai, it's me. It's Kharon."

Scrunching her face, her eyes scan between me and my company. "Son of Mollusk!" she rasps as her eyes linger on Hestas. Her eyes twinkle as she stares at him, and Hestas offers a small smile. It's almost as if she expected to see him. Quickly turning back to me, she smiles wide. "Brother! It's really you!"

"Yes, it is." I force aside my curiosity on why she seems so happy to see Hestas. "Stay back. Krillen will jar the cage, and I'll pull you out." Moirai stands but leans away from the golden bars as

Krillen pulls them back with his sharp teeth, breathing fire as he does. "That's it! Come on, Moirai!"

Krillen manages to yank the bars back enough for me to pull Moirai out. Just as her feet cross the threshold, her body glows an almost blinding radiance. Her eyes shine like the sun, and I know the power of the Great Eye is restored within her.

Tossing my trench around her, I look her over. "Are you okay?"

She smiles, pulling me into her embrace. "Yes, brother. At first, I feared you were an imposter, but when I saw Hestas at your side, as fate decreed, I knew all was well. Wait, where–where is Rae?"

"Back at the castle. Let's get out of here."

Moirai tugs my forearm, her eyes darkening some, but she forces a smile. Knowing my sister, she wants to say something more, but she clenches her jaw, restraining herself.

"Wait," she says, tightening her hold. Her eyes scan the area before bouncing back to mine. "You made a promise to Sincade DeLuca. You must fulfill it."

Snarling, screeching sounds grow from the distance. Everyone turns, watching for danger.

"How did you–" I stutter and stop myself short. Moirai has the gift of foresight. Of course she knew about my promise to DeLuca.

"We need to get out of here, sire," Roark warns, looking around as the light from the cage dims.

"Sister, let's go," I try to push her forward, but she won't allow it.

"Not before you fulfill your oath."

Gritting my teeth, I rip out the paper from my pocket. Opening it, I see a name written on it and a message.

Huffing, I blow out a sigh. "Sebastian St. John!" I shout into the dark. The prison chambers remain quiet, all except one. Something stirs in an iron cage near our exit. Walking closer, I'm slightly thankful I didn't have to look far. When I see a handsome man, haggard by imprisonment, step toward the thick bars, I am surprised. I half expected a woman to be the cause of DeLuca's request.

"Who's asking?" The man's voice is hoarse, as if he hadn't spoken in years.

"I have a message for you," I say, and lean forward to whisper the rest in his ear per DeLuca's request. Stepping back, I watch as a gentle smile crosses his face. "Thank you," he replies, as if I just freed him.

"Shall Krillen open the cage, sire?" Hestas asks, and I shoot a look at Moirai.

Looping her arm in mine, she shakes her head. "His time has not yet come, but you have provided him more comfort than you'll ever know."

"Let's get out of here!" Roark hurries us along, pushing us through the narrow corridor.

As I take one last look back, the man holds onto the bars, and I see a lone tear drip to his chin. I have no idea why the Changelings are keeping him prisoner, but I am happy to know I've given him a sliver of hope.

As we race from the cavern, a shrilling sound grows near. A loud, cackling howl pierces my ears as shadows lift from the ground, funneling around us. The shadowy wraiths claw at us until one snatches the leg of one of my sentinels and lift him from the ground. Tearing him in two, the wraiths throw his hollow husk aside.

"*Son of Erebus, come to stay? Son of Erebus, lie in wait. There's nowhere for you to run. Set her free, now take the plunge,*" the Wretched Ones declare.

"I'll die first!" Roark exclaims, stepping in front of me.

"No, Roark, get Moirai to safety. This is my fight!" I shout, turning so our backs are together.

Suddenly, a light brighter than the earth's sun shines through Moirai's hands, and she thrusts the embers emanating from her palms toward the wraiths. They scream as the light hits them, and Hestas stands with Moirai, shooting his light toward the vile creatures. The remaining sentinels continue fighting the shadows ascending from the ground, as does Roark, swiping his blade through their misty forms.

Looking around the cavern, I notice just how familiar it feels, and the thought disturbs me. When the Changelings sent me to the earthbound realm, they placed me in a cave. Distraught from all that happened when Moirai and I were given by Erebus, I never questioned it. Even Rae must wonder why I lived in such a hovel when a palace was my home?

For too long, I allowed the Changelings to rule over every facet of my life. Not only did they deceive me, but because I lived the path they chose, I almost lost the love of my life. I'll not allow them to conquer me. No longer will I allow my life to mirror the path they set.

Thinking about how I brought down my cave in Nova Scotia, I summon my dark fire from within, hurling a gale around the cave until the rocks crumble and the inner walls shake.

Two gangly faces appear within the shadowy form of the Changelings, and I see their blackened lips and hollow eyes peering beneath their sackcloth.

"You think you've won, but you will fail. Our will in motion will prevail. The love you seek denies you still. Her fate is set, her doom is sealed." They seethe their filth as the rocks crumble around them.

"Now, brother!" Moirai shouts as she and Hestas continue blaring their light fire at the Changelings, Krillen joining in.

Roark reaches into my satchel at my back and passes the Jinn jar to me. As I rip the cap off the jar, the Changeling jinn is released and floats into the sky. The two wraiths holler, and the piercing sound of their voices bloodies my ears. The Jinn flies about aimlessly, like a headless bird. Desperately, the Jinn tries to connect with her sisters, but she cannot. A thick, dark cloud encapsulates them as the curse of chaos takes over, sucking them into the dark flume.

"Let's get out of here!" Roark yells, pulling Moirai first, then me.

Hestas keeps his light fire going at our rear as the guards fight off the remaining shadows. The sentinels look at me, knowing we won't all make it out. Sharing a brief nod, I tap my heart twice, and once at my forehead. *"Good journey,"* I whisper.

"Good journey," Roark repeats, pulling my arm once more. "Sire, Hestas, let's go!" he shouts, and Hestas turns to leave.

As he does, a shadow whips around one of the sentinels, knocking him down, pulling the hood of Hestas' cloak. Screaming, Hestas tries to get the murky flume off him, but to no avail. Roark pulls Hestas, trying to find a clear way to use his blade to separate him from his coat without hitting him. Using his light fire, Krillen breathes a fiery mist, jumping up to Hestas' hood, tearing him away. Spinning on his heel, Hestas turns with a broad smile of gratitude, but there's none to be had as the shadows overtake Krillen from behind, dragging him back into the cave.

"No!" Hestas cries out, working aimlessly to use his light fire. The cave crumbles, and Krillen and the remaining guard are caught in the rubble. Running toward the cavern, Hestas screams, profusely shouting Krillen's name as he falls to his knees.

"Come on, lad," Roark protests, grabbing Hestas at his waist. "Bid him good journey. We have to go!" He pulls at Hestas as rocks fall from the top of the dwelling down the slope.

Running forward, I scoop up my sister, dashing to the ship, ensuring she's safe before turning back to Roark and Hestas. "Daybreak is upon us. We need to go!"

"Krillen!" Hestas' sobs send more rocks down the mountain side. Large boulders roll down the hill, narrowly missing Roark and Hestas. Dodging a few, Roark lets Hestas go, leery of the rocks.

Running past, Roark jumps into the ship. "Come sire, let him be. There's no saving a soul lost to his grief."

Grunting, I turn to get into the ship and sail off, but I cannot. I promised Raja her brother would not meet the true death on my watch. "Damn it!" I shout, using my fire to blast the rocks as they tumble toward me. "Come on, Hestas!" I say, lifting him over my shoulder.

Turning toward the ship, my leg is pulled from a small hole in the cave. Looking down, I see the shadowy face of one of the Changelings peering up at me through a small hole. For the first time, it looks more feminine than its typical gangly form.

The Changeling laughs as curdling black blood spills from her mouth. *"Save him, you might. She dies still. Her path is set, according to her will."* With her dying breath, the Changeling lifts an accusing coal finger, pointing it toward Moirai.

My eyes bounce to Moirai. Her face is like stone. Emotionless. Without a care. Lifting myself and Hestas above the rocky terrain, I carry us to the ship. Tossing him inside, I look at Moirai, but she looks away, tightening her lips.

Fiery rage wars within me, and both the Changeling's insinuation and my sister's response sends me into a fury. With one yelp, I release streams of fire from my hands, burning the mountain side. Jumping back inside the ship, there's only one person on my mind.

Rae.

Fifty

RAE

Pella and I spent the better part of the morning watching the parade from the balcony. Remaining behind the glass so that no one sees me or Pella in her true form, I enjoy learning about the different creatures in the Netherworld.

Clasping her hands at her chin, she bobs her head as her diamond eyes dance. "Oh, it's more than exciting, Lady Vereen. Just knowing we were able to save anyone from the snares of the Underworld is reason enough to celebrate."

"Yes, it is. This is all so surreal. Who would've thought the ferryman was capable of saving lives?"

"I would." Pella's quiet tone remains soft, but there's no doubting her sincerity. "Well, at least I can say he saved me. When my village in Viridian was destroyed by mongrels, he saved me. I am all that's left of my people."

I cover my mouth. "That's horrible! Is that why you can't reveal your true form?"

She only blinks in acknowledgment. "If others knew, the consequences could be dire. For centuries, we've led others to believe we horned sprites spring up from the ground. It was our way of thwarting the wayward desires those who sought all manner of contempt. In the early times, our women were violated. Since then, we've remained as nothing more than fireflies to keep up appearances."

"I am so sorry you had to go through that, Pella," I whisper, patting her back.

Her eyes lock onto mine for a moment, but she forces a smile. "Oh, look! I bet you recognize these stags, don't you, Lady Vereen?" She changes the subject, pointing out of the terrace.

Of all the creatures spared in Purgia, caravanning down the promenade, the centaurs are my favorite. I'm surprised Kharon let them stay after their faux pas with Queen Raja and the flirtatious dancing, but it's nice watching them shift into various creatures in the parade.

"I'm still shocked Kharon let them stay," I chuckle, watching a stag shift into a bull as he marches to the music. "That is very kind of him."

Pella giggles. "I'm sure that has more to do with you than it does with kindness. He's pretty shrewd when it comes to who gets to stay in Purgia, but seeing how you fancied them was likely all the provocation it took."

My eyes widened. "I never thought of that. I hope they stay on their best behavior. I'd hate for them to end up in the Fountain."

"Trust me, he wouldn't hesitate to send them to their demise. Either that, or he'd have Roark reap their souls from their bodies."

I bite my fingernail at the thought. "That sounds painful."

Jumping up from her seat, Pella shrugs her shoulders. "I suppose it is, although Roark seems to get a jolt from it. I think he rather enjoys reaping." Pella's eyes fall distant as she stares over my shoulder.

Turning behind me, I make sure no one is there. When I look back to Pella, her eyes are dancing again. "You know, you always get a twinkle in your eye when you mention him."

"Huh?" she shakes her head, and pixie dust flies across the room. "I'm sorry, you were saying?"

"I was talking about Roark. You like him, don't you?" I chuckle, playfully poking her arm.

Her big eyes grow wider as her mouth slowly falls open. Collecting herself, Pella purses her lips tight before looking away from me and back again. "I–I don't know what you mean."

Taking her arm in my hand, I give it a squeeze. "It's okay. Just us girls here. You can tell me."

Pella's eyes glass over, like ice crystals forming around two moss ponds, as the sweetest smile curves her lips. "*I love him,*" she confesses, and a lone crystal tear falls to her cheek. Quickly covering her mouth, she flits her eyes to the ceiling, trying to resist more tears. I gasp, wanting to reply, but I don't know what to say. Her head dips as she wipes her face. "But we can't. It's forbidden."

"By who?" I ask, surprised.

Her expression fades into something between sadness and fear. "Prince Kharon."

"I don't understand. Why would Kharon forbid you to be together?"

Clasping her hands together, she saunters slowly across the room. The music from outside is still loud, so I close the door.

"It's not that he's outright forbidden it. He doesn't know

about us. But it's as I told you. After he rescued me, we ensured no one knew anything more about me. If others knew I could conceive, I could be captured, or worse. My people were known to carry the one thing all those of the Netherworld are deprived of: life." Pella pauses, staring at me, ensuring I heard every word.

Thinking back to when Kharon said the two of us couldn't have children, I remember him saying he was born of death and I was of life. "I don't understand. I thought everyone in the Netherworld was dead."

Pella chuckles, her eyes twinkling once again. "Well yes, technically. As legend tells it, my clan is all that's left of a mixture of humanity and Nether-breed. While I'm not human like you, there lies an essence of humanity within me. Kharon fears others would try to usurp my power for their own."

"Yes, but surely Roark wouldn't do that."

Pella smiles, batting her eyes to block her tears. "No, he wouldn't. Still, I know Prince Kharon would be afraid of others finding out."

"Surely Roark wouldn't let anything happen to you," I reply, taking her hand in mine. "Would you like me to talk to Kharon for you? I mean, if I can sway him to save the centaurs, I only hope my powers of persuasion could extend to you and Roark. I know what it's like to be told you can't love someone openly. Where I'm from, Kharon and I must hide our love. It makes no sense for you and Roark to have to hide yours."

"You would do that for me?"

"Of course!" I exclaim, taking her shoulders in my hands and bringing her in for a hug.

"Thank you, Lady Vereen!" Pella cries into my embrace as her wings flutter wildly at her back. "How can I ever repay you?"

"Your friendship is all I need. That, and helping me pick out something to wear," I laugh, pointing to the gowns Kharon left for me.

"I think you'll look beautiful in either one, Lady Vereen," Pella says, holding up both a gold and pewter gown. "Of course, I am partial to this one." She darts me a wink, shaking the purplish one in my face.

Grabbing it from her hand, I twirl in front of the massive, floor-length mirror. "I think you're right, Pella. I like this one too!"

A loud trumpet blares outside, and we hear a series of claps and cheering. Flying to the terrace, Pella pulls the curtain back and looks outside.

"They're back!" she exclaims, clapping and jumping with happiness.

I race to her side. "I don't see anything," I say, squinting.

"Oh, Nethers me," she chuckles. "Human eyes. I forgot. Well, they're docking now, just over that ridge."

I can only make out the large body of water, but not much else. "You can see them? Are they okay?"

"I can see Prince Kharon and Roark, but they're too big for me to see around them. I'll need a closer look."

My heart flutters in my chest. While I'm glad Kharon is safe, I hope he was able to rescue Moirai. "Why don't you go make sure they're okay? I'm sure you want to see Roark," I tease, shoving her shoulder.

Her eyes betray her, brightening as her wings flap rapidly at her back. She bites her lower lip, her pensive gaze darting between me and the terrace. "Prince Kharon told me to stay with you."

"Yes, and you have. Now he's back, and all is well. Besides, I need to freshen up before he arrives."

"Are you sure?" Pella asks, lifting slightly from the ground.

"Positive," I reply with a brief nod. "Now go. I'll see you shortly."

Pella gazes around the room for a moment before a bright light flashes and she returns to her pixie size. As she darts out of the keyhole, I smile, knowing she's thrilled to see Roark. I know I'm looking forward to seeing Kharon again and finally meeting Moirai.

As fast as I can, I undress, immediately slipping into the pewter gown. It's so pretty and shimmery; I can't wait for Kharon to see me in it. Although I think he could have a decent go at being a fashion designer in my realm, I don't mind having him to myself.

I fuss with my hair in front of the mirror. I'm not sure if I want to wear it up or down. Kharon has never said whether he has a preference, so I linger in the mirror a little longer than usual, wondering what works best with this dress. As usual, I opt to wear it down. If nothing else, having it down gives me something to do with my hands when I get nervous.

My stomach rumbles and I grab it, realizing I haven't eaten. Kharon left me with a few snacks, but I've been so enthralled with Festivus and worrying about Kharon that I haven't thought about eating. I suppose, knowing he's safe, my body is finally telling me I need to eat.

There's an assortment of fruit, berries, and something that resembles wine on the small table. I pick a few small berries, nervously taking a few bites. I know Kharon said I shouldn't eat from anyone other than him or myself, but the thought of eating Nether food makes me nervous.

I drop one of the berries on the gold tray and lean on the table. As if I'm waiting for something bad to happen, I keep watch of myself in the mirror. Sighing hard, I laugh when nothing happens. I shake my head, thinking how silly I must seem. Just as I pick up another piece of fruit, there's a knock at the door. My heart thumps as I take slow steps toward it, wondering who it could be.

"Rae, it's me!" I hear Kharon say from outside.

"Khar!" I exclaim, happy to hear his voice.

"Let me in," he says. Without a thought, I open the door, happy to see his face staring at me as I do.

I'm surprised to see he's returned to his earthbound size. "Baby, what happened? You're smaller," I say, puzzled.

Leaning against the door with his forearm, he winces, holding his waist. "Saving my sister took a lot out of me. I need to sit down."

Taking his arm in mine, I lead him to a chair near the table. "Oh, I'm sure it did, Khar," I say, keeping a tight hold on his forearm. Pulling my hand from him as he sits down, I notice my fingers are covered in soot. Strange, since I don't see any on his skin. "What's this?" I rub my fingers together.

His eyes darken as he gazes up at me. "Changeling dust," he replies with a cagey grin.

"Well, that must mean–"

"They're gone!"

Gasping, I cover my mouth. "That's wonderful, Khar, but where is Moirai?"

"She's coming," he hurriedly answers. "I just wanted a minute with you, just us. I thought we could celebrate." Still smirking, Kharon seems different, like there's more on his mind than he's telling me.

"Sure, I'd love that, but first, you should tell me everything. What happened with the Changelings? Are they gone for good? Is Moirai okay–"

Grabbing my wrist, Kharon squeezes, hard enough to get my attention. "We'll talk about all of that, but first, a drink. Let's toast to our new beginning."

Jumping up from his seat, Kharon quickly pours two glasses of wine. Turning to me, he smiles, offering me a glass.

"To new beginnings," I say.

Lifting our glasses, Kharon clanks his to mine. Just as I tilt the glass to my mouth, I see a dark shadow mirrored in my glass. It's Kharon's reflection, except it's not. Holding the glass from my mouth, my eyes grow wide at the sight of a darkened figure grimacing back at me.

"Something wrong?" Kharon's voice sounds different now. Deeper. Darker.

Lowering the glass from my mouth, I watch as Kharon's eyes darken. They don't resemble the typical stormy hue I've ogled from afar. No, these eyes are vacant, almost black.

Swallowing the hard air in my throat, I try to maintain a modicum of pretense. "I'm not thirsty."

Darting a smile that doesn't reach his eyes, he lifts his glass once more, reaching across to lift mine to my mouth. "Come on, for me. Just one sip."

I try to step back, but he wrenches his arm around my waist, pulling me to him. With blackened eyes and a shadowy current brewing beneath his skin, he snarls, sniffing my neck. "Drink," he growls, forcing the goblet to my mouth. I try to turn my head, and he drops his glass to the floor, grabbing my chin. The sound of the glass shattering pierces my ears, and I try to wiggle from his tight hold. "You. Will. Drink!" he sneers, and the curdling stench emanating from him is nothing like I remember. Staring into his dark, beady eyes as he holds the glass to my mouth, one thing is clear.

This is not Kharon.

Fifty-One

KHARON

"I'm sorry, my prince!" Pella cries from behind me.

"Sire!" Roark shouts after me as I run through the courtyard.

Throngs of parade participants cheer at the sight of me. Most know I'd normally share in the celebration with them. This time, however, the last thing I can do is rejoice.

Between the Changeling's accusation and my sister's silence, I knew from the minute we reached the shores of Purgia that something was wrong. When Pella met us at the docks, instead of being at Rae's side, my instincts gnawed at me.

Lifting from the swarms of gatherers in the courtyard, I fly up to Rae's balcony. Kicking the terrace doors open, my eyes singe with fire when I see Rae in the arms of a shadowy creature that resembles me.

Glass clashes to the marble floor as the creature shrieks. It's a Changeling incarnate, a formless monstrosity that can only take the form of another, except these beings cannot occupy the same space as the one it mimics.

Just as the heel of my boot pounds on the marble floor, the Changeling returns to its shadowy nature for a moment and transforms into Leila Greene, the woman Persephone saw at the marketplace.

"You spoke a name in the wind, that's how we found you. You said a name in the night, that's how we'll bind you," the Changeling, cloaked in Leila's face, sneers.

Shit. I inwardly berate myself for not taking all of Rae's memories. Leaving Ross in her memory allowed her to speak his name. When Rae mentioned him, the Changeling spy must have heard it and discovered she was here. A costly mistake on my part.

Still holding Rae, the creature snarls, hissing at me as it holds the glass to her mouth. Rae's eyes grow wide as she stares at me, fighting hard to get out of the monster's grasp. I know she wants to scream, but she keeps her lips pressed tight, refusing to drink.

"Let her go!" I shout, my hands blazing with fire at my sides.

At that moment, Pella and Roark burst into the room, along with Thelios. Pella flutters to the creature's side, throwing pixie dust, burning the creature. It winces, but it manages to keep a tight hold on Rae. Roark whips out his scythe, but even he knows it's of little use. The creature is already void of a physical body, so there's nothing he can separate. Thelios holds his rod high, waiting for me to give him the go-ahead to send the creature into the abyss. I won't give that order while Rae is in its arms.

Once more, Pella throws her dust at the Changeling, but this time, it uses a free hand to grab her in its clutches.

"No!" Roark growls, banging his scythe across his chest. His blade burns with fire. He looks like a mad man, but I know that look: the look of a man in love.

Damn it. I don't have time to even consider what that would mean.

"Drink this or she will die!" the Changeling snarls, squeezing Pella in its hand. Pella screams, but her small voice sounds like a buzzing bee. Her face grows red as the creature squeezes her tight. Any harder, and it will crush her. If there was a moment I wish she would transform, it would be now. Yet, with the stronghold of the Changeling, her powers to shift are useless.

"Take me!" I offer, dousing my fire. "Leave Rae and Pella alone!" I say, stepping forward with my hands raised. "It's me you want."

"No!" Thelios yells, banging his rod into the floor, revealing a murky chasm.

"One step closer, and they both die!" The Changeling shrieks. "You killed my sisters. I will kill the one you love." It watches both me and Roark with daggers for eyes.

"Please, no!" I roar back, taking another step.

The creature tightens its hold on Pella, and her body goes limp as she gasps for air.

"No!" Rae cries out. "I'll drink it," she says, tilting her head back as tears drop from her eyes.

"Rae! No!" I scream as scorching fire blazes through me.

Darting me a goading, malevolent grin, the creature hisses as it pours the wine into Rae's mouth. Crumpling to the ground, Rae chokes, gasping for air. The Changeling drops Pella, but Rae reaches out her hand, letting Pella fall into her palm.

As they do, Roark swipes his blade through the air, narrowly missing the Changeling as he fights through a tearful haze. The Changeling evades his blade, but Thelios lifts his chasm, and it sucks the Changeling in like wind. Still, the Changeling fights back, shrieking, and we all lose our balance. Thelios falls back, bumping his head, knocked out cold as his chasm fades.

Rae continues gasping for air on the floor near the edge of the bed. She drops Pella from her hand and grabs the derclanite. The power is fading, fast. No doubt the drink is messing with her jewel.

Being one of the Netherworld, purely of death, no one else here can give Rae food or drink but me. It is a rule the ancient ones placed to ensure our two realms remain separate. The only reason I am able to do so is because our love breaks all curses and spells.

The Changeling charges me head on, and I know what it wants. It wants to kill me and take over my form once and for all. This has been the Changeling plan all along: to sit on the throne of Erebus.

Hurling a flame at it, I hit the Changeling in the chest, but the wound closes as quickly as it opens. Dark fire cannot drive out dark fire. I left Hestas on the ship, still mourning Krillen. I should call upon his light fire to assist me, but I am not weak. I will do everything I can to end this lifeless creature myself.

As I hit it with another flame, the creature winces a bit. I grab it, wrangling it down on the terrace floor. Strangling it to the ground, my fiery hands dig into its hollow body. The creature falls limp, and I turn to grab Thelios' rod. I can summon a chasm of my own and send this creature away.

My eyes bounce to Rae and Pella, and I see Roark now holding her in his palms. I can't tell whether she is alive or not, but the look in his eye strikes fear in my heart. Still, it's the sight of Rae's pale face that gives me worry. She's holding her heart, and I can hear the erratic thump of it, no longer in sync with the Netherworld.

Lifting the rod in the air, I clang it across the floor, mustering my remaining strength to summon a grim-chasm. I feel the winds of the chasm whip around me as I utter the incantation.

"No!" I hear Rae scream as I feel strong arms behind me, and a sharp object punctures my abdomen. Looking at my waist, I see a long piece of glass protruding from me.

All I see is Rae, howling from the floor. Her eyes grow dark as she watches me fall to the ground. Digging her nails into the floor, she screams again, pushing herself up and lunging toward me.

It's all I want, to feel Rae's arms around me one last time, if this is to be my end. It doesn't quite feel like death. Then again, how would I know the difference?

Yet instead of feeling Rae touch me, she presses past me, locking her arms around the Changeling, tackling the creature off the balcony.

Whipping my head around, my eyes grow wide, burning with tears when I see Rae falling into the Fountain, taking the creature with her.

Fifty-Two

RAE

I NEVER KNEW love like this before. A love worth dying for.

I always knew I loved Kharon Nyx, but this is far from a schoolgirl crush. With the power of the derclanite leaving me, plummeting into darkness once I ingested the drink at the hands of that wretched feign, I knew my life was over.

That is why I do what I do now.

Holding the creature tight at its waist, I take one last moment to marvel at the merriment ringing around me. While some stand in awe at the sight of me and the creature falling toward the Fountain, some remain oblivious as they continue with their celebrations. Even that is a blessing.

Whatever remains of my heart rejoices, knowing that some here are celebrating because they have been spared this misfortune, if you can call death a misfortune.

Pella called it a finality, a cessation of all things. That is exactly what I hope for. I hope to finally put an end to the filth of the Changelings. It is my sincere wish that, whether in this realm or my own, their villainy would cease.

We hit the dark liquid of the Fountain, and my skin burns. A searing pain like I've never felt waves over me as we sink into the molten liquid. The sounds of screams, and even the faint shrill of my name called in the distance, are the last things I hear as my head sinks below the surface.

My face feels like it's melting, and I'm desperate to breathe.

The wraith claws at me one last time, seeking to hold onto me, but it fades away. Or have my eyes liquefied? I cannot see. My last breath is squeezed from me as I feel the beat of my heart pound within me.

Accepting my fate, I hold two faces, Ross and Kharon, in my mind, hopeful they will give me an ounce of comfort in my final moments.

I am surprised to find memories too old for remembrance flashing through my mind: hazy images of me and Ross in our mother's womb, our first steps, riding bikes, comforting me through the searing pain of burning alive. Thoughts of us laughing, playing, and even arguing while just as quickly making up ring aloud in my forlorn memory.

As hard as I try to hold on to my lasting memories of Ross, I press past thoughts of him only so I can glimpse Kharon one more time.

I see him, getting off his ferry for the first time. His wavy blonde hair blows in the breeze, and his stormy gray eyes lock with mine. Thoughts of him watching me from across the room, snatching me from the arms of Kevin Addy, and keeping me warm on the ski lift flicker by.

There are even memories of him outside my window that I've never seen before, recollections of him in my dreams that give me one final pulse of pleasure I never thought possible in death. Fading thoughts of Kharon on one knee, holding me in his arms, bring consolation to my dying heart as the pounding of my heart ceases.

Just as I settle my soul to accept my fate, something happens. My heart beats. A strong thump reverberates through what is left of me, reviving the shell of my body. Strangely, I feel my skin tether and twist, weaving itself together like the threads in the Soleil. My flesh feels warm, but cooler than before. I feel my body take shape, forming, sculpting every rounded curve and lean limb in one motion.

A whiff of smoke blows through the hollow crevice along my face and my eyes pop open. Through a flaming fire, I see my hands and feet wading in the water. I feel stronger than I've ever felt. I turn about, in awe of it all.

Still, I don't take time to comprehend it when I see light above me. Perhaps in death, I've reached heaven, or the Higher Place, as Kharon calls it. He promised he'd meet me on the other side. I hear his voice calling to me from above the dark waters, and I swim, hoping to see his face one more time.

With each stroke, memories long forgotten ring through me. Two faces I know and love, ones I never thought I'd see again, appear first. My parents. The sight of my mother's warm smile beneath her beautiful brown skin echoes through my memory, invigorating my heart. It's the dashing view of my father's dirty blonde hair and perfectly crooked smile propelling me fast toward the light.

Other memories score through my mind, but there's one face I never thought I'd see again. Winter. My beautiful cousin. The closest version of a sister I've ever known. Her sweet smile, her caring eyes, and memories of her laughter serenade my soul.

Every memory Kharon took to protect me from the Changelings is revived. For that, I am thankful. Knowing I'll have these lasting memories in the High Place gives me comfort. My loved ones will always be with me.

My legs kick wildly beneath me, and my arms push out from my chest as I near the top. I swear I see Kharon's face in the distance, hovering over the water, and I hope I'm not imagining things.

As my fingers swish through the waves, my head lifts above the water, and I feel a fiery warmth hovering all around me. For a moment, I fear I had arrived to the other place, *burning in hell*, but when I see Kharon's smiling face as I ascend to the top of the water, I know that couldn't be farther from the truth.

Like a gust of wind, I am lifted high above the water, and nothing but a warm light envelops me. The light shining from me is brighter than the sun, and the warmth I feel from it comforts me in ways I never knew I needed.

Looking around, I'm surprised to see the same courtyard outside of Kharon's castle, Festivus in full swing. I didn't know there would be a need for Festivus in the High Place. Maybe it's not the same celebration? Perhaps it's the welcome wagon, ushering me to my eternal rest.

Whatever it is, it's of little consequence because he's here. Kharon is here, just as he said he would be. Waiting for me on the other side, just seeing his face as the wind propels me above him, is a joy to behold. His eyes are bright and full of wonder as he watches me.

Slowly drifting to the ground, all I want to do is run to his embrace, but when I see Roark and Thelios standing next to

Kharon, I am confused. I look for Pella, but when I don't see her, my heart sinks. That is, until I see her tiny face poking out of Roark's pocket, waving at me. It does my heart good to see her.

There's a woman beside Kharon I've never seen before, and Persephone is here, too. I'm not surprised any of them would reach heaven's gate, but to say I'm shocked is an understatement.

"Kharon," I try to speak, but my voice sounds different, like two tones in one, making my throat tickle. Everyone gasps, their hands covering over their mouths, stepping away from me. Everyone, that is, except Kharon and the woman at his side.

I say his name again, and he smiles as rivers leak from his eyes. He reaches his hand to touch my face, and the hesitation I see in his eyes makes me worry. What's wrong with me? What does he see when he looks at me? Am I some hideous burnt creature, too vile for his eyes?

Turning away before his hand can reach me, I am surprised to find the Fountain behind me. What is it doing here? I don't take time to worry about it. Instead, I lean over the marble stone until I can see my reflection.

I have no words to describe the woman I see looking back at me.

Fifty-Three

KHARON

How can I experience loss and joy at the same time?

The way my heart nearly leapt from my body when Rae tackled the Changeling off the terrace to save me nearly tore me up inside. Watching her fall, trying desperately to save her while being held back by Thelios and Roark, nearly ripped my heart in two. It was the sight of the Fountain catching fire as Rae sprouted from its core that revived the shell of a wretch I'd become in the minutes I thought all was lost.

Looking at her now, cloaked in fire but not consumed, like the tree in legends of old, my heart bucks wildly in my chest at the chance to hold her again.

I've never seen Rae Vereen look more beautiful than she does now. Every perfected inch of her has been tried by the fire, and she has returned pure gold. From her more pronounced yet petite curves to the waves of fire burning in her hair, everything about Rae can be described in one word. *Beautiful*.

"Rae," I whisper, almost afraid to touch her. Still, I reach forward, patting her back. To my surprise, her skin feels cooler than it looks, and the beams of light surrounding her settle into a soft flame.

She turns to face me, wide eyes full of awe, the sweetest smile on her face. "Kharon," she breathes, as she scans herself from the tips of her fingers down to her toes. "What is happening to me? Am I dead?"

I don't answer her. Instead, I pull her into my embrace, thankful I still can. Just moments ago, I never thought I'd hold her again. Had she simply gone to the Underworld or died in her realm, I could fight the keepers of the grave to steal at least a moment at her side. Not so with the Fountain. It is the melting core of all things, the resting place of Fotia and Kapnos. Nothing that enters the Fountain ever returns.

Until now.

Squeezing Rae tight, I plant a kiss on her forehead as tears pour from my eyes. Rearing back, Rae looks at me, her fiery fingers trailing along my jaw.

"Rae, no one has ever done what you have done for me. You–you gave your life for me. What would possess you to throw yourself over that balcony?"

Shaking her head, Rae smiles as small balls of fire drip from her eyes. "For you, Kharon, I'd do it again. When I saw that thing hurt you–I–I just needed it to finally end." Rae's tone is dark but the surety of her words is clear. I've always known I would gladly strike anyone down for Rae. Now I know she would do the same for me.

Taking her face in my hand, I wipe the flaming tear from her chin. "No one has ever loved me like this before."

Looking up at me, Rae smiles, her eyes dancing and full of hope. For a moment her gaze drops to my waist and she runs her hand along my midsection. "You're healed!" she squeals.

I shrug my shoulders. "Yes, nothing a little Nether-magic couldn't heal." I throw a wink to Moirai, thankful for my sister's healing powers.

"Is this real?" Rae ponders as she curiously examines her flaming fingers.

"Yes, Lady Vereen," Moirai says, now joining us. "This has always been your fate, your destiny. You were chosen before light formed in the stars to be a daughter of Fotia and Kapnos. You were destined to be fire born."

Gasps echo around us as the crowd falls quickly to their knees in reverence. Rae's eyes widen in surprise as she gazes around the courtyard. Shaking her head, trying to make sense of it all, she crosses a stare between me and Moirai. "Wait a minute! I died. I felt it. I felt life leave my body."

"Your old life, yes," Moirai answers quietly. "You were reborn. You are no longer mortal. You are much, much more."

"Moirai, you knew this would happen," I say, thinking of my sister's quietness once we left *Men-an-Tol*. "Why didn't you say anything? You could've prepared me."

My sister's face falls for a minute, but she purses her lips and lifts her head. "Brother, you know as well as I that death never announces itself." Pausing, Moirai gives me a look. She knows I understand that more than most. "This was Rae's journey to take, not yours. It was always *her* path."

"When she fell into the Fountain–" My words stagger and my heart stings as the memories of Rae falling from the terrace haunt my thoughts.

Rae squeezes my hand, looking up at me. "It's okay, Khar. I'm right here. I'm okay."

"For that, I am sorry, brother. We always knew it would come to this," she continues, darting her eyes to Persephone. Stepping forward, Persephone shares a smile between me and Rae.

"You were in on it, too?" I belt out, staring at the Queen of the Underworld. "What about that story you told me? Was any of it true?"

Lifting her palm in caution, she smiles. "Everything I shared is very real, except the trinket was never meant to bind her to me. Call it insurance."

"Insurance?" Rae questions.

Moirai nods. "Yes. Fate had decreed you'd become fire born, but I asked the Queen to wrap you in pomegranate to ensure your transition. Since the curse of pomegranate was manifested by the will of Kapnos and gifted to Hades, we knew it would work on you."

Rae's brows crowd the center of her forehead, her eyes laced with worry. "Does that mean I can no longer return home?"

Persephone chuckles and takes Rae's hand in hers. "Of course not, my dear. How do you think I was able to travel to your realm? We are of the few who can straddle both realms. Us and of course Prince Kharon. Being the Ferryman, it's his duty to live between both worlds."

"But Kharon, we destroyed the Changelings, right? You don't have to be the Ferryman anymore," Rae whispers.

I run my hands through her hair, enjoying the warmth of her face in my palm. "Not quite, beautiful. I'll always be the Ferryman, but since I'm no longer indebted to the Changelings, they can't force me to bring souls to them. Now, my sister is free."

Rae nods with understanding and her face beams. "Moirai!" she says, lunging toward my sister and wrapping her arms around her. "It's so nice to finally meet you."

Moirai laughs, squeezing Rae as she does. Fates aren't accustomed to being touched, something about it messing with their gifts of foresight. In this case, however, I'm happy to see my sister make an exception.

"I'm pleased to meet you too, Lady Vereen." Moirai kisses Rae's cheek quickly before I pull Rae back into my arms. I'm never letting her go again.

"Okay, one more question," Rae says, looking between me and Moirai. "Why am I glowing? Will it go away?"

Moirai looks over at me and smiles. "You carry the power of the Great Fire within you now. Before returning home, you should stay here for a while, at least until you understand your powers. When you are ready for the glowing to subside, it will."

Taking a deep breath, Rae exhales, and the light around her dims. There's still a radiant glow to her, but the fiery embers settle into her skin.

"Well then." Persephone adds a faux cough. "It would appear my work here is done. I shall expect you to make good on your promise, young one." She winks at me. I nod with understanding. "Until then!" Lifting her hand, a funnel of smoke whips around her, and she vanishes from our view.

"All hail Prince Kharon and Lady Vereen!" Thelios cheers, motioning his arms for the onlookers to rise to their feet. I hadn't realized everyone remained bowed this entire time. Cheerful claps echo through the courtyard as I hold Rae's hand in mind, lifting it high.

Rae looks at me, surprised our arms almost meet in length. "I'm taller!" she rasps in surprise as she looks herself over. She tugs at the golden dress she's now wearing in awe. "I like the gowns you make for me better," she whispers.

"I like taking the gowns off you better," I groan in her ear.

Rae's cheeks blush as she smiles at me, and I know we're both thinking the same thing.

Fifty-Four

RAE

Walking down the promenade, Kharon and I enjoy the remaining activities of Festivus. Kharon introduces me to some of the officials in his court along the way as we take in the sights. He even teaches me a few of the songs. It's surprising to learn how musical the citizens of Purgia are, but it gives me a whole new appreciation for purgatory.

The fiery remnant within me still flashes without warning, but thankfully, no one here seems to be bothered. Kharon just squeezes my hand intermittently, reminding me to take deep breaths. It seems to calm the frenzy within me.

As the celebrations conclude, we make our way back to the castle, settling in to hear the business of the day.

"This shouldn't take long," he whispers as we take our seats. "Just a few particulars and then it'll just be us." Winking at me, he smiles before turning his attention to the court.

Roark is the first to enter, Pella now seated on his shoulder, swinging her legs. I notice one of her wings looks damaged, which explains why she isn't flying. Either way, I am glad to see she's doing better.

Moirai is ushered in by Gao and Oru and seated on the other side of Kharon. Kharon said that she'll return to her palace soon enough so she can oversee the duties of the Fates, but she normally visits for Festivus.

Another man arrives, one I haven't seen before, dressed in a black suit with two female creatures on his arm, a gorgon on the left and a nymph on the right. Although they're fully clothed, these women resemble the naked women from yesterday. My nose crinkles at the thought.

"I'm so sorry I'm late, Great Prince," the man says, casually sauntering across the floor with a sly smile beneath his dark beard. Running his hand through his coal black hair, he gives Roark a nod and small fist bump. "I was busy um—entertaining," he smirks.

"I bet you were, Thelios," Kharon groans, shaking his head.

"Thelios?" I rasp, wondering what happened to his skeletal face and grimly garb.

"Ah yes," Thelios snorts. "I'm sorry, Lady Vereen. You met me in my ritual Festivus attire. This is me," he says with his arms outstretched, like he's walking a catwalk.

While he may seem a tad self-assured, Thelios is quite handsome. He's no Kharon, but it's not surprising he has women nearly falling at his feet.

"Please, Thelios, our prince has better things to do. Let's get on with it," Roark grumbles. Roark has been quiet for most of the day. I'm sure he's worried about Pella, but something else seems to be troubling him.

"It's quite okay, Roark, as long as Thelios gets to the point," Kharon says coolly.

Bowing gracefully, Thelios proceeds to give Kharon a rundown of the newest residents of Purgia. Roark, on the other hand, discussed who had been recruited to the watchkeep, protectors of the citadel.

"Well, sire," Thelios says with a sly smile. "We've shared our news. Are you ready to share yours?"

Kharon feigns a frown, but his lips curve into a soft smile. He gives me a look before rising from his seat. "I suppose you've heard I've proposed to Lady Vereen?"

"What did she say?" Oru blurts out, peeking out from behind Moirai, but Gao pulls her back.

Kharon turns and offers me his hand. Taking it, I stand next to him. "Yes. I said yes!"

Everyone claps, offering congratulations, but none louder than Thelios, who whistles his congrats. "I knew from the moment I saw you two together that she was more than a damsel. I knew she was your mate but *your wife.* It does me good to see you happy, sire."

"Thank you, Thelios."

"Yes," Roark chokes out his words. "We are all very happy for you indeed."

Gently letting my hand go, Kharon takes a step down the staircase. "Roark, is there something you want to say?" Lifting his brow, I see how quickly Kharon's mood is changing. "Anything you care to share before my court?"

Lowering his eyes, he bows his head. "No, my prince," Roark mumbles. I watch as Pella scrunches closer to his neck. Even she looks worried.

Pacing the riser, Kharon folds his arms behind his back. "Many of you may not know this, but when Lady Vereen and I fell in love, we had to hide our feelings. I had to feign interest in someone else and Rae had to act as though she despised me. Then, she went against her entire family and even her own sensibilities and confessed her feelings for me. From that day forward, we loved one another in secret, but never publicly. All of that changes now, not only here in the Netherworld, but when we return to her realm. It's for that reason I refuse to allow anyone under my hand to bear the weight of love in secret. It is too great a weight to bear."

Coming to Kharon's side, I loop my arm through his. I shoot a look at Pella.

Kharon kisses my forehead. "That is why from this moment forward, I declare the Grand Reaper of Purgia and the last daughter of Viridian may pursue their love without the weight of secrecy."

Gasps echo through the hall as everyone stares at Roark and Pella. Pella stands up on Roark's shoulder, jumping and clapping her hands. Roark's eyes grow wide as he looks up in disbelief.

"Well, damn," Thelios breathes, surprised at the revelation. It's clear even he didn't know.

"Your Highness," Roark begins, kneeling before Kharon. "It was never my intention to set a course against you."

Motioning for Roark to rise, Kharon pats his shoulder. "The sails of love chart their own course, my friend. And it is a course you must take–you, that is, and Pella." Leaning toward Roark's shoulder so only Roark and Pella can hear, he continues. "I'll let you two decide when or if you show your true form."

Pella smiles, looking at Roark. "It's up to you," Roark says to Pella.

Running off Roark's shoulder, Pella bursts into a ball of light before revealing her true form. More murmurs echo throughout the courtroom, and a tinge of worry bubbles through me.

"What the fu—" Thelios blows out an air of shock.

"Pella, you may showcase your true form in this castle and within the walls of your own solarium. Outside the castle gates, I'd like you to remain careful. Of course, you have Roark here to keep you safe," Kharon says.

Roark wraps his arm around Bella as she nestles into his chest, winking at me as she does.

Moirai stands, taking a step down to her brother's side. "As it has always been, the privacy of this court is without exclusion. Breathing a word of what happens here is tantamount to treason."

The room goes quiet for a minute before the crowd bows before Kharon.

Fifty-Five

KHARON

I HOLD Rae in my arms as we cross the threshold of my chambers, and my heart soars knowing we can finally begin our new life together.

"I love you, Rae Vereen." Crushing her mouth to mine as I carry her to my bed, there's only one thing on my mind.

"I love you, my prince," she smiles against my lips, caressing my beard. Rae squeals as I throw her onto my massive mattress, giggling and squirming to the center of the bed.

"Oh, you're not getting away from me that easily," I growl, leaning over her, planting playful kisses across her skin.

"Wait, Kharon," she rasps, holding her hands up in caution.

I growl again, my teeth tearing at the hem of her dress. "I'm not a patient man, my lady."

"That's not entirely true," she hisses, shoving my shoulder with a fiery finger. I wince, although it doesn't hurt, looking up at her. "I mean, you did wait years before we ever came to be."

I grunt, stalking my way up her body with her dress between my teeth. Tearing the loose fabric, I let it fall to the side, revealing her rounded hips. "Yes, and now that I have you, I'll never wait again." I thrust my face between her breasts, palming one and licking the swell of the other.

Moaning, Rae's head falls, her back arching and her breasts pressing forward, giving me an eyeful. Sucking in a breath, a faint mewling sound rolls through her, but she tenses, and she lifts my head by my chin so I am staring her in the eye.

"Kharon." Her deadpan tone gives her away. It's the tone no man wants to hear in a moment like this. Whatever this is, it must be serious.

Pushing myself up on my elbows, I hover over her, feigning interest in whatever she is about to say as my mind wanders towards the many things I'd like to do to her.

"Yes, beautiful?" I reply, running my hand across her shoulder.

"I think we should wait." Rae's eyes search mine, as if she assumes I know what she means.

"Wait? You mean wait to return to your realm? I know Moirai said–"

"No, Khar, not about returning to my realm. Well, I mean yes, but no. Actually, I meant let's wait to have sex."

I sit up on my knees. I'm still between her legs, and I've got a pretty piece of her thigh in my view. She wants me to wait? "We've already had sex. I think the time for waiting has passed, don't you?"

Rae pushes herself upright, leaning against the mountain of

pillows behind us. "Okay sure, in theory we've already had sex, but–"

"It's not a theory, it's a fact."

Her pointed glare digs at me. "You want facts? Fact: we made love when I was human. Also fact: I am no longer human and we haven't made love."

"All I hear is a problem to rectify," I answer slyly, scooting next to her.

"How about we protect my Nether-virginity?"

My throat nearly closes. "You can't be serious."

"Dead serious." Rae's eyes narrow, and the glint of fire I see now resting behind her eyes lets me know two things: she is serious, and she is, in fact, no longer human. "At least until after our wedding." Her face softens a bit, and she casts me a crumpled smile.

I tug on her arm. "Well, fuck, let's get Moirai back here before she leaves. She can officiate the ceremonies. Better yet, I'll ask Gao to do it."

Snatching her arm back, Rae shoves my shoulder. "Kharon! I'm serious."

Sighing hard, I run my hands through my hair. "Are we really doing this?" Palming my face, I mute my screams. "Where is this coming from? Fate gave me a second chance with the woman I love. I'd be a fool not to make the most of this opportunity. Do you realize how much I want you right now?"

Rae's eyes glass. "Yes, I do, because I feel the same way. I've got a second shot on a whole new life with you, Kharon, and I want to do it right. I want to discover us together. I want to know more about you, and I want to do that without complicating it with sex. I know making love to you now will be different because you won't have to hold back. I also know once we go down that road, I'll spend every waking second so needy for you, I won't be able to think. I'm about to become the Princess of Purgia. I want to know what that means, understand the ways of the land. Even more than that, I want things to be well with my family. I want to make love to my husband without a care in the world."

The way her eyes are dancing makes my heart melt. "I like hearing you call me your husband," I begin as the tops of our heads press together. Kissing her forehead, I rest my lips at her hairline for a minute. Taking a deep breath, I pull back and look her in the eyes. "Sadly, beautiful, there's no such thing as no care in the world, but I understand what you're saying. I appreciate you wanting to slow things down a bit, and I'll agree to maintaining your Nether-virginity, albeit with a few conditions."

Rae smiles wide. "Anything, Khar."

My eyes darken as I trace my thumb along her bottom lip. "First, you'll have to sleep in your own chamber while we're here, at least until the wedding. There's no way I'm sleeping next to you and *not* fucking you." I pause as her cheeks redden. She nods, sucking in a breath, and I swear I hear her pheromones singing to me. "Second, when we return to your realm, all bets are off."

I growl, leaning into her, inhaling her scent. "When you return to the earthbound realm, you'll appear more human, which means we can have human sex. Is that clear? It won't be Nether sex, so technically, you'll maintain your Nether-virginity."

Her eyes are dancing again. "Anything else?"

"I'm not finished."

"Please continue, *my prince*," she laughs with an eye roll.

"While we are here, you will train with me to learn your powers, test your limits. I'm sure there's much to learn," I say, repositioning myself on the bed so I'm in front of her again. Making my way between her legs, I pull her knees apart. She grunts, but I pull her gown back so that she's bared to me.

"Khar," she moans, her glistening little pussy now on display. "What are you doing? I thought you just said–"

I place a finger over her mouth. "One last proviso. You may

retain your Nether-virginity, but a man still has to eat. Now, lie back so I can enjoy my meal."

Fifty-Six

RAE

I never thought it would feel so strange to return to the earth-bound realm.

While we only spent what felt like an additional day and a half in the Netherworld, Kharon reminded me that it's been months in my realm. We didn't want my family worrying about me any more than they already have.

Finishing up my brief training, Kharon took care of a few court affairs, then assigned Thelios and Roark to manage everything else in his absence. Pella, on the other hand, has the tough duty of planning our wedding ceremonies. Although we plan to have one in my realm, it's important for the whole of Purgia to take part in the festivities. Just the thought of it makes me both excited and nervous.

"It feels different," I whisper over my shoulder as the ferry nears the riverbank.

"How do you mean?" Kharon asks as he motions his hands to lower the sails.

Shrugging my shoulders, I smile, turning to see Kharon now returned to his earthbound size. I glance over myself and notice I'm back to my normal height, plus an inch or two. I barely felt the transformation, since I've been wracking my brain over how to tell my family I am no longer human, especially Ross. I know he won't take kindly to the idea.

Kharon squeezes my waist, bringing me back to the moment. "Rae?"

"Sorry, my mind keeps drifting. I guess I keep thinking about how I'm not human anymore. I can feel it. I can't explain it, but I know I'm not the same woman."

Taking my shoulders in his hands, Kharon brushes his thumb along my skin. "I may not ever understand what it's like to be human, but I do understand what you mean. Coming to this realm, it feels like my powers are stripped away every time. I'm only left with earthbound methods of flight and some elemental strength. It's weird, but you get used to it."

"Will my family?" I moan, sighing hard.

"We'll find out soon enough," Kharon says, pointing to the side of his cavern. I smile, thankful to see just a remnant of home again. As much as I wanted Kharon to find somewhere else for us to live, and I still do, it feels good seeing this place again.

So many good memories. I blush at the passionate thoughts twirling around in my mind.

"Shall we?" Lifting me in his arms, Kharon carries us onto dry land. As we reach the cavern, Kharon's eyes roam around, likely assessing what he'll need to do to put it back together again. "Thankfully, it's just a matter of securing an entry point. For the most part, I left everything the same."

Kharon begins to wave his hands, summoning his power, but I stop his movement. He glances at me, his brows caving in a bit.

"Do you think I can try?" I ask, wanting to see how my powers work here.

An appreciative smirk grows on Kharon's face as he stares at me, his chest slightly puffed. "Give it a go," he says, gesturing his hand for me to proceed.

For me, there are no incantations or limericks to recite. Instead, my power comes from a deeper place. All I have to do is *call upon my power and it will answer me*, as Moirai once told me.

With a wave of my hand, a whiff of smoke blows until small fissures of crackling fire whirl in the air. Rotating my wrist, I move my hand in circles until I see the thick wall of the cave breaking down. A small hole, barely enough for my head, is all I can manage. Huffing, I blow out a sigh that sends my curly bangs flying away from my face.

"Ugh! My arms are tired. This is harder than it looks," I grumble, folding my arms.

Firming his hand on my shoulder, Kharon grants me a caring smile. "It's okay, Rae. You just have to keep practicing. We're in the earthbound realm now. Our powers take a lot more willpower here than in the Netherworld. It'll take some getting used to. For now, why don't we try doing it together? How does that sound?"

I smile as I lift my hands back up. Kharon gives me a wink and we both press our hands forward, allowing our fire and smoke to melt through the thick block of stone. Not even a minute passes, and we've opened the entire entrance.

Together.

Looking over at Kharon, I know I'm wearing the world's biggest grin, but that's how he makes me feel. Kharon, however, is smiling, something calculating behind his eyes that has all my lady parts dancing.

Entering the cave, Kharon whirls a gust of wind around, settling the interior back into its prior form. I stand in the center, gaping at the wonder of it all. It's more beautiful than I remember.

Wrapping his arm around my waist from behind, Kharon kisses my neck. "Are you ready?" he breathes, and the husky tone of his voice buckles my knees. A part of me wonders if he's asking me whether I'm ready to see my family. Yet, with his hardened member poking into my backside, I know what comes next.

His erection presses against my abdomen as I turn in his arms, and his darkened gaze locks me in place. Firming his hand at my neck, he crushes his mouth to mine, kissing me as if he hadn't kissed me in days. Although it's been a few days since we've had sex, we've surely kissed quite a bit. Not only have we kissed, but his mouth has been everywhere, feasting, as he likes to call it. In fact, I taste the remnants of myself in his kiss right now from his *morning breakfast,* as he likes to call it.

Our "no sex" rule has actually been quite fun. My soon-to-be husband has become creative these last few days. From intense moments of making me touch myself while he watches, only so that he can drench me in his cum, to rolling flames of fire over my body in a motion so erotic I combust, it doesn't feel like we haven't had sex at all.

Just practicing my skill, as he likes to call it.

"Khar," I moan as his hands sweep along my body, disintegrating my clothes to threads at my feet. "Wait," I say, pushing my hand to his chest.

"What?" he grits through his teeth, grunting desperately as he eyes me.

Standing before him, clad in nothing but the widest smile, I give him a wink. "I want to try something. You'll have to trust me."

My grin grows wider as I stalk around him, eyeing him up and down.

His chest rumbles as he grunts, staring at me. "Make it quick."

Stepping behind him, I put my hands at his sides, thinking of my next action. With my improved vision, my eyes narrow in on a tiny thread nestled at the side of his trousers. Using heat from my hands, I sear the thread, pulling only a tiny flick of fire. This is different from the weaving I did in the Soleil; this is Nether-magic on full display. As I burn the thread, the remaining pieces of fabric give way and fall to the ground, leaving Kharon bare before me from the waist down.

His eyes pop wide in shock as a proud smile crosses his face. "Not bad," he smirks as his shirt falls to the floor. Gathering me in his arms, Kharon carries me to the bed. Laying me in the center, he spreads my legs with his knees. As he begins lowering his face, I knock my knees together.

"No!" I protest, peering over my knee to see only flames in his eyes. I don't give him time to counter when I slowly part my legs. He sits upright, and my fingers find their way to his length. Stroking him hard, I tug a little. "You. In. Me. Now" I order, and his eyes flash brightly.

"As you wish," he smiles, and slams into me with one, hard thrust.

"Yes, baby!" I writhe beneath him, allowing my hands to score the muscles of his back.

"If my baby wants a strong, hard fuck, that is exactly what my baby gets." Once more, Kharon slams into me, and my eyes roll back. This is exactly what I needed.

Fifty-Seven

KHARON

Damn.

I knew I would miss fucking Rae, but that is an understatement. If I didn't know we had other important matters to tend to, there's no doubt we'd still be going at it right now.

Instead, here we are, standing outside of Elysian's office. I reached out to Melchior and let him know we'd arrived. Rae wanted to call Ross first, but she changed her mind, tearfully stating she knew she'd be nothing but a puddle of tears the minute she heard his voice.

Rae's eyes dart around the cobblestone courtyard outside her uncle's office. Her nose twitches a bit, and she manages a small frown.

"What's wrong? Is this too soon?" I ask.

She shakes her head, shrugging her shoulders. "No, it's just that the air smells different. The scent of pine is strong."

I look around, noticing the leaves are noticeably different. It must be late Fall. "You're right. Maybe–"

The squeaky sound of Elysian's door opening catches our attention.

"Pippin!" Ross cries out, throwing his now-bulky arms around his sister, yanking her from my side. Twirling her around, he thanks everyone from heaven to groundhogs for his sister's safe return. Placing her back down, he holds her hands, his eyes scanning the entirety of her. "Goodness, how I've missed you! Don't you ever leave me like that again!" he shouts, throwing his arm around her once more.

"Okay, move it along and let me see my niece," Elysian barks, coming to the door. He seems rounder than I recall as he perches his stout frame at the threshold. "Come here, my girl," he bellows past the loose cigar hanging from his mouth. "You are quite a sight for these old eyes."

Elysian nods at me over Rae's shoulder, giving me an almost bashful look. He tightens his lips under his thick mustache as he eyes me while leading Rae inside his office.

Ross gives me a sturdy hug, and I'm surprised with how much he's bulked up since we were last here. "It's good to have you both back," he says, gesturing for me to follow Rae.

Inside, we find Melchior and Stephen. They both wave at me while greeting Rae with light hugs. Even though this is her family, it's still hard for me to watch her being passed around a room of men. I suppose I'll never get used to it.

A cough from Elysian's desk startles both me and Rae. Her

eyes widen and her mouth drops as we see her aunt stand from Elysian's chair.

"I'm glad you are safe, my dear," Vivian says as she pulls Rae in for a hug. Rae looks at me, shaking her head in surprise. "We've missed you."

Pulling out of her aunt's hold, Rae's eyes bounce through the room and back at me. We both stare off in both surprise and confusion.

"Um…" Rae begins, pacing back to my side. I throw my arm around her, hopeful to settle the nervousness gnawing within her. "It's good to see you too, Auntie. I hadn't expected to see everyone once I got back from my apprenticeship." She trips over the last phrase, looking to her brother for some sense of direction, but he's too tearful at his sister's return to notice.

Melchior saunters into the middle of the room with his hands in his pockets. "It's quite alright, cousin. Vivian knows *everything*," he says, leaning hard on the last word as he darts a sharp eye to me.

Shit.

My arm drops from around Rae. How could I be so stupid? I inwardly berate myself as the puzzle pieces form a clear picture in my mind.

Rae looks up at me and around the room. "Khar, what is going on?"

Throwing me a cagey grin, Melchior shakes his head, laughing a little as he walks past me. "After all this time? You still haven't told her? Impressive, Ferryman. Very impressive," he mumbles nonchalantly as he makes his way to the side bar.

"Tell me what?" Rae grits through her teeth. Her cheeks flush, and I know she's pissed.

"Now, now," Elysian grovels, quickly coming to Rae's side. "There's no need for you to get upset, least of all with Mr. Nyx."

"Ah-hem," Vivian interjects, narrowing her eyes at her husband as she leans against the wall with her arms folded. "Perhaps my niece isn't too keen on secrets, especially not from the man she loves."

Breathing out a sigh, Rae looks over her shoulder. "What secrets?"

"Listen, Rae, I wanted to tell you but–" I begin, my hands lifted in caution.

"But what?" she fires back, her eyes glowing with flames.

"Sister!" Ross gasps, stepping forward, surprised at this new reveal.

"Stay back, Ross!" Rae snaps, lifting a now fiery finger.

More gasps echo through the room, and I swallow the thick air in my throat, trying to find the best way to break it to her.

"But what?" she repeats, glaring at me. "You were going to tell me but–"

Elysian crosses between us. "But they weren't his secrets to tell," he softly answers, and Rae's eyes bounce between me and her uncle.

"What?" Rae breathes back, confused.

"You should probably sit down for this, cousin," Melchior offers, taking her hand and guiding her to the small sofa.

"If she doesn't burn it down," Ross sneers, glaring at his sister. "What the fu–" he hisses into Stephen's ear.

"I'm sure she'd rather remain standing," Vivian grunts with a curled lip.

"Will somebody just spit it out?" Rae barks out, taking a deep breath as settles down into the leather seat. "What secrets are we talking about?" She shoots me another hard stare.

"Mine," Elysian admits, taking small, sheepish steps across the room. Rae's face crumples as her brother takes a seat beside her. "It's for that reason that I owe you my deepest apologies, my boy." Offering me his hand, Kingsley Elysian does the one thing I never thought I'd see. Apologize.

Fifty-Eight

RAE

"Wait a minute!" I blurt. "What are you apologizing for, Uncle El?"

My uncle's eyes shift to Aunt Vivian and Melchior a few times before turning back to me. "An old man like me carries many regrets, but I can say the hurt I've caused my family weighs the heaviest."

Melchior takes his place next to his father, patting his shoulder before turning his attention to Kharon. "I suppose I should apologize to you too, Nyx, if for no other reason than not believing better of you. I should have known you'd never cast a withering spell upon my father without reason. For that, I am sorry."

Looking up at Kharon, my eyes plead with him. "Baby, what is everyone talking about?"

"They're talking about the reason I withered Elysian."

Shaking my head, I force thoughts of Kharon pursuing Winter aside. None of that matters, not anymore. "Khar, really, we don't have to talk about that."

Ross rubs my knee, taking my hand in his. "You should hear him out, Pip," he says, with a wink.

"I should also apologize to you Kingsley, and to you, Vivian. I should have known leaving this realm would nullify the forgetting spell."

Groaning, my eyes narrow. "Why would you cast a forgetting spell on my aunt and uncle? Even more, why wouldn't you tell me?"

"I'm sorry, Rae," Kharon replies, taking small steps toward me. "I promised the truth."

"Yes, you did, even if it's hard to tell. Now spit it out."

Lifting his hands in caution, my uncle shakes his head. "Please don't be mad with Kharon. He was only trying to protect us—protect me."

"Protect you? From what?" I ask, watchful of the glassy tears forming in my uncle's eyes.

"From myself," Uncle El whispers.

Aunt Vivian comes to his side, rubbing his shoulders. "It's okay, honey. We're okay," she adds with a strained smile.

"Years ago, there was a woman who worked for me, Leila Greene. I considered her a friend, someone here to help me get things together—you know, the administrative side of the estate. After we lost Melchior, things changed. I grew cold and distant toward Vivian. I suppose I felt guilty I had an affair while Mel's mom was ill, and then Mel disappeared. I became more distant. Before I knew it, I fell back into old patterns as a means to comfort my sorrow. But a friend—Kharon, caught me. He told me to stop, or I'd destroy my family. I didn't listen. Vivian found out and she threatened to leave, take you and Ross, tell Winter everything. Kharon caught us fighting."

My heart thumps wildly in my chest upon hearing my uncle's reveal. How could he do such a thing? All this time, he blamed Kharon. Then, it hits me.

"So that's when you cast a withering and forgetting spell," I exclaim as the weight of it hits me hard.

Kharon offers a small nod. "Yes," he confesses. "I know it may seem hard to understand, but I loved this family. I still do. The thought of you breaking up because a grieving man lost his way hurt me more than you can imagine. I know all too well what it looks and feels like when families fall apart. I did not wish for such a fate to be yours."

I jump up, speeding to Kharon's arms. "I can't believe you held onto this all this time," I say, running my hands through his hair. Locking my gaze on his, it hits me. "Leila Greene. She's the woman from the marketplace!"

Aunt Vivian steps forward, her hand softly patting my shoulder. "Yes, Rae. You remember her?"

Kharon turns to my aunt. "Well, not for the reasons you think, but we did find out Leila's return was as a Changeling Incarnate. It wasn't really her at all."

"Wait a minute," Ross chimes in. "How did the Changelings get to Leila in the first place?"

"Kharon, dear, you don't have to say anything," Aunt Vivian counters, and I wonder what she knows that I don't.

Blowing out a heavy sigh, Kharon firms his hands in mine. "I wanted to get Leila as far from your family as possible. She was half-Altrinion, so I knew killing her was out of the question, but there was one place I could take her. So, I ferried Leila to the Underworld."

My eyes grow wide at his admission. I can't believe the lengths he went to for my family. Still, I can tell Kharon isn't as shaken up by this as I am. Ferrying someone to the Underworld is just another day for him.

"Unfortunately, the Changelings must have intercepted her from the Underworld," Kharon continues.

Gasping, Uncle El sways, leaning on his cane. "For what purpose?"

"Once Melchior was taken, they had to find a way to try to ensnare you again. She found Aunt Vivian. She reported her findings to the Changelings, and they planned to exact their revenge. Thankfully, they're gone for good."

Everyone's eyes are glued to Kharon as he speaks. This time, however, there's an admiration that permeates the air. I know one thing is true: in their eyes, Kharon Nyx is no longer the villain of the story.

"Kharon," Melchior begins, offering his hand. "It appears we owe you a debt of gratitude."

"Me, most of all," Uncle El admits, coming to Melchior's side and squeezing Kharon's shoulder.

"Think nothing of it," Kharon replies with a small grin. "That's what family does for one another. It is because I care for this family that I want to make it official. I want you all to know I've asked Rae for her hand in marriage."

All eyes turn to me, and Ross pops up from his seat. "Pip!" he shrieks, racing to my side, Stephen following close behind. Taking my hand in his, he searches for a ring. "Well, sister, what did you say?"

I look around the room until my eyes find Kharon's waiting and watchful glare. The care I see in his eyes, knowing just how much he loves me and my family, swells my chest with so much pride.

"Yes," I squeak out, my cheeks warming red.

The entire room rejoices, and both Kharon and I are squeezed to near suffocation. In all my life, I've never felt so loved, so embraced... *so seen*.

Fifty-Nine

KHARON

This welcome wagon has been one for the books. Never in a million years did I think the Elysians would ever welcome me with open arms. Apparently, I can still be surprised.

"This calls for a toast!" Melchior announces, clanking his glass of bourbon. I inwardly groan, wondering how many drinks my friend has had so far.

"Let's save the toasts for another day," I counter. I try to keep my tone as mild as possible. I'm not sure if everyone else has noticed Melchior's drinking problem. Now that I'm back, I'll do all I can to help him through it. Thankfully, no one seems the wiser as they continue hugging Rae and me. Melchior, however, gives me a look. He knows I'm only trying to help.

"Kharon is right everyone," Rae adds. "Besides, I can't toast until I talk to Win. By the way, where is she?"

Just like that, all the air is sucked out of the room. Everyone's faces go rigid and red.

"What is it?" Rae asks, her brows furrowing a bit.

The room stays quiet for a few seconds longer than Rae likes, and just when she parts her mouth to ask again, Ross adds a cough. "First let me say, Win is safe. She is okay."

Rae sighs hard with a hand to her chest. "Well, that's good news. Why do I feel a *but* coming?"

"That's because things have been a little tough for her as of late. Sure, she's missed you, but with her traveling and finishing school, she's been quite busy," Vivian begins, sauntering to the center of the room. "She even spent a little time visiting New Orleans, and that's when everything turned upside down."

"What do you mean?" I ask, walking to Rae's side.

"It's Lord Marchand," Elysian answers. "He's become undone, returned to his full monstrous self. With it, the entirety of the city has gone into disrepair."

Rae gasps, looking up at me. "I don't understand. What does that have to do with Win?"

"Lux needed to get her out of there in a hurry. He stayed behind with Cedric to help," Melchior adds. Turning his attention to me, he continues. "I fear Lord Marchand has fallen to his fate. He's met his fated mate and she did not accept him. I'm sure you can understand the rest." His eyes linger on me for a moment, and my heart feels heavy.

Even though I had no thoughts of endearment toward Marchand, I do not envy his situation, nor what it could mean for the earthbound realm in general. All I know is that I will do my best to keep Rae and her family from the throes of it all.

"I still don't understand what this has to do with Winter," Rae asks again.

"Mainly, she's just beside herself with worry. Night and day, she sits in her room, waiting for Lux to call, just to know he's okay," Ross replies. "I'm sure having you here will give her reason enough to smile."

"She can add one more reason to that list," Elysian continues, his solemn face fixing into a broader smile. "Lux called. He's leaving New Orleans. He's ready to marry Winter."

Rae and Ross beam from ear to ear as does Vivian. Still, Melchior and I trade glances. We know there's more to what Elysian is sharing.

"And?" Melchior groans, motioning for his father to continue. "This all seems like good news to me. What are you not telling us?"

Even Vivian looks concerned as she stares at her husband. "Dear?"

Elysian huffs, taking out a handkerchief to wipe his balding head. "Win has been through so much. All her stress, worrying over Lux. I'm not sure it'd be fair to spring the news of everything on her so suddenly. Can this at least wait until after the wedding?"

Rae's face pales, and Ross squeezes his sister tight around her arm. "Uncle, you're not asking my sister to continue this charade. I mean she's been to hell and back! Look at her! I know I'm not the only one who's noticed there's something different about her. She has flaming fingers, for goodness sake! Her eyes are like little candles, too. All of that and she managed her way back to us with the man she loves. Why should Winter's happiness be more important than Rae's? I'm tired of my sister taking a backseat."

Vivian and Elysian share worried glances before turning to Rae.

"And what about you, babe?" Stephen groans, tugging Ross' arm.

"Not now," Ross grits through his teeth, shaking his head.

Rae steps beside Stephen. "Ross? What is Stephen talking about?"

Hunching his shoulder, Ross sucks in a breath, rolling his eyes at Stephen. "Nothing."

"Oh, so Stephen proposing to you is nothing?" Melchior snips from across the room, laughing.

"Mel," Ross seethes. "I told you that in confidence."

"Ah, so you want us to remain a secret?" Stephen barks back.

Sighing hard, Ross throws up his hands. "Oh, you're just being dramatic. I told you I wanted to wait until my sister returned. That's all."

Grabbing Ross by the wrist, Rae halts his motion. "Well, I'm right here, Ross." She smiles wide. "You are such a gufflebup! Come here, you!" Pulling her brother in for a hug, everyone claps, patting Stephen on the back.

"We're getting married!" Rae shrieks, jumping up and down. "Wait, you did say yes, right?"

Looping his arm with Stephen's, Ross leans on his broad shoulders. "Look at him! Of course I said yes." Kissing Stephen's cheek, Ross mouths *I love you*, and he plunges himself deeper into Stephen's embrace.

"Well, well! Look at that, Vivian!" Elysian cheerfully announces. "It looks like all of our kids are getting hitched. I'll be a poor man sending all of you down the aisle," he chuckles, pulling at the seam of his pockets.

"Oh, not to worry, Uncle. Kharon is loaded! He has a palace!" Rae giggles. Ross and Vivian's eyes grow wide, and they rush to Rae's side, pulling her from me to get all the details.

Rae indulges their interests, even as Stephen and Elysian's curiosity is piqued by Rae's description of my realm. I note how she's careful to keep the negative details of the Changelings or her fall in the Fountain at bay.

Still, there's one person isolated from it all. Melchior remains apart from the huddle, casually sipping his bourbon in the side chair.

"I'm happy for you, old friend," Melchior says, tipping his glass toward me.

"Thank you," I reply, taking a seat next to him. "Now, are you going to tell me what happened between you and my sister?"

Curving his mouth to the side, Melchior sets his glass down on the table. "Ah, so I'm guessing Moirai didn't tell you what happened, huh?" Pausing, he keeps his eyes fixed on me. Circling his finger along the glass rim, he shrugs his shoulders. "Well, when the person you love doesn't see you in her future, it does you no good to argue with fate."

Despite the laughter surrounding us, seeing my friend in pain hurts more than I can describe.

"I'm sorry, Melchior. Moirai didn't mention it to me. In fairness, I was trying to remain neutral. As hard as it seems right now, I'll tell you what I've told Rae. Fates still only see in part. They do see the future, yes, but the details are not theirs to know or even understand."

Biting his lower lip, Melchior looks at me and then over my shoulder, glancing at his happy family. "Yes, but how can I make her see we can still be together when what she sees tells her we have no future?"

"Trust your heart. Fate told me to pursue your sister, but I always knew my heart belonged to Rae. In the end, it was my heart that paved my way to happiness. If you want to be with Moirai, let your heart do the leading, and your fate will follow."

He lets out a small chuckle, and slaps my hand. "That's good stuff right there!" an appreciative grin spreads across Melchior's face. "Damn, Nyx. When did you become an aficionado of love?"

I shake my head and point at Rae. "Believe me, my friend, I'm still learning."

Sixty

RAE

Two Months Later

"Are you nervous?" Kharon asks as I nestle deep into his embrace. His bulking biceps keep me warm as we lay on top of our satiny sheets.

Although I mentioned us getting a place of our own, I've grown accustomed to our little love den. Sure, it's drafty and cool, but between myself and Kharon, we're like our own heat lamps. I don't get cold like I did when I was human.

"Baby?" He taps my shoulder and kisses my forehead.

"A little," I reveal. "I mean, last night was Win's wedding. Now

I'm expected to walk into her new home and tell her I'm in love with someone she hates. That, and oh, he's about to become your in law. Yeah, I'm sure that'll go over well."

Taking my chin, he turns my face up to his. "We've waited long enough."

Pushing up, I lean back against the mound of pillows. "I know. To be honest, I am ready to get it over with."

"So am I. I'm ready for us to start our lives together. Besides, I have a surprise for you."

I clasp my hands together, grinning wide. "You do? Tell me!"

Shaking his head, Kharon folds his arms. "Not until we get done with the heavy lifting."

"Come on, Khar!" I poke his shoulder, but he playfully turns his head away.

"Nope."

"You know I could always persuade you," I say, straddling Kharon's waist. Lifting a brow, Kharon smirks, but he doesn't let up. His hardened length juts at my already-slick center, and I line him up with my entrance. "Would you like me to convince you?" I tease his tip, and I hear him suck in a breath, his eyes popping wide as he stares at me.

Taking my waist in his hands, he licks his lips as his eyes flash with fire. Pushing me so that I'm impaled on his shaft, he grunts. "If you think I'll stop you from riding me, you still have a lot to learn about your husband." Firming his hands on my waist, he rolls his hips, forcing me to grind down hard.

"Khar," I moan, arching my back. Using the opportunity to plunge his face between my breasts, he sucks, nips, and licks everything his mouth can reach.

Fisting my hair in his grip, he cranes my neck into a kiss. Slowly trailing his tongue along my neck, he growls into my nape. "I'm sending you out good and fucked. I want them to smell me on you. I don't want there to be any doubt of who you belong to."

Laying me on my back, Kharon continues pounding hard into me. Holding me by my ankles, he gives little room for me to move as he plows into me with a need so unrelenting, you'd hardly know we just did this not even thirty minutes ago.

"You said you wanted to convince me. Convince me this pretty little pearl is mine."

I can barely think straight, he's fucking me so hard, but I find the strength to pull my legs from his grasp. Stretching my legs insanely wide, I show him everything. "It's yours, Kharon. All yours," I breathe as he sits back on his knees, admiring our connection.

"Damn right," he growls, driving himself deeper. "Now, isn't that a beautiful mess we've made," he smirks as his release leaks out of me.

I'm not done with him yet.

"Oh no you don't," I begin as he holds himself at my entrance, admiring his work. "You made the mess, Mr. Nyx. You clean it up." Lifting my brow, a sly smile crosses my face as a gleam of surprise fills his. With my foot on his shoulder and my hand on his head, I push Kharon down.

Offering me a graceful nod, he dips his head low. "As you wish."

"It is customary after the mating ritual for the pack–or family, in this instance—to commemorate with a meal. In this, we mark our connection as family. Always and forever," Lux states as we gather at their table.

As lovely as everything is, I wish Kharon was here with us. He's not far, waiting for me to give him the signal to join us.

I almost wonder whether Win notices the glances we've all traded. I know everyone is wondering when I'll finally let the cat out of the bag. Knowing I'm nervous, my brother keeps everyone enthralled in tales from his and Stephen's honeymoon.

Contrary to my brother's typical, live-out-loud personality, he and Stephen chose a quaint ceremony at the lumberyard. They vacationed at a lovely mountainside resort in Vermont, where Stephen is from. The happy couple even brought Win and Lux a bottle of maple syrup from a tree they tapped together. Although I can't get the crazy story my brother shared of him and Stephen having their first fight as a married couple covered in syrup out of my mind, I use it to fixate on happier things instead of what I know is to come.

"I am so happy to have my whole family here," Uncle El begins, standing with a glass of champagne. "To you, Lux and Winter. Stephen, you've made my nephew a very happy man and finally took him off the playboy list," he laughs, winking at Ross. "Having my son returned is a joy I never thought I'd behold, but Melchior, your presence is the best present an old man could ever ask for. To my wife, thank you for enduring me. I know I can be a hard man. Ah, and I almost forgot, Cedric and Abigail. Welcome to our family."

Everyone lifts their glasses, cheering, but Winter casts a worried stare at me. "Wait!" she calls out. "Father," she grits, narrowing her gaze. "You forgot someone," she says, leaning her head in my direction.

My uncle parts his lips to speak, but I quickly rise from my seat. "It's okay, Uncle El. I've got this one." Taking a deep breath, I look down at Ross, and he and Stephen nod for me to continue.

"Rae?" Wins starts, but Lux squeezes her shoulder, cautioning her to let me continue.

"I am so happy for everyone. For you, Win and Lux, and my brother and Stephen. For everyone here. It's good seeing our family together and happy, but there is someone missing." Closing my eyes, I blow out a sigh.

"There is?" Win says, looking around.

"Before I answer, let me just say, for the longest time, I only had my heart set on one man. Every day and practically every night, he's the man I dreamed about. He's the only one I wanted. For a moment, I thought I was just foolish, that I was chasing the wind. I wasn't foolish. In fact, it was the wind driving me in his direction."

"Rae, where are you going with this?" Win groans, now standing.

"Look, Win, I know this may not seem to be the right time to tell you, but I need you to know the truth. I'm in love with Kharon Nyx." Heaving a heavy sigh, I blow out another breath.

Sucking in a gasp, Win folds her arms at her chest. Lux stares around the room while Cedric and Abigail offer knowing glances, and his mouth falls wide.

"Rae, look, I know you loved Kharon, but you have to let him go. He's history. Gone. He and his lies went up in smoke."

"Win," Uncle El begins, walking to the door. "That's not entirely true, my dear."

Opening the door, there's Kharon, every bit as dashing as I've ever seen him. If my family weren't here right now, I'd continue our earlier activities.

Growling loud, Lux's eyes flash to gold, as do Winter's. I'm slightly impressed to see the imprinting took and she's now sharing her husband's wolfen traits, but I need her to back down.

Snarling and hissing, Win and Lux are respectively held back by Cedric and Abigail. "Hear them out, brother," Cedric warns, nodding toward us.

"Lord and Lady Decanter," Kharon says, remaining at the threshold. "My apologies for my unexpected arrival. By no means do I wish to sully the sanctity of your nuptials. However, I do come to ask that you hear us out."

"Speak quickly," Lux bites back.

We spend what feels like hours explaining everything to Win and Lux. While Lux seems at least understanding, Winter has no interest in seeing Kharon as anything but the villain.

"You just want me to believe that some entity controlled everything? That Nyx was just a pawn? I lost my brother, Rae! My brother! Do you know what he stole from me?"

"No, my dear," Uncle El starts, "Nyx didn't steal that from you. I dare say not even the Changelings stole that from you. *I did that.*" Gasps echo through the room at my uncle's admission, and my aunt perches herself at his side.

"We did," Aunt Vivian affirms, rubbing his shoulder. "Win, dear, after we thought Melchior died, we made you responsible for everything we lost. Nyx didn't do that. The Changeling's didn't. We did. For that, we are the ones who should apologize."

"Even more, you have no idea the lengths Kharon Nyx has gone to protect our family, the things he's done to protect us, even from ourselves," Uncle El continues.

"You can't seriously be defending him!" she quips.

"I can," Melchior chimes in. "I can tell you sister that no one fought harder to keep me safe—no, to keep us safe— than that man right there!"

"That's not entirely true," Kharon whispers.

"I bet!" Win gripes, but Lux cautions her to keep listening.

"Sure, I may have done what I could to take care of Melchior as well as look out for your father and his interests, but no one, not even I, has done what Rae has. She did more than risk her life to travel with me to the Netherworld to avenge my sister and your family. She gave her life for that purpose."

"Kharon," I rasp. I'm not sure if I'm ready for my family to know everything that happened in the Netherworld.

"No, Rae, they need to know the truth." Stepping over the

threshold, Kharon enters the room. My uncle closes the door behind him as Kharon walks to my side. "In your realm, the first book ever printed in the words of men states there is no greater love than to give your life for another. This woman has shown such great love, not just for me, but for this entire family. It was Rae's bravery of charging a Changeling head on and plunging not only the vile creature, but herself, into death, giving her life for us all. She single-handedly is the hero of the story."

Ross jumps up from his seat. "Pip! Is this true?" His eyes leak with tears. Nodding, I mouth *yes*, and he pulls me into his arms. "I knew something happened to you! I could feel it."

"The purity of her heart caused the great powers of old to grant her a new life. A life born in fire. Rae Vereen is now Netherborn."

"I knew something was different about you," Lux says, staring at me and Kharon. "You smelled different. I just didn't want to say anything," he confesses to Win. "But brother, you knew?"

"For a while," Cedric admits. "You know if I thought there was danger, I would have told you."

"Win," I say, turning my attention back to my cousin. Her eyes are thick with tears; I know this is a lot for her. "Look, while I'm not asking for your permission, I do need you to understand. This is happening. I know this is an awful lot to take in. I'm sorry, but I just couldn't go on without telling you."

Winter wipes her eyes. "You're right, Rae, this is a bit much." She glances over her shoulder at Lux and he nods, offering a small smile. "If you promise me you're happy—and I mean truly happy—"

Like a flash of lighting, I bolt to her side. Everyone gasps at my reveal, but no one says anything. "I am, Win. I promise, I've never been happier."

"That's all I ever wanted," Win croons in my ear, pulling me in for a hug.

The room buzzes with joyful congratulations and plenty of hugs. While Lux and Kharon seem to share a semblance of moving forward, Win remains noticeably wary. I know it may take some time for her to come around to things, but I'm simply happy the truth is out now.

Looking around, I can't help but smile.

It may not be perfect, but this is my family.

Sixty-One

KHARON

Rae's hand is warm in mine as we make our way down the gravel path. She shoots me a pensive gaze while forcing a few quaint smiles while we walk.

It's been almost fifteen minutes and I'm surprised she hasn't asked me where we're going. Although I know she won't admit it, it doesn't take a genius to know she's bummed her cousin stood her up for lunch earlier.

The last few days since we announced our relationship to Winter and Lux have been interesting to say the least. While Lux and I are hardly friends, it's clear that he's accepted that we are now family. I'm sure Cedric and Abigail have more to do with that than I'll ever know, but whatever the reason, I am thankful.

Winter, on the other hand, is a different matter entirely. She remains cautious. Reserved. As much as she tries to hide it, it's obvious she still doesn't like me.

Honestly, I am pretty sure Winter never cared much for me before all of this. Even when her father tried to play matchmaker, she remained cool toward me. Maybe she always thought I was disingenuous. I don't know nor do I care.

I only care about Rae.

She is all that matters to me.

Thankfully, Winter and I have that in common. It's for that reason she forces the biggest smile when Rae is around, doing her best to show support of our relationship. Not that Rae is totally oblivious to her cousin's overtures, but I think the now Netherborn side of Rae isn't as people pleasing as she was in her mortal life.

But today isn't about Winter or anyone else.

It's about us.

"Kharon, where are we?" Rae stops in front of a tall brick building. "We've been walking forever," she groans, as her eyes scan the quiet street.

"I'm glad you asked," I smile, waving my hand toward the large black doors. Narrowing her gaze, Rae scrunches her nose as her eyes drift between me and the building. Before she has a moment to say anything, the surprise bubbling within me rushes out. "We're home."

Rae's eyes pop open and she covers her mouth in a gasp. "Khar..." she breathes out, squeezing my hand, lifting on the balls of her feet to kiss my chin.

"Come, let's see our new home." Taking her arm in mine, I lead us through the broad, black double door entryway, where we find a sizable foyer.

"Wow, baby! This place is huge!" Rae shrieks as she turns about, scanning the long hallway. Her eyes roam up and down the four levels she can see from where we stand. "Which one is ours?"

A sly grin hovers at the side of my face. "All of them."

"What? Kharon, you can't be serious!"

I narrow my gaze. "Dead serious."

Rae's eyes flicker with a fiery glow in return as she bites her bottom lip.

"This way we'll have more than enough room to house our family one day," I add, throwing her a wink. "Let me show you around."

The first level has two offices on the immediate left for me and Rae, while the family room and kitchen are on the right. Rae can hardly contain her glee as she twirls around the oversized kitchen.

"Khar, baby! This is so lovely!" She whizzes through the kitchen, leaving her fiery mist behind as she runs her hands along the extra long kitchen island. "And big," she coos, stretching her arms across the marble slab.

"I think they said we could seat at least eight at the island alone. Sounds great for morning breakfast and pizza nights."

Rae's eyes dance with tears, but her bright smile spreads from ear to ear. "That sounds nice," she whispers, trailing her hands along the large mixer wrapped with a large red bow. Before she has a chance to mention the mixer, she whips her head in my direction and frowns. "Wait a minute, Khar. Who told you how many people could sit at the island?"

I smile. "I thought you'd never ask."

Gesturing my hand behind her, Rae turns around only to find Ross and Stephen coming through the kitchen terrace.

"Hey Pip!" Ross chuckles, leaning his head on Stephen's shoulder.

"Ross!" she balks, surprised to see her brother and his husband. "What are you two doing here?"

Stephen and Ross share knowing glances, and Ross points over Rae's shoulder toward me. "Why don't we let your nether-honeybun answer that for you."

Leaning against the island, Rae's eyes follow the small steps I take toward her. "If you remember, when we first returned from my realm I told you I had a surprise. Well here we are. However, that surprise would have never been possible without Ross and Stephen."

"That's right sis!" Ross adds. "You have your handsome brother-in-law to thank for not only overseeing all of this awesomeness, but he also did quite a bit of heavy lifting."

Stephen nudges Ross's chin. "Don't sell yourself short, beautiful. All of the interior was all you," he smiles, planting a quick kiss on Ross's cheek.

Throwing her face in her palms, Rae is a mix of tears and joy. Shaking her head, she wipes a few stray tears away with her wrist. "I can't believe you did all of this! How? When?"

"Kharon sent very precise instructions before he left. All we had to do was follow the script," Stephen says.

"Before you left?" Rae breathes as she begins to put it all together. "Wait! Are you telling me you arranged this *before* we left for the Netherworld? Before you asked me to marry you?"

Closing the space between us, I take her hand in mine. "Yes. I always knew I wanted to spend my life with you." Adding a kiss to her forehead, I squeeze her hand. *"Forever."*

"Forever," Rae repeats, pressing her head to my chest.

"Damn it!" Ross whines, fanning his face. "Now I'm crying."

Rae peers out from under my hold and laughs. "Well get yourself together, Merry. This is my moment."

Stephen and Ross laugh, as the two share an embrace.

"You're right, this is your moment," I continue, turning her back to me. "So let's continue with your tour."

Rae's eyes light up. "There's more?"

"So much more," I groan, kissing her.

Once more, Rae's eyes twinkle and I realize my only goal in life is to see that same light in her eyes for a thousand years.

Sixty-Two

RAE

I am speechless.

From the large bedrooms to the luxurious bathrooms through-out, I am at a loss for words. Not only do we have room for a sizable family one day, but there are little touches that I know only came from Kharon.

There's a quaint den adjacent to the kitchen full of pictures of some of the food I've made and a desk with my recipe book in the center with extra pages added. Knowing how much Kharon cares about my dreams means more than words could ever express.

Making our way to the top floor, there's a double door at the center of the hall and the look in Kharon's eyes tells me exactly what is behind those doors. Yet, when he shakes his head, tugging at my wrist before I have a chance to enter, I know he's up to something.

Ross and Stephen chuckle in the background as they stand near a pair of French doors that lead to what looks to be a rooftop deck.

"Like I said, beautiful: *so much more*," Kharon whispers in my ear as we step outside.

My eyes pop open and my mouth parts wide at the sight before me. Beautifully stringed lights are aglow, illuminating everything in my view. A lovely fountain sits in the center, pouring into a large hot tub, encased in ornate stone. Fragrant foliage and pine outlines the terrace, overlooking the beautiful cityscape from above.

Still, for as breathtaking as it all is, it's the sight of my beautiful family standing under a large gazebo taking my breath away.

Gasping, thick tears fill my eyes at the sight of my cousins, aunt, and uncle all standing with smiling faces as Kharon and I remain just beyond the doorpost.

"Khar," I rasp, trying to get my words together. "What's all of this?"

As though it were answer enough, Kharon takes my wrist in his hand, bringing my knuckles to his lips, planting a soft kiss. "It's time I make you my wife," he says just above a whisper.

My eyes leak, falling like little balls of fire, landing just where Kharon's lips had just been on my hand. Kharon's eyes flicker as he stares at me, the flames dancing as he stares at me and it makes my heart pound.

"But I'm dressed like this," I sheepishly counter, tugging at my skirt and leather jacket.

"You look beautiful," Kharon answers, running his hand through my hair. "We can do all of the pomp and circumstance when we have a ceremony in the Netherworld. I just refuse to wait another day to make you mine. I hope that doesn't bother you, but if you really want me to make you something—"

Lifting my palms in protest, I smile. "No!" I shriek, and small bouts of laughter stir through my family. "I can't wait another day." Squeezing Kharon's hand in mine, I bite my bottom lip, as thoughts of everything that will come after the nuptials swirl in my head.

"Are you ready, sister?" Ross breaks me from my abandoned thoughts, now stepping into my view as he offers his hand. I scrunch my nose, my gaze shifting between my brother and *my man*. "You may be fire born now, but you'll always be my sister. With that comes certain privileges." Lifting his chin, Ross sucks in a breath, forcing away his tears. "Like walking you down the aisle," he adds, opening his arm.

Kharon steps to the side, nodding at me briefly before making his way toward the gazebo.

Looping my arm with my brother's, I lean my head on his shoulder. Ross plants a small kiss on my forehead and squeezes me into his hold.

"I'm ready Ross," I begin, as my gaze travels to Kharon standing at the center of the gazebo. I lock my sights on him until I see no one else. Although it now makes sense why Win stood me up, none of that matters. In this moment, there's only one person who has my full attention, my devotion, and my heart.

I've withstood the nocturnal creatures, disapproving family, and even the realms of darkness. I now know there's nothing in either this world or the next capable of keeping me from the love of my life. He is my air. My reason. He is the flame to my fire.

I have stared death in the face as darkness and fire consumed me. Yet through it all, I learned one thing.

For him, I'll let it all burn.

Changeling Epilogue

Kill our sisters they will see, the life they plan will never be. Not fire nor brim from us can hide; swift wings of death for both groom and bride.

Stay Tuned!

Return to the Netherworld
Kharon & Rae's story continues.

More from L.C. Son

Explore the books and short stories of the Beautiful Nightmare Universe:

<u>Books</u>

Beautiful Nightmare (Book One)

Hearts Eclipsed, A Beautiful Nightmare Novella

Awaken: Beautiful Nightmare (Book Two)

Untamed: A Beautiful Nightmare Story

Beta Rising

One Winter's Kiss: A Beautiful Nightmare Story

Flirting with Darkness (Anthology)

Fire Kissed & Fire Born Duet (Netherworld Series Debut)

<u>Coming Soon</u>

'Till Death Do Us

Chaos & Curses (Anthology)

Beautifully Dark Things

Dawn of Descent: Beautiful Nightmare (Book Three) TBA

For more info on my books, visit: My Books & Short Stories - L. C. Son Books (lcsonbooks.com)

Remember leaving reviews makes you an MVP!!

About L.C. Son

Known for her Amazon Best Seller, *One Winter's Kiss*, and the series starter, and epic fantasy novel, *Beautiful Nightmare (Book One)*, L.C. Son is the happy wife of more than twenty years to her high school sweetheart and a loving mom of three.

Growing up, she spent hours reading comic books she "borrowed" from her older brother, which inspired her love of heroes and all things fantasy and paranormal.

Much like the characters she adored, she lives a duplicitous life. By day, she works tirelessly to champion the employment of persons with severe disabilities. By night, she puts on her wife-mom cape, sharing with her husband at their church and juggling their kids' highly active schedules.

Presently, she's working on the next installment in the Beautiful Nightmare series.

For the latest info and to join the member-only newsletter, visit: www.lcsonbooks.com.